HER INNOCENT WAR

By

Betty C. Hatcher

Her Innocent War

ISBN-13: 978-1497583115
ISBN-10: 149758311X
Copyright ©2014 by Betty C. Hatcher

Published by Frugal Press, Oklahoma City, OK
Cover art by Anne Osborn
Cover design by Bill Boudreau

This book is dedicated to Marcia Preston,

its godmother,

and to the support group of writers called Gadflies.

Her Innocent War

PROLOGUE

During World War II thousands of young girls left home for the first time to work on stateside training bases. They saw none of the horrors of combat, only the home front scars: Fears and rumors, lovers and friends who marched away, some maimed, some never to return. They coped with scarcities as though doing without was a badge of honor. They lived among strangers they never would have met in an ordinary lifetime.

How could any of them know war wasn't just waving flags and knitting socks for 'our brave boys,' saving bacon grease and rubber, giving up sugar for the war effort? How could they know it wasn't glory and triumph for the fighting men either?

Never again would any of them be the same, nor would the nation. America lost her innocence then.

Nineteen, unaware of her beauty, Louella Tolbert's only knowledge of men is one chaste kiss from Stith Bonham before she goes to work on Seacomb Army Air Base.

If lovers are lucky, their lives change in parallel ways. How could the changes coming for Louella parallel those of Stith's overseas?

CHAPTER I

Louella pulled the shabby suitcase from under the cape jasmine where she had hidden it. Dew clung to its varnished cardboard in the moist half-darkness before dawn. The scent of flowers was strong in the damp South Carolina air. Rising, she turned to face the weathered house, her home for all her nineteen years. Below a flat drift of pale smoke from the kitchen chimney, the once grand house seemed to float above the blackness of the earth, partly submerged in the gray lake of ground fog. The wide porch was full of shadows, the black cavities of windows staring at her.

Shivering, she lifted her eyes toward what had been her bedroom. A pale face appeared. Her little sister Cora Sue held up one white hand, fingers crossed. Louella grinned at the goodluck sign and turned toward the road. Leaving her sixteen-yearold sister to deal with Papa felt like deserting. How different might it have been if Mama was still alive. Of course, Cloteel, dear, loving Cloteel was there to help, just as she'd been from Louella's youngest memories, brown arms always ready to gather them in and comfort their childhood sorrows.

It was useless to waver now; Cora Sue and Cloteel had encouraged her decision. When Papa awoke she'd be gone, headed toward something better, somewhere closer to Stith. Four miles to the Air Base and she had better hurry before Brent Tolbert missed his oldest daughter and came to fetch her home.

She had reached the mailbox at the end of the path when a sound like a rifle shot froze her steps. The slam of the front screen door reverberated through the fog like a living presence searching for her under the dark trees. Half strangled by dread, she turned.

Out of the porch shadows a tall white figure appeared at the top of the steps, a black square where a heart should be. Louella held her breath. Papa, in his nightshirt, clutched his Bible to his chest. His heavy body descended the stairs and marched down the path, parting ground fog like Moses at the Red Sea, his face a blank in the dimness, heavy white hair like a ghostly halo.

Her suitcase handle slipped in suddenly sweaty palms. She clutched it more firmly and turned to run.

"Lou — el — la!"

The roar of her name stopped her in one step. Even the trees seemed to listen. Determination grew enormous within her and she gripped the damp sand under foot with clenched toes.

At the mailbox he faced her.

Grateful she could not see his penetrating eyes in the gloom, Louella lifted her chin and waited, her suitcase held like a shield before her.

"Running away, are you? Sneaking out like a thief in the dark?" When she did not speak, he commanded, "Answer me!"

Louella found no words and her silence increased his anger.

"I reared you as a God-fearing daughter and this is the thanks I get, you breaking God's commandment to honor your parent?" he roared.

"I am going, Papa." She held her chin up, winning her voice not to tremble. "No way you can stop me. I'm nineteen, full grown."

"You're not too big for whippin'. "Spare the rod and spoil the child," he quoted. "I reared you an obedient daughter..."

"I've got to go help, Papa. Help make the war end."

"What?" he roared again, waking a bird into a querulous cry. "What does a spindly things like you think you can do about ending a war!" He roared in laughter. "Get yourself inside, Louella. You ain't too big to thrash, you ungrateful..."

"I'm going, Papa."

He took one step toward her and she backed against the mailbox, shuddering.

"Good-bye, Papa."

She spun around before he could reach her and ran down the road, expecting the bruising grip of his hand on her arm. Twenty feet away she glanced back over her shoulder.

He had not moved, looking more ghostly as she moved farther away. "If you run off, don't never expect to come through my door again as a daughter of mine!" With a dramatic sweep of his arm he pointed the black Bible toward the shadowy porch, sending fog wraiths swirling. "Any girl works at the Air Base is a harlot to damned Yankees, beyond redemption and no kin of mine!"

The sight and his words burned into her brain and she ran faster. It was a long time before she slowed to a walk, breathing hard.

Papa hadn't always been so hard-hearted. There were soft memories of early times, but since Mama died so mysteriously when Louella was eleven, he spent days with his Bible, withdrawing until, one by one, his friends gave up.

"I can't change what is," she whispered, "but I'm sure missing you today, Mama." She increased her speed in the coolness before full sunup.

It was her love for Stith Bynum that had given her courage to leave home and defy her father. For a year and a half he'd been fighting overseas in a place she could not imagine. His letters, safe in her suitcase, said only that he missed her.

But now it was June 29, 1945. Even VE Day hadn't made any difference, except he was out of combat, stationed in Paris. World War II went on and on. Perhaps it would never end.

Staying at home to hoe cotton and work beside Cloteel, cooking and cleaning for Papa wouldn't help end the war.

The one time Stith had come courting, Papa had chased him down the road shouting so loud she became afraid he'd have a seizure. If Mama had still been around, things might have been different. Louella kicked at the sandy ruts. Papa wouldn't let them even mention Mama's name, like it was her own fault she died.

She shifted the suitcase to the other hand and lengthened her stride.

"I won't go back. Ever!" she vowed to the ancient oaks.

A sluggish breeze swayed the hanging moss behind her, pale in stronger light. Something slithered and splashed into the bayou beyond the trees.

She shivered in the heavy humidity. Her father's black anger about the Air Base worried her. She hadn't told her destination but he obviously had guessed. With her free hand, Louella covered one ear to shut out echoes of his voice. Would God punish her if she worked there? Other women could be harlots; she would remain a virgin for Stith.

By full sunrise she had reached the wooden bridge where the bayou crossed the road. Hungry for the biscuits and bit of sideback saved from last night's supper, she climbed down into cool shadow under the wooden planks. Sluggish brown water nudged reeds near the edge. The water would feel good on her sandy feet, but she'd better not waste much time. She dropped her suitcase and waded in.

Movement caught her eye and her breath stopped.

"'Mornin', Miz Louella. I'm right proud to see you."

It was a soft, familiar voice and Louella relaxed. The old black man had been her friend all her life.

"Good-morning, Elijah. How are you?"

"Tolerable. Jest tolerable." Thin and ancient, he sat on a scrap of old carpet spread over a rock, his splayed feet bare beneath frayed overalls. A faded sweatshirt, once red, covered his sharp shoulder blades and bony arms. Under grizzled hair, his face was a contented mask. One hand held a cane pole, the other curled around a corncob pipe which he pulled from his wrinkled mouth, his shiny black eyes on her suitcase.

"'Pears you's going someplace, Miz Louella. You done run off." It was not a question.

Holding her long cotton skirts above the water, Louella considered. Papa was such a hard master to the old man, she felt fairly sure of Elijah's silence.

"Going to get a job at the Air Base, 'Lijah," she announced.

"You knows your Papa, he's gonna come fetch you home, Miz Louella, sure as catfishes swim in this here old bayou."

"Once I'm in that gate, he can't reach me," she answered defiantly. She waded out of the stream and offered part of her meal.

Corncob pipe back in his mouth, he spoke around it, one flat foot patting the dust. "Law, Miz Louella, I done et a long time ago." A puff of smoke circled around the pipestem. "Reckon I hain't seen you this day, beings as anybody asked. Reckon I just been fishin' here and ain't nobody been by at all."

"I appreciate that, 'Lijah, indeed I do." She patted his shoulder and took a seat on the boulder beside him.

It was peaceful in the shadow of the bridge with the water sounds, the scent of his tobacco and the smell of fatback and biscuits. They kept the silence of old friends between them. Hurriedly she finished the last bite and shook crumbs from her skirt. Moving around the curve of the stream, out of sight of the old man, Louella pulled on her good pair of black lisle stockings and the flat black slippers. When she returned and picked up her suitcase, she was conscious of his calm eyes.

"Well, I reckon I'd best be getting on down the road before Pa does catch up with me," she said. "One day I'll be rich and then I'll fix a place for you and Cloteel, promise I will." Suddenly conscious of his great age, she realized it would have to be soon.

"Watch out for Yankees, Miz Louella, and take care, now." His ebony eyes were solemn.

As she climbed the bank, she realized she had left another part of her life behind. Cloteel and Elijah were not just servants but friends.

Some quarter mile down the road, the trees ended and shestepped out into hot sunshine. Without the live oaks and pines, humidity and sun bore down. Here the land had been cleared for the flat cotton fields on either side of the concrete highway. Among the green masses of dust-covered leaves, pink blossoms showed. Good cotton weather this year, she calculated, and I hope I never have to pull one more boll.

As she walked down the long stretch of tarmac from the highway to the guard's hut at the base, the angular shapes of the air base's buildings on the horizon were an uneasy target. This part she had imagined many times; everything beyond was a strange dream. She felt a brush of fear, like bat wings in the dark.

The guard, immaculately creased and clean in the early morning heat, garrison cap an inch above his right eyebrow, stared at her with round expressionless eyes.

Louella was conscious of the sand on her slippers. For confidence she touched the cotton fabric of her dress with its tiny pink rosebuds. She had ironed it crisp and fresh last night but now it hung limp.

"I'm Louella Tolbert and I've come to work. The radio says you're hiring."

The guard's eyes seemed to revolve in his head like an owl's. He puckered his lips in a soundless whistle and took a full minute to look her over.

Louella slumped her shoulders, wishing she was not so tall with such a big bust. She kept her eyes on the shiny toes of the soldier.

"So that's what they're saying in the boondocks, huh?" He stepped into the hut. Through the window she saw him turn crank and speak into a box. She could not hear his words beyond: "You'll never believe this, but….."

What's not to believe? Louella wondered. Am I the very first to come look for a job?

He returned with a slip of paper and pointed her toward the nearest building some distance down the black asphalt. His face was not blank now but had a sort of hungry expression on it. Somehow he reminded her of a coon dog begging table scraps. What a perfectly silly thought, Louella decided and started walking.

No live oaks here. No trees at all. Just the low wooden buildings, gray paint above neat grass. Men in khaki moved everywhere. Over a low hill came the roar of airplane motors. This may be a hard day for me, she thought, but it isn't easy for Stith overseas, either.

She found the building with 201 painted on the corner, a clapboard structure with darker gray asphalt roof. There was not a single peeled place on the paint nor the white trim that gleaming in the sunlight. Even the square stacks of bricks and mortar at the corners supporting the whole building looked newly painted

A truck filled with soldiers drove by, whistles shrill. Louella felt her face flush. Were they Yankees?

Juggling her suitcase, she tugged at the heavy wooden door. Now it begins, she thought.

CHAPTER II

Glen Hart leaned over the Personnel Officer's desk to rap it twice.

"Just tell me how you expect me to run the Post Exchange without any employees. You've got me pruned down to one secretary, one accounting clerk and Barbara — and she's due to domino any minute." He pounded the desk a third time.

"Hell, she's going to have that baby between the desks if you don't get me a replacement! Maybe you expect me to wait until her kid's old enough to type?"

The fussy little officer squirmed in his chair. "Now, look, Hart, don't yell at me. Everybody's chewing my ass." His round face reddened. "Look out that window, pal, and tell me what you see. Since VE Day, GI's from the European Theater have flooded this base. Everybody on the whole post is crying for help." He leaned into Hart's face.

"You think I can cut a stencil and just crank out a dozen clerks or so? There's nobody left in this grand metropolis of Seacomb. All the smart ones went for high-paying jobs at assembly plants. And you know all that." His face was now a mottled red.

Hart remembered the little man had trouble with high blood pressure and eased back. He shoved fingers through his thick pepper-and-salt hair and ruffled it like a cock's comb.

"Buddy," Hart sighed, trying another approach, "keeping that office going is like shoveling out the Aegean stables. One load of paperwork out and two come sliding in."

The desk telephone rang and Hart turned to find a chair, ready to continue his demands. On the telephone, the Personnel Officer was noncommittal, limited to a terse 'yes' or 'no.' His eyes on Hart held an expression that smacked of amusement as the color ebbed from his cheeks.

Hart shifted his big frame to the other foot. Without this man's assistance he was helpless. He felt his temper rising.

Telephone back on its cradle, the Personnel Officer looked at Hart across the arch built of his fingers, each fingertip meeting its duplicate.

"This is your lucky day, my friend. Instant action. You request; I comply."

"How's that again?"

"Some camp follower just showed up at the gate looking for work."

"And?"

"She's all yours, big fellow. You do the interview. I've got other fish to fry." He scooped up papers from the desk top, shoved them into a briefcase and snapped it shut. The silver bars on his uniform winked when he gave Hart a sarcastic salute and walked out the door.

New arguments prepared, Hart felt the letdown. It took a moment to adjust. He circled the desk and sat in the vacant chair, which was too low for his long legs.

Checking out the knot in his tie, he shot his cuffs out of his blue suit jacket, noticed they were threadbare and tugged the jacket sleeves down again. Guys in the Army Air Corps had the advantage of not trying to match up shirts and suits, jackets and pants. He thought of his wife Irene at home in Texas. He'd sure be glad when....

A shadow fell on the upper glass of the office door.

Camp followers had little need for brains. He waited, full of hope she at least knew the alphabet. If she couldn't do anything else, God grant she could file. Every flat surface at the PX office had disappeared under shoals of paper. Fruitless time was spent searching documents. It was as though the war had burst a dam, drowning them all in paper. Anybody strong enough to walk through that door and clear security check would have a job, he vowed.

But he was not prepared for Louella.

She wore thick black stockings and flat shoes dusted with sand below a long, flowered cotton dress that clung damply to her body. Tall, with full breasts swelling above a tiny waist, her thick black braids seemed a coronet too heavy for her slender neck. Shyly she held her head down.

Dropping the suitcase of varnished cardboard before the desk, she raised her face to him. The impact of long dark lashes over large gray eyes flecked with gold made him catch his breath.

"The radio said you're hiring folks. So I came." Her voice was soft, her accent slow and Deep South. "My Stith is away fighting overseas and I want to help."

She offered her pass and Hart pretended to examine it. Finally he cleared his throat.

"Ever worked anywhere before, Miss Dollbutt?"

"Tolbert. It's Tolbert."

"Dolbert?"

"Tolbert. Louella Tolbert," she repeated. "Not for pay, except for picking cotton. But I made A's in typing at Consolidated High School and I'm real good at figuring." Her gaze did not waiver. "I'd sure be proud to try."

He thought of this beautiful, shy girl surrounded by fifteen hundred lonely men. In hesitation he stared at the desk. She seemed so vulnerable in her strange clothes.

"Do your folks know you've come?" he asked.

"I'm nineteen."

Perhaps that was a direct answer, he realized. The face of his oldest daughter June, also nineteen, flashed in his memory and he felt his fatherly instincts rise. "Do you have a place to stay?"

"I can pay." She fumbled with catches on the suitcase, drew out a flat shabby purse and held it toward him.

He gestured it away. "There's a six-month waiting list for housing on this base, but visitors can stay four days free in the guest house. After that, you'll have to find something else."

Shoving application forms toward Louella, he said, "Get to work on these and I'll give the Housing Officer a ring and get you in the guest house."

When she was settled at an empty desk, Hart returned to the telephone. Maybe he clutched at brittle vines, but he did need help. He had sweet-talked his pregnant clerk into an additional month already. If Barbara, who had sworn Friday was her last day, could stuff enough information into this new girl, just maybe....

He glanced at the tall tense figure hunched over the forms across the room and felt a pang of concern. War has all kinds of casualties, he thought, here as well as overseas. I can't protect her; she'll have to grow up fast.

He dialed the officer in charge of the guest house.

It took Louella a long time to fill in the many pages required to be accepted for Civil Service, forms with small spaces that cramped her round handwriting. It was hard to concentrate surrounded by distractions of typewriters, telephones, conversations and the constant thud of airmen's boots on the wooden floor.

She tucked a loose strand back into her braids and touched away beads of nervous moisture on her upper lip. Mentally she sent a thought of gratitude to her high school typing teacher. She remembered the rickety machine with letters that stuck and a ribbon worn to holes. Surely they'd have better here. Daily her teacher had repeated that typing was a skill offering her a chance to move up in the business world. It couldn't hurt that math was Louella's best subject, either. Her glance met the eyes of the man at the desk.

"Finished? Bring it on over."

Again she stood before him, half holding her breath. Time stretched before he laid the papers down, shoveled one hand through his hair and looked up.

"Okay, Miss Tolbert, we'll put you on temporary until the security check clears."

Louella's smile grew from the inside out and her hand flew to her mouth in delight.

"You'll start as a GS-2. The salary is thirty-two dollars a week. At the end of six months it will probably be more. If you do good work." His voice continued in a litany of job information.

Louella heard nothing beyond "thirty-two dollars a week." A fortune! It had taken a very long time to accumulate the twenty dollars in her purse. Dragging cotton sacks was a slow way to earn money, but her goal had been enough to pay for bed and food before her first paycheck. Now she would have thirty-two dollars every seven days! She wrenched her mind back to his voice.

"...the MP's will issue you a temporary pass. I've signed you up for Room 12 in the guest house until next Monday." He stood to shake her hand. "I guess I didn't introduce myself. My name is Glen Hart. I'm the manager of the Post Exchange and you will work for me. Report to the office in the Post Exchange as soon as you're settled."

It was early noon when she left Building 201. The usual moisture hung in the bright sunshine. She walked down the paved street, a wide grassy area like a park on her right. Beyond she saw a small chapel with its identifying white cupola above the standard white and gray clapboards. That's where I'll go Sunday, she decided, surprised to find a church on the base where they learned about war.

In the center of the smooth green grass a large flag hung limp on a tall silver pole. Men marched back and forth in close block formations, elbow to elbow, reversing directions in response to the soldier who shouted commands.

As one group drew near, Louella heard its leader shout, "Eyes left!" Every man stared at her, the sound of their boots in unison a soft shush on the grass.

"Hip, hip!" called the man in charge.

"Hurray!" they answered, watching her.

"Hip, hip!"

"Hurray!"

"Eyes right!" Heads turned away as they marched on past Louella.

Too interested to be self-conscious, she swiveled, suitcase banging against her knees. Was Stith marching on a Paris street like that right now? She had never seen her love in uniform, except for the photograph he'd sent, which she'd hidden from Papa under her mattress. She had it with her now. The photographer had made a mistake, though, when he tinted Stith's hair. It was auburn, not carrot red.

She watched until the men disappeared from sight behind a building, then frowned. Why wouldn't they send Stith home now? All the Germans had surrendered. VE Day was long past. But what if the Army sent him to the Pacific instead of back to South Carolina? She shoved the dark thought away.

The guest house surprised her. It was not a house at all, just another long one-storied building with the same gray clapboards and white trim. She entered a narrow hallway full of windows on her right, a row of closed doors on the left. Which one was hers? Confused, she paused, listening to the silence. Examining her key, she saw the number twelve stamped in the metal, located the correct door and entered.

Across the small room stood a gray oak bed with an oak chest also painted a matching gray. Both were lined against a lighter gray cinderblock wall. She had found her home—at least for four nights. She closed the door and leaned against it. To her left was a tiny closet alcove. A venetian blind with wide slats was half closed against the outside glare at the single window where a fan droned, stirring humid air. In the opposite corner sat a sturdy oak chair, painted like everything else on the base— gray. A small table beside the bed held a lamp.

Louella took two steps forward and dropped the suitcase. Her very own room! A bed with clean sheets she had not washed herself! A closet all her own! The khaki blanket folded like a package at the foot of the bed was not very pretty, but who needed one in this weather?

Tentatively she touched the white sheet. It was drawn so taut it seemed to resist and she drew back her hand. The room was not unfriendly; it simply tolerated her presence.

There were no sounds in the building, other than the window fan which droned like heavy breathing. Louella wondered about the rooms down the hall. Were there others just as uncertain behind those closed doors? Or were they all happy, easy folks come to visit kin? Surely on other bases across America there were rooms where girls like her tried to bolster their courage. Where was the person now who last slept in this bed?

Louella shook herself, mentally and physically. This is silly, she taunted herself. I did what I set out to do: left home and found a job. This is my room now — at least for four days.

Excitement renewed, she kicked the suitcase under the bed and dropped to hug the flat pillow. A job! A room! She'd prove to Papa she wasn't a bad girl. Now she'd be able to buy pretty clothes like those in the movie magazines hidden with Stith's picture under the mattress. Won't sister Cora Sue be happy when she brings her something fine!

Stith, my love. She hugged the pillow tighter and stroked her cheek against it. They had never had any time alone together, except once, that Sunday afternoon she'd slipped out to meet him.

Now there wasn't time to remember that wonderful day when Stith Bynum wove a grass ring for her, a promise to marry when he returned from overseas.

Wrenched back to the present, Louella released the pillow and rolled over. Now was now and she'd better hurry. Reluctantly she pushed up from the bed.

CHAPTER III

Headquarters functioned as the brain of Seacomb Air Base, but the heart was the Post Exchange. It was the one place where military brass with fruit baskets of ribbons on their chests rubbed elbows with raw privates in ill-fitting fatigues. Pilots back from flights in the unheated fighter planes sweated in fleece-lined leather jackets, proud kings of the hill. Men ate and joked, stood in lines to buy or flirt with the clerks. It was an escape over a hamburger and fries to forget bad news from the front or from home. It was relief from SOS at the end of the month's rations when the company cook served chipped beef on toast three nights in a row.

The GI leaving, held the door open to watch Louella's timid entrance. She blinked in the dimmer light and he winked back. Confused by noise and movement in the huge room, she never saw his overture. He shrugged, released the door and walked away to concentrate again on a toothpick and his back tooth.

To Louella's left were numerous counters piled with merchandise. Girls behind glass cases dispensed glittering wares. A stack of T-shirts glowed a luminous white against the piles of khaki pants stacked beside them. She recognized jewelry, boxes of stationery and pens, shoes and boots, fishing rods, hunting knives, cosmetics, lacy nightgowns. It's just like a great big Ben Franklin dime store, she decided.

Against the righthand wall behind a cluster of small chromeand-lineoleum topped tables a jukebox blarred "Don't Sit Under the Apple Tree," accompanied by a clatter of dishes and cutlery, scrape of chairs and babble of voices. Loudest of all rose the orders of two harried waitresses who shouted orders through a small window to a perspiring cook in a tall white hat. Under the glare of florescent lights, the crewcuts of the soldiers were like thick paint brushes shaded from wheat stubble to black.

Bewildered, Louella stood in the aisle to get her bearings. Servicemen passed on both sides. When one turned back to stare full in her face and whistle, she jumped, heart thundering. In all this confusion, where was the office? Finally she noticed the sign over an open hallway announcing: PX OFFICE. She realized she'd been holding her breath and filled her lungs once more as she hurried under the placard.

After the hubbub of the open PX, the hallway was very quiet, her footsteps hollow on the wooden floor. Two solid doors on her left gave no clue to what hid behind them. The murmur of voices and the clack of a typewriter led her to the door at the end of the hall. Through the glass in the top half of the door she saw a group of people busy at gray metal, linoleum-topped desks. She recognized Mr. Glen Hart, the one closest to the far wall.

A brown-haired, very pregnant girl propped against a filing cabinet was speaking. Through the closed door her words were faint but clear.

"...and he said now he was to the place where food was more important than sex, well, he had a mirror installed over his dining room table!"

There was an explosion of laughter from the others just as Louella stepped into the room. It stopped immediately and five pair of eyes turned toward her. Unable to move, she stared back, clasping her purse before her in both hands as a protective barrier.

Glen Hart half stood, leaning his tall body across his desk. "Welcome, Louella." He pushed back a lock of pepper-and-salt hair and without pause for her answer, announced, "Meet Louella Tolbert, everybody."

"Am I glad to see you!" the pregnant girl said.

Louella lowered herself to the edge of the chair Hart indicated, her body stiff.

"You'll replace Barbara Brousely here." He waved a hand toward the bulky brunette. "That's Frances Maynard in the corner, queen of the Kardex."

The older girl on the tall stool quit flipping cards in the tall black case and grinned in Louella's direction. Her face was tan as a saddle under short brown curls, her movements quick.

"Hutch here is our leg man, runs interference with the Air Force's chain of command for us. For some reason the civilian way is never the way of the Army."

The baby-faced young soldier flushed up to the roots of his sun-streaked brown hair and moved his plump body uneasily in his chair. "Pleased to meetcha."

"Most important of all," Glen Hart continued, "is Brenda Burnstein, my secretary, who really runs this place."

The blonde with wise eyes, dressed in bright blue crepe, lifted her hands from the typewriter keyboard to pat her hair. Blue stones in her large earrings glittered. "Glad to have you, honey." Louella could see through the careful makeup that Brenda was older than the Kardex queen.

"That's all of us—except for Donald Monahan my assistant manager, who's on vacation this week. You'll meet him later."

The smile on his lips reached his eyes. "We're like a family here. There's too much to do and we all pitch in to get it done, help each other. If you have any problems at all, just ask. We're not military or..." He broke off to consider his words. "I guess we just like each other."

Hart resumed his seat and reached for a stack of papers. "Barbara, get her started while I finish this dictation."

When Louella rose, Brenda scooped up pad and pencil and took the chair. Louella heard Hart's dictation begin before she had reached Barbara at the filing cabinets.

Hutch disappeared through the hall door, pulling his garrison cap down over his stiff crewcut. Frances hadn't broken the rhythm of flipping cards and writing information.

"What's your name, again?" Barbara asked with a warm smile.

"Louella Tolbert."

"Well, Louella, you just don't know how glad I am you're here! I'm way behind on filing because I can't bend over far enough to reach the S's through Z's." She laughed. "I told Mr. Hart in other week I wouldn't be able to get close enough to open the top drawers, either!" She shifted her bulk. "Baby's due in three weeks. That's too darn close."

Louella felt herself relax under the flow of words. Barbara's voice was Southern, like her own. "You come from around here?" she asked.

"Forty miles west. My husband's back from the war." Barbara hesitated, laughter gone. "He lost a leg over there. But now we're starting our family." Her smile was back. "Along with every animal on our place. Our mare just had her foal. We've got a new batch of baby chicks hatched yesterday and the dog's due to whelp her litter the same time this one's due." She patted her belly lovingly, with a hearty laugh. "Mr. Hart said it sounded like we had a stallion on a merry-go-round out at our place."

Louella's cheeks burned. Maybe Barbara wasn't born around here after all. Southern women didn't talk out loud about sex. If Barbara saw her blush, she ignored it.

"Steinmetz through Zurchowski. Manufacturers of what we sell in the Post Exchange. Those go in the lower drawers, most recent date in front. I'll handle Adams through Rochester."

The minutes raced by and Louella's confidence grew. By five o'clock her stack of invoices had dwindled by half.

"Quitting time!" Glen Hart declared.

Rising from her stooped position, Louella stretched tall with relief, suddenly conscious of the ache in her back.

"Where you staying, honey?" Brenda asked as she dropped the cover on her Royal typewriter.

"Through Friday at the guest house, they call it. After that I'll have to find something in town, I guess."

Frances waved good-bye over Brenda's shoulder and ducked through the door. "'Night, everybody," Brenda said and hurried after her.

"You're a godsend, Louella," Barbara said again as she angled her bulk through the door. "See you tomorrow."

Glen Hart walked down the hall with Louella. Apparently aware of her fatigue, he patted her shoulder as he stopped by the first blank door and inserted his key. "First day's the hardest. Tomorrow will be easier."

Louella moved on toward the smell of food and the chatter in the open PX. It's been an interesting day, she thought, and it's not over yet.

Technical Sergeant Leon Cobb sat at the food counter in the Post Exchange. For the last thirty minutes his thoughts had blocked out the sounds around him while he pondered a problem.

To gain his goals, he always moved through obstacles, not around them, but the current block was different.

Come the end of the war, he intended to own the biggest, flashiest nightclub and bar in Miami Beach. Never again would anyone look down on him then. No more common labor for some landscaper and the humiliation of overbearing bosses and snobbish landowners in their mansions.

But VE Day had come and gone. Men were arriving daily from the European Theater. He simply had to speed up operations to meet his financial deadline. The owners of the club he had an option on didn't look like the patient kind.

Being a sergeant in Supply was full of advantages and he'd used them all. Moonlight scrounging was easy, a pleasure. Someone always needed an extra clothing allowance, a few gallons of gasoline for a three-day pass or some of the tenderloins that never showed up in the messhalls. Now he had things rolling in the black market sugar and booze business, profits could reach a thousand a week — if he was careful. Add in the profits playing poker with a bunch of farmboy GI's whenever they could sneak a game in. He'd have to be extra careful about poker, though. Some losers were catching onto his deals.

He was proud of his horse-trading talents. To get a man what he needed when he wanted it had built a bank account with no relation to his Tech Sergeant's pay of $117.90 a month. He couldn't understand the fools who said black marketing showed he wasn't patriotic. Hell, he was in the Army, wasn't he? Somebody else would get them what they wanted, if he didn't. And he had a need for the money.

By keeping his ears open he'd learned just whose buttons to push, when and where. Friendships didn't put a nickel in the bank and he'd get there a lot faster without dragging a dozen stupid "friends" along with him.

His eyes flickered with contempt over the chummy GI's at the tables reflected in the mirror behind the counter. Two stools away he caught a glimpse of Melba waiting on a customer and he swiveled around into the aisle. He preferred not to bump into her this evening. After you rolled them in the hay, they seemed to think they had some kind of hold on you. Women, he thought, he'd have to be careful of any snares there. One-night stands were necessary, of course, keep a man healthy. Maybe twice if she was really good, and then move on.

He eased the seven-inch pocket knife out of his pants pocket, unfolded it and began to ream under his left thumbnail, which was half an inch long. Showed he didn't have to do manual labor, like those old Chinese guys with the foot long claws. Maybe he'd let his grow, see how long it would get.

His thoughts returned to the business he'd built in bars for a twenty-mile radius around the base. A No. 10 can of peaches was damned near worth its weight in gold, what with sugar rationing. But a sack of sugar, well, that brought double, along with any female companionship he cared to indulge in.

Booze, it was the best money maker. Sell a bottle without making the customer buy a fifth of the plentiful rum, like civilians had to do, and he could almost name his price. It was the booze business that boosted his bank account high enough his Florida banker now called him by name. But that account would have to be a lot bigger quick. The war was ending too fast to suit him.

He reviewed his plans to take over as manager of the Non-Commissioned Officers Club. That's where the real gold lay. For every bottle he'd filched out of the Officers Club on the base, there'd be ten at the NCO Club with him in charge. Then he'd be sure of his Miami Beach club, even have the training for it.

It would happen very soon. The current manager, Master Sergeant Woods, had a bad case of ulcers. Cobb messed up the NCO Club's supplies every few days and he could tell it was hard on Woods' stomach. He was so damned grateful when Cobb straightened things out again, believing he'd been done a personal favor, that Cobb had to laugh. Woods and that pint of half-and-half he carried around as medicine for his belly! Stupid guy should stay off the hard stuff, too.

Cobb snapped his knife shut, gave it a toss from one hand to the other and tucked it away in his pocket. His eyes misted. That NCO Club was a real dilly. Three years back Woods had pulled a real smart deal. For that he saluted the man mentally. By Federal wartime regulations no liquor was allowed enlisted men on military bases. The prestige of the gentlemen's liquor at the Officers Club lost its glamour when the NCO Club opened down the road. Woods restored an old Southern mansion, but ghostly Southern ladies and gentlemen sure wouldn't recognize the inside now.

He licked his lips. Just give him six weeks and his future in Miami Beach was nailed down. He shoved his long legs further into the aisle and focused on the conversation at the nearest table among the three GI's hunched together over hamburgers.

"Now that's what I call a real 'double-breasted' woman," said one. Another snickered, "Yeah! Some front porch!"

Cobb swiveled to his left to face the object of their regard as a tall brunette in freaky clothes slid onto the stool beside him. For a second her wide gray eyes flecked with gold met his. An expression he could not read flashed for an instant before she turned aside. The way she held her head and the coil of black braids like a crown made him think of royalty, in spite of the way she was dressed.

Glen Hart's words, when he left her, had warmed Louella. Now her hunger pangs rose with the smell of onions and coffee and she hurried ahead. There had been no lunch and it was many hours since the biscuits and sideback eaten by the bayou with Elijah. She decided on a quick supper, a warm shower, then bed—but she must write Stith, too.

There was only one vacant stool at the PX counter, next to a thin soldier with a blond crewcut, who half sat, half leaned against the counter. Lean as a knife, his long legs crossed at the ankles extended into the aisle between tables, defying passersby. Oddly, his uniform looked crisp in spite of the heat and humidity. No dark sweat stains like the others.

Louella slid onto the vacant stool and faced him for an instant. His eyes startled her. They were like icewater, cold and pale, the pupils large and black. Before she could look away, she had the strange feeling she saw down ebony tunnels into his skull.

The jukebox, now silent between numbers, clicked and a new record began. A tableful of GI's across the room sang along with enthusiastic rudeness about "Right in Der Fuhrer's Face."

Louella read the posted menu behind the counter, careful not to glance again at the man beside her, aware of his attention. With effort she concentrated on what to order for her first meal in a public place alone. The muscles of her face felt stiff, her hands trembled. A quick glance at other plates was no help. No rice, no cornbread.

The waitress bustled toward her but stopped to put one hand on the shoulder of the thin soldier seated beside Louella, who was uncomfortable with the sight of the white bulge of the girl's breasts above her pink uniform when she leaned over the counter.

"Hey, honey! How you tonight, Cobb?" The waitress fondled the side of his neck and ran a finger around his ear. "How's my favorite lover?"

Louella's face burned and she turned toward the glass case of pie on her left.

"Get your hands off me, Melba, damn it! You stink of dishwater."

"Well, shit, honey," the girl spit out, jaw slack, face turned angry red, "that sure as hell ain't what you told me last night!"

"Who could smell stink in bubble bath?"

Louella gulped in shock. Surely they hadn't been naked in the bathtub together! She stared at the girl's sullen face.

"What'll you have?" the waitress asked Louella in a choked voice, then whispered, "Stay away from that one, honey. He's a one-time-Johnny."

Unable to comprehend, Louella blinked and ordered the only familiar food on the menu: A hamburger and coffee.

Head in the air, her face still pinker than her uniform, the waitress moved away. Her reflection in the mirror made a two-girl parade. She ignored Sergeant Cobb and shouted Louella's order through the kitchen window.

Louella stared at her own hands folded on the edge of the counter. Her imagination saw two naked bodies writhing in a tub of bubbles. This was what Papa had said about the base, about sinful people. Well, she didn't have to be like that just because she was working here now. She wrenched her thoughts back to her surroundings.

Voices from the tables were too quick, harsh speech so fast she couldn't understand much of it. She stiffened as she realized it was Yankee voices she heard. Horror stories from her childhood flooded back. Yankees killed the Valiant Boys in Gray, ruined the great South and its gracious ways of living, burned Atlanta and raped Southern ladies. She shivered.

Gathering courage, she examined faces reflected in the mirror behind the counter. They didn't appear mean. They looked a lot like the boys she'd known in Consolidated High. Anyway, she reassured herself, they helped Southern boys beat the Germans and now they all fought the Japs together. She released her breath and relaxed.

"That's fifteen cents, honey," said the waitress as she plunked down a plate before her.

When Louella shoved the coins across the counter, Sergeant Cobb joggled her arm. She dared not turn in his direction. When her hunger eased, she slowed down to savor the last of the food. Even the pickle and potato chips were delicious. But the coffee was awful. She missed the chicory. This is Yankee coffee, she thought.

She sipped at her cup, conscious the man beside her drew her thoughts. Finally she slid off the stool, meal finished. Despite her intentions, she caught the reflection of his eyes in the mirror. They were so pale it was as though he had no irises, making his pupils seem blacker. Like burned holes in a blanket, Cloteel used to say.

She turned her back and threaded her way through the tables to the outside door. Were those strange eyes following her? She resisted the temptation to turn and see. Resolutely she headed to the guest house.

Cobb had inspected the tall girl beside him intently. Her profile was excellent—all the way down to slim ankles. When he tried to catch her eye in the mirror again and twice bumped her arm—accidently on purpose—she ignored even his apologies. Too damned good for him, was she? Nobody, but nobody was going to put him down ever again as trash. He'd see about this one.

It was not hard for Cobb to spot her light-colored dress outside the PX in the early muggy evening as she walked down the road between its edges of white-washed stones. Only a few figures moved under the hazy streetlamps. He relished the sway of her hips below the narrow waist. He could teach her a few things.

Doubling the length of his steps, he caught up and slipped his left hand under her elbow. "Want a little company, sweet thing?"

"Oh, my!" She flinched and jerked away, her face a pale oval in the fading light. "No, no!" She began to run.

He remained where he stood, debating another approach. Maybe it was his conversation with Melba that turned her off like that. When she turned in at the guest house, he gave it up. Probably somebody's wife come for a visit, although she wasn't wearing a ring. Some of the dumb slobs were too poor to buy a wedding band.

Forget that prude, he told himself, and headed back to the barracks. Tonight he'd be there for bed check, for a change.

CHAPTER IV

Brenda Bernstein dropped her purse into the desk drawer and took out pad and pencil, ready for the day's work to begin. The first one in this Friday morning, she made coffee and took time to examine her face in a small mirror inside her middle drawer. Hell, she didn't look so bad considering what last night had been. She patted a strand of blonde hair into place and frowned at her reflection.

"Those lines are deeper," she said aloud, looking at the corners of her eyelids. "Well, laughter lines is what they are. I've laughed a lot in thirty-five years and I intend to keep on, no matter what." She glanced at the door. Anybody who caught her talking to herself would think she was some kind of crazy.

She dropped the mirror to survey the office. Who'd have thought she'd land on this small air base in the hick South? I was born for big cities and bright lights, she thought, but that sure's not what life dealt me this round.

Back in the Bronx she met Master Sergeant Flint Burnstein, and in one short weekend married him and arrived at Seacomb Air Base. She picked up the mirror again and frowned at her image. Had it really been that great with Flint? There had been only three weeks together before Uncle Sam swooped him overseas.

The chemistry had been there, all right, but now she could not be sure what he was really like, other than a big bear of a man with brown hair. After three years it was hard to even picture her husband. He'd sure known the ropes, though. Landed them a two-bedroom apartment in the housing area on base— and those were scarcer than diamonds mined under Times Square.

Should she still feel guilty about Eddie after two years of having him in her life? With Flint unreachable overseas, she wasn't a nun and Eddie was right beside her every free hour. Soon she'd have to make a decision about that.

Her eye fell on Louella's desk. That one sure dresses like a Halloween party, she thought. Black lisle stockings! Even her own grandmother wore nylons these days. The girl could be a knockout with the right clothes. She seemed scared but determined. Probably needed somebody to take her in hand.

Brenda rose to check her stocking seams and be certain there was no more mud on her platform pumps. Half the streets weren't paved on this damned base and that gumbo dried like concrete. The door opened and she straightened.

Glen Hart entered, both hands pushing back unruly hair, his grin a sleepy grimace. "'Morning, Brenda."

"Certainly is."

"Any coffee?"

"Coming up."

Over thick mugs they sat in silence, staring at the opposite wall, half asleep.

"What do you think of the new girl?" he asked finally.

"Seems shy."

"Reminds me of my nineteen-year-old daughter June. Acts a lot younger, though. Hope she'll work out." He yawned. "Trouble is, all the good workers are either in some high-paying war job or in service themselves." He ran one hand over his chin and encountered the scrap of toilet paper stuck to a shaving nick on his face. "Got a feeling we're lucky with Louella." "Umhh."

"Hope the security check turns out okay."

"You think maybe she's some kind of spy?" Brenda gave a short laugh and rubbed her temple. She was a little hung over after all.

"You never know about the family," Hart said and grinned. He scribbled a note on his desk calendar. "Better check with the housing officer again. I got her one extension on the guest house until Monday, but I'm afraid that's it. There's a six-month wait for base housing and I hear the town's full up. I'd hate to lose her for lack of a place to hang her hat."

Hart shook his head. "Damned glad Monahan and I've got rooms across the hall." The movement shifted his hair and reminded Brenda of the mane on a policeman's horse she'd seen in Central Park.

"I've seen beds curtained off in a back porch with hijack-high rent unloaded on some of the GI's families," Brenda commented. "While they were still doing construction on the west end of the base, I met one guy lived in a chicken house in town. A chicken house!"

"Hope they shoveled out the shit first," Hart said after a long sip of coffee. "Some people don't let patriotism get in the way of making a buck."

"Well," he continued, "let's get a running start this morning on the dictation. No end to paperwork on an Army Air Base. Bet we could sink a Jap freighter from the sheer weight of the files in just this one office."

"And seven copies of everything," Brenda added. "I met a guy from the RAF once. Showed me his orders to come to the States. Just a note scrawled on the back of an old envelope by his commanding officer. Hate to think the British are smarter than we."

"Ours not to reason why," Hart replied. He loosened his tie before he lifted the first document. "Dear Sirs — make this one to the supplier of those fatigues that ripped at the seams — regarding your shipment...."

With an ear tuned to Hart's voice, her pencil flying over the stenographer's pad, Brenda still noticed when Louella entered the office. The girl was a worker — rare in these parts with most natives full of malaria. She didn't look so strange today in a white peasant blouse and full blue skirt. But, oh, those stockings! Didn't she know she could buy nylons in the PX? Maybe she didn't have any money, poor kid. Ten more days until payday.

At noon Barbara pushed the top file shut with a sigh. "Thank God that's all for now."

Frances Maynard slid off her tall stool. "Want to get a burger and some sun?" she asked Louella and Barbara.

"Meeting my Jack today," Barbara answered. "He's taking us both to lunch." She patted her bulge.

"How about you, Louella?"

Louella straightened with a grunt. "My, it's good to stretch. I'd be happy to go."

"Count me in," Hutch said, ambling with them toward the door.

They left Brenda and Hart to their chicken salad sandwiches from greasy PX brown paper bags.

Down the hall Louella gestured at the second closed door. "What's in there?"

"That's Mr. Monahan's room," Hutch replied, trying to tuck in an escaping shirttail.

"Mr. Monahan?"

"Yeah. He's assistant manager. Nice guy. Went home to California on leave, I think."

Louella heard a faint rustle behind the door and hurried to catch up to the other two.

Lugging hamburgers and iced tea, the three stepped out into sunshine and claimed a small metal table on the concrete patio. Three nearby tables held enlisted men, their khaki uniforms dull under the glow from bright yellow umbrellas.

"Not so hot today. There's even a breeze," Louella commented as they took their seats.

"I love the sun," Frances said. "My home's on the California desert."

Amazed someone would chose a desert to live on, Louella asked, "Isn't that kind of...barren?"

"Lord, no, child! Lots of things live on the desert. After a spring rain it blooms, miles of flowers everywhere. People come all the way from Los Angeles every year to see them. The air's so clear you can see all the way to the horizon. Sun, sure, but icy cold in winter when the wind blows. Come see me when this war's over and I'll show you goldmines, cactus and Joshua trees. Lots of things." Frances was solemn behind her half-eaten hamburger. "I sure miss it. This humidity's about to warp my soul."

"How did you wind up here?"

"Followed my man." Frances wiped a dot of mustard from the corner of her mouth. "They sent him overseas from here and he's due back before long, if I count right. Ought to have his thirty-six points any time now."

"Thirty-six points?" Louella asked.

"One for every month of service, more for overseas." She bent her head over the table, her short brown curls bouncing. "Hope they don't need him in the Pacific now VE Day's come and gone."

Hunger eased, Louella nibbled the last potato chip. The heat felt good between her shoulder blades. At the next table four GI's hunched over a portable radio. A reporter painted a word picture of the rubble of conquered German cities, telling of people who scrounged among ruins to fight over garbage in the streets. She shuddered, wondering about the lives of the hated enemy now. Somehow she couldn't control a feeling of pity.

Hutch's shirt was damp, his face pinker. He dabbed at his forehead with a paper napkin. Obviously uncomfortable, he still managed a smile. Such a cheerful soul, Louella thought.

"Where's your home, Hutch?"

"Kingfisher, Oklahoma," he answered, leaning forward into a little more shade. "Well, not right in town. My folks have a farm three miles west, but I went to school in town. Would have graduated from high school this spring, if I'd stayed with my class." His round face was rueful.

"All those guys that came home on leave looked so great in uniform, talked about places they'd been and things they'd done. Crossing the Rhine River. Battle of the Bulge." He shrugged. "Well, I kept after Pa until he signed for me to get in, but nothing exciting's happened to me yet. Just Seacomb, South Carolina." He dropped his damp paper napkin into his paper plate. "Those guys stretched things some, I reckon."

Louella was astonished when she calculated Hutch was at least a year younger than herself. Maybe it was the uniform that made the difference.

"Oklahoma," she said, trying to remember. "Which side did they fight on in the war? The Civil War, I mean," she added hastily.

Hutch looked at her in surprise. "Don't know, really."

"Probably Indian Territory back then," Frances offered.

"My great-grandparents homesteaded in the Run of '89 when the Cherokee Strip opened," Hutch said.

Louella pictured half naked savages in the one cowboy movie she'd been allowed to see. "Are there still Indians?"

Hutch laughed. "Indians are like everybody else, go to school, farm and all. Got a little Indian in me, too, on my Mom's side, but you can't tell it. Choctaw, like Will Rogers." He ran his hand over his streaked brown hair. "Mostly I'm Czech. Czechoslovakian, you know. Lots of folks around Kingfisher are." He leaned toward Louella. "Tell us about you."

She stiffened, not ready to share her life. "Not much to tell, really. Pa raises cotton near here."

"We've got ten acres of cotton back home." Hutch rolled blue eyes at them both. "Know what? I just realized I miss my three little brothers! Imagine that. They were always getting into my stuff."

Louella felt a pang. "I miss my sister Cora Sue, too. There's just her...and Pa."

As she spoke she heard a hiss. A bitter smell hit her nostrils, burning intensely. Something stung her eyes, tears welled. Behind her she heard two more hisses.

"Chemicals!" Hutch shouted. "Run!" He grabbed at Louella's shoulder.

Louella turned and faced two khaki figures approaching, hoods over their heads, round glass eyeholes glittering. A long black tube, like a snout, curved down to something round and metallic which sizzled in short bursts of yellow fog.

They couldn't be real people, she thought wildly. Martians! Everything disappeared in the blur of her tears. Hutch's fingers were painful, urging her up. Not Martians; they must be Japanese! The enemy had invaded, dropped from the skies!

In panic she leaped to her feet. Her chair crashed over. With every breath her lungs seared. Through a Niagara of tears she saw Frances, hands clamped over nose and mouth, scrambling away. Figures from other tables shouted and ran. The abandoned radio announced progress of the signing of the charter for the United Nations, the voice a center of calm in the whirlpool of escaping people.

Louella choked and tried to escape the hooded figures. She heard their hollow laughter nearer now. Arms extended in blind terror, she screamed when she struck the edge of a metal table. Fingers entangled in the octopus tentacles of the umbrella fringe, the table swayed and went over, carrying Louella with it. Frantically she fought a cage of pedestal, table and chair legs.

When hands touched her, Louella gave up, seized with a fit of coughing, helpless.

"Louella, it's just me." It was Hutch's voice.

She tried to still her panic, fighting a new convulsion of coughing. Flat on the concrete patio, she laced her fingers over her head in fear.

"Come on, Louella, it's just a little tear gas." The small sandals beside Louella's watering eyes belonged to Frances, whose words came between her own coughs.

Hutch, his face a scarlet blur, helped Louella to her feet. She rubbed at her stinging eyes and caught a glimpse of the hooded figures, now far down the street. Finally able to draw breath, she straightened sheepishly.

"You all right?" Hutch asked, mopping his face on his sleeve.

"Oh, heck, it's on my shirt, too."

Gulping air, Louella gasped out, "Have we been invaded?"

"Oh, shoot no, Louella. This happens every now and then. Guess we should have warned you." Frances sniffled and dabbed at her reddened eyes. "Headquarters thinks it keep everybody on their toes to have a little teargas attack. All part of the training, they say."

Embarrassment swept over Louella, making her feel very awkward beside her new friends. "But I'm not in the Army," she protested, thankful for the oxygen in her lungs again.

"Ever hear of civilian casualties in wartime?" Frances asked, ironically.

"If you ever hear a hissing sound again, move fast," Hutch instructed. "That hiss means chemicals."

"Well," Frances said matter-of-factly, "they've never sprayed inside the PX yet. Let's get back to the office." She marched ahead of them through the sales counters and down the hall stomping in indignation.

By the time they had passed the first closed door, the limp spaghetti feeling had left Louella's legs. Again she heard a small sound behind that door, like the squeak of bedsprings. Mice, probably, she thought.

When the three entered the office door, Brenda looked up and laughed. "Yeah, we heard about it. Keep down wind of us, will you?"

Brenda glanced at Glen Hart before she added, "I'll give Louella something to be happy about. Looks like she needs it right now. Honey, you passed security."

"You're on permanent now, Louella. Congratulations!" Glen Hart added.

The announcement startled Louella. "My, that is mighty fine," she murmured. It hadn't occurred to her before she might not have the job after all. What would she have done? No job; no money; no place to stay. Shivers spun down her spine and she dropped into her chair, knees weak again, although she kept the smile frozen on her face.

CHAPTER V

Still uneasy that evening, Louella closed the door to her room in the guest house. Tomorrow she'd have to find a place to stay in town. She spread the contents of her purse on the bed.

"Almost fifteen dollars left," she said aloud, stacking the dollar bills carefully. "Food costs more'n I expected. What a room will be, I have no idea yet. Bus fare into town is ten cents. That's twenty cents round trip. A whole dollar a week, at least! I must have been out of my mind to buy that Old English soap and a lipstick with payday still a week away."

Frightened by the uncertainties, she peeled off her right stocking. Through the black lisle a circle of white flesh shone at the heel of her left foot. She blinked back a mist of tears. There's no money for another pair; I'll have to mend it. She wondered where to find a place where she could wash and iron her few clothes.

Dangling the offending stocking, she stared at the chest of drawers across the room. Problems towered over her. She shook her shoulders to remind herself she was tired from the strain of her new job and all the adjustments she'd needed to make. It had been a long day with the tear gas fright plus everything Barbara had crammed into her head. Today was Barbara's last day. She wasn't sure she could do the job without her.

She rubbed at the dull ache behind her temples. "But I will do it! I've got to!" she announced to the chest of drawers. "I knew it wouldn't be easy. I can't go home again."

She pulled off her clothes, put on her cotton robe and headed for the showers. Alone in the latrine, she enjoyed the caress of warm water, pure pleasure against her tired body. The Old English Lavender lather was like scented whipped cream, a delight after all those years with the sterile smell of Ivory. She turned off the shower and listened for sounds of anyone else in the room. There was only the drip from the showerhead and the drip-drip-drip echoing from cast-iron faucets at the row of washbasins, plus one of the stools that kept running.

With thick foam piled in her hair, she decided to experiment with a new hairdo to match her new life. For a moment she hesitated. What if someone saw her nude? Lifting her chin she walked to the mirrors.

"A woman's hair is her crowning glory." Pa's words rang in her ears. He'd have a fit if she cut her long braids. She made a face in the mirror. Pa wasn't in charge of her any more.

How would a windblown bob look? She pulled the lathered mass close around her face. Maybe a pageboy? First payday she'd do something different. Get it cut if she found the nerve. At least buy a chenille snood like Brenda's.

Suddenly beside her own reflection a ruddy face appeared in the mirror. She couldn't tell if it was a man or woman. But why would a man be in here? Her thoughts scurried like mice. A patch over the left breast of the person's fatigues said only JOHNSON. A thin line of tongue licked at lips in the broad jaw, gray eyes moved down her naked body.

Louella whirled, felt the blush move up her chest. She shrank against the edge of the basin, icy against her buttocks. When she saw the crepe-soled sturdy oxfords, she realized why she hadn't heard anyone enter. She threw up one arm to cover her breasts, shielded her crotch with the other as she fled to the privacy of the shower stall.

Shaking in fright, she turned on the water full force, frantic to rinse away the soap and escape. At the corner of her eye she saw movement. Her robe was sliding away over the partition where she had hung it. With a desperate grab she caught its hem and pulled. It didn't give.

Over the noise of the water she heard the hall door open. Someone said, "Oh, hi. Are you making repairs or something? I can come back."

Louella did not hear an answer as she wrung out her hair and pulled on the robe. She peered cautiously out of shower and saw the fatigues disappear into a toilet stall. Safe in the outside hallway, she met a pretty young brunette swinging a pink enema bag.

"Caught you in the shower, didn't he? They're supposed to holler out or send in a woman to check first."

Too shaken to speak, Louella pulled her robe closer; a trail of wet footprints followed her down the hall to her room. Inside, she slammed the door and locked it. Leaning back against the wooden panels, she caught her breath.

Suddenly she was furious. He sure got a good look, didn't he? And he scared me. I'm getting so jittery if a cat sneezed I'd jump, she thought in disgust with herself. Still, he might have...that pretty girl showed up just in time. She must be constipated, poor thing, using an enema bag.

She shoved the night table in front of the door and checked the bolt again. "Well, I can't write Stith tonight," she said aloud. "He might guess I'm scared half the time." She kissed his picture, pulled on her cotton nightie and turned out the light.

Tomorrow she'd meet her sister Cora Sue at the drugstore in town at two. Somewhere they'd find a room for her to rent. Over her bedtime prayers she heard the plaintive notes of Taps and turned her face to her pillow. They played that when a soldier died, too. Was Stith all right tonight? She fell into uneasy sleep.

In her dream she sat at her desk in the Post Exchange office surrounded by towering stacks of paper. Frances poked her head through and shouted, "That's wrong! You did it wrong!" The huge figure of Mr. Hart emerged, looming over her. "I'm not sure you'll do at all," he growled over and over. Brenda appeared in a large black snood on her yellow hair, mouth a circle of scarlet. "Ain't this fun, kid?" she screamed. Then they all began to shout at once.

Suddenly she found herself swimming down a stream of gray water. Overhead her own home towered like an enormous dark ship. From its roof her father shouted, "Trash! Yankee lover! You're no daughter of mine!" The water turned to black gelatin. Her arms ached with effort and she couldn't swim away from the menacing ship. Her father's voice roared in her ears and the fellow in fatigues labeled JOHNSON joined him on the roof.

Louella bolted upright with a strangled cry, sweating and shaking. Wildly she looked around the silent room. A dream, just a dream. She hugged her shoulders and waited for her heart to slow its heavy beating. The small breeze of the window fan dried her damp body and she lay down again.

Deliberately she turned her thoughts to Stith. Once again the memory of the last Sunday afternoon before he went away comforted her, the happiest day of her life.

That wartime Sunday morning in 1942 Louella had been sitting beside her father with the congregation in the brush arbor. Without moving enough to attract his attention, she could look past her father and see Stith Bonham across the aisle. Stith returned her glances while Preacher, in earnest sweat, thumped his Bible and shouted of hellfire and brimstone. She dawdled behind her father when the service ended so she and Stith could make plans to meet down the road later.

At home, the minute her father's door closed to signal his Sunday afternoon nap, she slipped out of the house and ran to the first bend in the road. When she glimpsed Stith's old pickup, her heart thudded. Through the flashes of sun on the windshield another head showed. There was someone else with him! She stopped, disappointed.

At that moment Stith threw open the door and jumped down. It was not until Cousin Delbert stuck his head through the side window and grinned at her that she relaxed.

"Hey, Louella," Stith called, voice eager, a smile on his tanned face. He reached for her hand and threw back his head to toss an auburn lock out of his eyes.

A tingle ran up her arm when he squeezed her fingers and led her back to the pickup. Under the cypress branches overhead sun glinted and disappeared. Young leaves met, bowed and retreated in a minuet born of a cloudless day and a gentle wind. From somewhere there was the scent of wild honeysuckle.

Louella had smiled up at Stith's profile. His eyebrows and lashes were almost black below the dark russet of his hair. She smelled his freshly ironed shirt, the scent of shaving lather. His chin showed promise of what would be a heavy beard in a year or two. Already shaving! They weren't children any more. She shivered.

"What is it?" Stith stopped and turned toward her.

"Just good being with you," she said, ducking her head, "and wishing you weren't going away."

His brown eyes were serious when he took her other hand and drew her toward him, standing firmly in the middle of the road. "A man's got to protect his country. And those he...loves."

Her heart pumped an extra beat. "I purely admire you for it, Stith, but you aren't even gone yet and I'm missing you already."

A grinning Delbert broke the spell. From the open door of the pickup he called out, "Hey you, Louella? Thought you lovebirds might like a little music." With his battered guitar he struggled up into the bed of the truck. His back against the cab, he plucked solitary chords.

"Well, practice good, pal," Stith said. "Louella and I are going to take a little stroll along the bayou. You sing out, if anybody comes along, you hear?"

"Sure will." Delbert didn't lift his head from concentration on fingers and strings.

Stith reached inside the pickup and lifted a 16-gauge shotgun from its rack over the back window. With it cradled under his left arm, he held his right around Louella's waist. Together they left the sandy road and walked toward the sound of lazy water.

"I'm sorry, Louella. Delbert's a good kid but awful young. I reckon he just don't know what it means when you want to see your girl alone."

She had only dreamed Stith would choose her. It gave her a warm sensation to hear him say it aloud. Most fellows wouldn't make the effort after a try or two, Papa being the way he was about boys coming to the house.

The path became too narrow to walk side by side. Stith moved ahead to hold branches until she passed before he released them to whip back into place. Soon the guitar chords had faded behind thick vegetation, bird songs clearer. Somewhere near a wren called, "Tea kettle, tea kettle," and a catbird mewed its answer. Heavy wings beat overhead and they both ducked.

"Owl," he said.

When they broke through the last of the bushes, they were on the bank of the bayou. Side by side again, they watched the heavy weights of cattails on slender stalks moving with the brown water.

"Look," Louella said, and pointed at a canvas stool beneath the lacy green of a tall cypress.

"Usually it's muddy 'round here," Stith said and flushed. "It's my favorite fishing spot and I come here sometimes just to think." He laid the shotgun beside the seat and brushed away a twig.

Poised self-consciously on the canvas, Louella drew up her knees and circled them with her arms. In all her eighteen years she had never been alone with a boy before and it was hard to breathe normally. If Stith was about to go to war, he wasn't a boy; he was a man. She hoped he could not sense the wild beating of her heart.

He hunkered down on one knee before her, intent on the tall grass at his feet, and began to work with three long stems in his square brown hands, weaving them into something Louella couldn't see.

The heavy growth on both banks blocked any breeze. She watched a single drop of perspiration race down the side of Stith's face and longed to blot it away. She gripped her knees more tightly and felt a trickle between her breasts.

"Louella..."

She looked up quickly.

"Reckon you could write me now and then while I'm gone, tell me how things are and all? If you could, well, I'd write back when I could—if I wasn't in an actual battle or anything." His face glowed in the green light under the cypress leaves. "If you don't want to, you wouldn't have to, though...."

"Oh, Stith!" Louella unclasped her knees and pressed her hands together. "I'd be most proud to! You'd be my own fighting man. I'll save up sugar and when I have enough I'll bake you cookies. Maybe I can learn to knit...."

The picture of the girl in a blue ruffled apron in the Pillsbury advertisement grew in her mind.

"...and I'll get a blue star and hang it in the window for you...." She broke off. "No, I reckon I couldn't do that, Stith. Papa might get mad."

"Reckon he'd mind if you wrote?"

"Reckon he wouldn't have to know." Louella grinned. "Cora Sue and I get the mail in every day. Don't suppose he'd ever know a thing about it."

Louella tucked a damp strand of hair back into her braids and jumped up. "Law, it's hot, Stith. Suppose we could wade a little?" She unbuckled her flat slippers, turned her back and drew off the black lisle stockings. One toe into the water, she felt Stith's eyes on her bare legs. The water was cool. Perched on a ledge, she kicked her feet, beating up a foam like cream on the chocolate colored water.

Stith crouched beside her, holding her hand and laughing at her pleasure. If only the day could go on forever, she thought. A mockingbird on one of the cattails across the stream folded its white and gray wings. Its long tail a balancing pole, it watched them with one bright eye.

"That old bird looks like a lady hiding her white petticoats under a gray dress," she laughed.

Stith said nothing. Drawing her left hand into his, he spread her fingers. Over the third knuckle he slid a small green band of woven grass stems.

Louella stilled her feet.

Stith sank down on one elbow, gazing up at her. There was no smile as he said, "Louella, it will be a long, long time before I come home again and can do it right. But maybe we could sort of let this be a promise to be engaged for real when I return?"

The sun was golden on his russet hair when he lowered his head. "Maybe it's all too quick," he said, "and you want to think about it some. But I don't have much time. I report to Seacomb Air Base tomorrow for induction. Then they'll send me somewhere for basic training."

"Oh, my dear Stithie," she breathed, "I don't need to think about it. I love you, Stith, and I'd be so proud to be your girl. Someday, when the war is over, we can tell Papa and the whole world."

In one motion he was on his feet, pulling her up toward him. The ground was warm under her toes. Was it the heat of the earth or his arms around her...? Before she could decide, he kissed her.

The feel of his lips surprised her. They didn't look soft in his lean face. She trembled and kept her balance only because his arms tightened to pull her against him. Her head found a nest on his shoulder, her lips against the pulse in his throat.

"Louella, Louella...."

His lips against her forehead, she caught the scent of his breath like sweet meadow grass. For a long while they stood holding each other under the cypress tree until she felt a change in the shape of his body against hers. Wondering, she looked up at him.

Face grave, he slid his hands down her arms and moved a step back. He straightened his shoulders and lifted his chin. "Now I have something to fight for, someone to come home to, someone to be the mother of my children someday." She felt lost in his brown eyes.

"Someone beautiful and...innocent. Someone to protect."

She memorized his wide brow, the shape of his straight nose, the small indentation in his upper lip, the curve of the lower.

When his brows lifted and his eyes widened, it startled her. His grip was suddenly painful on her arms.

"Don't move," he commanded and stepped away slowly.

It seemed she only blinked and the gun that laid beside the stool was in his hands. In one swift gesture he pumped it and fired. Frightened, Louella jumped and whirled toward his target. A foot behind her the body of what had been a snake writhed, head missing.

"Cottonmouth moccasin," Stith said. "God, it was a big'un!"

"I thought they never bothered anybody unless they were bothered first." Her whole body shook.

"Probably had a den around here and we stirred it up some...."

The rustle in the bushes behind them sent Louella into new fright. Stith drew her to his side, arm around her waist, still gripping the shotgun.

Cousin Delbert burst through into the clearing. "Y'all all right?" he demanded, skidding to a stop. "I heard a shot. Figured I'd best find out was you two all right."

"We're fine." Stith didn't appear pleased to see Delbert.

"He just saved my life, is all," Louella announced. "Lookie yonder."

"Heck, Louella, it wasn't so all fired dangerous as that," Stith said, but she noticed he walked taller while they returned to the pickup.

Alone on the way home, Louella turned the grass ring around and around on her finger, feeling like she had swallowed sunlight. It was the most important day in her entire life. To be eighteen, to have found her love returned made the whole world perfect. She hugged herself in joy, then kissed the grass ring.

CHAPTER VI

Not knowing the Saturday bus schedule, Louella sat on the high curb outside the security guard's kiosk. For the tenth time she rose impatiently to dust her navy skirt and fluff out the white frill on her blouse. Once more she opened her purse to count her change for the fare. It seemed hours before the bus turned in a cloud of exhaust fumes and crunched to a stop on the gravel.

Louella mounted the high step, handed the driver two nickels and took the seat behind him. Except for four Negroes side by side on the wide seat at the rear, the vehicle was empty. Faces impassive, the four avoided meeting her eyes in the driver's rear view mirror.

With a whoosh of compressed air the folding door closed and the old bus lurched into the ten-mile trip to the town of Seacomb. As it rattled and clattered down the highway, dust sifted through open windows like pale powder onto her skirt. The only movement of moisture-laden air came from their forward speed.

"Hear tell there's a storm came inland in Floriday," the driver said. He shifted a toothpick to the other side of thin lips, eyeing Louella in his mirror. "Reckon we'll get a good rain out of that. Maybe something more. Feels like cyclone weather." When she did not reply, he added, "Cotton needs a good rain."

Louella acknowledged with a nod, not willing to encourage him. With a shrug the driver hunched over the steering wheel. Soft talk and chuckles came from the four on the back seat, their Saturday excitement high.

While the bus swept past white cotton blossoms in the fields under the leaden sky, Louella also saw the small weathered cabins surrounded by yards bared of vegetation for fear of fire.

Through windows empty of screens she caught glimpses of black children watching. Again she wondered about cold nights in the unpainted shacks on their spindling supports of stacked bricks. Even here in South Carolina there was frost on the grass sometimes. She remembered ice once. She smiled at a dark figure waving a languid hand from a broken chair under a chinaberry tree.

In town the bus pulled to a stop outside the drugstore. Louella dusted her skirt a final time and drew on her gloves. The veil on her pillbox hat adjusted, she stepped down onto a sidewalk full of jostling black folks, laughing among themselves. Every Saturday seemed a high holiday for them, she thought. What they found to laugh about in their painful lives puzzled her. Did they really have extra joints at hips and knees like Papa said to account for their loose, ambling strut?

The clock in the furniture store next door said two-thirty. Half an hour late. But where was Cora Sue? Perhaps inside the drugstore.

It took a moment for her eyes to adjust to its dim interior. Just inside the door she breathed in mingled scents, identifying medicine smells, perfumes, milky odors from the soda fountain—all overlaid with the heavy smell of sawdust sweep used on the wooden floor. The huge plate-glass mirror over the marble counter to her left reflected many bottles and boxes behind the glass doors of the dark wooden cabinets which lined the opposite wall.

No Cora Sue.

With a sigh she climbed onto one of the high wire stools. "A cherry Coca-Cola, please," she said to the old man in the immaculate white jacket behind the spigots.

"Comin' right up, Miss." With a flourish he scooped crushed ice into a tall glass, pulled at the white porcelain soda faucet and added a squirt of cherry flavoring from the bottle with its long narrow spout. He set the drink before her as though he presented it to a queen, his lined face beaming.

"That'll be five cents."

She pushed the coin across the marble surface and returned his smile around her straw, savoring the sweet liquid. Then she asked, "Do you know of any rooms to rent?"

The old man's face saddened. "Been lots of folks in here asking," he drawled. "I'm sorry. I don't know of a one. Seems like all the kindly folks with room to spare already has it filled. Other folks is just too stiff necked, I reckon." He continued to polish the counter as he spoke. "Your man out at the base?"

Louella ducked her head over the tall glass. "I'm working at the Post Exchange office," she answered, peering at him through her veil.

Something in the wrinkled face snapped shut. There it was again. The fast girls took the first jobs and now everyone in town thought a single girl on the base meant only one thing. She heard her father's voice again, "Only trash work there."

The druggist tucked his rag under the counter and turned his back on her, heading back to the pharmacy.

Louella stared at her pale face in the mirror. What would she do if she couldn't find a room today? And where was Cora Sue?

Suddenly beside her own reflection Cousin Delbert's freckled face winked at her. One sandy cowlick marred his slicked down hair. She whirled on the stool.

"Delbert! I'm just so glad to see you!"

"She ain't coming."

Louella grasped his hand and slid off the stool. "Is my sister all right?" she asked.

"She's fine, I guess," he answered. "Your Pa, though, well, he won't hardly let her out of his sight. She said he's turned strange, won't talk or nothing. Cora Sue says he spends all his time reading his Bible." Delbert's ruddy face was strained. "I stopped by this morning and he didn't say nothing to me neither. Cora Sue said you'd be in town and to give you this." He handed her an airmail letter.

"From Stith!"

"She got to the mailbox first or he might have tore it up." He knocked his straw hat against his knee. "Anything you want me to tell Cora Sue?"

Louella took a deep breath and let it out in a rush. "Tell her...tell her I love and miss her and...oh, Delbert, I got a job in the Post Exchange on the base making thirty-two dollars a week! Now isn't that just the greatest luck you ever did hear?" She felt the joy of her first job rise again, then ebb. "Right now...well, I can't stay at the base's guest house after Sunday. I've got to find a room in town." She took a step closer. "Do you happen to know of anybody who has — "

"Don't know no town folks," Delbert said. He shoved one hand into his pocket. "Louella, tell me about soldiering. I reckon to go my next birthday — if it ain't all over by then."

"But you'll only be sixteen!"

"From what I hear, they don't check too close." He straightened his stocky frame. "I'm big for my age...and strong. Time
I've done basic they'll know they got a good 'un."

"Oh, Delbert!" Louella hugged her cousin hard and caught the disapproving glare of the druggist over his shoulder. "I don't know what I can tell you. Haven't seen any of the training part. The base is like a little town, even has a picture show, a post office and all. And a tiny church." She bit her lip and ignored the druggist. "But they'd send you someplace far off. I heard tell Uncle Sam ships boys as far away as he can so they won't go running home again."

"Always did want to see something more than South Carolina." Delbert peered at his dusty shoes, then raised his head to look directly into her eyes. "Well, I gotta go. You take care of yourself, Cousin, you hear?" He moved toward the brighter street outside. "I don't believe all those stories about...well, about trash and all that. You know." He cocked his sandy head, gave her a lopsided grin and was gone.

Louella savored his words. She gathered up purse and gloves from the marble counter and left the drugstore. Outside it was hard to breathe in the heavy air pressing down under gray clouds. Rain by night, she thought. She needed to hurry and find a room.

Next to the depot, odors from the fish market were sickening in the still air. She held her breath, glancing in at the rows of pink and white flesh on mounds of crushed ice in glass counters. It passed her mind to wonder why they never served the plentiful local catfish at the PX.

In the dark train station at the Travelers Aid desk the prim elderly lady looked at her in dismay. "A room to rent?" She repeated Louella's request and pursed thin lips. "If I could find a room it would go to that young mother who slept here last night." She pointed toward the nearest wooden bench. "For a single girl who works at the base? Certainly not!"

Louella followed her pointing finger and saw a haggard young face leaning over a fretting baby while a toddler pulled at her skirts.

"Oh, my, oh, my, the poor thing," Louella breathed.

The rigid woman at the desk relaxed. "I declare I don't know what they're all going to do. I just feel so sorry for...."

Louella sighed. "Maybe something will turn up, I hope."

When she passed the young mother, she smiled into the troubled eyes. The pale face smiled back.

Through the dark room Louella's footsteps repeated in an echo from the dirty tiles. Perhaps if she knocked on a few doors someone would know of a room.

There were only two residential streets in Seacomb, each four blocks long, but it took a while to work up the nerve to ring a doorbell. Four times she reached a door; four times a face peered out at her through a narrow opening and shook its head. Each time Louella felt her courage shrink a little more.

At the last house on the second street she spotted a small sign: Tourist Home. With a lift of spirits she hurried up the porch steps past a motionless swing and rockers with cane seats. Crisp curtains showed through gleaming windows. The door pull beside the beveled glass door echoed faintly. A broad figure came toward Louella and opened the door a cautious crack.

"Do you have a room to rent?"

"Don't take children." The voice was harsh; the ruddy face with veined blue eyes stared her up and down.

"It's just for me," Louella explained. "I work at the base." Then wondered if she should have mentioned that.

"Humph." The blue eyes were colder. "Come along."

Louella followed, hope growing. On the second floor the woman opened a varnished door and motioned her inside.

The small room smelled of soap and disinfectant. Muslin curtains hung at the tiny window near a large walnut bed which sat heavily on a faded rose-patterned carpet. A massive washstand filled the opposite wall, a worn towel draped on a rod above a cracked pitcher and bowl.

"It's...very nice," Louella said, trying to picture the room as home. "I...I think I'll take it."

"Five dollars a day. Pay in advance."

"Five...." Louella's body stiffened, hope gone. Five times seven was more than she made. Suddenly her salary seemed very small. "I...I guess I can't take it, then. I just couldn't afford...."

"Humph." The woman led the way downstairs. "Dunno what you girls," she sneered the word, "that work on the base expect!"

Louella flinched and brushed past. Feeling hostile eyes on her back as she walked down the sidewalk, she did not turn. At the bus stop her shoulders slumped. What could she do? She couldn't go home again. She felt rigid with fright.

Brightly dressed black folks enjoying their Saturday good times pushed past, laughing. Service men in olive drab walked by in groups of two or three. Civilians in light summer clothes moved close to the buildings. The curbsides were for jovial folk with darker skins.

Louella saw it all and registered none of it. Miserable, she glanced up at the lowering clouds. Maybe they'd let her sleep in the PX? But she knew better than that.

"God," she whispered, "I need help. Can you hear me?"

But what would the Creator of all the universe care about one girl in Seacomb, South Carolina? Too scared to cry, her eyes were dry.

It was late the next morning when she wakened. Still groggy, she rolled over to rouse Cora Sue. Reality brought her upright. The stockings and cotton panties she had rinsed last night hung over a chair. A dark spot on the floor showed where they had dripped. Today there was no sound of planes overhead.

Sunday! Church.

Rain fell from the eaves. Heavier patters on the flat composition roof combined with the whisper of raindrops over the whole base. Through the venetian blind she saw a few figures in khaki rain slickers moving along the wet streets.

She'd have to wear her peeling old raincoat. It wasn't nice enough to wear to the Lord's house on her first Sunday but she had no choice. Her stockings were still damp. She wasn't made of sugar; she wouldn't melt.

At the door of the guesthouse she held her yellow oilcloth slicker like a tent over her small navy hat, poised for the dash to the PX for breakfast. Running through the rain, she hoped they'd have grits today. She knew she'd probably have to settle for scrambled eggs and toast again. What she wouldn't give for a plate of turnip greens for supper, too.

After breakfast she hesitated at the PX door. The distance to the chapel seemed twice as far today. Her body felt clammy under damp clothing. Sighing, she raised the slicker again and scurried through the shower, hopping to avoid the deepest puddles. Almost to the parade grounds, she heard a car behind her.

"Get in. I'll take you to the guesthouse."

Surprised, Louella reminded herself the base held many kind people. Smiling, she turned her improvised tent toward the voice.

The soldier's face was dim in the shadow of the small coupe. The single wiper on the windshield beat a merry rhythm, sending a spray over the dark green roof. But when the driver moved closer to the window, Louella caught her breath. It was the man with the no-color eyes.

"I...I'm going to preaching," she faltered.

"Preachin'," he mocked. "You mean church." He heaved an elaborate sigh. "Get in, then."

"Thank you, but I'll just walk," she answered primly with raised chin. Her slippers squished with every step.

For a few steps he kept the car even with her. When she didn't stop, he growled, "Okay, Duchess. You've got it!" He rolled up the window and sped away.

Louella jumped aside to avoid the wave of water. Why would he be angry at her? Lowering her slicker, she dashed into the foyer of the chapel. Beside the dripping khaki raincoats, she found an empty peg. With every step on the red carpet to the closest pew her shoes oozed.

Only a few soldiers were seated, their olive drab uniforms dull under the gray light slanting in the narrow tall windows of plain glass. At a small portable organ a man in khaki with major's insignia played a quiet hymn she didn't recognize.

When the music stopped, a tall officer rose, gave a short prayer for those who suffered destruction in the Florida storm, read a scripture and talked about doing one's best. Hand gestures made the gold cross on his lapels catch the light. When he finished, the congregation rose to sing about "those in peril on the deep."

Louella felt bewildered. He hadn't raised his voice once, did not threaten hell for their sins. In fact, he never mentioned the word. He hadn't made her feel guilty a single time. What kind of preaching was that? It was more like a talk at assembly in high school.

The soldiers moved down the aisle to shake the speaker's hand in the foyer. At the door, the man with the gold cross took Louella's hand and smiled at her.

"Don't believe I've seen you at chapel before. Are you new to the base?"

"I work in the PX." She added, "I just came Wednesday."

"I'm Chaplain James," he said, releasing her hand. "It's very pleasant to see a young lady at services. I hope you will come again."

"Oh, I never miss preaching." The last to leave, Louella noticed the quiet of the room without the organ music. "One thing," she said, "there wasn't a collection taken. Is there a place where I can put my offering?"

"We have no expenses here not met by Uncle Sam." The answer puzzled her. "Perhaps you would like to send your contribution to your home church."

How strange not to make an offering to the Lord on His day. She raised the yellow slicker overhead.

"If you ever have any problems you need to talk about, I'm here to help," Chaplain James called out when she reached the bottom step.

Back in her room, she dropped the wet slicker in a heap inside the door. Empty hours stretched ahead. On the edge of the bed she counted her money again. Enough for food until payday next Friday. Ten dollars left over. That wouldn't pay much rent, even if she could find a place. Returning the cash to her purse, her fingers touched damp paper.

Stith's letter! Agonizing over the unsuccessful hunt yesterday, she had actually forgotten it! Here was something good for a change. She drew the letter out of the envelope, careful not to tear the single thin sheet of V-mail. How she wished it was Stith himself she touched, with this war over and her safe in his arms. His fingers had held this paper once. She bent and kissed the damp onionskin.

"*Dear Louella,*

"*It's been a long time since I've heard from you. Guess mail is held up somewhere again. I think of you often. Are you still wearing my grass ring?*

"*Things are sure different over here. The food is not like home. I've met a family here who's had a bad time of it, really bad. They almost starved, but they talk a lot about when our Army marched into town. How people kissed the soldiers and pushed roses and bottles of wine at them and everything. Wish I'd been there!*

"*It's not too bad being stationed here. My buddies and I explore the city. It's real old with lots of interesting things I'll tell you about when I come home. There's rumors we'll go to _____. If we do, I may be home for a few hours on the way. –Stith*

Louella fingered the hole the censor had cut out of the letter which would have told her where Stith was headed. She raised the page again and kissed his name. Twice more she read the letter, trying to see behind his words. "I've met a family here...."

Did that family have a daughter, someone young and pretty? His other letters had talked about plans for them when he came home. This one seemed rather cold, about things you would write to a stranger. She shivered and kicked off her wet shoes.

If only the censor had not cut out part of the last sentence. She didn't even know where he was. France? Italy? She'd heard there was still fighting in Italy. The thought of seeing him again, even for a few minutes, made her tremble, quickly dulled by fear of where he might be heading.

And why had the word "Love" been missing above his signature?

CHAPTER VII

Monday morning Brenda snuffed her first cigarette of the day just as the office door opened on a soggy Louella lugging a wet cardboard suitcase. She watched Louella push her burden into the corner, then hang a dripping yellow oilcloth slicker on the coatrack. What a sad apple the girl looked today.

"Guess you found a place?" Brenda asked, waving her second cigarette at the suitcase.

"Found one in town, but it was five dollars a day and I couldn't...." Louella bent over her desk fingering a yellow pencil.

"Another patriot!" Brenda snorted. "Hell, you could stay at the Waldorf for that!" She surveyed her makeup in a pocket mirror and ran fingers down her pageboy bob to smooth it under. Good lipstick color, she decided. Mirror in the drawer, she slammed it shut. Decision made.

"I've been thinking," Brenda began, "I've got an extra bedroom here on base in the housing area and...well, if you can't find anything else...." Brenda was startled by the blaze in Louella's gray eyes, her head lifted now.

"We could try it for a couple of weeks," Brenda continued lamely, "see if we could stand each other."

To Brenda's discomfort, two large tears rolled down Louella's cheeks before she buried her face in her arms on the desktop.

"You could help with the rent some. Not much," Brenda added quickly. "Maybe bring in some groceries now and again...."

The dark braids came up from the desk and Louella's mouth worked but no words came out. Then she smiled, a smile so wide and bright that Brenda blinked. "I just didn't know what

I was going to do! I couldn't go home and I had to get out of the guest house. Oh, my, I'd be so proud...."

"Hell, it's nothing," Brenda said and waved her hand. "We'll work something out."

Damn it, she thought, what have I done? Saddled myself with a hick Southerner just because that damned housing officer has been on my neck to give my place to some GI with a family. She jerked the cover off her typewriter. At least I won't have to move now. "Want some coffee?" she asked.

"I'd purely appreciate a cup," Louella said. "I couldn't eat any breakfast for worrying."

"No breakfast for me, either," Brenda said, fluffing up the ruffle at her throat. "Too much beer lately and I gotta watch my figure or nobody else will. Beer's fattening."

The office door opened again. Frances and Glen Hart arrived together. Another week had begun.

Glen Hart leaned back in his chair, full attention on the busy people around him. Good group, he thought, my family away from home. His mind turned to his wife and daughters back in Texas and he felt defenseless against the sharp pang of homesickness which stabbed him.

Directly in his line of vision, Louella caught his eye. The same age as his oldest daughter June. What hell it was to miss his children growing up. Each brief time he'd been home June was more and more a young lady.

Well, there was nothing he could have done to prevent his absence. When they quit building Fords in '42 his business had stopped cold. He admitted the dealership hadn't ever made much profit, but it kept their heads above water. Somehow he'd never learned the knack of piling up money, always too concerned about the circumstances of people buying his cars. For too many he'd shaved the profits too thin.

Who'd have thought he'd wind up on this small base in South Carolina for the duration? Matter of fact, he'd jumped at the chance. Too old for service, business gone, he had to do something and his best talent was managing people. So Uncle Sam paid him well to stay away from home. All those actions taken so far away in Washington affected millions everywhere. Sherman had sure been right: War was a lot of hells, small ones and large, overseas or here in the States.

Consider his assistant manager, Donald Monahan, a little leprechaun of a guy with white hair over an Irish face. He was a nice fellow faced with a huge medical bill for his invalid sister, now that her man had been killed over the English Channel. Even the GI insurance hadn't wiped out all the bills. He and Donald, old men in a young man's war. Displaced as much as any GI and trying to cope. His thoughts made Glen realize how glad he'd be to welcome Monahan back today. He was surprised at how much he missed the little man.

He glanced at his watch. Ten o'clock. Donald was late. He'd possibly missed connections somewhere between here and California, train and plane schedules being what they were. The West Coast was a long way to go under wartime travel conditions. Probably only left him a couple days with his sister. He wondered again why Donald hadn't taken his full two weeks, but was selfish enough to be glad there had been only ten days without his support.

A shadow fell across the glass of the hallway door and it opened slowly.

Hart shot out of his chair. "Donald Monahan, I was just thinking about you...." He took a deep breath, catching alcoholic fumes. "My god, what's happened to you?"

The little man's white hair was shaggy over his ears, his face white velvet. His dark green suit hung on him like clothes on a hanger. When Hart gripped his elbow, he felt only bird bones. Hart was doubly alarmed when he read shame in Donald's green eyes.

Monahan slumped into the chair beside Hart's desk, clenching and unclenching his fingers.

Hart realized the little man was trying to stop their tremors.

Around them the office was suddenly silent. Brenda's typewriter ceased, her hands in midair. One glance in their direction and Brenda quickly turned her head away. Louella stood with one hand half way to another file document. In the corner Frances muffled an exclamation. At Hart's frown, normal office noises began again.

Hart filled a mug at the coffeepot and handed it to Donald, who took it in both hands, managing to keep the coffee from sloshing.

"Now," Hart said, "tell me what happened. When did you get back?"

Monahan stretched his neck out of a loose collar and lifted his chin. "So now you know," he said in a voice aimed at the entire office.

"Know what?"

"About the drinking." The little man ducked his head and Hart saw two raw scrapes between half-inch patches of whiskers missed by an unsteady razor. "I went to bed with a bottle. Several bottles."

Hart was incredulous. "Here? You mean you never left the base? Right there in your room across the hall?"

Monahan nodded, staring at his coffee mug, not meeting Hart's eyes.

"My god!" Hart had slept next door to Monahan and heard nothing. Perhaps he'd blocked out sounds, assuming the room was empty. "Didn't you eat? You're so thin...."

"Little cheese." Monahan didn't lift his head. "Crackers once, I remember." He tried to push himself up from the chair, coffee dribbling. "I'll go pack."

For a second the words eluded Hart, then realization made his voice louder than he'd intended. "Whatever for? Sit down, friend." He paused to consider. "How many times does...."

"Made it two years this time."

The sadness on the velvety features wrenched at Hart. "Things just got to me. All those bright young men...my sister's husband...my sister...." Again he pushed half up from the chair. "Well, I'll be moving on."

Hart leaned across the desk and glared at Monahan. "The hell you will." He kept his voice clear and emphatic. "You're not saddling me with all the work, buddy!" As Monahan flinched, compassion softened his words. "If it's just getting cigarettes and pop to the troops, it all counts. And last week was a bugger without you. You're not quitting on me, old pal!"

Monahan held his head a bit straighter. "Couldn't promise." He laced and unlaced his fingers. "Most times it's just a social drink, you see, and no problems. But then sometimes...."

"First things first," Hart ordered. "You're coming to lunch with me. Your problems will not be mentioned outside this office — or in it, either. You're family, man!" He made sure the others were paying full attention.

Visibly pulling his pride together, Monahan glanced at the others. "If you're sure...."

"Give me five minutes here," Hart said. "I'll pick you up on the way out."

When the door closed behind Donald Monahan, Hart let out his breath. "I'll be damned!" For a few seconds he rearranged the papers on his desk, pulling his thoughts together. Finally he pushed back his chair, conscious of glances darting his way. With his hand on the knob, he turned.

"Remember: In this office we're a family."

CHAPTER VIII

"I'm just so excited!" Louella announced that evening after work as she and Brenda walked to the housing area. "It's the strangest thing. Just a week on the base and this all seems like home now, especially now I have a place to stay. Thanks to you." She swung her suitcase high and skipped a step to match Brenda's stride. "All the uniforms and buildings and the planes going over, seems like I've always been here."

The day had seemed incredibly long for Louella. Her curiosity about Brenda's apartment had been hard to contain. It was certain to be different from the guesthouse room. Perhaps it would be as elegant as Brenda herself. She glanced at the shorter woman beside her. Brenda even had earrings to match all her clothes.

Louella switched her suitcase to the other hand. "I can tell now if somebody's from Boston or New York just listening to them talk. Remember that fellow from Texas who came in the office this morning? I knew right off he was from Mr. Hart's state."

"There's a mixed bag on base, all right," Brenda said.

They reached the small concrete-block housing units not far from the Post Exchange. Tiny scraps of grass surrounded the low structures. Twigs of trees, wrapped and wired, attested to the newness of the base itself. Each small lawn was edged with whitewashed rocks that stretched down the street like dotted lines.

Louella entered the tiny living room behind Brenda and caught her breath. It was different, all right. But the same, too. The block walls were painted the same gray; the furniture similar sturdy oak. But the clutter!

Movie and confession magazines spilled over the heavy scarred coffee table, topped by cups with dried brown coffee stains. Two orange-colored ashtrays overflowed with cigarette butts and ashes. The dusky green couch listed toward one end. At the sagging end was a paper plate with dry sandwich crusts and a petrified pickle. One of the two chairs with thick wooden arms boasted a pillow which read "Myrtle Beach, South Carolina" against bright blue waves painted on fringed pink satin. Beside the other chair two empty beer cans leaned together like friendly drunks.

Dismayed, Louella came to a full stop, unsure of what to say.

"A mess, ain't it?" Brenda led the way across the room through the door on the left. Sweeping up a stack of dresses from the bed, she announced, "This room's yours."

Louella dropped her slicker and suitcase. Except for the brightly flowered cretonne curtains at the small window, faded where the sun had touched them, the room was identical to those in the guesthouse. The bedspread matched the curtains. The oak chest of drawers, painted the eternal gray, held a collection of cosmetic bottles and jars, reminding Louella of the drugstore in town. Through the open closet door she saw bright clothes jammed together above a jumble of shoes and wire hangers.

From her own room beyond the bath separating the two bedrooms, Brenda called, "I'll get rid of some of that for you."

Discouraged, Louella sank onto the bed. It was obvious Brenda just wanted some free household help, an unpaid servant, someone to do her dirty work. What does she think I am? Louella wondered, some brainless retard? But like an iron bell rang the thought: She had no other place to go! She'd have to stay at least until payday. Maybe by then something would open up in town.

"Make us some coffee, huh?" Brenda's voice rose over the sounds of banging drawers and rattling hangers.

Louella found the small dark kitchen separated by a shallow offset from the dining area. A bare iron faucet dripped with a tinny sound onto a stack of greasy pans in the cast-iron sink.

She's already issuing orders, Louella thought resentfully.

She dumped stale coffee grounds from the blackened aluminum pot into the step-on garbage can after a minute's hesitation to figure out how it worked. Letting the water run to clear the rust from the pipes, she filled the pot. On open shelves by the stove she located a can of coffee and spooned it into the basket holder.

When she turned to the squat black gas stove she felt a moment of confidence. Maybe she hadn't known about step-on garbage cans but Cloteel had taught her about gas stoves. Before the flames caught with a pop, she inhaled the sour odor of the gas.

From the corner of her eye she caught a glimpse of Brenda circling the living room, picking up trash and clutter. With a sigh she hoped she'd been wrong about the servant bit.

"Quite a party here last night," Brenda commented when she added the paper plate and beer cans to the garbage. "Quite a party several nights lately. The guys get lonesome." Her eyes were sharp. "Hope you like parties."

"Don't really know," Louella answered, stacking dishes on the foot-square counter and filling the sink with soapy water. "I've only been to one or two where I come from."

Brenda stared at her. "Must have been a pretty sad sack life for a pretty girl like you."

"You think I'm...pretty?"

"Don't tell me no guy's ever told you that. Bet you've got a lot of boy friends back home. Wherever that is."

"Just Stith Bonum." Louella savored the taste of his name on her lips. "He's overseas and that's why I'm here. To help. Although I can't figure out how filing invoices will shorten the war any. At least I'm helping support our soldiers. I love Stith and I want him to come home safe."

Brenda was silent for a long moment watching Louella. Then she waved a dustcloth, swiped at the rickety dining room table and took a stance within arm's reach. "You know you really could be a lot prettier if you did something to your hair. And those stockings!"

Louella brought her ankles tightly together. Brenda's criticism rankled.

"My god, we can get nylons at the PX, you know."

"We can?" Clothing was supposed to cover your body, not reveal it, but the thought of nylon hosiery was temptation.

"Matter of fact," Brenda said, one thumb on her lower lip, "I've got an extra pair." She turned toward her bedroom and returned waving nylons like a fragile banner. "Anything to get those black babies off you!"

Louella wiped her hands on the dishtowel. "Come payday I'll replace these. Oh, my, I do thank you." She held the stockings carefully, running a fingertip down their length to savor the smooth feel. How she'd envied the town girls in high school with their shiny hose. Flushed with pleasure, she carried them into her room and spread them on the bed. She could see the cretonne flowers right through the nylon.

The good smell of onions and potatoes frying filled the apartment while Louella finished washing dishes. Brenda added two slices of ham to warm at the sides of the skillet. When Louella remarked on spending so many meat ration stamps, Brenda said, "Hell, this is the start of something special: A new roommate. Let's live a little."

Reassured about her status of helper, not slave, Louella began to enjoy the evening. It was nice to have someone to talk to about the day at the office. By dark they had eaten and once again they tackled dirty dishes. The songs of Patty, Maxine and Laverne lilted from the radio. This time Brenda washed, keeping time with her hips as they sang "Bugle Boy from Company B" along with the trio. Louella felt a giggle bubbling up. It would be fun living here, after all.

Finally Brenda spread the dishcloth to dry on the edge of the sink. "Damn, but women's work is boring! Come morning, it's all to do over again." She turned toward Louella's room. "Let's attack your closet so you can get unpacked."

Cross-legged on the bed, Louella stroked her new nylons while Brenda dropped dresses and hangers beside her. "You sure do have lots of beautiful clothes," Louella said, fingering the red taffeta on top of the stack.

"I get a box of remainders every season from an uncle in ready-to-wear in Jersey. More'n I need." Brenda's head was in the closet, her words muffled.

"What's `remainders'?"

"What's left, samples he didn't sell." Brenda peered around the closet door. "Maybe some will fit you. I've gained a little weight lately...." She held the red taffeta dress under Louella's chin. "Red's good with your black hair. This might be too short, but it's long on me. Try it on." She wiggled the hanger until Louella took hold.

Louella felt a blush burning when she dropped her skirt and blouse to pull on the scarlet gown. She had never undressed before anyone but her sister.

With a delicate rustle the skirt belled out around her knees. "Waist is loose, but I can fix that," she said. In the small mirror over the chest of drawers she inspected the oval neckline and puffed sleeves. It was kind of bare, but if she was really going to change.... She pushed back thoughts of her papa's outrage. No other female on the whole base, except the WACs, wore long sleeves or high necks. How she longed to be like the others.

"Now that's more like it," Brenda commented, leaning against the door jamb with a load of shoes.

Louella unbuttoned the long row of shiny buttons and returned the dress to the hanger. "Maybe I could borrow it sometime...for a party?" She pulled on her old cotton robe.

"It's yours, honey. Too small for me now." Brenda carried away the shoes. Returning, she frowned at the cosmetic bottles and jaws on the dresser's top. "Don't need all this stuff, either. Can't imagine why I ever bought it. Keep it all, if you want.

Otherwise, I'll pitch it out." She kicked off her shoes and flopped on the bed to watch Louella unpack.

"Guess you didn't have time to take much when you left, huh?" Brenda commented. She hopped off the bed, dumped the contents of two drawers into the flowered wastebasket and carried it into her room.

Louella folded her cotton panties and nightgown into an empty drawer, hung up the rosebud dress and her two skirts and blouses. They looked drab against the red taffeta.

Brenda returned with her arms loaded. "Here's a plaid skirt I can't get into. The collar and cuffs on this navy need washing; might fit...."

By the time Lux Radio Theater signed off, Louella had more clothes than she had owned in her entire life. She silently vowed to do most of the cleaning to repay her generous roommate until she had money of her own. "What a day to remember," Louella said aloud as she joined Brenda on the listing couch.

Under the light from the wobbly floor lamp, Brenda's hair looked rumpled. She grimaced and yawned. "Yeah, life's just one laugh after another in wartime." The notes of "Taps" sounded in the distance. "I'm turning in. Didn't get much sleep last night and this wartime news gets me down. This time I'll take the bathroom first. 'Night, new roommate."

Too excited to rest, Louella turned off the radio news broadcast and thumbed through a copy of "Photoplay." June Allyson's pert smile caught her eye, plus the full skirt that swirled around the movie star's dancing feet. The red taffeta dress hanging in the closet looked a little like the one in the magazine's photograph. Louella's pleasure grew. Lots of parties, Brenda had said.

A small apprehension nibbled away at her pleasure. Would the people at those parties like her? It was all so different here. Well, I'm different now, too, she thought.

And tomorrow I'll wear my new nylons.

On the Fourth of July, three mornings later, Brenda and Louella, still in their robes at noon, finished the breakfast dishes together.

"The 4th here is certainly not like our celebrations at home," Brenda said. "Back there the Polish always had a big do. With fireworks. They had those big pinwheels going 'round, rockets lighting up the sky. All those colors...." She sighed. "It's hard to believe my niece, who's four, has never seen fireworks because all the gunpowder that used to make them now goes to real shells for the war. I'll sure be happy when we can really celebrate again."

"I miss the Christmas fireworks, too," Louella replied.

"That I can't understand about the South. Why at Christmas?"

"Might be because we don't have snow and all." Louella had never questioned what was normal for her. "I don't really know."

"I'll put on the potatoes for salad." Brenda pulled a sack from under the sink. "Hope this'll be enough. The Commissary is closed today for the holiday."

While Louella cleaned a chicken for frying, her thoughts were on the day's beach party to come and Brenda's green and white nylon jersey swimsuit she would wear. Even with its gathered skirt, she felt naked in it. Consoling herself with the knowledge everyone else would be wearing a swimsuit also, she concentrated on how good the water would feel after the hot kitchen.

"Eddie'll pick us up at four," Brenda said. "That Eddie's something else." She smiled as her fingers flew and the pile of peelings grew in the sink.

"He's a...good friend?" Louella poked at a sputtering chicken thigh in the skillet.

Brenda gave her a quick glance. "He's more than a friend, Louella."

"Uh, Brenda...." Louella hesitated.

"Yeah?"

"I was wondering...," she began again, alarmed at her boldness, "doesn't your husband mind? You going out with other men and all?"

"Flint mind?"

"I guess I shouldn't have asked, but...."

"Oh, hell, Flint's a big boy. He doesn't expect me to live in a convent while he's overseas. You can sure as hell know he's after every skirt that twitches, wherever he is. Now when he comes home, that's different. But I'm a growed-up girl and there comes a time a woman just has to have a man. You know?"

Astonished, Louella stared at her roommate. Need a man? Surely she didn't mean.... It was a man's nature to need a woman, she knew from the story of Adam and Eve, but a woman's needs....? Her face was hot from something besides the stove.

"You never have, have you, honey?"

Louella kept her eyes on the skillet and finally shook her head.

"You'll find out one day," Brenda said softly.

Louella changed the subject.

By four o'clock the sun had burned off the haze, revealing a brilliant blue sky. Only a few summer clouds drifted on the horizon as they loaded the picnic food into Warrant Officer Edward M. O'Brien's '42 Plymouth coupe.

"New York, New York!" Eddie spread his arms wide, captured Brenda's waist and whirled her on the sidewalk, his green eyes flashing. His black hair sprang back into waves from its careful combing.

"Eddie, you idiot, stop it!" Brenda protested breathlessly. She patted her own hair back into place. "You're not from New York, anyhow. You're from Brooklyn."

"Look who's talking, Bronx!" He opened the car door with an elaborate bow. "Enter, my princess!"

"You, too, countess," he said, ushering Louella in beside Brenda. Closing the door, he did a jig step to the driver's side. In the middle of folding his lean frame under the steering wheel, he stopped to give Brenda a resounding kiss. Ignition on, he put the car into gear and sang in clear tenor, "To the sea, to the sea, to the beautiful sea!"

At the security gate, the guard returned Eddie's salute and waved them on with a grin.

Louella felt happiness like a giant bubble as she watched the little shacks drift past on the highway. Had it been only four days ago that she would have been grateful to rent one?

"There's the Noncommissioned Officers Club." Eddie gestured toward a colonial mansion, tall columns brilliant white, the grass a smooth green rug before it. Rhododendrons flowered near the wide porch steps. "Sure makes the Officers Club on base look sick. Whoever pulled that off has my admiration."

He saluted the mansion. "Hear they've got a new drummer, guy from Massachusetts just back from overseas. How about we all go hear him Saturday night?"

"Okay by me," Brenda said. "How about you, Louella?"

"Three's a crowd."

"No way. The more the merrier," replied Eddie.

"I don't know how to dance, though."

"Then you'll have an expert teaching you," Eddie announced with mock modesty. "Used to instruct back in the Big Apple for a while. You'll get lots of practice. The GI's will stand in line."

A shiver ran down Louella's spine. Nylons. A swimsuit. Soon, dancing. Was this the road to ruin that Preacher back home warned about? What was so terrible about having fun? She had learned to love her Yankee roommate and Eddie seemed good-hearted. So were most of the GI's she'd met, even the ones from the hated North. Surely it would be good to forget the war for a few hours with friends. Maybe Brenda and Eddie were right and Preacher was wrong. The thought shocked her. She shook her head free of such heavy thoughts and concentrated on the feel of the breeze against her cheek from the open window.

By the time they'd parked at the seashore, the heat had begun to fade. Outside the bathhouse, two girls in bright brief bathing suits brushed past Louella and Brenda, leaving a wet trail of footprints on the weathered boards of the ramp leading to the sand.

In a dark booth which smelled of damp and mildew, Louella struggled into the green and white printed nylon suit. The contrast between her tanned hands and white thighs was apparent even in the dimness.

Brenda was squealing in the shower, then emerged to shake the water off her two-piece red suit. "Hurry up! Fun's waiting."

Louella caught her breath in the icy shower, then wrapped up in her beach towel to cover as much as she could. Together they walked to the surf.

Everything was in motion. Waves broke into suds on damp sand. Colorful beach balls made rainbow arcs between young soldiers and girls. White bathing caps and crewcuts bobbed in the emerald water.

Louella kept her eyes down, aware of whistles and wolf calls. For Brenda, she assumed. But it was her sense of humor that broke her stiffness. How funny all the soldiers looked in bathing trunks! Tanned faces and arms ended where collars and cuffs had been. Bleached shoulders with smooth or hairy chests and white legs were hilarious.

Laughing, she caught up with Eddie and Brenda at the waterline. Past the surf, she sank into the warm sea. Undertow sucked sand beneath her toes. Buoyant in the water, it felt good to be alive, to see smiles. The war dissolved in the salt spray. She floated parallel to the shore, staring up at white gulls doing acrobatics overhead. Once a swell caught her and she came up sputtering.

It seemed only minutes before the sun dropped behind a distant grove of trees. A shifting flight of small birds plummeted one at a time for small fish, wings brilliant against the aquamarine sea in the sunset.

Louella stripped off her white rubber cap and ran to join her friends on the blanket spread for their picnic. Eddie trotted up bearing a six-pack of beer covered with moisture beads.

"Hey, I met a bunch of guys and gals down the beach who asked us to join them at their campfire later for watermelon." He followed a long drag on his Budweiser with a swipe of his hand. "They're good joes from my company. How about it?"

"Sure," Brenda said, "but after we eat." She handed out their paper plates.

For Louella, her first sip of beer was unpleasant. It foamed in her mouth tasting like the pewter spoon her mother once had allowed her to use when she was very small. She swallowed quickly. Eddie and Brenda were obviously enjoying theirs. She took another sip. Not so bad. Plenty cold and I'm thirsty, she thought. Alternating chicken and potato salad with the brew, she finished the can. Add one more of Preacher's list of sins; she had been drinking. But she felt so fine, she giggled.

Eddie stretched to his feet and pulled at Brenda's hand. "Race you to the water."

She refused to move. "Shouldn't go in for an hour. We'd get cramps." Her eyes were sleepy.

"Hell, I didn't mean to swim!" He jerked her to her feet and whacked her on the seat. At her shout of outrage, he ran for the surf with Brenda close behind him.

Left to herself, hunger satisfied and content, Louella rolled over to the edge of the blanket and sifted sand through her fingers. A recollection stirred: A soft, loving woman who helped her build a castle by the shore. She strained to see the face, but it was a blur. There was only the memory of gentle arms, a voice and laughter. If her mother were only here now, there were so many questions.... She wished she had a picture of her mother to treasure, but Papa had taken them all away when she died, almost as though it was her mother's fault she passed away.

What would she ask her mother, if she were here? Would she be horrified at drinking and dancing and parties and her two new friends who committed adultery? Louella's confused thoughts swirled like mosquitoes, biting and frustrating.

She jumped to her feet and strolled along the edge of the surf, poking at an occasional shell, avoiding two lumps of dead jellyfish. Wolf whistles broke her concentration.

"Hey, tall honey, wait for me!"

"Will I do, sweet thing?"

There was no doubt these were meant for her! Her ears burned and she didn't turn, afraid to face them. Again she felt naked in the damp suit that clung to her body. Face stiff, she hurried back to the sanctuary of the blanket.

She found Brenda and Eddie wrestling with it, flapping sand and teasing. Eddie won the match, wrapping Brenda in the gritty fabric, announcing, "Time for the campfire!"

Louella draped her beach towel around her shoulders and they ran toward the cluster of people gathered around a pit in the sand. Were there four or five men and three girls? Louella couldn't be sure, for they shifted constantly.

"Hi. Glad you could join us," greeted the swarthy man with a chest like a black fur rug. "Have a Bud." He gestured toward an ice chest.

"Thanks, Joe. This is Brenda and here's Louella, everybody."

A chorus of names rang in Louella's ears. Except for Joe, she couldn't fit any of them to a face.

"Somebody find some newspapers so I can get this damned fire started," the burly man ordered. "And get more driftwood.

This handful won't last fifteen minutes." From the way he was handing out orders, Louella decided he must be at least a Sergeant, although in bathing trunks you couldn't tell ranks apart.

Gradually the navy blue night closed down, decorated with a shimmer of stars. A creamy melon-rind moon perched above the horizon over the sea with a rhinestone Venus nearby for accent. The sand beneath Louella was warm remembrance of the hot summer's day. There was taste of salt on her lips, an itch of dried salt on her body. Now and then a breath of air stirred the fragrance of the bonfire. It was luxury to stretch muscles with a good kind of tired in them, pleasant to longer feel naked and ashamed.

She watched the phosphorescent shimmers where small waves broke on the sand and the firelight flickering across the faces around the pit. This was the very best Fourth of July I've ever known, Louella thought, hugging her knees.

She sensed for all those around this fire the war felt far away and yet thoughts of homes hovered very near. Maybe the others remembered other 4ths and campfires on other beaches or in mountain campgrounds. Maybe on wide prairies or in thick forests or out on the desert where Frances lived.

Brenda's low voice broke in on her thoughts. "Sure glad they lifted the blackout here on the East Coast, now the war in Europe is over. A German U-boat got an oil tanker a hundred miles off this shore during that war. Last time I was here I got globs of tar on my feet."

"Let's sing!" Eddie was on his feet. "Row, row, row your boat...."

The round ended with an uncertain baritone and a shout of laughter. Old favorites followed. Here on a South Carolina beach young people sang of buffalo on the wide prairie, of Dinah in her kitchen, of working on a railroad, of the top of Old Smoky. But when someone started, "Home, Sweet Home,"

Louella caught her breath and thought of Cora Sue, Cloteel and Papa. The mood around the fire had sobered.

A shout of "Watermelon time!" cleared the air. A soldier's knife meant for quite a different purpose split open the long green melons with a satisfying crack that meant ripe sweetness inside. Chunks were handed around.

"Perfect way to eat a melon," Eddie commented, spewing a seed into the breeze, a minute projectile flashing in firelight before it landed. "No forks. Let the juice run down your chin." His watermelon finished, with a wicked grin he scrubbed Brenda's back with its rind.

Instantly there was a shouting rush of men bearing melon peels on high. Louella ran among the screaming girls for the shore. Shrieks ran out as sunburned shoulders were scrubbed. Bodies scrimmaged in the foam among microscopic sea creatures that glowed in the moonlit surf.

When the rind touched her back, Louella's scream was almost laughter. A small wave sent spray over her shoulders. It was utter joy to be held by stronger muscles, buoyant in the phosphorescent sea. The watermelon quarter brushed her arm as it floated on by. Someone pressed full against her in the warm sea, salt lips on her own. Pure delight to feel firm thighs that held her secure against the suck of the undertow. She gave herself up to the pleasure of the kiss. Stith had not kissed her with such a hunger. She was suddenly aware of feelings that stirred her depths beyond mere pleasure, echoing her own hunger she had not known existed.

Dimly she heard a shout. "Come on! Only an hour to bed check. Gotta leave now!"

At that moment she was alone. Ahead a dim form ran up the beach. Confused by the strength of the feelings in her own body, it was several moments before she left the water. The flames were dying in the fire pit as Joe kicked it full of sand. She hurried to catch up with Brenda and Eddie and tumbled into the coupe beside her roommate.

As they drove through the warm night, Louella closed her eyes, head back against the seat. I never saw his face, she thought. Her friends sang all the way home, but she felt lips touching hers and wondered who it was that had held her in the shimmering water.

Was the heavy heat she still felt deep in her body the woman's need that Brenda had talked about? Her face was hot against the breeze from the window beside her.

CHAPTER IX

Friday. Payday morning. Brenda and Louella were the first to arrive at the office.

"Gotta get our life's blood perking." Brenda picked up the coffee pot.

"Why is it the first cup's always the best?" Louella bent to check the seams of her nylons. Once again she rolled the tops of her hose, pulled the roll out into a tight twist and tucked it under. Next payday she'd own a garter belt like Brenda's, but maybe white instead of black. She dropped her skirt just as Donald Monahan entered.

"Top of the morning to you, Brenda, my pretty colleen!" His shirt was a crisp white against the dark green of his suit. Although his clothes were still loose, he was a rejuvenated man. His small round cheeks glowed. The silver halo of his hair repeated in snowy eyebrows like small pointed roofs above his emerald eyes. Reaching for Louella's hand, he said, "Don't believe I've had the pleasure."

"Louella Tolbert, my new roommate." Busy with the coffee, Brenda spoke over her shoulder.

He reminds me of an elf, Louella thought, smiling at the man who was no longer the shaking sad figure of Monday. "I'm pleased to make your acquaintance, sir," she said as she'd been taught.

"Ah, and do I detect a charming Southern accent?"

"Rare species," Brenda informed him. "A native."

"My dear," he said, rising to his toes to meet Louella's eyes, "my disappointment is deep that Glen Hart found you first, else I would have a beautiful clerk."

Louella smiled and moved toward her desk, pleased with her new ability to accept a compliment without blushing.

"He's the one who runs the harem in merchandising and the cafe," Brenda explained.

The day officially began when Hutch and Hart entered together, but it was fifteen minutes later when Frances skidded through the door with a guilty look. Bustling to her stool in the corner, she announced in the general direction of Glen Hart, "Sorry I'm late."

He waved a hand of acceptance.

"I swear," she said, adjusting her wiry body to the stool, "those pilots think they can fly on the ground! I saw three I recognized on the way in today and they must have been doing ninety!" She ran her fingers through her short brown curls. "You'd think they'd take better care of a car. It's not like they could buy a new one, with Detroit turning out only Jeeps and tanks nowadays." Without a noticeable pause, she turned toward Donald Monahan. "'Morning, Donald. When will the inventories be ready?"

"Whoa now, my dear, you're moving faster than the pilots," Monahan replied, both hands lifted. "Give me until Wednesday." He disappeared down the hall.

"Get your notebook," Hart ordered Brenda without looking up. When she was seated by his desk, he began his dictation.

"Dear Sirs and so forth—you can get the address from this invoice—regarding the four gross of T-shirts shipped to us on— what was that date?—the 27th of June, be advised the name of this Air Force Base is Seacomb—and spell that out— not Siccumb as it is printed in red on these shirts by your company. Period. Paragraph. One gross is being returned for replacement at your expense. Usual ending." He shoved the invoice over his desk toward Brenda. "Too bad headquarters has no sense of humor and pulled them out of stock. I would have re-ordered." "I bought Eddie one," Brenda commented.

"Bought four myself." Hart grinned.

At noon Louella excused herself from the sack-lunch-or-PX plans of the office force. "Been hankering for some red beans and rice," she told Brenda. "Think I'll put some on to simmer while we're at work this afternoon.

In the hazy heat she walked the three blocks to the housing area. A squadron of servicemen in fatigues, their sergeant supervising with one eye on Louella, pushed mowers over the parade grounds. Sunshine glinted on the flag's colors in a light breeze. Brilliant yellow marigolds surround the base of the silver pole. Overhead three Corsairs took off with a scream. A glimpse of camouflaged wings and they were gone, a distant drone above the sound of a truck motor backfiring at the motor pool. The sounds of the base had become so usual to Louella that she no longer flinched at flyovers.

At the edge of the housing area the music began. Through open windows a dozen radios accompanied her down the street.

"That's Bing Crosby," she whispered to herself. "And Vaughn Monroe," she added as she passed the next open window. A nonsense song babbled from the third housing unit and she chuckled. "Iskabibble with Kay Kaiser's band."

I really have learned so much in just five weeks, she congratulated herself. It felt good to walk tall, proud of her appearance. No more slouching to make herself shorter. Able now to accept the length of her narrow feet, too. If I didn't have so much turned under, she thought with a smile, I'd be a giant!

She'd had such a hunger to learn about the world. All her new knowledge was deeply satisfying. So many ways there were to live, to dress, ways to speak. Someday I'll see the wide prairie where Hutch lives, Brenda's Bronx and Eddie's Brooklyn, she thought. Maybe even California with Frances' desert and movie stars and flowers.

A low whistle nearby startled her. Over her shoulder she saw no one. Another louder whistle. Whirling, she stared down the empty street. Only an overturned child's tricycle down the block marred the rigid lines of concrete buildings and flat yards with their borders of white rocks.

It was a small movement beside the bush at the corner of the nearest apartment that caught her eye. She faced a grinning soldier, helmet liner tilted, rifle in hand. Astounded, she spotted another camouflaged man prone behind the building, his mottled olive drab and brown blending into the dusty grass. And another beyond those steps! Invasion? But they're ours, she reminded herself.

Flushed, she hurried down the sidewalk accompanied by a low chorus of sound, relieved when she closed the apartment door behind her. How invisible they had been! That's how the enemy crept up on you! She shivered and wondered where Stith was this day.

She drained the red beans she had soaked overnight in the big pot, added the ham bone with its scraps of meat, a cup of rice, a chopped onion, then tossed in garlic pods. Gas flame turned low under the pot, she made herself a peanut butter and jelly sandwich and ate it, idly strolling the room.

The listing couch had been repaired by Eddie. It now sat firmly on the multi-hued striped rug, the Myrtle Beach pillow banished to a closet. It had been a relief to know the eyesore was the taste of an admirer, not her roommate's choice.

She licked away the last of the peanut butter from her fingers, and laid down on her bed, careful not to wrinkle her plaid skirt and blouse. A pleasure to see all her new clothes in the open closet. Maybe they were castoffs, but they were hers. Soon she'd be able to buy dresses no one else had ever worn. She had her eye on a navy blue polkadot in Lerner's window in town. Maybe some white shoes with platforms? She had enough shoe ration stamps.

She thought of her roommate and frowned. Maybe Brenda was dating another man while she was married, but Stith doesn't have to worry about me. I have been eating with Hutch most evenings, she thought with a twinge of guilt, but he's just a chubby little brother I never had.

Stith. Why no letters for such a long time? Had he found some foreign girl? Maybe the daughter of the family he talked about? Stith wouldn't.... Louella pushed up from the bed to open her dresser drawer and lift out her woven grass ring. Now it was dried and brittle. No longer could she wear it. She held it on the tip of her thumb, gave it an impulsive kiss, then placed it carefully back into its nest of cotton balls.

A glance at the clock told her it was time to leave. She slid fresh lipstick over her mouth before the wavy mirror and hurried back to the office. The platoon on maneuvers was nowhere in sight.

Glen Hart looked up as she entered. "There you are. You've got a visitor."

"Visitor?" In the middle of a step she halted, then caught her balance. Had Papa....?

"He's waiting in the PX coffee shop." Louella could not move.

"Says you'd know him. His name is Stith."

When Louella reached the end of the hallway, she slowed, trying to calm down, wanting to see Stith before he saw her. Several steps into the aisle she saw the soldier at the corner table, head lowered, face brown and solemn. It was the streak of white in the auburn curl over his forehead that stopped her. His face was thinner, cheekbones high, shadows in the hollows. Was it really Stith? A stranger wearing his face seemed to sit there.

She was almost at his elbow before he looked up.

"Stith? Stith! This is just the finest surprise I ever did have!" It was the moment she'd waited for and her words tumbled out. "Does this mean you're home to stay and won't have to go to the Pacific? Oh, Stith, you've got to meet my friends. I'm living here on the base and my roommate...Oh, Stith, you're here!" Out of breath, she bit her lip, waiting for his first words.

"Louella." His voice was as hollow as his face. "It's good the troop train was routed this way. But we're headed for the Pacific front."

She tried to swallow the rock in her throat. He had pulled out a chair for her. In this thin tense man she found no trace of the gentle boy who wove her ring beside the bayou long ago. And now he was still in danger, heading to fight the Japs. He seems taller, she thought. Maybe because he's so...so gaunt. There was a hardness, a grimness to his bearing that puzzled her.

His eyes were on her hair and she reached up to check her braids. Then the need to touch him overwhelmed her. Across the table she caught his hand. "Oh, Stith, I love you so much!"

He did not return her pressure. Slowly he withdrew his fingers.

A sudden fear made Louella blink and she dropped her offending hands into her lap. No smile. No loving greeting. Had she really spoken of her love to a stranger?

"Can I order something for you, Louella?"

The boy she remembered had spoken her name as though he loved the sound of it. This man dropped the word like a hammer blow. In shock, she watched him jump to his feet.

"Let's walk." He dropped coins beside his coffee cup, took her arm in a firm grip and propelled her through the outside door.

The afternoon heat was at its peak. The buzz of cicadas competed with airplane motors overhead and on the flight line. Her arms ached to hold him but she silently hurried her steps to keep pace. Almost at a run, he stopped suddenly.

"Is there any place we can talk? Somewhere private?"

"Our apartment in the housing area. It's this way...."

"No." His tone was cold. "There. Beyond the parade ground." With a stiff finger he pointed to a marble bench in a tiny rose garden.

She had to trot to keep even across the hot expanse of grass. A brass plaque on the bench announced it had been the gift of the first flight school class of 1944. The odor of roses hung in the still air. A small magnolia offered scant shade, the July sun a coppery shine on its leaves.

Louella caught a scent of pipe tobacco, something that reminded her of trains, shaving lotion and a clean-man smell when she took her seat beside Stith. He took her hand and turned it over and over, as if he sought an answer in it. His touch deepened her hunger for him. She leaned closer, waiting for a kiss. For a long moment even the cicadas ceased their whine.

"I've been thinking about us for a long time," he said.

"I've thought about you every single waking moment of...."

"I'm not the guy I was when I left, that's for sure."

"Neither am I. I've learned so much...."

"Louella!" He barked her name like a top sergeant. "You're not listening to me. Hush! Try to understand."

She stared at his twisted mouth. He was actually rude interrupting her like that. Southern boys were never rude....

"Crazy things happened in a crazy world and maybe I'm crazy now, too."

Did he mean Section Eight? Eddie talked about insane men back from overseas awaiting Section Eight discharges. But this was Stith and she had promised him.... She felt a painful cramp when she tried to breathe. The odor of roses was strong.

With a start she saw a two-inch scar above the knuckles on his right hand, an angry red line. When he eased his grip and turned her palm again, she saw the same two inches inside. Revulsion churned for a moment.

"Bayonet," he mumbled.

She fought nausea and touched the scarlet welts with her fingertips. What other wounds did Stith have she couldn't see?

"Five of us, out on a scouting expedition. We came on them just over a small hill." His grin was terrible. "Him or me." Louella blinked.

"Death's been nearer than sunlight and air ever since. It's waiting. For me." His pupils had expanded until his eyes were black holes.

Louella drew back, frightened, and dropped his hand. But this is Stith! She touched the white streak in his hair and brushed back a lock over his forehead. If there was only some way to console him, bring back the smiling boy she remembered, banish this sorrowing, scared stranger. If she could just hold him, cradle his head against....

"He was a guy my size. My age, I reckon. But in the wrong uniform. When it's kill or die, you kill and we got them all that day. After a while it doesn't make much difference, you don't feel anything." He released a shuddering sigh. "When I wiped my bayonet that day, I knew. Death is coming for me." Louella shivered in the heat.

"Life's not the way we thought, Louella. I guess you don't know that yet, but what I've seen and done showed me clear." His face was like chiseled brown marble. "There was one thing I had to do: Get back here and tell you to forget about us in the future. There won't be any for me." He closed his eyes, his hands clenched on the edge of the bench.

"But...I love you!" The words burst out of her pain. Couldn't he stand even the sight of her any longer? The sunlight grayed around her and she looked up, surprised to see no clouds. She swallowed hard and said firmly, "Love will make it all right. It's just what you've been through and you'll soon forget when the war ends. It's just the war and the fighting makes you...."

"It made me, all right!" he said bitterly. "Showed me you got to climb over bodies if you have to, but get there. That's what I aim to do as long as I can dodge Old Man Death." He threw back his head, turning away from her.

"But we planned to marry and...."

He spat. "What dumb, stupid dreams. You wanted a family, tying me to drudgery to support a bunch of brats, fighting off creditors and boll weevils, malaria and taxes!"

"No children?"

"Struggle to keep a brood in shoes? Not for me." His eyes burned into her. "It's an ugly world and I aim to scratch me a place in it before I die. Alone."

Through the thunder of his words, the last one fell on her heart like a stone.

"That's what life's all about, Louella. Not drifting through your days, trying to live up to some dumb ideals that don't mean shit in a world with war, where kids become prostitutes to keep their families alive. And men like me get too drunk to remember how young they were."

Louella stiffened. Had Stith done what he said? A low moan escaped his lips and she could not look at this stranger.

"So that's how it's gonna be." He jerked to his feet. "Go find some innocent guy like you, Louella. Maybe you can find someplace to hide where the world can't get at you." He pulled back his left cuff and looked at his wristwatch. "I've just got time to get back to the troop train. Lucky we were routed this way with a layover." He threw back his shoulders. "I had to tell you face to face, like a man. Don't wait for me."

"But...Stith, that's crazy!" She bit her lip on the word. He really was deranged. "I mean...it's just your experiences and you won't feel this way when the war's over and you get back to a normal life. Time the war's over, then we could...."

"Forget me, Louella."

"But I left home for you. I can't go back. Everything's built on our future together. Without that...." She spread her hands toward him in appeal.

Already he had moved away. "I've got to hurry to make it," he said over his shoulder, stepping back toward the parade grounds.

"Stith," she called, not caring if there were ears to hear, "won't you even kiss me goodbye?" Tears were very near.

He turned and strode back to her, pulled her into his arms. His lips were violent on hers, his arms so tight her breath was gone. She felt her lip split under the brutal force of his mouth.

Her eyes open, she stared directly into his dilated pupils.

"Goodbye, Louella." He was gone, racing across the grass.

Louella tasted coppery blood from her lip. She took one agonized breath and sank down on the marble bench.

The bronze green of the magnolia leaves swam in a blur, the odor of roses gagging her. His khaki figure grew smaller and smaller, running out of her life. When she could no longer see him, she lowered her head into her hands. Tears trickled over her fingers and she let them flow until numbness conquered some of the pain.

He's taken away my world, she thought, discarded my love like rotten fruit. How can I build another world without him in it? I was strong when he loved me. Now I feel too weak to stand.

What is left to build on without him? What will become of me?

CHAPTER X

Brenda left the office early that afternoon, eager to inspect this star-spangled marvel that Louella had talked about. Her brief glimpse of Stith in the office gave only an impression of an ordinary GI Sergeant with a haggard face.

At the apartment, she rattled the knob before she took some time to unlock it. Give them a little notice, she decided, before she threw open the door.

"Well, where is he, honey, that wonderful man I've heard so much about? I want to meet the guy that my roommate raves about."

Louella raised up from the couch, her face puffy, eyes red.

"What happened?"

"You've heard about Dear-John letters?" Louella drew a shuddering breath. "I just had a Dear-Jane visit." Brenda swore.

"He's gone. Out of my life. He told me to find somebody else, that he's changed." Louella smiled feebly and dabbed at a trickle of blood from a split lip. "He talked kinda crazy, but maybe he meant I wasn't good enough...he didn't want me anymore." She clenched her fists and threw back her head when the last words strangled.

Half bent over the table, ready to drop her keys, Brenda froze into position. She felt her face flush as she shouted, "That goddamned son-of-a-bitch!" Keys clattered onto the table top and she shoved one fist into the air. "That double-plated brass bound goddamned son-of-a-bitch!" Too angry to stand still, she paced the room.

"Don't blame him, Brenda. It's me. I shouldn't have expected...."

Brenda halted and jerked Louella to her feet. "Stop it! That fool didn't know what he had. Quit beating on yourself."

Louella shrugged free. "He's mixed up and scared of dying, Brenda. In spite of everything, I can't help feeling sorry for him."

Brenda shook her roommate, gently this time. "What gives him the right to treat you this way? Hell, he's not the only fish in the pond. You can have any of the fifteen hundred men on this base. Any, you hear? Except Eddie, of course."

Louella smiled weakly and dabbed at her lip.

"And, by god, you're going to have your choice — or else I'm the Pope."

"I just wasn't woman enough for him." Enraged,

Brenda slapped her.

Louella blinked and covered her cheek with a hand.

"Oh, jeez, I shouldn't have done that, honey! I'm sorry!" Brenda cringed at the sight of the red welt. "It just makes me so goddamned mad to hear you run yourself down after what that bastard did to you." She cradled Louella in her arms.

Tears flowed over Louella's reddened cheek.

"Hell, yes, honey. Go ahead and cry," Brenda crooned, rocking Louella. "Then we'll get to work and show him. Don't fight it, honey." She held her at arm's length. "Want me to cut your hair, fix it different? Be a lot prettier with curls instead of those old braids," Brenda coaxed.

Louella sniffed a final tear and blew her nose on tissue from her pocket. "Why not?"

"All those braids remind me of a prune-faced history teacher I had back in the Bronx, the one with her knees bolted together."

"I think I'd like to fix my hair different," Louella said, tossing her head back and pulling pins from her braids to let them fall, combing them out with her fingers. "I've got to begin all over again, anyhow."

Brenda cocked her head in astonishment as the black waves fell down Louella's back. "My god, you can almost sit on it!

What a chore all that must be to wash." She put her hands on Louella's shoulders and turned her slowly.

Louella pivoted, her chin defiantly lifted.

"Let's take a real good look at you, see what we've got to work with." Brenda propped her head on one hand, the other supporting her elbow. "With a waistline like that, I have to remind myself not to hate you, roommate. You make me feel like a water tank on stilts. What's it measure?"

"Twenty-two, last I checked."

"With a thirty-six bra?" Brenda grinned an evil grin. "We'll drive them straight up a wall! How tall are you, honey?"

"Five eight."

"Might intimidate a few, but lots of little guys love to burrow noses into tall bosoms while they dance, the creeps!" Brenda placed two fingers under Louella's chin. "Nice cream-and-magnolias Southern skin. Shows your pores haven't been fighting city soot and crap."

Looking at her roommate's satin skin, Brenda was painfully aware of her own coarse skin and the small mole on her cheek. She shrugged the feeling away and continued the inventory. "I'll thin your brows some, just underneath. Are you sure those eyelashes aren't glued on?"

She was relieved to see Louella's smile becoming stronger. Good, she's coming back to life.

"How'd you chip that front tooth?"

"Lightning tossed me onto the mailbox when I was little."

"Wonder you weren't killed."

Louella giggled. "Lightning's a horse."

"That snaggle tooth keeps me from pure hate, honey. A little imperfection helps a sensitive type like me." Brenda's fingers were busy in Louella's hair. "Don't roll those big gray eyes at me. I'm only kidding." She hummed two bars of "Star Dust." "Maybe just over your shoulders. With lots of loose curls. Yeah. You're not the sleek Joan Crawford type. More like Ann Miller, the dancer. Tall, friendly, with elegant ankles."

Brenda led her to the table and wrapped a towel around her neck. "God, it's going to take forever with these," she clicked manicure scissors.

"I guess I couldn't ever be a little, cuddly June Allyson, could I?" Louella asked. "But Ann Miller's pretty dramatic. Maybe I could be more like Rosalind Russell or—better still—Dorothy Lamour. Real sexy."

"How would Stith like that, huh?" Brenda said, then bit her lip. Louella batted her eyes and she knew the tears were close again.

Slowly the black pile of hair grew around the chair. Neither spoke until Brenda announced, "There, that's it. Now to roll it up."

Louella shook her head, experimentally. "Feels odd with the weight of my hair gone," she said, running fingers through it. She winced when Brenda anchored the first pincurl with a bobby pin.

Twenty minutes later Brenda finished the last curl. "Tie a scarf over it tonight. Tomorrow morning we'll have the unveiling."

"Just in case I get to feeling too naked, I'm going to braid what you cut off, make a switch out of it. Then I can pin it back on...if I ever have to face Papa again."

Brenda shrugged. "If it was blonde, you could have sold it to Uncle Sam for cross hatches on Norden bombsights." She paused for a moment. "Louella...."

"Hmmmm?"

"Well, before..." She started again. "Before all this happened with Stith, we'd planned to go to the NCO Club tomorrow night, seeing Saturday was coming up. Eddie and I decided to make a party of it, a good way for us to meet Stith. We thought he was here on leave and..." She heard Louella's sudden intake of breath. "Maybe it wasn't such a good idea, after the way things have turned out. I'll call it off."

"A party?" Louella gave a strangled laugh. "I do declare a party is just exactly what I would most like. Show off my new haircut. Laugh a lot. Learn to dance." Her words were brave, but her face was miserable.

At least she's trying, Brenda thought. For now, it would have to do.

CHAPTER XI

Technical Sergeant Leon Cobb ran up the steps of the portico at the Noncommissioned Officers Club. Bougainvillea waved its scarlet blooms at him. He threw open the leaded glass double doors and entered. Small tables in the wide entry hall, now converted into a dance floor, held upturned chairs surrounding a Chianti bottle with myriad colored wax drippings.

A black hand scrubbed the floor of a small stage at the far end of the room, its owner hidden behind a set of drums. His entrance brought the hand and its scrub brush to a halt, followed by a hollow boom from the base drum which re-echoed up the curving stairway beyond. A black girl, whites of eyes showing poked her head over the rim.

"I never heard you come in, suh." She stood to wipe both hands on a gray skirt.

"Where's Master Sergeant Woods?"

"Up yonder." She gestured toward the stair, sank back to her knees, sloshed the brush in a pail of dark water and returned to slow circles on the stage floor.

Cobb ran lightly up the worn oriental carpeted steps two at a time. At the door facing, he rapped twice. Garrison cap tucked under his belt, he checked the knot in his tie, straightened his shoulders with a jerk and entered on the command, "Come."

In opulent days, the manager's office had been a bedroom. Faded blue plush drapes hung at the tall narrow windows. Here again bougainvillea trailed outside the glass, green leaves softening the glare of a Southern sun. Close by stood a Victorian fainting couch of sun-faded blue brocade. A small white marble fireplace in the corner emitted the faint acrid odor of old ashes. To his right two steel Air Force chairs sat under a brighter square of the flocked burgundy wallpaper where a picture once had hung.

Cobb pivoted to face Master Sergeant Wood behind his government-issue desk of scarred oak. The lamp beside his elbow revealed white in Wood's brown hair. Lines of pain showed in his narrow clenched jaw. Cobb realized his hunched position was not from concentration when Woods straightened with a grimace, clutching his midriff.

"Glad you made it, Cobb. Any news?"

"Got the orders right here." Cobb unbuttoned his shirt pocket and removed a folded paper which he placed in the exact center of the desk.

"Hell, don't stand on formality around here, man. Pull up a chair." He read aloud from the paper. "7 July 1945. Great! That means I can report to sick bay today. And none too soon. This ulcer is killing me!" He managed a grin. "Think you can handle the Saturday night crowd by yourself?"

"Right."

"It's yours, then. Supplies are in. Sam's a good man in the kitchen. You won't have any trouble there. Just keep order if somebody gets a snoot full. We don't bother the MP's, you understand." His eyes moved above Cobb's head, thinking. "Got a new drummer for the band. Pretty good—for a soldier."

Woods rose from his desk, lifted a carton of half-and-half from the floor and took a long swig. He wiped his mouth and sighed. "This helps some, I guess." He moved toward the door, then hesitated.

"Oh, yeah. You owe Flodeen a dollar when she's finished scrubbing. Take it out of petty cash in the lower right-hand drawer." He tossed a set of keys onto the desk. "All those civilians want their money the minute they're done. Lucky to find her, anyhow."

With one hand on the knob, he turned again. "Dunno just how long I'll be out. Doc talked about cutting. You know where I'll be if you have any questions."

Cobb gave him a half salute. "Good luck, then."

The door closed and Cobb circled the desk. Hands spread on the top, he eased himself down and grinned. Year-long goal accomplished, here where supplies weren't checked too closely. Mentally he saw his bank account multiply. And he'd have the know-how for his own club, too.

He heard Woods speak to Flodeen before the sound of the outer door closing. From his new vantage point he surveyed the room.

"Horrible," he said aloud. "Little paint, maybe." His eye fell on the brighter square of wallpaper. Better not make too many changes just yet in case old Woods made it back. Not likely, though. A poster of Betty Grable would cover that spot just fine. Easy to remove in a hurry, if need be.

He assembled the papers on the desk top and began to read.

That much chicken? And the meat! Amazing! Sam must really be a good cook to bring in that many customers when chow lines on base were free. It wouldn't take much to beat the slop served in the mess halls, though. His eyes narrowed on the liquor invoice. Toots would be good for a quarter of that and it wouldn't be missed. Not with a substitution of rotgut for the good stuff.

"Maybe I ought to take in a partner," he said to the desk lamp, then shook his head. He could handle this by himself. Keep it one man. Might be a little less profit but nobody gets a cut, either. Get too big and somebody always squeals.

He glanced at the closed door and clamped his jaw shut. Had he said anything aloud somebody outside could have overheard? No.

The scarlet flowers at the window shook in a sudden breeze and Cobb's eyes wandered to the blooms. With all forces now directed toward Japan, the war was bound to end soon. While his sun shone, he'd have to store all the hay he could. With a smile he snapped off the light and headed for the kitchen downstairs.

Time to let Sam know he had a new boss.

That night Louella looked around the NCO Club in the candlelight, determined to look as if she were having a good time for the sake of Eddie and Brenda.

Flat drifts of cigarette smoke eddied upward to flatten in slow swirls below high ceilings lost in dimness. The room was crowded with GI's and a few girls, conversation and laughter rising and falling.

She straightened her blue printed nylon dress, a loan from Brenda. It helped to have a new image to hide behind. Unfamiliar curls tickled her neck. When she had dressed that evening, it was a pretty woman who looked back at her in the mirror. Could it be that Brenda was right? What if...what if she acted as if she were pretty? It was worth a try. How wonderful it must be to be admired. It had been a long, long day with a bitter afternoon. Tonight she'd try to shed all thoughts of Stith, like a butterfly emerging from a tight cocoon.

Across the table Brenda's eyes shone in the reflection of Eddie's Zippo lighter held to her cigarette.

"Hungry?" he asked.

"A little nourishment always helps," Brenda replied.

"Chicken and a basket of fries all around?"

"Fine."

Louella nodded and felt her curls bounce.

At the half door separating kitchen and the tables into what must have been a breakfast room before, Eddie placed their orders. He circled by the bar against the wall and returned with a bottle and three wine glasses. Flipping his napkin over his arm, he opened the wine with exaggerated ceremony. Bent stiffly at the waist, he twirled an imaginary moustache.

"Ma'mzelles will enjoy zees wine. Of the very best vintage. Guaranteed to make ze feet light, ze heart happy!"

"Oh, Eddie, you nut!" Brenda laughed as he served her.

Louella lifted her glass to admire the beauty of light trapped in the rising bubbles.

"A toast!" Eddie lifted his champagne. "Tonight Louella learns to dance." He smiled at her over the rim. "May your feet always be light, your heart happy!" "I'll drink to that," Brenda said.

Louella smiled faintly and took the first sip. Tangy but cold. Sliding down her throat, it left a glow behind. "Good," she pronounced and took a deeper drink.

Behind her on stage musicians rustled music and instruments, moistened reeds. A clarinet and a saxophone tuned to the insistent single note from the piano. The drummer practiced a roll on the snare drum. A pause. The first notes of "Stardust" filled the room. Voices around her rose, accompanied by the shuffle of chairs and feet as a few couples moved to the dance floor.

"Before I go to work on Louella," Eddie said to Brenda, "zees dance is ours, Ma'mzelle."

Louella watched them moving across the floor as one, Brenda's blondness sharp contrast to Eddie's dark head. Their steps were intricate, effortless. Oh, how I want to be able to dance like that, Louella thought, to move with the music with a partner, like drifting in a dream. With the last note, Eddie dipped and bent Brenda in a tight embrace. Full of laughter, they returned to the table.

"More wine, Fred Astaire," Brenda demanded.

The band struck up "It's Been a Long, Long Time."

"Now for it, Louella," Eddie commanded. He guided her to the edge of the dance floor. "Remember always to move your left foot back for the first step as your partner starts forward. Now follow me. We'll just do a step in place for now. Right foot back; that's correct. Put your weight on your left foot. Now the right. You're doing fine."

Eddie held her firmly, swaying them both, exaggerating their steps. "Now the same thing in a circle."

Inside Louella the wine glowed. She had finally relaxed, the heavy weight she had borne was growing lighter. The music matched her heartbeats. Other dancers swirled around them.

"Now we separate a step and I'll turn you. Just follow my hand." With the twist of his wrist, she turned, keeping the beat. "That's it! That's great. You're a natural."

Eddie moved faster now and Louella managed to follow. The movement of her body in time to the music thrilled her. Great fun, the best she'd ever known. The brush of her nylon skirts against her thighs was sensual. When Eddie led her back to the table at the end of the number, she felt glorious.

"You really caught on fast," Brenda commented. She reached for Eddie's hand. "Come on, Astaire, that's `Pennsylvania Six Five Thousand.'"

Louella sipped her wine, watching their feet. Faster and faster they moved until their bodies began to blur before her. Brenda's white dress belled out in the swings. Two by two, the other dancers moved back to watch. On the last notes Eddie lifted Brenda to swing her right and then left of his body. They ended in a tight spin to the whistles and cheers of their audience.

"Eddie's the best damned dancer!" Brenda said, breathlessly, as she dropped back into her chair.

Eddie returned, bearing their food. "Begin the Beguine" was faint background music over laughter, clatter of dishes and silverware. Conversation between the three ended while they concentrated on their meal.

"'Nother bottle of wine." Eddie headed for the bar.

By now the floor was crowded with dancers and he had to battle his way back, the wine bottle held overhead.

"Drink up, Louella. The next number is ours."

When "Stomping at the Savoy" started, once more the floor was crowded, Louella and Eddie among them. It was almost impossible to move except at the edges. Finding an empty corner, Eddie twirled Louella out and back, out and back.

The room whirled around her. It was like floating on sound. Relaxed, her fingers slipped from Eddie's and momentum spun her toward the wall. With a jolt she fell against a tall blond soldier. Without a word, he grasped her waist and steadied her too close against him.

Louella felt a shock. It was Sergeant Cobb of the strange eyes, his face a lean mask. She stood paralyzed in his arms.

He said nothing. Slowly he released her and slid one hand down her hip and cupped her buttock for an instant.

"I'm...sorry," Louella mumbled, stepping back. "I just...slipped." She couldn't look away from those colorless eyes. Her body tingled from the thrust of his against her.

When Eddie took her hand and led her back to the table, Cobb had not moved nor spoken.

"That was my fault, Louella," Eddie apologized. "I should have held onto you." He frowned. "Stay away from that one. I've heard rumors he's...no good."

"That was Tech Sergeant Cobb, wasn't it?" Brenda asked.

Eddie nodded. "Can't put my finger on it, but there's something wrong about that guy."

"I heard he used to wrestle alligators in Florida for a living. Looks like that might be the straight poop," Brenda said and laughed.

Louella glanced back at Cobb against the wall, startled to find him staring back. She looked away and felt herself flush. When she looked up again, he was gone.

A sudden shout from the far corner table caught their ears. Figures pushed and shoved. There was the sound of china breaking. Two angry voices rose above sudden silence. People turned, rose from chairs to watch. Two men dropped to the floor. A thud of blows echoed and one figure staggered up, wiping at a bloody nose, and was jerked down again. Between tables the men struggled.

For a few moments the band played louder. Then the music wavered and stopped. Louella gasped when a woman screamed. As the fighters neared, Eddie half raised from his chair, ready for action.

They were almost beside Louella when Cobb moved between the men, grabbing each by a collar, forcing them apart. The shorter man dropped his arms, but there was a flash of light from the knife in the hand of the other. With one movement Cobb thrust the short man aside and struck at the wrist that held the knife. It clattered to the floor at Louella's feet. Cobb crooked an arm around the man's neck, pinioned his wrists and frog-walked him swiftly to the outside door where he heaved him into the night.

Danger gone, Louella released a gasp of admiration for Cobb. The room was silent when he picked up the knife at her feet. He knelt and looked straight into her eyes. A thrill ran through her, a sense of danger drawing her. His strange eyes revealed no hint of his thoughts. Knife in hand, he rose and walked rapidly through the room and mounted the stairway, disappearing from her view.

How strong he is, capable in a crisis. A woman would be well protected with such a man. Protected—except from the man himself. How could she be both repelled and attracted at the same time? How could she even think about another man so soon after she lost Stith? Emotions in conflict, Louella bent her head over her wine glass, unwilling to let her friends read her thoughts.

The short fighter wiped his bloody nose and mumbled to himself as he turned toward the restroom door. The band struck up "Tangerine" at a fast tempo. Two or three couples moved onto the dance floor. Within three minutes the crowd was happy, laughing at what had been impromptu entertainment for the evening.

"That's it for tonight. Our party's over," Eddie announced. "I leave after the first fight. There's always another slob who can't hold his liquor."

That's the other side to alcohol, Louella thought, trailing her friends out to the car. It made me feel happy. Would more have made me want to fight? Or drink until I passed out, like Donald Monahan? Was that why Preacher got red in the face shouting about Demon Rum?

But I do feel fine right now, she thought. Surely there's nothing wrong if you remember moderation. It had been such a lovely evening, enough to almost erase Stith's memory. Almost.

CHAPTER XII

It was six p.m. Wednesday evening when Hutch rapped at Glen Hart's door, the last two knocks in louder cadence. "Bun and a weeny, hot dog!" he hummed to himself. He really felt good and he needed somebody to share his pride. While he waited, he sucked in his rotund belly and grinned.

"Come on in. Door's not locked."

Glen Hart was bent over a small wooden radio on the bedside table. "Glad to see you, Hutch. Just a minute until this thing warms up and I get it tuned in. Want to catch the six o'clock news." He maneuvered black knobs while the instrument crackled.

Hutch looked around as he sat in the only chair, a straight-backed wooden one. The green chenille coverlet on the bed was rumpled; two pillows were wadded against the gray-painted headboard under a clamp-on metal bed lamp. Newspapers, like huge fallen leaves, drifted over the bed down to the floor.

Above the snap of static, the nasal tones and precise pronunciations of Lowell Thomas rose from faint to audible. "Another string of Jap cities is on the death list. Today American B-29's dropped three-quarters of a million pamphlets on twelve more Japanese war centers, warning them to surrender or...."

Hart sank down on the edge of the bed, sweeping away the newspapers, his large hands gripped the mattress edge, his hair tousled, wrinkled white shirt open at the throat. Noticing his frayed cuffs, Hutch decided Hart was one of those men who can't manage without a wife.

Intent on the clear baritone voice, Hart looked up and smiled at Hutch. When the broadcast ended, he reached over and clicked off the radio. Hutch saw a patch of white skin showing through the heel of his right sock.

"Pamphlets!" Hart's tone was acid. "If planes can make it over their cities, why not bombs? Are we planning to wipe out the enemy by hitting them on the head with sheets of paper?" His laugh was sarcastic and he plowed both hands through his gray hair, leaving it in somewhat better array. "The files in our office might wipe out a village that way, though—if they dropped the file cabinets, too.

"So what's with you, Hutch?" Hart asked. "You look like something happy is on your mind. Cookies from home? I could sure use either good news or good cookies. This damned war is going to last forever. Bombing with pamphlets!"

In answer, Hutch leaned his round body toward Hart and extended his hand. On his open palm lay new Sergeant's stripes.

"Well, congratulations! It's about time!" Hart's smile was broad. "I realize since you're not attached to a regular company, Headquarters overlooks the strays for promotions. You've deserved these for months."

Flushed with pleasure, Hutch tucked the patches back in his shirt pocket. "I was wondering. Do you have some thread and a needle? I'd like to sew 'em on tonight."

Hart placed one thumb on his lower lip. "'Fraid not. Safety pins, yes. Needles and thread, no. God knows I could use a little mending myself. If my wife could see me...." His brow cleared. "How about the girls? Why not check with Brenda and Louella?" He glanced at the windup Westclock on the dresser. "It's early and a week night. They're probably home."

Hutch rose and hitched up his pants. "I wouldn't want to bother them. Never been to their place." He cleared his throat.

Hart smiled. "Girls don't usually bite, Hutch." His eyes narrowed. "It's Louella, isn't it?"

Hutch ducked his head. The room seemed suddenly very warm. He shoved his hands into his pockets and looked up at Hart. "She's...special."

"Ever tell her that?" When the silence lasted too long, Hart added, "Girls like to hear things like that."

"She's...sort of engaged."

"I didn't mean you had to propose to her."

Hutch caught the quiver in Hart's voice and suspected it was laughter. His ears burned and he wished the conversation at an end. "It's just that...she's older than me. I just like to...to be somewheres around her, that's all."

"Just crumbs from the table and not the whole meal?" Hart was smiling now. "Go on over. They'll be just as happy as I am to know you finally made Sergeant."

"Well, okay...I guess." Hutch fumbled with the doorknob. "See you tomorrow," he mumbled and closed the door behind him.

Walking through the PX, he thought it over. Maybe Hart was right. It wouldn't hurt anything and she is right here on the base. Not that he wasn't conscious of that every day. Many times he'd gone out of his way just to walk through the housing area, hoping he'd catch a glimpse of Louella. Once he'd followed but lost the nerve to catch up with her.

On the short walk to their apartment, he changed his mind twice. At the door he pulled out the new stripes like a talisman before he knocked.

Brenda answered, wiping her hands on a bright red, ruffled apron. Quickly she adjusted her look of surprise and drew him inside before he said a word. "Hutch, how nice! What brings you out of the barracks tonight?"

Louella entered from the bedroom, wearing a pink flowered robe. Under the ceiling light bobby pins winked from the pincurls framing her face. "Hey, Hutch! How you tonight?" she said, patting the seat beside her on the couch.

"I'm making coffee," Brenda announced, disappearing into the kitchen.

"I was wondering, Louella...." His voice seemed very weak and he tried again. "Louella, I wondered if you would sew these on for me?" The patches in his damp palm had curled from his death grip on them.

"New stripes? What do they mean? They're different from the ones on your jacket now."

Brenda set coffee mugs down on the table before them. "Sergeant's stripes! Congratulations!"

"That is better than Corporal, isn't it?" Louella asked.

Hutch's pride made him sit straighter as he nodded. He was very aware of the scent of Louella's shampoo and clean hair.

"How nice, Hutch. I'll get a needle and thread."

When she returned, he handed over his jacket, embarrassed by the perspiration stains under his arms.

"Toss me your shirt, too," Brenda said. "I'll do it."

Hutch froze. What a dummy he was, he thought. He hadn't thought about taking off his shirt, too, in front of them. He remembered his undershirt was clean that morning and relaxed. He turned his back to unbutton the shirt and wrestle it from his pants.

The girls bent over their work, ripping off the corporal's stripes.

Hutch lifted his coffee mug, which sloshed alarmingly. The first swallow burned his tongue. Feeling clumsy beside Louella, he breathed in her fresh smell. Both of them seemed different tonight, Brenda especially. Without makeup, her pale lips revealed her years. For the first time he noticed the deep lines that bracketed her mouth. When she moved, air currents brought wafts of the pungent scent of Woodhue perfume. Always could smell her before you saw her, he thought, and tried again to relax.

"It's too quiet in here. See if you can get some music on the radio, Hutch," Brenda ordered.

Grateful for something to do, he switched on the small Motorola on the table by the window. The big-band sounds of Kay Kaiser's orchestra filled the room with "Surrey with a Fringe on the Top."

"That's from Oklahoma!" Brenda said. "I got to see that play in New York right after it opened." She bit off a thread. "Gee, I miss seeing the big new hits. The dancing in that one was fantastic." She looked up from her sewing. "Did you know Louella is learning to dance?"

"Will you help me practice?" Louella asked. She rose to her feet.

He shrank back against the couch. "Sorry. I can't do anything but polka. And `Put Your Little Foot.' I could teach you that, but we'd have to have different music and...." He fell silent. "Maybe you could teach me to jitterbug when you learn how," he burst out, shocked at his boldness.

"Tell you what," Brenda interrupted. "Let's have a party, have a bunch in and everybody practice. Today's Wednesday. How about Saturday night?" She held out his shirt for inspection. "You know Warrant Officer Eddie O'Brien, Hutch. And he could get Sergeant Cerly and his wife. She's nice. And there's Palermo and maybe Ohio from Eddie's company." Brenda tossed the shirt to him. "Get in a little beer and some cheese, maybe...."

"A party would be fun," Louella agreed, holding out his jacket.

"I'll come, bring some pretzels or something," Hutch said and retreated to the privacy of the kitchen to pull on his shirt. Pants rebuttoned, jacket in position, he returned, head twisted to admire his new stripes. He straightened and said, "I sure do appreciate this," directly to Louella, then added, "You, too, Brenda." Unable to think of anything else to say, he pulled his garrison cap out of pocket and slapped it against his knee. "Well...."

"Glad you came by," Brenda supplied.

She's telling me goodbye, Hutch realized. Louella opened the door for him and he took her hand. "Louella, you're...." His voice was too low for Brenda to hear. "Louella," he said a little louder, not caring if Brenda did overhear, "You're so special! I just wanted you to know that."

He was already off the step, hurrying off into the darkness before she could reply. Special? Louella closed the door slowly. There's nothing special about me. Everyone in the whole world is more special than Louella Tolbert, she thought. But Hutch is a nice boy, a little-brother friend. It was sweet of him to say it. She switched off the porch light.

The narrow gray metal stall in the apartment was like showering in an upright coffin, Louella thought again on Saturday night. At least the plastic curtain of red roses made a little color. Toweled dry, she tried once more to stop the drip from the rusty showerhead. The small bathroom steamed with the fragrance of Old English soap. She mopped at the small mirror over the cluttered lavatory to unveil her wavering reflection.

Dampness had softened the tight pincurls that framed her face. She ran her tongue over the irregular line of her front teeth. If she kept smiling, nobody seemed to notice that they weren't perfectly straight and that one was chipped.

She pulled on the black panties and bra Brenda had given her and glanced down at the pointed cups. Two black ice cream cones. But nobody could see what she was wearing underneath her clothes. It made her feel sexy, built up her confidence. Not that she needed quite so much reinforcement these days. There had been several dates with servicemen, two officers and one pilot. Tonight it was great to look forward to a party without dread. In these short weeks with Brenda she had learned other people were more concerned with their own appearances than hers. That small fact discovered had brought relief, freed her thoughts from herself.

Through the thin wall she heard Brenda in the kitchen rattling dishes. Music filled the apartment. Louella clamped an eyelash curler on her right lashes. One day she'd learn how to use mascara properly. Last time she'd tried, she'd looked like a clown. Left lashes curled, she was ready for the party.

All lamps lit, the little apartment shone with the scrubbing they'd given it that morning. The colors of the flowered drapes were festive. In the kitchen Brenda diced cheese, her red apron good contrast with the slinky black rayon dress she wore, her hair like newly minted gold under the ceiling light.

Louella squeezed her roommate's waist. "What can I do?"

"There's a jar of pickles somewhere. Stick some toothpicks in these cheese cubes and open some potato chips." Brenda resumed humming along with the radio.

"Oh, what a beautiful morning...!" Louella sang. When the song ended, she said, "I hope they all can come. Tell me about Tony Palermo. I like his name."

"He's a big guy from the Bronx. Had a deli down the street. Company cook now. Italian and bigger'n a barn. But he's okay."

"And Ohio?"

"Sort of a kid-brother type off a farm near Columbus, Ohio." Brenda continued arranging the cheese platter. "Hope we don't run out of beer." She pulled the drip pan from under the icebox, emptied it into the sink and replaced it. "There, that's the last thing."

Brenda uncapped a bottle of Budweiser and sat on the couch. "Lord, my feet hurt already!" One leg extended, she inspected her pump. "The silver buckles dress 'em up a bunch, don't they?"

Palermo was the first to arrive. His portly body filled the doorway, khaki shirt already dark with perspiration, a smile on his swarthy face. "Here." He shoved a brown paper bundle at Brenda with thick hands.

Brenda peeled back one corner and shouted, "By god! Tenderloins! I haven't even seen any since the war started! How on earth...?"

"Don't ask," Palermo grunted. "Didn't have no GI serial numbers on 'em. Thought they might get lost in the mess hall."

"Louella, meet Tony Palermo, a neighbor from home," Brenda called back, her head in the icebox stowing away the steaks.

"Glad to meetcha." Tony wrapped one hand around Louella's, then eased his bulk down onto the couch. "Hot, ain't it?"

"You'd be hot at the North Pole from all the beer you drink," Brenda retorted, putting a cold bottle in his hand.

It was Louella who answered the triple rap at the door. The tall thin boy with a blond widow's peak under his crewcut flushed, "I'm Ohio."

"I'm Brenda's roommate," Louella answered and behind him saw a stiff khaki figure down the walk, accompanying a tiny woman dressed all in brown. As Ohio brushed past her, she called out to them, "And you all must be Sergeant Cerly and Ellen."

"Richard Cerly." The man's eyes were steel balls. He gave her hand a single pump and moved past, leaving his wife on the doorstep.

"I'm Ellen," the woman said, her brown eyes large as a doe's behind dark-rimmed glasses. One hand held a red purse that clashed with her brown dress. In the other she carried a small paper sack tied with butcher's twine.

Inside, Ellen handed the sack to Brenda. "I brought a little sugar. Richard and I can't cook in our room in town and I had an extra ration stamp." In the bright light, the shy woman reminded Louella of a sparrow.

"Sugar! Great honk! I've been drinking coffee black so long it would give me the blind staggers!" Brenda held the sack high. "We'll make fudge."

"Fudge and beer?" Palermo snorted, pot belly shaking.

"Well, I'd like some," Ellen said. At her husband's frown, she moved to stand beside him.

Brenda rummaged in the kitchen. "Hell, we're out of cocoa, anyhow. Guess it'll have to be another time, Ellen." She waved a hand in Louella's direction. "Get acquainted, everybody. Louella's a rare bird. Native."

Louella caught a flash of contempt from Cerly, but Ellen, after a glance his way, said, "It's lovely country around here. All those pines and bayous."

Cerly expelled a contemptuous breath. "Got anything to drink?" he demanded of Brenda.

"In here," she answered, waving at the kitchen. You other guys rally 'round. Beer's on the house."

The door popped open and in bounced Eddie singing, "New York, New York!" He grabbed Brenda and waltzed her past the couch.

Palermo growled from his seat and wiped his mouth with a heavy hand. "You'd think you was the only one from the Big Apple. Brooklyn ain't any closer than the Bronx."

Eddie's square grin widened and he slapped Palermo on the back. "You may be from the Bronx but you sure aren't Irish, you old wop!"

Louella caught her breath at the slur.

"Thank God for that, you mackerel snapper!"

Louella relaxed, realizing the trade of insults revealed a friendship shared.

A light tap on the door revealed a nervous Hutch, cap in hand. "Come on in," Brenda said, "and meet the crowd. This guy Hutch Hutchinson just made Sergeant," she announced to the group.

Hutch was flushed as he took the beer Brenda offered and joined Louella. Over his shoulder she saw Cerly's nose wrinkle and he brushed at the stripes on his own sleeve. There was one bar more than Hutch's and she realized Cerly outranked him. Palermo also wore the extra bar.

"I'm Tom Sandane, but everybody calls me Ohio." He pushed his hand out to Hutch. "How long did it take to get those stripes? Man, I'm wondering if the day'll ever come for me." So that made him a Corporal, Louella thought. She was beginning to read the Air Corp's strange symbols.

"Everybody out of the kitchen," Eddie ordered. "Time for the dance to begin." He supervised rolling up the carpet and pushing back furniture. "Here we go. Turn up the radio and find a partner." He reached for Louella's hand.

Ellen rose to her feet expectantly. "Not me," announced her husband, tilting his chair against the wall. The light left her face until Ohio stepped forward.

"Will I do?" he asked.

For a second Ellen hesitated, looking at Cerly. Then she turned her back on her husband and followed Ohio.

"You and me, babe," Palermo grunted. One of Brenda's hands disappeared into his paw.

Hutch leaned against the kitchen counter watching.

In two minutes Louella had picked up the beat and gave herself over to the pleasure of movement and music. In the next dances it was not difficult to follow Palermo's firm grip nor Ohio's lithe body, his gold-capped tooth winking at her from a friendly grin. But without firm guidance, she had trouble dancing with Hutch, who held her like a cut-glass vase. For the third time, his shoe brushed her foot.

"Sorry, Louella. Guess I just wasn't meant to foxtrot. Let's get a beer."

Just as they turned away, the radio struck up a polka and Hutch's face brightened. "Now this I can do!" This time his grip was firm. Whirled faster and faster, Louella laughed aloud. It was impossible not to follow his quick steps and their logical sequence. The room spun around and her curls swung out on the turns. The music ended with a one, two, three and she fell into a chair.

"Oh, that was great!" she gasped, fanning herself with one hand.

"If you can polka like that, you can learn 'em all," Eddie assured Hutch. "Just takes practice."

Across the room, Cerly rose from his chair. He peeled back his cuff and consulted his watch. "Time to go, Ellen." He had been so silent and rigid all evening it was as though a statue had spoken.

"But it's just ten o'clock on a Saturday night." Ellen's cheeks were rosy from the dancing. Now her face was a pinched mask. "I guess we'd better go, Brenda," she said with a sigh. "Thank you and Louella for a lovely evening."

Sergeant Cerly nodded at the girls once and pulled his wife through the door.

Eddie's anger exploded as it closed. "Why she married that stuffed shirt, I...." He shrugged it off. "Next time invite Ellen when he's on night duty, Brenda. She sure needs a little fun, shackled to that toad." He motioned to the remaining men. "You'll have to sit out every other dance."

"Oh, hell, Eddie, it's too hot in here now and my feet are killing me." Brenda kicked her pumps into the corner. "How about some poker?"

"Sounds good to me," Palermo agreed. His face dripped. Even the cuffs turned back on his shirt were damp.

After they wrestled the carpet and furniture back into place, Brenda produced cards and a cellophane sack. "Beans will have to do for poker chips. I'll be banker."

Louella took a small breath. Drinking and dancing. Papa wouldn't approve for sure, but would Cora Sue be ashamed of me too? She felt a pang of loneliness for the sister she'd left behind. Poker would be another step down the road to perdition if Preacher was right. She sipped at the warm beer she'd been nursing most of the evening. If the first two had already condemned her to hell, she might as well learn to play cards as well.

"I don't know how," Louella announced to the room.

"Boy, your education had been sadly neglected," Eddie said.

Ohio checked his watch. "I go on guard duty at midnight and I'll have to cut out pretty soon."

"I'll sit behind Louella and help her," Hutch offered. "There's only room for six at the table, anyhow."

"You start in my place, Ohio," Brenda said. "I'll sit in when you leave. Give me a chance to make some more snacks, too." To the others she asked, "Poverty poker?"

"Yeah. It's a week till payday," Palermo groaned.

"Okay. Everybody put up a dollar for beans. You're still in the pot when you run out."

Three hours later the game ended. Louella was thirty-five cents ahead. It would have suited her better to lose money. When Hutch refused the coins, she tucked them away for her little sister.

The last to leave, Hutch held Louella's hand at the door, his blue eyes shining. "See you Monday, Louella. I sure had a fine time." He released her hand reluctantly. "I sure did."

When he disappeared down the walk Brenda said, "Good party. Except for that bastard Cerly." She dumped the last of the beer bottles into the garbage sack and pinched her nose. "Phew! Smells like a smokehouse and brewery combined in here." She fanned the open door to force fresh air inside.

Louella emptied the last ashtray, her thoughts confused. She could not rid herself of guilt. "Brenda," she asked, "do you think it's wrong?"

"What's wrong, honey?" Brenda closed and locked the door.

"You know. Dancing and gambling and drinking."

"Gambling? You mean tonight? Honey, that wasn't gambling. Nobody lost enough to matter. Money just added a little spice to the game."

"But...."

Brenda rubbed red eyes. "Every now and then you drop a bomb like that. Doesn't that religion of yours allow any fun? In my book life's hard enough without something to laugh about sometimes."

Feeling defensive, Louella retorted, "Preacher says dancing, drinking and card playing are instruments of the Devil."

"Seems to me," Brenda said, dropping her apron on the kitchen counter, "I've seen a good deal more of the Devil in some of those backbiting do-gooders always quoting the Bible, honey." She bent to pick up her pumps from the corner. "God, let's don't get into religion tonight! I'm whipped." In sock feet, she padded into her bedroom.

In her own room, Louella stripped off her clothes and pulled on a fresh cotton nightie. Too tired to take off her makeup, she tumbled into bed. In the darkness she stared up at the low ceiling. Echoes of the music and laughter rang in her mind, her thoughts still on religion.

I know Brenda believes in God, she thought. All Jews do. But she never goes to services. And she eats ham. Jews don't believe in that. If Brenda doesn't believe in Jesus will she go to Hell? The thought of her dear friend suffering eternally agonized Louella and she rolled into a tight ball. Before she fell into troubled sleep, she said a long and earnest prayer for Brenda.

Again the old gray house floated on gray water toward her, her father astride the roof. He thumped the black Bible in his hand and shouted, "Hell fire! Eternal damnation! Carousing Jezebel!" His face dissolved into the lantern jaw of Preacher, hair like fire, skin an eerie green.

Louella jerked upright, sweating. Wildly she looked around the quiet room until she realized she was safe and could quiet her racing heart.

I've got to talk to Chaplain James about this, she thought, and fell into a dreamless sleep.

At Sunday services the next morning Louella hung behind the other worshipers when they trooped down the red-carpeted aisle. Ahead she saw Ellen wave before she hurried to catch up with her husband. Louella hoped to be alone when she reached Chaplain James at the door, but it was not to be.

"How's my beautiful young friend this smiling day?" Donald Monahan touched her elbow.

He's so different now, Louella thought, from that shaking figure the first time she'd seen him. Today his round little cheeks were ruddy and he seemed to prance beside her.

"I'm really kind of sleepy today," she answered.

"Been partying? That's nice. Young folk need pleasure in these days."

There it was again, she thought. Wasn't Life real and earnest, like that poet said? Chaplain James suddenly seemed unapproachable. She shook his hand and escaped down the steps.

"Would you care to lunch with an elderly admirer?" Monahan asked when he caught up to her again.

"I'd be proud to, sir," she smiled, knowing it would be hours before Brenda would be up.

"Let us, then, hasten to partake of the culinary delights of the PX." He doubled his steps to match hers. His running commentary on the beauties of the day carried them all the way to the door.

Sunday was a quiet time at the Post Exchange. Every soldier who could escaped the base. Most of the others were either busy with assigned duties or catching up on sleep. A bored waitress leaned against the counter examining chipped red fingernails, one by one. The only sounds came from two voices beyond the pass-through, arguing baseball in the kitchen.

Louella and Monahan chose a table and the waitress forwarded their order to the cooks, then returned to contemplation of her nails. The rattle of pots and pans began and the baseball discussion continued.

"Mr. Monahan...," Louella began, and lost her nerve. She lifted her glass to sip at water.

"Yes, my dear?"

"Everything's so different here. I get confused sometimes...about what's right and what's wrong. Even chapel. They don't take up an offering, you know."

Monahan's face was watchful. "Separation of church and state does get rather thin in wartime."

His words made no sense and she blinked. "It seems strange to have a church in a place where soldiers are learning to kill. But I am glad it's here. I need to worship."

"It gets most important in wartime, my dear," he said. He leaned closer over the table. "This is pretty deep, Louella. What's really troubling my pretty friend?"

She wiped at a spilled drop of water and shifted her knife and fork before she answered. "Well, I've met such nice people since I've been here. Although I miss my sister Cora Sue, they've all become like my family." She struggled to put her thoughts into words. "But...they do things my preacher back home says are sinful. They're good people and I...." She gave it up.

A small smile worked at Donald Monahan's mouth, then vanished. "What things, my dear?"

"Well, things I've been doing, too. Things like dancing. I've had wine and beer. And last night I learned to play poker for money. Just pennies, but that's money."

Monahan's face looked like he was struggling to make it blank. Was he pursing his mouth to keep from laughing at her? He reached across the table and took her right hand in both of his.

"A pretty girl like you needs happy people. Was it fun?" he prodded.

"Well, yes, it was, but...."

He wiggled his leprechaun eyebrows at her. "Irish folk think God likes the sound of laughter, too."

"But Preacher says...."

"And is your preacher a happy man?"

His question startled Louella. 'Grim' was the word that flashed to her mind. "No," she said slowly, "he's not really." "Then he's refused the gift of joy, which is Heaven sent." He smiled and released her hand.

"Then you don't think it's wrong for me to learn to dance and all?"

He laughed and the overhead light made his white hair shimmer. "An Irishman is no one to be asking about that, my dear. I do a dandy bit of stepping meself now and again. Always seemed to me another way to express happiness to my Creator, glad as I am to have a healthy body when there's many cannot step at all, at all." He winked at her. "Be happy, my dear. A good father does not want his children sorrowful and in pain. Enjoy what He has given you."

The click of high heels announced the arrival of the waitress with their lunches ranged on one arm from wrist to the lacy handkerchief pinned to her flat chest. "Anything else?" she asked.

Monahan questioned Louella with a look and answered, "Not for now."

Slipping a coin from the pocket of her pointed pink apron, the waitress clicked over to the jukebox. Soon a baritone sang of the blue of the night and the gold of the day while they ate.

Louella's thoughts were as busy as her fork. All her years she had thought everyone believed like the Preacher. Now she found her world stretched infinitely wider than before. And she had yet to leave the sand and pines of South Carolina. What could it be like in other countries? Millions and millions of folks on the round earth. Did they all struggle too to know the answers of right and wrong? And were their answers not the same as hers, but still correct for them? What if she got the answers wrong and wound up in Hell after all?

Louella glanced up to find Donald Monahan watching intently.

He swallowed his last bite and blotted his mouth with a paper napkin. "No one knows for sure what God thinks, my dear. Just that He loves us all, saint and sinner, and gave us wonderful gifts and a beautiful world." He winked an eye that twinkled. "One day at a time, my young friend."

When he rose, Louella picked up her purse and gloves.

"Speaking of one day at a time, this day I must check the inventories, be it Sunday or not." He smiled up at her when she picked up her purse. "May I say you have given me much to enjoy this day, Louella? Your beauty has brightened these Irish eyes." He patted her hand. "Can you find your way home, my dear? I must get to my figuring."

"Of course. And thank you, Mr. Monahan. I'll have to think about what you said."

His steps were brisk walking toward the hall that led to the office. When he reached the open archway, he turned, made a small leap and clicked his heels together in midair. As he disappeared down the corridor, a laugh echoed behind him.

Maybe just being happy is the answer if it doesn't hurt anyone else, Louella thought and adjusted her hat. She walked into the sunshine smiling.

CHAPTER XIII

At the end of the month all their meat ration stamps were gone and Louella suggested a fishing expedition for fresh bass. "Eddie'll take you, honey. I don't have to go," Brenda said. "Fishing and me don't get along together."

Louella's face reddened. "Oh, I couldn't go alone with him."

Finally Brenda gave in.

On Saturday morning as Eddie's coupe lurched down the sandy road toward Magnolia Park, Louella watched the moving background of tall pines and live oaks with drifting moss. For the first time all week she felt alive, suddenly aware of the longing to see it all again, a homesickness she'd shoved down too long. She missed her little sister Cora Sue and old Cloteel. Had it been a mistake to leave, now that Stith was no longer hers? Did Brenda guess she was hungrier to see these piney woods she grew up in than for the fish?

"Not much like the Bronx," Eddie commented under his breath poking Brenda with his right elbow.

"There it is ahead! See the gate?" Louella strained forward.

The rusted elaborate gates of Magnolia Park stood open, one side leaning from its hinges like a drunk. The trees had opened out to a broad grassy bank that bordered a small beach on the edge of a dark lake. Huge cypress trees with fine leaves grew in the murky water, thrusting knobby roots like sprouting horns around them.

"There's the boats! Let's hurry! Oh, isn't it fine?" Louella hopped out of the car and spread her arms wide.

"This is spooky." Louella heard Brenda whisper to Eddie. "Never fear; Eddie's here." He slipped an arm around her waist.

The small wooden building near the beached boats showed vestiges of white paint. Where boards were bare, they had weathered to a soft gray that blended into the dim light under a huge magnolia. The scent of the bleached blossoms was heavy in the motionless air.

When an elderly black man limped out of the door, Eddie joined him to dicker for a boat and bait.

Slippers in hand, Louella skipped back to Brenda. "Isn't this something, Brenda? Oh, it used to be even finer than this, my Papa said. But after the war—the Civil War—seems like they didn't have any money to fix it up and all." She turned on one toe and surveyed the park like an owner. "Come on. I want to show you something—if they're still there. I haven't been out here for seems like a coon's age."

Brenda followed to a row of four small cages made of old weathered boards and chicken wire lined with fine mesh screen. Louella heard a rustle reminding her of a mouse in dry leaves. A buzz began like dozens of grasshoppers at once and then a rattle that made Brenda jump back in alarm. Each of the cages held an enormous snake, bodies thicker than Eddie's muscular forearms. Their coils flowed over themselves, scales rippling like patterned water. Triangular heads lifted, tongues flickering like frayed red threads tasting the air.

Brenda shuddered, but did not turn away.

"Rattlesnakes," Louella pronounced. "They're something, aren't they?" She was as proud as if she had invented them. When she slapped the nearest cage, the rattles grew louder. She jumped to her feet before Brenda could move and called over her shoulder, "Come on. Let's get to fishing!" Impatiently she waved Brenda on and then dropped her shoes at the water's edge.

There was green everywhere, overpowering green. Far to the right was a small sandy beach, white in the dim light. A low building of native stone sat back a hundred yards. On a low bench by the door a thin black woman lolled, her woolly hair fastened into a topknot with a twig. The bony figure waved a greeting in Louella's direction. The woman's feet were bare, her shapeless dress repeating the steel of the sky overhead.

They all took seats in the boat and under Eddie's hands the oars creaked in the stillness.

"Where'd you learn to row?" Brenda asked.

"Central Park, where else?" Eddie said, head cocked to watch for hazards.

Louella watched the oily water slide by, leaving a long rolling vee behind them, the watery sun flickering through the lacy leaves overhead.

"Never saw anything like those trees," Brenda commented.

"Cypress," Louella answered. "That's cypress knees poking up around them. When they're polished they make nice ornaments. One would look good in our apartment," she suggested, but Brenda didn't seem enthusiastic.

No one spoke as Eddie rowed deeper into the lake, out of sight of the shoreline. Somewhere nearby the sad cry of a bird made Brenda jump.

"A loon," said Louella. "Oh, look! Egrets!"

A dozen birds high among the branches soared away at their approach, their legs shining black in the green light under the trees like arrows following the wide strokes of their white wings.

For a moment Eddie lifted the oars like dripping wings. Clouds overhead thickened, making darker shadows.

"Here'd be a good place to anchor." Louella pointed to a slender tree trunk at the boat's prow.

Eddie looped the painter around the trunk and let the boat drift. Hand in the bait bucket, he caught a minnow and hooked it through the stomach. Brenda quivered.

"Now for some bass," he announced and cast toward a growth of cypress knees.

Louella had finished rigging two short cane poles with red and white bobbers. She impaled two minnows on the hooks and handed one pole to Brenda. "Now, we'll have us a special supper tonight."

Brenda's grip tightened on her rod. "This is sure different than excursion boat fishing off the New Jersey coast where the catch is not as important as the beer and laughter," she commented, watching her bobber make tiny circles. "Why's my line doing that?"

"Probably the minnow," Louella said. "It's not a fish." In the dimness it was cooler now. An occasional breath of air moved the delicate leaves overhead. Long strands of gray moss drifted like a movie setting for a scary picture. There's beauty in the black water, Louella thought.

Eddie cast again, the silence broken by the whir of his line. "Got him! By gosh, I've hooked one!" Eddie reeled wildly, his pole bent double. Just as Louella squealed and jerked back on her pole, he landed his fish. At once there were two bass flopping on the bottom of the boat.

Brenda pulled her feet back, watching the shining fish, heir gills flapping, bodies white against the weathered wood.

"Put 'em on the stringer, Bronx," Eddie ordered.

"Not me. Cook 'em, yeah. But I don't touch until they're ready for the pan."

"I'll do it." Louella tucked her blue skirt under her bare legs. She slid the cord through the gills, tied one end to the oar lock and tossed the fish into the water.

"Roommate, you amaze me," Brenda said.

Eddie and Louella had landed four more when Louella said, "It's going to rain, sure. Bass bite best just before a storm."

As if in answer, a rumble echoed in the west. Nearer and nearer the thunder came. By the time the first drop fell, four more bass filled the stringer. A whisper started among the leaves overhead and the rain began.

For the first time Brenda's cork made a sudden dive. Her jerk on the pole was automatic. A fish leapt from the water twice the size of the others. It twisted in the air, scales flashing, but struck the side of the boat and splashed back into the black water to a trio of groans.

"Too bad. He was huge!" Eddie said and leaned over to kiss Brenda.

The rain fell steadily now and Eddie pulled an old tarpaulin from under the seat to shelter them. Its stiff cracked fabric was more strainer than protection. A flash of lightning lit their faces, an immediate crack of thunder echoing among the trees like an explosion in bass drums.

"That was too damned close." Brenda shifted uneasily.

For five minutes the rain poured, then stopped as suddenly as it had begun, the air fresher, cooler. Sun now glinted on black ripples.

"We've got plenty of bass for supper. Let's go swimming," Louella said.

"Couldn't be much wetter than I am already," Brenda agreed.

When the two roommates approached the stone bathhouse to change, the old black woman on the bench brought a twig she'd chewed into a brush around to the opposite side of her puckered mouth. "Hydy," she drawled and showed stained teeth. "Waren't much of a storm, ware it?"

"Hey, Auntie," Louella replied. "Sun's nice now."

Brenda followed her into the dank building. Swimsuits on, quickly the girls escaped back into the sunshine. Testing the ebony water with one toe, they found it warm as the air. Beyond the sand of the beach, they felt mud soft as butter under their feet.

Louella tossed her bathing cap onto the beach. Paddling beside Brenda, her hair floated like a fan around her white shoulders. Farther out, racing parallel to the shore, Eddie's body gleamed cutting through the water.

Brenda rolled on her back, floating with her eyes half closed. Strange how Brenda seems out of her element here, Louella thought when I love it so.

"Snake!" Eddie shouted.

Brenda panicked and sank. Finding her footing in the shallow water, she thrashed toward the shore, choking. She shrieked, fighting the water that held her back.

"Where's a snake?" Louella called, standing to shade her eyes.

"There it goes."

She joined her frightened roommate on shore. "Law, Brenda, it's a long ways from us." A narrow head like a tiny Viking prow undulated across the middle of the lake.

"But what was it I stepped on that m-moved under my foot?" Brenda asked, still shaking.

"I...I think I'll go in," she said.

The old black woman followed the girls into the bathhouse. When Brenda picked up her towel, she said, "Here now, Missy. Just you let old Auntie do that. You needs a nice rubdown after that fine swim."

"Hey, Auntie, will you give me one, too?" Louella asked, wringing her hair out over one shoulder. To Brenda she added, "She's really good at massage."

Brenda stretched out, face down, on the wide bench along one wall. Black hands dried her with the towel, then began to knead the muscles in her back. When the soft voice said, "Now it's your turn, Missy," to Louella, Brenda said, "I'm so relaxed I can't move."

Louella moved onto the long bench beside her. "You got any children, Auntie?" she asked as the old woman began the rubdown.

"I done got five living, Missy. Most grown and gone, they is." After a silence, she added, "Your friend. Don't seem like she's from around here."

"Now aren't you the one, Auntie, to figure that out! She's from New York."

"Well, do tell." There was a rich chuckle. "I got me a son up thereabouts. Wants his mama come visit Christmas. Sent me money. I ain't never seed his babies yet."

"You plan to go?"

"Been thinking on it some." The old woman was toweling Louella's hair.

"Then you'll see snow, Auntie," Brenda contributed.

"Snow?" Her wrinkled black face peered around at Brenda. "Ain't never seed snow. Don't reckon I'd like that none." Her brush twig rotated. "Reckon I'll just do me some more studying on it."

When the girls had dressed and joined Eddie, Louella said, "I'd best give her a little money. That's all she gets is what folks give her for massage."

"My lord," Brenda said, "can't be ten women in this place in a month's time. How can she make it on so little?"

"She doesn't need much," Louella said, unconcerned. "Just enough for snuff and cornmeal. Raises her own greens. Catches fish. Sells a rattlesnake now and then."

"God," said Brenda, "next to that I'm a millionaire. Maybe the blacks were better off when they were slaves on some plantation. No! Better to be free with a bony fish than a slave with a side of beef. At least this black soul's kids are out on their own. Second generation should have it better."

They took a different road home, following Louella's directions, although she realized Eddie and Brenda probably thought it looked the same with its identical rutted sandy tracks, same drifting gray moss on the oaks. But this one led home, she thought, and felt that homesick pang again.

"Slow up a little, please, Eddie," Louella ordered suddenly. "Someone I know lives here."

There it was, the Tolbert house set back into heavy pines. The rusted mailbox leaned toward them and Louella wondered what her friends would say if they knew it was her home. It had been a fine place many years ago. Now the thick wooden columns that supported the roof over the wide porch were bare of paint. Double doors stood open and Louella could see through the central hall into the ragged garden behind the house. It had been her joy but Cora Sue and Cloteel probably had their hands full without tending to roses, she thought.

Cora Sue's white cat Snowball was cleaning its fur on the broad steps, and for a moment Louella considered jumping out of the car and picking her up. There was no other movement in the silent house. The curved balcony which ran the width of the second story was empty. From the tall chimney a curl of pale smoke flattened in the sultry breeze. Near the sagging barn a black horse with a white blaze watched them. So old Lightning was still alive.

"Those white blossoms on that magnolia tree look like a huge bouquet," Brenda said. "The whole place reminds me of a black and white pen-and-ink sketch."

"Wonder why they have a fire burning on such a warm day?" Eddie wondered aloud.

"Keeps out the damp," Louella said shortly. "Guess nobody's home." Her face changed and she shrugged. "Let's hurry. We've got fish to fry."

"God, yes," Brenda said, "let's hurry. Feels like nobody out here has laughed for years and years."

She doesn't know how right she is, Louella thought.

"And I want a cold Bud," Eddie added.

CHAPTER XIV

"Did you hear?" An excited Hutch burst into the office.

Hart looked up from his paperwork and the three girls swiveled their chairs toward Hutch.

"They dropped an atomic bomb on Japan! Last night! Over Hiroshima!" Hutch blurted. "Headquarters is in an uproar over it. Japs thought they'd been blasted by hundreds of B-29s loaded with regular bombs. Guess we about wiped out the whole town!" He turned and spun out the door.

For a moment Hart was thoughtful. "I get it. Truman met Stalin and Atlee last week. Then the pamphlets." He combed his fingers through his hair. "Paper falling wouldn't even give 'em a headache, but if we warned 'em.... Sure. That's the American way." He leaned back, hands locked behind his head. "That atomic bomb must be a foretaste of Hell. Thank God it's ours. This ought to speed things up a bunch!" Looking at the three girls, he doubled his fist and shot up two fingers in the victory salute.

Louella and Frances shared a grin and returned to their work at the desk in the far corner.

"Big Apple, here I come!" said Brenda.

"God, Brenda," Hart said quietly, "I'll be glad to get back to my wife and the girls. Man wasn't meant to live alone. These years in South Carolina taught me to appreciate what she's done for my comfort—and my clothes." He was homesick for the sight of Irene's calm hazel eyes and her smooth brow.

"Not long now," he murmured under the clatter of the typewriter as Brenda returned to her work.

Concentrating on the figures before her, Louella jumped at the sound of the pencil snapping.

Frances held the pieces and frowned. "If only Charlie and I could just go home!"

Louella laid down her own pen to give her friend full attention, alarmed at Frances' grim face.

"It's been a long, long time following Charlie from base to base the last three years, taking whatever jobs I can find, and then stuck here when he went overseas." Frances tried to fit the pencil pieces back together. "It's a wonder I haven't grown moss in this humidity." She gave Louella an embarrassed glance. "Sorry. I know you grew up around here, but it's the dry desert air I need." She edged forward on her chair.

"Dawn's wonderful in the California desert, Louella. The sun comes up in this wide mauve light. Silent, so silent. It sits for a moment on the rim of the earth. Pink and gold on any thin clouds."

Surprised at the poetic outburst from her matter-of-fact friend, Louella did not interrupt.

"Golden sparks reflect from the night's moisture on the needles of the Joshua trees before it evaporates in the sunlight."

Suddenly curious, Louella asked, "What kind of a house do you have in the desert, Frances? Is it like the ones around here?"

"Lord, no! It's long and low with adobe walls." At Louella's blank expression, she added. "'Dobe is bricks made of mud and straw or something."

Louella realized Frances was seeing it all on the office wall like a movie screen.

"On the hottest days it's cool inside. And there's a 'dobe brick wall at the edge of our place that keeps the snakes out — more or less."

Louella moved uneasily in her chair.

"Wonder if Duke will remember me."

"Duke?"

"Heinz 57 mutt. He was old before we left him with the neighbors. And that's been three years...." Frances hurled her pencil's pieces into the wastebasket in a fury. "Bomb 'em all. Bomb all those damned Nips! Let Charlie and me go home!"

~~

"It's really coming to an end, isn't it?"

Brenda kept her voice low as she laid the finished correspondence on Hart's desk for his signature. She sank into the chair beside him. Across the room Louella and Frances were deep in conversation.

"An end?" Hart echoed. "Looks like it. I hope."

Brenda bent her head over her steno pad. "And then I'm going to have to decide."

"Decide?"

"Between Flint and Eddie." She traced a row of O's with her pen and did not look up. "I wasn't searching, you know. I mean...for anyone. Eddie just showed up."

Hart leaned back in his chair listening closely.

Brenda recrossed her legs. "Not that there hadn't been several others who drifted in and out, good for a drink and a laugh or two."

Hart held his silence. If talking would help, he'd be glad to listen. It was the first time she'd come for advice, but there had been many, many others who talked while he listened. Sometimes he felt he should have chaplain's bars. "Go ahead, Brenda. I'm all ears."

"Eddie's kept me so busy, there hasn't been time for anyone else. Maybe it's just for the moment, to share being displaced in wartime, but...but we've kind of drifted into something...." Brenda lifted her head and looked straight at Hart. "God knows when Flint'll show up. Not a line since early August and that said `somewhere in the South Pacific.'"

"Mail's never been dependable."

"There's the religious thing, of course. Seems like the war dissolved most religious prejudices...let us see the whole person." She tossed hair out of her eyes. "Judaism hasn't been very real for me. My folks never went to temple or anything and I only remember about three words in Hebrew. Flint couldn't care less. He hasn't been to temple since his bar mitzvah." She rotated the pen in her fingers. "But Eddie...well, he's strong about being Catholic. That damned St. Christopher medal on his dogtags, sometimes it looks big as the moon to me."

She's a realist, Hart thought. She hasn't a single hypocritical bone. Never tried to hide she and Eddie are lovers.

"Didn't Eddie pose a little problem when Louella moved in?" he asked.

"Louella's the goddamnedest innocent nineteen-year-old I ever met!" Brenda's smile was rueful. "Hell, I knew the facts of life before I was ten. Checked them out before I was twelve." Her laugh was low and she glanced at the girls across the room. "Behind the laundry tubs in the basement of our apartment building! Wonder what ever happened to that curly-headed kid. He was as dumb as I was."

Hart grinned.

"I wonder sometimes about Flint when I see some of the shell-shocked guys coming back who are waiting for Section 8 discharges. There was one in the PX yesterday who looked as if the Devil rode his back." Brenda shivered, then shrugged. "Hell, not Flint! That big guy could plow through Hell without singeing a single hair." She ripped the sheet of doodles from her pad and crumpled it.

This woman has strength, Hart thought. He'd miss her common sense and zest for life.

"Eddie wants me to go to Myrtle Beach with him next weekend," Brenda continued. "We'll have that, at least." She straightened in her chair, her gaze direct. "Thanks for letting me blab."

"Anytime," he said. "You know that." It was rare she admitted a need.

"So..." Her voice rose. "Maybe we'd better start earning these magnificent wages Uncle Sam bestows upon us."

"Who's running this outfit? You or me." Hart raised a hand facetiously. "I know, I know. You always have."

Some of the tension had left Brenda's face. The listening ear is sometimes oil on troubled waters, Hart thought, and smiled at his mixed metaphors.

"Gotta go to the powder room," Brenda announced. She dropped pad and pen on his desk. "Back in a minute."

The hall door opened and a calmer Hutch entered with a stack of mail. Hart examined the chubby boy/man before him. If Louella was his surrogate daughter, here was his surrogate son.

"Sit down for a minute," Hart said, indicating the chair Brenda had vacated. "What'll you do when the war ends?" Hutch sat, rubbing pudgy hands on both knees. "Back to the farm for me, I guess." His round blue eyes clouded. "That sounds awful dull now. I'll probably have to wrestle my little brothers to get all my stuff back. They always was in my things."

"And what about Louella?"

Hutch started and flushed, throwing an anxious glance at the girls across the room. "Reckon...reckon she'll be gone out of my life." His plump cheeks sagged. Then he smiled. "But she's still here now."

Hart realized the boy just wanted to hang around somewhere near her.

"I've got another year on my enlistment, anyhow," Hutch said.

Maybe, Hart thought to himself. There had been early discharges granted already as the government began to reduce its armed forces.

"Anything for Headquarters?" Hutch asked, ending the conversation.

Hart shook his head and watched the young sergeant amble out the hall door. He swiveled to inspect his bailiwick. Not long now before this rooster must let his chicks scatter into their worlds. He hoped not too many hawks were hovering.

The first atomic bomb had fallen on Sunday, August 5th. The tempo of the war picked up immediately. Everyone listened to Lowell Thomas' six o'clock broadcasts. The base became one huge radio. On Wednesday Russia entered the war on the Allies' side, declaring war on Japan to pick up a few crumbs from the staggered enemy, striking the Kwantung Army of Mikado in Manchuria on Thursday. Friday Lowell Thomas reported Japan had discussed an offer of surrender by radio-telephone. The Monday report said Washington, D.C. thought they were stalling, that Tokyo was in turmoil. The air war in the Pacific still raged, but the smell of victory grew stronger.

To Hart, Seacomb Air Force Base seemed to alternate between exhilaration and despondency. Groups gathered to pass the latest rumors. "The base will close next Thursday." "Hell, no, we're all being shipped to the Pacific in ten days."

In the PX servicemen merged, then broke apart to join new groups. Squadrons had trouble concentrating. There were spurts of sustained effort, followed by sudden retreats from mental or physical duty.

Headquarters was a beehive packed with workers and drones. Workers elbowed their way through the drones, who loafed in doorways, hoping to pick up a word or two.

Another week and a half passed. Lowell Thomas reported MacArthur had conveyed instructions of the United Nations to the government of Japan and Imperial headquarters. On Tuesday, the 21st day of August, the actual surrender began.

Hart, knowing high emotions were hard to sustain over a long period of time, anticipated the slow return to normal on the base. But the news of the collapse of the Japanese brought a wild surge of excitement.

Late one afternoon Eddie dashed in the office door. "This is it! Come on, let's celebrate! The town's gone crazy!"

Hart sighed and waved the office staff out the door.

Louella, Brenda and Frances stacked themselves inside Eddie's coupe. Hutch mounted the running board and kept a grip on the window post while they headed for town. The grinning guard at the gate returned their V-for-victory salutes and waved them forward.

On the crowded highway, cars formed parades in both directions on the two-lane road. The air filled with car horns and shouts. Small American flags waved from windows of Packards and pickups. Vehicles were packed with people in ragged clothes, in khaki, in business suits, cotton dresses, overalls. White teeth flashed from grinning faces, black and white. The V-for-victory sign was everywhere.

Eddie's car reached the top of the one small rise between the base and town. He cut the motor exactly at the middle of the little bridge over the bayou. The Ford approaching from town, its paint gone in rusty patches, stopped beside them. The occupants of both vehicles poured out to meet on the pavement cheering. Cars behind halted and more people emerged.

From his glove compartment, Eddie pulled out a pint of bourbon and took a long drag. "Hurrah for Truman! Hurrah for MacArthur!" he shouted and passed the bottle to Hutch, then to the red-faced towhead beside the rusty Ford.

Down the line in both directions other bottles passed hands. A cluster of black folk began to slap hands in rhythm, their small children kicking out a shuffle, pigtails flying. White folk were quick to pick up the beat.

Eddie grabbed Brenda and swung her around and around, laughing. Frances, Louella and Hutch watched from the shoulder of the highway. Unable to see over the crowd, Frances kept making small leaps. Finally she crawled onto the hood of Eddie's car to sit, beating time on the metal.

Louella swayed with the cadence by the fender. "Oh, my, oh, my," she kept saying, like a song.

Hutch watched only Louella, aware of her Evening in Paris perfume. It was a perfect day in the midst of history being made. Sun shone on the multi-colored crowd, reflecting from chrome, brightening the flags. He tried to absorb it all to remember some dull day when he was driving the tractor.

Louella suddenly turned and threw her arms around Hutch and kissed him on the lips. "Hutch, Hutch, isn't it wonderful? The war's over!" Her arms were tight around his neck and she arched against him.

Convulsively he encircled her waist and then pressed his lips against her throat.

Her face aglow, Louella broke from his embrace and spun in a circle, hugging herself. "Stith will be safe now, won't have to fight any more!"

Hutch felt the breath go out of him. It was just an impulse when she'd kissed him, just her excitement with the news. He turned aside to hide his face, his body aching from feel of her. Well, he'd had that much. Enough to fill his dreams for a while. He turned a sad smile toward the glowing girl, who hopped up beside Frances on the car hood.

"Police." The word rippled down the crowd like wildfire. Far down the line of vehicles that stretched toward Seacomb were flashing red lights and the sound of a siren, faint above the noise of the crowd. Bottles disappeared. People climbed back into their vehicles and motors turned over, an underlying roar to the still cheering crowd.

A portly member of the Highway Patrol in a Sam Brown belt pushed his way down the center stripe of the bridge. Under his broad hat brim his red face shone with perspiration. His yellowed teeth grinned around a cigar. "Okay, time to break it up, folks," he yelled in a gravelly voice. "It's been a fine celebration but it's time to get on home now, you hear?"

Eddie grinned back at the officer, gave him a sharp salute and slid under the steering wheel. The three girls scrambled off the hood and fitted themselves in beside him. Hutch closed the door and mounted the running board.

Speed regained, Eddie began to hum, "Oh, beautiful for spacious skies...." The girls picked up the words, their song floating in snatches to Hutch by the open glass.

He clutched the window post tighter and jammed his garrison cap on firmly with his free hand. He blinked against the wind, eyes sightless, mind on the feel and scent of Louella in his arms.

After the others had left, Hart remained seated at his desk. Hands locked behind his neck, he tilted back in his chair. From what he'd been able to glean, Seacomb Air Force Base had sprung into existence from a cotton field. Now it would close.

He looked up at the white enameled reflectors and bare bulbs overhead and wondered what the future held for him. There would be a scramble for jobs with all the GI's wearing `ruptured duck' discharge buttons. And a time lag before car assembly plants could gear up once more, reverting back to automobiles from tanks and jeeps.

Mentally he calculated how long his savings would last. Might be a good idea to drop Ford a line, inquire about his old franchise. Not that there would be anything to sell for a while. Still, if he could line up a couple of good mechanics, cars still on the road after four years would need maintenance until the first new models rolled off the assembly lines.

Maybe this time he would be able to make his agency successful financially. There would be GI's with money to burn, eager for cars—plus civilians who had gone without.

Another upheaval for his family was coming, too. After his long absence it would take all their efforts to be close again. Would they be four strangers? He dropped his hands from his head and straightened. Not Irene. Her letters and love were the constants in his life.

He looked around at the utilitarian room. He'd spent most of his waking hours for the last four years here. What about his surrogate family? Frances would return to her beloved desert; he would miss that wiry efficient woman. And Brenda; he couldn't have accomplished so much without her wry humor and level head. Louella. He smiled, thinking of her innocence. That one deserved a happy life with her soldier. Maybe Stith would come to his senses back home. The day was bound to come when Louella's eyes wouldn't hold happy innocence. Life has a way of taking that away in a single heartbeat sometimes, he thought. He wished his surrogate daughter well.

And Donald Monahan. Suddenly he wondered where the little man was. Celebrating with the clerks? Celebration meant liquor.

He frowned and pushed his lanky body upright. Monahan was a sensitive man. But then Hart had never met an alcoholic who wasn't. When life got either too seamy or too happy they always tried to thin down their emotions with something from a bottle. He'd better check on Donald.

Down the hallway, noise reverberated from the open PX, voices shouting back and forth accompanied by sudden cheers. He stopped at Monahan's door. For a moment he hesitated, then rapped twice.

"Come in. Come in."

Monahan stood before the gray oak dresser, a full bottle of scotch in his hand. He flushed when he saw his visitor. "Just in time to celebrate," he said. "I'll find you a glass." He shot a wary glance at Hart.

Hart cleared his throat. "Not for me, Donald. Just dropped in to invite you to lunch at the Officers Club, seeing this is a big occasion." He kept his eyes on his own right thumb. It was several seconds before he had his answer and he looked at his friend.

"You're right." Monahan's voice was soft. "Future seemed ominously near just now." He set the bottle on the dresser and ran his hands over his white hair, then tightened the knot on his paisley tie. "Let's go." He turned his back on the unopened bottle and glasses. "You dropped by at just, as they say, the propitious moment."

It took two of Donald Monahan's steps to match one of his own, so Hart slowed down. "I was thinking today that after this base closes down I'll be needing a good man at my car agency. How do you think your sister would like Texas?"

He reached the hubbub of the open PX before Hart turned for an answer. The little man was ten feet back down the hall, his lively look gone, replaced by something like wonder. Monahan caught up and placed one hand on Hart's arm.

"Are you sure I'm your man?" He cleared his throat. "I do have a...that little problem."

"We can work something out." Hart turned away from the hope that burned in his friend's green eyes. He laid one arm around Monahan's narrow shoulders and together they left the building.

CHAPTER XV

In the early evening after their momentous VJ Day Louella finished dressing at seven p.m. She dumped change and lipstick into the sequined purse Brenda had loaned her and walked into her roommate's bedroom.

"How do I look for the party at the NCO Club?" She whirled for inspection in her red taffeta dress, the first time she'd had the courage to wear it.

"Spectacular!" Brenda gave her only a brief glance as she dropped a sheer black nightie and panties into an overnight bag.

Stunned, Louella asked in a small voice, "Are you...going somewhere?"

"Haven't had a chance to tell you, honey." Brenda's back was turned. She took a sundress from the closet. "Eddie's got a three-day pass and we're off to Myrtle Beach for the weekend."

Uncertain, Louella said nothing. She caught a sharp glance from Brenda and adjusted her face. "That's nice."

"We'll work on our tans, swim a little. Do some bar-hopping. Be good to get away a couple of days." Brenda still did not look directly at her roommate. "You'll be all right?"

"Don't worry about me," Louella said. "Delbert let me know Cora Sue will come to town tomorrow and meet me. You and Eddie deserve to get away. I'll be fine." She was looking forward to spending time with her sister.

As the two girls entered the Non-commissioned Officers Club an hour later with Eddie and Hutch, it was like walking into a solid wall of sound. The efforts of the small band were feeble against voices from the tables.

Louella touched the red carnations in her hair. It was sweet of the boys to produce corsages on such short notice. She admired the contrast of the white gardenias on Brenda's black-clad shoulder. The flower scents mingled with the odor of tobacco smoke and alcohol.

Someone shouted at Eddie from a back corner table and they pushed their way through. Louella found herself wedged between Hutch and a thin sergeant with a white square of adhesive tape over a shaving nick on his long chin. Names were yelled over the din but—as usual—she could not attach them to particular faces. Everyone at their table was drinking champagne.

Louella watched candlelight flicker on the bubbles in the wine stems. Bearing a magnum of Paul Masson and four glasses held upside down between the extended fingers of his right hand, Eddie nudged her chair. Carefully he righted the glasses beside her on the table.

"A bit of the bubbly, Ma'am?" he asked and filled her glass to the brim.

When he had served all four, he raised his wine. "To VJ Day, my friends, and to the Ruptured Duck. May we service types all be wearing one soon!"

"Hear! Hear!"

"I'll drink to that!" echoed around the table. It was obviously one of a good many "tastes of the bubbly" for the others.

The sergeant beside Louella returned to his argument about the advantages of California with the corporal across the table who upheld the State of Maine. Beside the corporal two rosy-faced soldiers discussed dry land farming versus irrigation. At the far end a red-eyed technical sergeant showed snapshots from his wallet to a sympathetic buck sergeant, who brought out his own wallet.

Louella's champagne was cold and smooth, the bubbles a pleasant tickle. Thirstily she emptied her glass and demanded, "Another, please, Eddie."

The second was even better. The warm glow spread to her fingers and toes. What a glorious day it had been! She concentrated on the sparkling bubbles. It was fun here with happy people celebrating the end of the fighting. She felt festive in her red taffeta dress she had saved for a special occasion. The level of her champagne dropped to the bottom and she met Hutch's eyes over the rim of her glass.

"Louella, uh, you're supposed to kind of just sip it."

His round face held so much concern she burst out laughing. "But it tastes so good, Hutchie." She leaned forward to inform him seriously, "The Bible says, 'Take a little wine for your stomach's sake,' you know."

"But you haven't had anything to eat yet and...."

"Time to practice your prancing." Eddie stood over her chair. One hand on her elbow, he helped Louella to her feet.

The music in the hall was louder and she began to sway with the beat. On the dance floor with Eddie, the foxtrot completed the warm sensation of the champagne. The spicy scent of her carnations and the swish of her taffeta skirt added to her pleasure. It was good to dance with Eddie. Dance with anybody. Just to move with the music in strong arms.

When the tune ended, she gave a great sigh. "So fine. So very fine."

As they reached the table, the sergeant with the white patch on his chin rose and bowed. "Me next?"

Someone had refilled her glass and she swallowed it down in a hurry. The bubbles went up her nose and she choked. In concern, the sergeant slapped her on the back.

"Got some down my Sunday pipes," she laughed.

When they reached the dance floor, she told him, "Don't do anything fancy. I'm just learning."

Her partner was swift on his feet and she had to concentrate to follow. After him came the stiff corporal from Maine, then the two farmers-turned-soldiers. The tech sergeant with the snapshots did a two-step by the bandstand while he told her at the top of his lungs about his wife and kids. During the next dance she learned about the buck sergeant's family.

There was only time for quick swallows of the wine between each partner. Swinging her skirts on a turn, she suddenly thought, why, I'm the belle of the ball! She felt as petite and pretty as June Allyson, even if she was tall and dark, with a crooked tooth.

When the buck sergeant returned her to the table, Hutch touched her on the arm. She turned unsteadily. His face was a fuzzy balloon. Laughter bent her double.

"Are you happy, Hutch? Be happy, Hutchie." She squeezed his fingers and leaned closer. Her head felt curiously loose on her neck.

"Louella, I've ordered fried chicken for you," he said in her ear. The puff of his breath moved her curls and tickled her neck. "You still haven't eaten anything and all that wine on an empty stomach...."

"Oh, law, Hutchie, I don' wanna eat. Jus' dance! I'm having a purely delicious time. I jus' wanna dance. Dance and have some more of that wondaful bubbly stuff." Her tongue felt thick and she struggled with the words, wriggling her nose at him to make the fuzzy balloon smile. "Let's us dance, Hutchie!" She jumped up from the chair and tripped over its leg. Irritated, she pushed at the offending chair.

Hutch steadied her with a firm hand on her elbow and led her to the dance floor. She was surprised at how pink his round face had become. But the dance with him was not so much fun. He held her clumsily and stepped on her toe once. A little deflated, she stood beside him at the edge of the floor when the music stopped.

"How about me, little lady?"

Turning made her dizzy and it took a moment to focus on the blond blur with two black holes that was a face. Sergeant Cobb!

Hutch grunted and jerked at her hand.

She steadied her wobbly head to smile up at the taller man. "Why ever not? I'd be most pleased, I'm sure."

For a moment Hutch did not move, then left them. To Louella his face was a scarlet blur. Looks just like an angry short, fat turkey gobbler with red wattles, she thought, and laughed again, slapping at Cobb's shoulder.

His grip was firm on her waist when the music began. He pulled her closer, his body like steel against her breasts, his steps smooth and expert. She arched backward to look up at him, conscious of his warmth. It was nice to dance with someone taller than she was. The shape of his lifted chin reminded her for a moment of the triangular heads of the rattlers at Magnolia Park. Well, maybe I can cage him, she thought. Her breath caught on such a reckless idea.

"Lots of folks out tonight cele...." She took another stab at the word. "Celebrating."

Cobb relaxed his hold and bent toward her. "Good business tonight."

"Where you from, sir?" she asked, suddenly curious.

"From around." His dark pupils expanded. "You?"

She was surprised he had not answered her question. Most of the soldiers were eager to talk of home. "I'm from around, too," she said. "Around Seacomb, that is." So witty! She giggled and stifled a hiccup.

Smoothly he swung her among the crowding couples. She felt the rhythm of his breathing, the beat of his heart. Delight in following his lead raised her happiness another notch. She felt as light as a chiffon scarf.

The end of the number found them beside the bandstand. He did not offer to return her to her table. She stood comfortably in the circle of his arm. The room blurred into a rainbow of colors.

"Having a good time?" he asked.

"Oh, yes!" She let out her breath and leaned against him.

Cobb said a few words to the drummer, who tapped the bass man on the shoulder and they passed a word through the band. "Begin the Beguine" brought more dancers to the floor.

Once more Louella was in Cobb's arms, breathing the masculine smell of his shaving lotion. Other couples whirled around them. Once she opened her eyes to see the serious faces of Eddie and Brenda at her shoulder. She wiggled her fingers at them behind Cobb's back and they finally danced away. Hope they're as happy as I am, she thought.

With the last note, Cobb stopped at the foot of the staircase. His dip was close and personal before he released her. She almost fell and caught at the newel post.

"I'm thirsty," she announced. "Let's get some more champagne." She tugged at his hand.

"Plenty upstairs," he answered and maneuvered her ahead of him up the steps.

Her legs felt oddly heavy and she ricocheted between the balustrade and Cobb. Although she willed her feet to obey, the stairs seemed ready to slide out from under her. She tried carefully again. "How funny, funny, funny!" she crooned, peering up at Cobb beside her.

Behind him the noise of the crowd seemed much louder. The band had taken its break and songs rose from several tables, half shouted, a battle of tunes. For a moment she stopped and stared down on the scene. The movement made the room spin like a lazy-susan. She tried to pick out her table and thought she saw Hutch sitting alone, but the room whirled again and she gave up.

With a grand wave of her free hand, she tackled the stairs once more and giggled as Cobb urged her on. The steps were alive! They kept shifting and she grabbed at him and giggled again. It was a relief when they reached upstairs and Cobb pushed open the door across the hall.

Beads of perspiration dampened Louella's forehead and she blotted at them with an unsteady hand. "Hot in here," she said, swaying in the dim room.

"Yeah, baby," Cobb replied. "Let's get you out of that red overcoat."

Something was wrong with his words, but she couldn't focus her mind on the problem as his fingers worked at her buttons. Her dizziness increased. "Gotta put my head down," she mumbled.

"Yeah, baby." He steadied her. "Here's the couch."

She sat, her eyes closed, holding her head to keep the room steady. She heard a drawer open, then close, and felt the coolness of a bottle offered her. She tipped it to her lips. "What's that?" she asked. "Better'n cham...." She made a mighty effort. "Champagne."

"Sloe gin."

"Slow? Well, I declare. Have you got some fast gin, too?" She fell back against the couch giggling.

"This ought to be fast enough, baby," Cobb answered as he slipped off her shoes and stroked her instep. His body pushed against her when he kissed her, arms under her waist, his mouth soft at first, then hard and hungry.

Just like Stith, she thought, and gave herself up to the pleasure.

His fingers circled her breasts. How good to be held, caressed, loved. Her eyelids were too heavy to open, but her body was awake to his touches. Was it Cobb? Or was it Stith who stroked her? It must be Stith. Pretend, her mind ordered. Slowly she wound her arms around Cobb's neck, fingers in his hair, accepting a searching tongue.

"You have a beautiful body, pretty girl," Cobb murmured in her ear. His words were soft. His hands pulled away her clothing, found her bare breasts.

She arched her back and pulled him toward her, finding the pulse in his throat with her lips. The rhythm of his hands and body measured her breathing. It was a fine, fine feeling. Someone loving her.

Faintly the babble of the crowd and muted music floated from downstairs to mingle with the rustle of her slip when his hands explored her thighs. She shivered convulsively and pushed feebly at his fingers. She shouldn't. He mustn't.

But the stroking continued, lower and more insistent. Touching meant loving, and she had been so lonely.

Somewhere deep inside she felt a hollow growing, a hollow that demanded to be filled.

Cobb's moonlit face was buried on her breast, eyes hidden. For a second she wondered again where those dark tunnels led. I must ask him. Does he love me? She could not find the words and his mouth moved over hers.

The hollow inside was beating now. His lips slid down her throat. She felt her hard nipples, her breasts swell. More, more, her body demanded. She shut her eyes again against the revealing moonlight. Cobb's full weight was on her now. She tried to roll away, but her body was master, her whole being on fire.

With a great sigh she welcomed him and the hollow filled with one brief stab of pain. A rhythm built like great waves beating on a shore, tossing her. Against her eyelids sparks and crimson flashed. Suddenly the waves built to a great crescendo that hurled her high into rainbows and stars, higher still into a convulsion that left her heart hammering, her body moist and limp.

Cobb's weight was gone and the colors faded behind her eyelids. With a deep sigh of content, she stretched in luxury. Smiling, she rolled on her side, tucked one hand under her cheek and passed out.

CHAPTER XVI

It was the same old nightmare that woke her, the shout of her father from the roof of the gray house on the fog lake. "Whore! Jezebel! Tramp!"

She started up. The odor of musty brocade brought back reality and she covered her bare breasts with her hands. Her head throbbed and her stomach lurched. She stared into the shadowy corners of the room. I can't have slept for long, she thought. Music and laughter still rose from downstairs.

But where was Sergeant Cobb? The room was empty. She staggered to her feet, sickened. He's gone! Why would he leave me now after.... He must love me or he wouldn't have.... But he's gone!

In the moonlight she saw the shape of a desk lamp and snapped it on. Sharp pain behind her eyes at the brightness sent her hands to her temples. Her taffeta dress lay in a crumpled heap at her feet like a pool of spilled blood. It took several attempts before she could fasten her brassiere and button the dress.

She sank down on the couch again, holding her head. Slowly she rocked, shamed. Cobb loves me. He must love me. He has to! Perhaps he had to go take care of the club and he'll be back soon. Another fight broke out perhaps. That must be it.

She continued to rock and began a soft moan of grief.

Hutch sat alone at the table. It had been almost an hour since Louella and Cobb had gone upstairs. He stared at the empty place beside him. Grease had congealed on Louella's untouched chicken. Wine stains on the tablecloth were as ugly as his thoughts.

Thirty minutes ago Cobb had descended to the dance floor, a thin smile on his lips. Why hadn't Louella been with him? Hutch shifted on his chair. Something was wrong. He pushed himself up from the table and shouldered his way through the dancers until he found Cobb beside the bandstand. Feet planted, he touched the taller man on the shoulder.

Cobb whirled and stared down, his face a cold mask. "What do you want?"

"Where's Louella?" Hutch waited for a flicker of expression. None came. He must not be human, he thought, the man doesn't even sweat.

"You mean the girl in the red dress?" Cobb examined the nails on one hand. "Mind your own business, Sergeant." Turning on his heel, he walked away.

Hutch felt his ears burn. To hell with Cobb, he thought, I'll go and find her. Pushing his way back through the dancers, he mounted the stairs. The hallway on the second floor was dim except for a faint sliver of light under the door directly ahead. His clenched fist pounded on the door, sounding like thunder.

"Who...who's there?" It was Louella's voice.

"Me. Hutch."

The noise of the crowd below filled the silence. When she did not answer, he pushed open the door.

She drooped on the couch under the open window. Head down, her hands gripped the faded blue cushions on either side, her hair and dress disheveled. One of his red carnations lay at her feet, crushed. Above the scarlet dress, her face was faintly green.

In two steps he sat beside her and touched her clenched hand. Her damp black curls hid her face. "What is it, Louella? What's wrong?" He forced words out of a tight throat.

She raised her pale face, her eyes hollow, then turned her head away. "Oh, Hutch, I'm sick!" Her voice was faint. "Please take me home."

"Of course, I'll take you home." Hutch stood and pulled her to her feet. Cobb was a monster to leave a sick girl alone.

She swayed beside him, head still low. "I...I can't go down there like this," she whispered.

"Oh, heck, Louella. Everybody down there but me has had too much booze by now. Nobody's going to notice. Just lean on me." If necessary, he would carry her all the way to the base. Her weight against him felt good as they descended the stairs.

At the bottom step Eddie and Brenda met them, faces concerned. "What's wrong with Louella?" Brenda asked.

"Too much champagne on an empty stomach, I guess," Hutch replied. "I'll see she gets home."

"Take my car." Eddie dropped the keys into his hand.

When the club door closed behind them, Louella ran to the edge of the portico. Grabbing the rail, she sank to her knees and vomited into the rhododendrons.

One arm around her waist, Hutch supported her clammy forehead with his right hand until the spasms stopped.

"I'm sorry; so sorry," Louella sobbed, stumbling beside him toward Eddie's car.

"Nothing to be sorry about, Louella," Hutch answered gruffly. He eased her into the passenger's seat. "You didn't eat. You drank too much. Sergeant Cobb, the louse, shouldda come after me when you got sick." He bit back words a lady should never hear. He wanted to ask why she'd gone upstairs with Cobb, anyhow. Maybe curious what it looked like? Probably not that. Then what? Well, he wasn't about to ask.

All the way back to the apartment her lament continued. "I'm sorry, so sorry...."

Hutch helped her inside and flipped on the light. "Can you...manage?"

She hiccupped and nodded, as the bathroom door closed behind her and Hutch heard her retch again. He felt sick with her, miserable with her misery. When she reappeared, one hand on the door frame for support, he had not moved.

"Hutch, you're so good. A true friend." Her face had lost the greenish cast but her eyes held dark shadows. "I'll be okay now." She moved through her bedroom door.

Hutch longed to rush through the barrier now closed and take her into his arms, stroke back the black curls from her stricken face. Anything to make her well and happy again, the way she had been on the bridge that afternoon. For long minutes he stood, shifting his weight from one foot to the other.

"Well," he said finally to the closed door, "I'd better return Eddie's car." He waited another minute. No answer. Quietly he let himself out and drove back to the NCO Club. Hunched in misery over the wheel, he slapped at the rim and said aloud, "If only she'd eaten first...."

For a time after the outside door closed behind Hutch, Louella lay limp. She was an empty shell, sick in mind and body.

Suddenly she leaped from the bed, tore off the red taffeta dress and jammed it into the wastepaper basket. She pounded it down again and again with her fists, sobbing. Never again could it bring her pleasure, only painful memories. She fell back into the bed and shivered under the sheet.

I've known a man, like it says in the Bible, she thought, therefore I must be evil. She shook with icy fear. Maybe Papa was right; maybe working at the base did turn you into a Jezebel. For a long time she sobbed into her pillow.

When she grew calm again, she rejected the thoughts. If she was truly bad, she wouldn't feel this pain and sorrow. She felt ill and used. But now Cobb would have to marry her. Or would he? Frantic to still her racing mind and the demons that taunted her, she sat up and dropped her chin on her drawn-up knees.

If only she could run away, never have to face her friends again. She thought of the dark waters of Magnolia Park, and of swimming away from the white beach through the black lake, farther and farther, until she sank forever among the sprawling cypress roots.

But suicide was a greater sin to God than this, she told herself. I'll live through it, somehow. Face them all and live it down. Brenda will stand by me.

With an ache in her heart, she lay down again. But tears were waiting and once more she sobbed into her pillow. "I'm sorry, so sorry. Stith, it should have been you."

It was long after midnight when Eddie cut the ignition in front of the apartment and Brenda took up the argument again.

"Look, it's just until morning. Louella needs me tonight, poor kid. I'd better stay here, get her on her feet." She hurried the last words as she saw Eddie's jaw tighten before he turned off the car lights. "By noon she'll be okay again."

Hell, Brenda. I don't get a three-day pass every day! Take away the rest of tonight and there's only two nights left." He slid his arms around her shoulders and kissed her hungrily. "It's been too damned long." Eddie gave her a little shake. "Ever since Louella moved in you've been a mother hen. Hell, she's nineteen!"

"Yeah, nineteen going on twelve." Brenda rubbed her lips against his taut jaw. "Been missing you, too, you know." Eddie glared at her, jingling the keys hanging in the ignition. "Aw, come on, Bronx. We could be there in a couple of hours.
She's got to learn some time."

"I'll be ready by noon. Promise."

"I already have the reservation for tonight in Myrtle Beach!"

"Noon tomorrow. I promise."

"Goddamn it, Bronx!" In the dim streetlight inside the car, Eddie's eyes glittered.

Brenda held herself very still, very calm.

Finally he released a long sigh. "Twelve noon, then." He leaned across her to open the door.

Purse and shoes in hand, she slid out. Before her key had released the apartment door, he had gunned the motor and raced away. VJ Day had certainly turned into one great day to remember, she thought. Flipping on the light, she dropped her gardenia corsage turned half brown onto the coffee table. Eddie would get over it as soon as they were on their way. Her yawn was huge.

Outside Louella's door she stopped to listen, then opened it quietly to peer inside. The light behind her was a pale yellow wedge over the rumpled bed. Louella turned a flushed face, tears shining on her cheeks.

Brenda sank down on the edge of the bed and pushed the damp hair from Louella's forehead. "Been tossing your cookies, honey? Want some AlkaSeltzer?" She was surprised to see Louella still wore her slip. "How do you feel now, baby?"

Louella grasped Brenda hand and held it against her feverish cheek.

There was an alarming amount of heat in that cheek, Brenda thought. She tried to remember her first binge. First hangovers were the worst.

"I feel terrible, just terrible!"

I'll just bet that's right, Brenda thought wryly.

"I'm pregnant." Louella's word emerged through a hiccup.

I didn't hear that right, Brenda assured herself. "You're what? Say again."

"I'm pregnant."

"My god, Louella!" Brenda felt as if someone had hit her midriff with a large rock. What had she gotten into with this innocent acting girl of the wide gray eyes? Had she been fooled into taking in a floozy, suckered by the innocent act? "But you told me you'd never...."

"Tonight Sergeant Cobb and I...well, he did, anyway."

Jumping up from the bed, Brenda began to pace in a tight circle. That goddamned s.o.b.! All the time she and Eddie were dancing, having a wonderful time, that bastard had Louella upstairs and....

"I thought he loved me, because...." Louella turned her hot face into the pillow, voice muffled. "I just felt so fine with the champagne and all...and he started feeling my...well, I got so's I wanted more and more...."

Brenda felt her fingernails bite into the palms of her hands.

And now I'm going to have a b-baby...." Louella's shoulders shook. Eyes brimming, she looked up. "What shall I ever do? Will I have to marry Sergeant Cobb?"

Brenda dropped onto the bed and pushed back Louella's damp curls. "Stop it, Louella! Listen to me. You can't know you're pregnant yet."

"Oh, but I am. We...we did it."

"Damn it, Louella, how can anybody be so dumb? Didn't your mother tell you anything?"

"Mama died when I was twelve." Louella's eyes opened wide, pools of misery. "But when Papa took the cow to the bull, every time she had a calf. And when the cat...."

Brenda heaved a sigh and slapped her own knees. "You don't run on four legs," she interrupted. "It's not like that with people...usually. My god, you must know married couples who don't have children."

"I thought they just didn't." Louella's face looked puzzled.

"Honey, I guess you're my daughter to raise now." Brenda forced a smile. "Listen to Mother Brenda and listen real good. You're only going to hear it once from me." She took Louella's limp hand into hers. "You're young and healthy. Your body has its own rules. Sometimes they get more important than what your brain tells you. Especially now since your body's sort of come awake tonight."

"Is that why...?"

"Let some guy get his hand up your skirt or into your bra and in no time at all he can get you so worked up you won't know your ear from your elbow." Brenda rose, hands on hips, looking down at her roommate. "You gotta have some information to hold off all the studs on this base — if that's what you decide to do.

For the average GI sex is like Chinese food; give in and an hour later they're after you for more." She paced the floor as she spelled out what her roommate needed to know, grateful she'd had a young aunt who explained sex with no frills, just the facts and left it up to Brenda what she did with the knowledge. Her own mother had been too embarrassed to talk about it.

As Brenda talked, Louella sat bolt upright, changing emotions flooding across her face.

"So that's how it is," Brenda finally finished. "You'll just have to wait and see if Cobb's seed is going to sprout. God, I hope not."

"So if I get the curse next week like always, then I'm not...."

"If that's when you're due."

"Never again," Louella whispered.

Brenda sat again to roll down her hose and pull them off. "Now it's time you and me both get some sleep." She shook out her nylons and rose. "You okay now?"

"Uh-huh."

Tensions released, Brenda yawned again and moved toward the door.

"Brenda...." The small voice followed her.

"Yes?"

"I know you meant to leave with Eddie tonight and...well, thank you."

"Sure, honey."

"And Brenda...."

Brenda paused at her own bedroom door. "I...I guess I know now why you and Eddie...."

Brenda did not turn around.

"I mean...part of it was just...just so...wonderful."

"Welcome to the real world, Louella. You're not a kid anymore."

CHAPTER XVII

The next morning Louella lingered over her coffee, still in her robe. Brenda and a cheerful Eddie had gone. Today the apartment seemed strange. No Brenda puttering in the kitchen, no drift of cigarette smoke trailing behind. The window fan rattled. Her stomach roiled, though she managed a little scrambled eggs and dry toast. She snapped on the radio, but the blast of music intensified the throb in her head. Click. Off again. After a shower and a first-time fumbling douche, she felt clean again physically, if not mentally.

The clock signaled she'd better hurry if she was going to make the bus to town. Surely Cora Sue would be there this time; Cousin Delbert had been certain.

She pulled a green and white nylon dress off its hanger and looked with longing at the bed. How she would like to crawl back into that comfort, think about all that Brenda had told her. Today she felt empty, incapable of any feeling toward Cobb, confused by the new sensations that had swept her last night. She was sore in mind and body. And alone.

"Well, it was a new world I wanted when I came here," she said aloud. She tugged on the dress and brushed her hair, the bristles of the brush like claws against her scalp. Bright lipstick was a little help to the pale face in the mirror.

All the way into town on the jolting bus her mind felt foggy. Waking thoughts had always turned on Stith. Thinking of Cobb was worse than the void. She tried to make her mind a blank.

She was aware of soft chuckles and happy talk from the back of the bus. She was the lone white passenger. Once by accident she caught the driver's eyes appraising her. Could he tell? Just by looking? She felt the heat in her cheeks.

How she wished there'd been no last night, no Sergeant Cobb. She wanted to go back home to simpler days. No! See it clearly, she scolded herself. Your only hope is to make your own way. When the war ends, take a job somewhere away from Seacomb. Charlotte maybe.

With a hiss and a sigh the bus jerked to a stop at the drugstore. She stepped out onto the curb, straightening her skirt and arranging a smile for Cora Sue's benefit when she entered the dim doorway.

No Cora Sue.

Perhaps a Coke would settle her stomach, she thought, moving toward the fountain. Perched on a stool, she sipped the sweet fluid and watched customers reflected in the mirror ahead. Bright clothes and dark. White faces and black. The clink of fingered merchandise, murmur of voices, clang of the cash register. She felt transparent, a watcher alone.

Glass drained, she slid off the stool. She needed air. She'd meet Cora Sue outside.

Louella leaned against the drugstore window, eyes blank to the bustle of pedestrians passing in two streams. Most of the blacks walked at the edge of the curb or in the street. It was several moments before she became aware of one small dark figure trying to attract her attention from the edge of the sidewalk.

Elijah stood patiently in dusty gray overalls and cracked shoes with holes to ease his bunions. He turned a stained felt hat around and around in gnarled hands, black face anxious, dark skin stretched over old bones.

Louella moved to meet him. "Hey, 'Lijah! How are you?"

He bobbed his head. "Miz Louella. Mighty proud I done found you." He gave the old hat another whirl. "Miz Cora Sue, she sent me could I find you."

"Is...is something wrong, 'Lijah?" Alarmed, Louella touched the old man's arm. It was as thin as bird bones.

Elijah ducked his head and revolved the hat completely around. "Yessum. Your daddy, he...he sick. Plumb outen his head most days."

"Does Cora Sue need me?"

"Don't rightly know, Miz Louella." For a moment he was silent. "She say, 'Tell my sister.'" His troubled face cleared. "I reckon she could use some help. He been actin' kinda.... Cloteel, she helping all she can, but I dunno..." His soft voice trailed away.

"You did right, 'Lijah." Louella pushed a fifty cent piece into his leathery palm. "Now you just find some pretties for your grandchildren, you hear? I'll go see if they need me."

"Thankee kindly, Miz Louella. I'll just do that."

She watched the old man shuffle toward his mule tied to the lamp post at the corner. Then she ran across the street to catch the approaching bus. The Coke had done its work and her headache had eased, too. But her stomach clutched again as she thought of her father. Was he still angry? On the bus she stared out of the window, alternately dreading and longing for her first visit home. After a few attempts to engage her in conversation, the two GIs across the aisle gave up.

It was half a mile after they had left the bus at the base when she stepped down onto the sandy road that led four miles to her home. Before she had passed the cotton fields along the highway she realized high-heeled pumps were a hindrance on uneven ruts. In the shadow of the first pine she slipped off shoes and hose. Shoving the nylons into the toe of one slipper, she tucked them under her arm and made faster time.

The sand felt good under her bare feet. Such a long time since I've felt that, she thought. How time could stretch and condense. Had it really been less than three months since she walked this road in the other direction?

The leaves of the live oaks looked as tired as she felt. They were covered with dust, weary from months on the boughs. A few dry leaves sifted onto the drifts of pine needles at the edge of the road. The scent of rosin under the sun refreshed her. The silence was broken by the sigh of branches in a light breeze and the rustle of a small creature back in the palmettos. A lone bird called.

Nearly home, her footsteps quickened. But at the leaning mailbox she stopped. The house looked more worn, certainly not the threat of her nightmares. Chewing a wisp of hay, Lightning watched over the sagging fence. Snowball curled in a puddle of sunshine on the lowest step.

"Puss, puss," Louella called softly as she reached toward the cat. At first sound its yellow eyes opened. When she touched the soft fur, the cat arched its back, its tail swollen, and hissed at her, then fled around the corner of the house. Even Snowball didn't want her back home.

She slipped her pumps back onto her bare feet, and straightened her small hat and veil. In the open door she called, "Cora Sue." Only an echo answered, then silence. From her father's room upstairs she heard the murmur of voices, one deep, one light. She heard his door open and footsteps along the second floor hall.

Cora Sue appeared at the head of the stairs carrying a basin which sloshed half its contents when she saw Louella.

For a moment her sister didn't look familiar. She had grown taller, her figure beginning to swell against the dark cotton of her dress. The brown braids coiled on her head were fuzzy with escaping wisps. It was no longer a child's face she saw. Cora Sue's chin was firm, lips narrow, but she still had the amber splotches of freckles across her nose.

Oh, god, what did I do, leaving her to run the house and care for Papa! Only sixteen and she looks haggard. But I could not have known, Louella thought, as she met her sister at the foot of the stairs.

Cora Sue set down the basin on the newel post and hugged her. "Oh, Louella, Louella! I'm so glad you've come." She pushed back. "My, you look pretty! And your dress, it's grand." She fingered the green and white nylon, her rough fingers snagging the fabric. "You've cut your hair!" She turned a curl against Louella's cheek. "Papa won't like that."

Arms around each other, they walked down the front hall into the kitchen. "Cloteel, Louella's come! Isn't that fine?"

The round old black woman bending over the sink turned her head in its faded blue bandanna. She beamed through the mist from the steaming water, then wiped her hands on her white apron.

"Miz Louella, ain't you a sight for sore eyes! My, my, but you's fine!"

Louella smiled for the first time that day. The dear old soul hadn't changed any. She threw her arms around Cloteel and kissed the dark cheek.

Cloteel pulled a cane chair from the round oak table and beamed at them both. "My babies has all growed up! Now, Miz Louella, you just set yourself down while I pours you a nice cup of coffee you likes so much. There's some hot in the pot." Cloteel bustled over to the stove for the granite coffeepot, her bare feet slapping on the worn linoleum. "And Cora Sue, you just rest yourself too, you hear?" To Louella she added, "That chile been caring for her Papa night and day. She's nigh wore out."

"What's wrong with Papa?" Louella asked, savoring the chicory brew in spite of her worry.

"Don't really know," Cora Sue answered. "Wouldn't talk for days after you left. Just read his Bible and stared out the window." She looked at her hands. "'Lijah and me, we got the cotton in, best we could. Didn't make much this year, but it paid most of the bills. So far, anyhow."

"You reckon it might be the malaria?"

"I doubt it. Times past he worked even when the chills were bad." Cora Sue paused. "Doc Cutler said something about his heart tiring out." She sighed. "Papa talks about the long ago when he talks any."

"Does he ever talk about me?" Louella leaned over the round table, holding her breath for the answer. Cora Sue shook her head and Louella asked, grasping at her only hope, "You reckon Papa's gone back to living in the past? Maybe he's forgotten about me leaving."

"I flat don't know, sister. He never mentions Mama. I wonder about that some." Her face was pensive. "Louella, do you remember Mama at all? Sometimes I try but I can't see her and I can't find a picture."

"Chile, he done burn every picture the night she died," Cloteel said. "She was real pretty, your ma."

"Sometimes I can recall her voice when she sang, but her face won't come to me, either." Louella patted her sister's hand. "You were just a baby." She finished her coffee and set the cup down in the saucer with a click. "Well, if I'm going to face Papa, I'd best get at it." Taking a deep breath she wondered if she should even try.

"He seems more clear this morning," Cora Sue commented.

Louella placed her hat in the exact center of the table. "Fix him a cup of coffee, Cloteel, and I'll take it up to him."

Mounting the stairs, her hand trembled, sloshing the coffee. At her father's door she hesitated, then rapped once and turned the knob.

His hair against the white pillow was a lifeless gray, long around his ears. His face was turned toward the window where the light emphasized the heavy gray bristles over his doughy skin. The room smelled of sickness, a fetid odor of a bed long used. The dark carved headboard loomed above his long body which barely raised the white sheet covering him. His gnarled fingers picked at the fabric. He's so thin! Louella thought. Slowly Brent Tolbert turned his head toward his oldest daughter and focused his dark eyes on her face.

How ill he looks. How could I fear this weak old man? She felt a rush of love flood through her.

His hand gripped the sheet and he stiffened.

"Papa, I heard you were sick so I came home."

His lips pursed under the unshaven tufts of hair, ebony eyes staring into her soul.

With firm steps she moved closer to the bed and bent to offer the coffee. The moment froze. She ached with pity for the man so limp on the bed, her once strong father.

Grimacing with effort, Brent Tolbert struggled into a sitting position. His eyes never left her face. With a sweep of his thin arm he struck the cup and saucer, sending a cascade of scalding coffee down Louella's skirt. She gasped and yanked the fabric from her searing leg.

"Gone off to the Yankees! Come home wearing trollop's clothes! Shorn yer hair!" The weak voice became a roar in her ears. "Jezebel! You're no daughter of mine! Get out of my...."

The shout descended into a terrible gurgle. His ashen face twisted and he raised a trembling fist.

Louella stopped breathing. Her nightmare come true! She took one step backward. She could not turn away from the contorted face.

His sneering mouth worked, a thin trickle of spittle emerged. His right eye opened wide, the right side of his face sagged. His raised fist fell limply to the sheet and he flung himself back, body arched, convulsing without a sound.

Louella could not move. Only one of his eyes remained open, the right one, black and glaring. Staring at her.

Louella shuddered and backed into the hall. Covering her face with her hands, she slumped against the wall. He's had a stroke and she was the cause of it. Have I killed my own father? She ran down the stairs, her entire body shaking. Numbly she stumbled into the kitchen.

Cloteel sat at the table smiling up at a faded calendar picture of two small girls under a blooming apple tree.

"Papa's...papa's had a stroke, Cloteel. I've got to call Dr. Cutler. Oh, god, Cloteel, maybe my coming home has killed my father."

With one startled glance at her sister, Cora Sue dropped her coffee cup into its saucer and ran for the stairs.

Cloteel padding behind her, Louella headed for the telephone in the front hall.

"Hit don't work. Phone man cut it off." Already Cloteel was pulling her bulk up the stairs. "Best go to your Uncle's place down the road. Quick as you can, honey."

Louella's mind cleared. My god, her father was dying. She had to get Dr. Cutler to help! She ran outside, threw a bridle over Lightning and kicked him into a canter. "Faster! Faster, you old bag of bones!" she shouted, tears wet on her face. "Papa's going to die. Faster, damn you!"

Half a mile down the sandy road Delbert stood at the gate, hands full of mail from the rusty box. He looked startled at sight of Louella.

She pulled her skirt back down over bare thighs and shouted, "Get Dr. Cutler on the phone! Papa's dying!"

When he ran for his house, she turned Lightning toward her own home.

Huddled on the porch steps, Louella rested her head on her knees. Even the sun on her shoulders could not warm her. It had been a very long time since Dr. Cutler's car had spun into the drive scattering dust. With his small black bag he had taken the steps two at a time, not stopping to speak.

Miserable, Louella clutched her knees and rocked. She was afraid to return to her father's bedside, terrified of his single staring eye, afraid sight of her again might kill him outright. Now there were no more tears to cry.

She felt a soft movement beside her and turned to find Snowflake strapping her leg with a loud purr. Puss remembered her. A new flood of tears gushed. She scooped the cat into her coffee-stained lap and rubbed her cheek against its fur, soft as whipped cream. When she heard the voices of the doctor and her sister approaching, she wiped away the tears and released Snowflake.

At the doorway Cora Sue said her thanks to Dr. Cutler and returned inside. Louella realized that for the moment they had changed places and her sister was protecting her.

Sighing, Dr. Cutler eased his trim body onto the step beside her.

"Is...is he dead?" Her words were hard to force out.

"No, Louella, but it's too early to tell if he'll make it through this. The right side of his body's affected. That means there's a blood clot on the left side of his brain."

Louella caught her breath.

"The clot forms when a blood vessel bursts." He fiddled with the handle of his black bag. "If it's a small clot, there's every hope his body will absorb it and he'll recover just fine." After a pause he added. "But it takes time."

"It's my fault, Doctor. I did it to him. Went to the base to work. Cut my hair...." The lump in her throat closed off her voice completely.

"You're wrong about that, Louella," he said, smoothing his gray hair. "He did it to himself. He's a hot-tempered man. Always has been. Warned him years ago he'd better learn to control his anger." He slapped at his knee. "But he's stubborn. That very stubbornness may help him now." His gaze was on the road when he continued.

"Young people have their own lives to live, Louella. I brought you into this world and watched you grow up. You've got everything it takes to make a good life—if you give yourself the chance. It was fine news to me when I heard you'd struck out on your own." He slapped his knee again and rose, satchel in hand.

"When Cora Sue's time comes, help her. It's always hardest for the first one, the one who breaks the path." At the foot of the steps he turned back. "Give your papa time, Louella. Recovery will be slow."

At the end of the walk he climbed into his car and waved before he pulled the door shut. The coupe disappeared in a golden haze of dust caught by the setting sun.

Slowly a feeling of life returned to Louella. Dr. Cutler was a man she could trust, a man concerned with life and death. His words had worked a healing and the tightness in her chest eased. Snowflake curled against her thigh again and she stroked the soft fur.

"Well, I've got to make it now," she said aloud, "for my sake and for Cora Sue's." She pushed her shoulders back. "First of all, I've got to send her the money I've saved to get that phone hooked up again. With Papa so sick, she'll need money for medicine, too." And she didn't want Dr. Cutler to have to wait too long for his fees, although she knew he would tell her not to worry about it.

She gave the cat a final stroke and with a determined step, she stood and went inside.

CHAPTER XVIII

Glen Hart pushed the papers back on his desk and lit a cigarette, his eyes on Louella bent over her desk. Dark curls slid over her face and she flicked them behind her ear without breaking her concentration.

Something different there and he'd bet it wasn't just her father's illness, either. He'd been puzzling about it for two weeks now. Tracing it back, something must have happened around VJ Day.

The door opened on a thin sergeant with creases like knives in his uniform. Hart idly wondered how the man did it, starched and polished in all this everlasting humidity. For a moment he could not place the face. Then he remembered. Sergeant Cobb, temporary manager of the NCO Club while Woods had surgery.

Cobb stood at attention before Hart's desk. "The NCO Club's down to a three-day supply of paper plates and napkins. Any word on delivery yet?" he asked.

"Sit down, Cobb. I think there's been something...." Hart sorted through a stack of shipping invoices on the corner of his desk. "Um, yes. Shipped Tuesday from Minneapolis. Should arrive any minute."

Hart raised his eyes from the invoice to find Cobb's full attention on Louella, his profile sharp against the lime green wall. Louella glanced up, her mind obviously still on her work, but the transformation on her face startled Hart. Her gray eyes widened, animation gone.

"Louella." Cobb stiffly nodded.

A slow flush moved up Louella's cheeks. Her eyes didn't waiver from the sergeant's face. A smile flickered and then disappeared. The look between the two was so intense Hart felt the air vibrate. Pain on one face. Smugness on the other.

Brenda's typewriter ceased clacking. Hart heard the rustle when she walked to Louella's desk between the two, breaking their gazes. She slapped down a paper and said too loudly, "Here's the next one, Louella, and Frances needs it right now!" Brenda's back was rigid.

Her face totally blank, Louella seemed to have trouble comprehending. Then awareness returned to her eyes. "In a minute, Brenda. I'll be right back." She disappeared through the hall door.

Cobb's voice caught Hart's attention. "Today, maybe? Well, give me a ring when the stuff comes in, okay?" As the door closed behind him, Hart heard his footsteps recede down the corridor.

He felt sick. Cobb and Louella? Surely not Cobb! Hart dredged up everything he could remember about the man. Rumors whispered black market. Nothing concrete, but still.... Cobb and Louella? Surprised to find the invoice wadded into a ball, he smoothed it out. Brenda would know.

When she took her seat at the typewriter he asked, "After you take notes at the eleven-thirty meeting in Headquarters, how about us detouring by the officer's club for lunch?"

Brenda wiped the scowl from her face and smiled. "Sure, boss. Beats a peanut butter sandwich every time."

Waiting in the warm hallway, Louella shivered. When Cobb approached, she tried to read his face, but the alternate glare and shadow from the bare bulbs overhead hid his expression. As he reached her, he ended his steps in a soldier's one-two-halt and nodded. "Louella."

She couldn't tell if it was a greeting or a question. "I...I wondered when I'd see you again...."

"It's a small base." One corner of his mouth turned up. He cocked his garrison cap farther back on his blond crewcut. "Any time, baby. Knock before you come in, though."

It was as though he had drenched her in cold dirty water. She stepped backward, hands behind her pressing against the wall. "I...I thought you loved me. And that was why you...we...."

"Sure I love you, baby." His grin was wide. The light glittered on his white teeth and colorless eyes. "I love all pretty broads. One at a time." He gave her a mock salute. "Like I said, any time, baby."

Shamed, she dropped her head, listening to the echo of his footsteps fade into the noise of the PX. After a long time she became conscious of pain in her fingers, jammed against the wall. Inside her something was more painful. She felt brittle, like an empty eggshell. With effort she moved her hands and relaxed her tense muscles. Then anger flooded her and she straightened her head. He had taken her without a thought but his moment's pleasure. He had held her in strong arms, spoken gentle words and she had been lost, falling into the deep black tunnels that were the pupils of his strange light eyes.

I was a fool once, she thought. I will not be again.

It wasn't until Brenda finished her pie in the quiet atmosphere of the officers' club dining room that Hart brought up the subject on his mind. "I've noticed a change in Louella lately," he said. Looking at her expectantly, he leaned forward and lit Brenda's cigarette.

"Different?" She tapped her Camel against the ashtray, not meeting his eyes.

"Something happen around VJ Day?"

"Well...." Brenda rolled the burning cylinder between two fingers. "Well, she was pretty sick that night at the NCO Club. Too much wine."

"More than that."

Brenda took a deep drag of tobacco smoke, her eyes on the waiter at the next table. The silence lengthened.

"Look, that girl's like one of my own daughters to me. If there's anything, any way she needs help...."

Brenda turned an angry face toward him. "She'd never had but a drop of champagne before and she didn't eat anything and...well, Cobb had her upstairs a long time before we missed her. Eddie and I were dancing!" She slammed the table with a clenched fist and their coffee cups clattered.

Hart felt his chest constrict, squeezing his lungs. The blood roared in his ears. Could she be pregnant? He pushed his spoon against the tablecloth and it bent double. "Upstairs? At the NCO Club?" he asked, incredulous.

"That goddamned bastard son-of-a-bitch!" Brenda spit out the words.

When the roar in his ears subsided, Hart asked, "Ever see a bird hypnotized by a snake, Brenda?" "In the Bronx?" she snorted.

"The bird can't escape. Can't even move. Louella looked like that this morning when Cobb came into the office."

"I warned her about him. We all did. But he's got those strange eyes and hands like an octopus." Brenda mashed out her cigarette. "She was dancing with everybody, having a ball, when he cut in, Hutch told me. If Hutch wasn't such a kid himself, he could have dragged her off the dance floor. They're two such innocents!" Her last word sounded like a curse.

"I swear to you," Hart growled, "he won't get away with it. He'll pay."

"I could kill him!" Brenda's voice was loud in the quiet room. An officer at a wall table glanced their way.

"Pretty strong," Hart said. "There are other ways." The thick metal of his spoon resisted his efforts to straighten it. "I intend to find out what makes him tick and stop his clock for good. A dishonorable discharge, hopefully. We'll do it the Air Corp way: slow, sure and final."

"You have an idea?" She hitched her chair closer. "Eddie and I have talked about it until we're blue...."

"We'll give him enough rope to lasso himself and then hang him with it. I've heard rumors about Cobb and black market. Know anything about that?"

"I've heard them, too. Nothing for sure. He's in the beer joint in town a lot, but that's not unusual. There's nothing else to do in town except that, the movies and the NCO Club."

"Your friend Eddie. In the quartermaster outfit, isn't he?"

"Last I heard," Brenda grinned.

"It'll be dull and slow, but...records. There've got to be records on every item issued. Put a little pressure on the clerks in his unit, him being a Warrant Officer with the clout. If nothing shows up, it ought to dry up his supplies, at least. People do odd things under pressure." With his full strength, Hart still could not straighten his damned spoon.

"I think," he continued, "someone needs to keep an eye on the NCO Club and Hutch probably needs to spend more time in town." He gave up on the spoon. Let the busboy be surprised when he cleared the table. "What did you say the name of that beer joint is?"

"The Daisy May."

"Eddie might poke around the NCO Club, pull a few pop inspections. Go over the records there, too."

Brenda seemed skeptical. "Well, it sounds too damned slow, but I'll talk to Eddie and Hutch." She leaned across the table. "That poor dumb Hutch still doesn't know what happened — and I won't be the one to tell him. He adores Louella and hates Cobb already."

"In the meantime," Hart added, "you'd better stick pretty close to Louella." If there was a pregnancy, he thought, Brenda could help her. An abortion? The thought made him sick.

"Close, hell! I've sat guard on her bedroom door every night and checked out her dates making sure they were squeaky clean!" Brenda's eyes were moist. "She's having a damned rough time of it, you know. Feels guilty about her pa having that stroke when she finally got up enough nerve to go see the old goat." She sniffed loudly. "Being poor is bad enough without being so innocent the world shoves you around."

"People get over innocence, Brenda. They don't always get over being poor."

"Well, she has grown up some since her pa's stroke. Having to think about her little sister's welfare made some difference, I guess." Brenda smoothed down her blonde hair. "I'm not old enough to be her ma, but damned if I don't feel like it. Eddie calls me Mother Hen." She smiled ruefully.

He shoved back his chair, fumbled for change in his pocket and dropped coins on the tablecloth. "Mother Hen?" He laughed, his hand on Brenda's elbow as they left the dining room "Then just called me Father Heart."

Several hours later, back in the office, Louella crooked a finger at Brenda and whispered, "I want to show you something." What now, Brenda wondered, bending over Louella's desk. Her roommate pulled open a bottom drawer and pointed to a box wrapped in brown paper wedged into the very back. Brenda saw a blue cardboard flap where the end was torn open. Louella tugged at her elbow. "I had to buy some Kotex."

In sudden realization, Brenda hugged Louella and planted a kiss on her cheek. "Well, glory hallelujah," Brenda whispered. She rubbed off the lipstick print of her lips with two fingers and grinned at Louella.

When she passed Hart's desk he lifted his eyebrows in silent question.

"Women's secrets. Women's secrets," she murmured as she passed.

Thank God, she thought. One less thing to worry about.

CHAPTER XIX

Technical Sergeant Leon Cobb shifted in his manager's chair as he shuffled papers at the NCO Club. This was no time for tightly tied loose ends to unravel. That damned Swartz in Supply suddenly had announced there'd be no more sugar. Claimed his sergeant even counted bowls on the mess tables. Not even reminders of past favors had dislodged Swartz from his unreasonable attitude, although his red face did sweat profusely. It had taken thirty minutes of verbal arm-twisting before he came up with a single ten-pound sack. Hell, that wouldn't begin to cover any of the markets he'd set up at backdoors around town. The bakery alone took ten a week.

Well, there was nothing to do but tell that pasty-faced baker 'no' this week. Might not turn out all bad, though. When Swartz loosened up again, the price would rise.

Everything was still fine at The Daisy May. His business with Toots had been so good, his banker at home knew his name, a real buddy! Since he'd become manager of the NCO Club it had been no problem to find rotgut and cheap wine to replace the good stuff. A few of the GI's had complained, but what could they do? Cobb grinned at thought of the labels on the substitute booze. Not Southern Comfort; not Golden Wedding. Golden Comfort! Mentally he saluted the smartass who'd come up with that one. Close enough to pull in the dumb ones, anyhow.

There was never enough Chivas Regal and Beefeaters gin for his market. He decided to raise the prices again. Multiply by three? Not having to buy a matching bottle of the plentiful rum every time, like the civilians had to do, was something, too.

He rose up from the desk. Better check with Sam about the hamburger meat. Toots needed more. Stale bread crumbs could stretch the NCO Club's ground patties.

172 ~ Betty C. Hatcher

In the kitchen Cobb found Sam grumbling over his pans, black face unhappy. He looked up at Cobb, then frowned down at his bread dough.

"Good morning, Sam."

"'Morning."

"Sam, we've got a few shortages we're going to have to work around for a while," Cobb began. "Sugar, for one. No supplies on that this week."

"Can't make no pies, got no sugar," Sam muttered. He rolled his dark eyes in Cobb's direction. "Them boys purely loves their pie."

"Everybody has to make sacrifices during wartime."

Sam grunted, black hands busy pounding the white dough. "Anything else, Sergeant Cobb?"

"Hamburger meat. We've got to stretch it. Use yesterday's rolls for bread crumbs and the GI's won't know the difference. What's on hand will make a lot more burgers."

"Don't reckon I could do that, Sergeant Cobb." Sam's black eyes were openly defiant now. "Them boys needs their meat. Can't be fooling with their meat, no, sir." His words were soft but clear. "When Sergeant Woods was here we didn't have no trouble about getting meat. Sugar neither."

Insolent darkie! Cobb set his chin. There were others who'd like Sam's position. "Are you saying you won't, Sam?" he asked, making his voice a threat.

Sam hesitated and then began to knead the dough faster. "I ain't persackly saying I won't." He kept his eyes on the bread board and his busy hands. "I just saying it ain't right, Sergeant Cobb. I sees big packages of meat come on the truck, but when I checks the meat locker, they's shrunk away." He stood very still. Cobb could see the whites of his eyes.

"Spit it out, Sam."

Sam dropped his head. "I ain't saying nothing. Just seems like things disappear 'round here."

Cobb felt a flush of anger. He glared at the black man. "Are you making accusations?"

"No, suh! I ain't saying nothing, Sergeant Cobb," Sam repeated. "Just looking out for my boys. They's the ones got to fight them little yellow slanty-eyes. They's the ones needs meat, not no bread crumbs."

"If you don't like it here...."

"I likes it fine." Sam's face showed strain. "Maybe next week the quartermaster'll bring more meat?" he wheedled.

"Things stretch during wartime just so far."

"Yassuh. I understand."

Cobb left the kitchen determined to find another cook. Toots might know one. He'd check tonight when he made his delivery.

Back at his desk, he stared at Betty Grable's blonde pompadour crowned with a froth of curls in the poster he'd hung on the opposite wall. She smiled back at him over her shoulder, her legs straight and beautiful.

The rap at the door startled him. He shouted louder than he had intended, "Come in!"

A warrant officer entered. Cobb snapped to attention and saluted his superior officer. What in hell did he want?

"Pop inspection, Sergeant. Headquarters is running a little check on things."

Cobb dropped his salute. Woods had never mentioned anything about unscheduled inspections. Did headquarters even have jurisdiction off the base? Could they do this? Don't buck the system, he reminded himself.

"Certainly, sir," Cobb replied, eyes on the man's insignia. "Where would you like to start?"

"Why don't we begin with your delivery invoices?" The warrant officer's voice was congenial and his accent was Brooklyn.

Cobb tensed, but offered a chair at the desk, dug out the papers and spread them before the man.

"Pull up a chair yourself, Cobb. This won't take long."

Cobb chose the chaise lounge, crossed his long legs and adjusted the creases in his trousers as the warrant officer checked off items and made occasional notes on a clipboard.

"Hmmm." He leaned back in his chair. "Only three cases of hamburger buns. Seems very little compared to the quantity of hamburger patties you receive here. How thick are the burgers you serve?" His pen beat a tattoo on the edge of the desk.

Cobb started. "Not all of the meat's used in burgers, sir." He sat erect and uncrossed his legs. "Some goes into...meatloaf."

"Meatloaf?" Sharp blue eyes inspected him, eyebrows lifted. "Can't imagine GI's ordering meatloaf at a club...."

"Did I say `meatloaf'? I meant meatballs. We serve a lot of spaghetti and meatballs. The Italian GI's go for it."

The warrant officer picked up his clipboard. "Well, that's about it for paperwork. Let's check the kitchen."

Cobb's mind worked fast while they descended the stairs. If Sam said one word, he'd slit that black throat with his own butcher knife. He tried to move ahead of the officer to warn Sam with a look. It didn't work. He followed the warrant officer through the kitchen door.

"Sam, this is Warrant Officer...."

"O'Brien."

"He's doing an inspection." Behind O'Brien's back he glared at the black man.

"Yessuh, Officer. I keeps a clean kitchen. None of them roaches here, nossuh!"

Cobb expelled a taut breath. Let Sam worry about a health inspection, keep his mind off the meat locker.

"Looks very clean." O'Brien lifted a pot lid. "Smells great, too."

"Little barbecue sauce, suh. Makes it from my pappy's receipt."

"Before this war's over, I'd like to take your `receipt' back to Brooklyn. Can't get any good barbecue back there, you know."

"Yessuh!" Sam beamed. "Ain't never writ it down nowhere, but iffen you drop by, reckon I can explain what all's in it."

"I'll do that. Thank you, Sam." The warrant officer moved on around the kitchen and stopped before a big pan heaped with rolls. "And this?"

Sam frowned. "Yestiday's rolls, suh."

Cobb intervened. "Sam grinds them for crumbs. You know, crumb toppings and such...on apple pie." He made sure Sam caught his eye.

Sam stared back and said under his breath, "And hamburgers."

"Did you say `hamburgers'?" The man had damned good ears.

"Uses it in hamburger meat to make meatballs, sir," Cobb intervened again. "Makes them lighter and less tough. Some of the meat we get these days is on the tough side."

"Hmmm." The officer's eyes were everywhere. "Let's see the meat locker."

Cobb led the way into the small room, feeling the small of his back tighten up with nerves.

The warrant officer ducked his head to enter and stopped to check the thermometer near the door. "Right temperature." He pivoted to survey shelves and hooks. "Doesn't seem to be much of a supply on hand."

Cobb cleared his throat and glanced over his shoulder to be sure Sam was still out of earshot. "Well, your inspection came on the morning we get delivery. As you see, we're about out of ground round and low on steaks, too. Since Sam isn't a butcher, we have to get our meat already packaged by the Army." He forced his face into congenial lines. "I've been thinking about replacing Sam, getting a man who can cut meat as well as cook. Save considerable time, since the Air Corp serves its own messes first and we're an afterthought."

With his back to Cobb, the officer fingered a white-wrapped package. "I'd hate to think of Sam not being around. From the scuttlebutt I hear, he's a drawing card for the NCO Club. Nice friendly fellow. Always happy." He slapped the package and turned around. "He seems a little out of sorts today, though, doesn't he?" He ducked his head exiting the meat locker. "Well, that's about it in here. How about the liquor storage?"

Cobb's muscles tightened again as he led the way to the area and unlocked the small storage room. He'd been very careful to keep the same number of cartons stacked, but if the first case of good stuff was lifted....

O'Brien raised a single bottle from each top case, read the label and dropped it back into place, face inscrutable. "That's about it for today, Cobb. I'll get back and write up the report." Cobb felt the tension drain out of him as he led O'Brien to the front door, skirting Glodeen on her knees, scrubbing in slow circles around the stairs.

She looked up and smiled a gap-toothed grin. "Hey, Mr. Eddie, how you?"

"Fine, Glodeen. Just fine."

Eddie? Eddie O'Brien? Of course! Brenda's friend. And Brenda is Louella's roommate, if that matters. He took a sharper look at the warrant officer.

O'Brien's face was bland. "Won't detain you any longer, Sergeant. Carry on." He returned Cobb's salute.

"When will I be getting a copy of the report?"

"In due time, Sergeant. In due time." The warrant officer ran down the porch steps to his car.

Cobb leaned against the doorway watching the Ford coupe turn and head back toward the base. Now what in hell was that all about?

CHAPTER XX

As she left the Post Exchange, Louella thought, Sunday afternoon and once again I've missed preaching. Since the night with Sergeant Cobb she'd been unable to force herself to enter the chapel for services. She could not shake her shame, could not rid herself of the dirty feeling, of being unworthy to enter God's house.

Probably there would be no one in the chapel at this hour. Perhaps she could just slip in and say a prayer for forgiveness and one for her papa's recovery. For a moment she hesitated, then hurried across the parade grounds.

It was a beautiful late October day with a fresh breeze. The colors of the flag were brilliant above the neat expanse of grass. Only a few dusty marigolds still bloomed after the long summer. When she approached the little chapel, the contrast of the white cupola against the blue sky made her eyes sting.

On tiptoe she went up the three wide steps and pulled at the heavy door. It opened without a sound. Sunshine through the small arched windows fell in stripes across the polished pews, touching the podium with yellow light.

Louella let the door close behind her. She walked three steps and slipped into the last pew. For a long time she stared at the pulpit, watching sun's rays inch across the chapel.

Finally she leaned her forehead onto the pew ahead on her folded hands.

"I'm here, God," she whispered. "Too many things have happened to me that make me feel guilty, too guilty to enter your house for worship. Do You know I'm here? Are You looking down on me now and do you know how I feel?" Tears trickled over her fingers. "If you hear this contrite heart, I pray for Papa. And watch over Cora Sue. I'm needed here to make the money for...."

She had not heard the outside door open and the sight of the shiny Air Force shoes and neat khaki trousers in the aisle beside her pew startled her. She shrank back against the seat, mopping at her damp cheeks. She recognized Chaplain James.

"Louella, how nice to see you again." He smiled down at her. As he noticed the tear tracks his face sobered. "I've wondered if something might be wrong." When she did not answer, he continued. "Would you mind if I sat and talked with you a while?"

Embarrassed, Louella shook her head and slid down the pew for him to enter.

He sat a distance away and did not look in her direction.

"It's beautiful here on a sunny day with God's good sunshine the only light," he said. "Sometimes on Sunday afternoons I come in like this just to be quiet and think about how good He's been to me."

Louella felt herself relax in the peace of the chapel and the calm man beside her.

"If you want to talk about it, Louella, I'm here."

Louella wadded a handkerchief between both hands, then smoothed it out. "I haven't been to preaching because...."

Her throat was tight and she could not look at the chaplain. "...because I've broken some commandments." Now he would despise her, too.

Chaplain James's words were soft. "I, too, Louella." He looked straight ahead.

"But you're a preacher!" The words were out before she could stop them.

"And a human being." He clasped his hands together and rested them on the pew ahead. "God's forgiveness is the most beautiful thing He gives us all." Now he turned and looked into her face. "Louella, we're neither of the Catholic persuasion and I do not hear confessions, but perhaps we can talk about what is troubling you."

Louella thought of all the actions she had taken that made her feel guilty. "There's liquor...and dancing...and playing cards," she began, clutching the damp handkerchief. "Preacher at home says folks who do those things will burn in Hellfire forever."

There was a long pause before he answered. "I wonder about that, Louella. The more I read my Bible, the more I am convinced that Jesus told us the most important things are to love Him and love our fellow men. And women." He touched her arm. "If I remember, the Ten Commandments do not mention liquor, dancing and playing cards." It was a question.

She stiffened. "It does adultery."

"I didn't realize you were married, Louella."

"Oh, I'm not."

"Then there is no way you could have committed adultery." His eyes were on the cross behind the pulpit. "Perhaps it would help if you read again the stories about women who did break that commandment whom Jesus forgave. The woman at the well. Mary Magdalene. She was what we would call a prostitute, but she was the first one He appeared to after his resurrection." He turned toward Louella. "You know, Louella, there are really very few saints in these pews. Just people who have to begin again over and over."

He gave her a long searching look. "There's something else, isn't there, Louella?"

She knew her tense body and clenched hands had prompted his question. "There's Papa. I didn't honor him like the commandments say. I just up and left to make my own way." She gulped, fighting tears again. "And when I went home to see him, he called me...called me things. He got so mad at me he had a stroke. And that was my fault, even if Dr. Cutler says no. If I hadn't gone home, he wouldn't be sick now." She saw again the naked glaring eyes of her father.

Chaplain James put one hand over her clenched fists. "God has a plan for all His animal kingdom—and we're part of that, too. Sometimes I think we humans have confused things a great deal."

There was comfort in his warm hand on hers.

"When young birds have grown their flight feathers, the parents push them out of the nest, forcing them to fly, just as God gave them the instinct to do." He sighed and released her hands. "But in the human family things get pretty mixed up. Sometimes young people feel a need to fly before their parents are ready to let them leave." He paused. "Would it help if I went to see him?"

Louella's eyes widened in alarm. "You mustn't do that, Chaplain James! Papa thinks everybody at the base is...everyone is a...Yankee." She ducked her head.

"I see." He sighed again. "I have met several other proud Southern folks like your father who have not accepted the way the Civil War ended. I shall not disturb him, then, with the sight of this uniform, Louella." For moments he was silent.

"The only advice I can give you is to stay as close to God as you can and keep on trying." His voice deepened. "Every soul in the whole world fights a lonely war of its own every day. When you know that, you can accept everyone, good and evil alike. But it's a constant battle to win your personal war."

Louella saw the lines of pain in his face, but his eyes were clear, a small glow like a flame in their hazel depths.

"There is a comfort in prayer when there is no other." He rose and smiled down on her. "I must go. But I will pray for you, Louella."

She stood and followed him down the aisle. When the heavy doors closed behind them, the gold cross on his lapel flashed in the sunshine.

"Thank you, Chaplain James. I will remember what you've said."

"God brought both of us here today, Louella." He touched his cap and strode away across the parade grounds toward the barracks.

God and country, she thought, watching him go. How hard it must be to serve both.

CHAPTER XXI

Hutch wrestled the spigot open at the crusted lavatory in the men's room at the Daisy May. A thin trickle of rusty water splashed over his hands. In the cracked grimy mirror he examined his face. His round blue eyes looked almost turquoise, reflecting the bilious green pocked walls around him.

"I'll probably look like a kid when I'm old and creaky," he said aloud. "I've been in the Air Force a whole year and a half and I still look like an Okie farm kid."

He rubbed damp hands over his chin, wondering if a beard might help. So far he only had to shave every other day. I'm hopeless, he thought. Hands dried on the stained roller towel, he pushed through the door, glad to leave the stench of the dirty toilet.

The only customer this early evening, he eased his bulk down into the corner booth, facing the nervous blink of the red neon beer sign in the window. The half-light that follows sundown made the open door a pale gray rectangle.

Bored, he moved his beer mug in circles, enlarging the damp spot on the wooden table. Maybe he should have chosen the other side of the booth so he could watch Toots tend bar. He could hear her moving around and the clink of glasses and bottles.

What was he doing here, anyhow? Eddie's instructions were, "Watch in case Cobb comes in." What good would that do? He lifted the mug and sipped the brew. It was flat, but he wasn't very thirsty. The silence of the empty room bothered him and he wedged his thick body upright and stuffed in his shirttail, which had pulled loose again.

Toots looked up from the glass she polished, an automatic smile on her small face. "Get you anything? How about a burger?"

"Thought I'd play the jukebox. Got change for a dollar?"

Toots leaned down to open a drawer and shoved four quarters across the bar. Hutch dropped the crumpled dollar bill beside her hand. In a magician's flash it was gone and he heard the drawer close. The speed of her movements made him blink. She picked up glass and towel again, her hands never still. "What's your name, soldier? Don't remember you being here before."

"Name's Hutch, Ma'am."

The wooden floor creaked under his boots on his way to the gaudy jukebox. Shaped like a headless matron, its lighted bosom pushed out to hold the printed numbers of the tunes. Red and green lights chased up and down its sides. With one hand on the ample bulge, he leaned over and considered his choices.

"Star Dust" for sure, because that's the one he'd danced to with Louella before Cobb cut in. "Don't Sit Under the Apple Tree" and "Deep Purple." Two more; five for a quarter. He closed his eyes and punched random numbers. Probably be some hillbilly tunes, he thought as he plodded back to the booth and faced the neon sign again.

"Sure you don't want a hamburger?" In reflective light Toot's eyes under her impossibly black hair glittered like black glass.

The odor of stale grease and onions hung heavy in the air over the smell of bygone beers, canceling the idea of eating what she offered. "Don't believe so, Ma'am."

Just went to show how low he was, though, refusing any food. The music was too loud, echoing off the rusty tin ceiling in the empty room. He thought of how Louella had changed. Like she'd gone as flat as his beer. Solemn now. Not full of enthusiasm as she was before. She was worried about her sick pa for sure, but it seemed like she'd changed even before that. Ever since the night she got sick at the NCO Club.

Cobb was involved somehow, but he couldn't figure it all out. Eddie and Brenda weren't talking but they were sure up to something. What, he didn't know. If spying around here would help Louella in some way, or put a crimp in Cobb's style, he was willing.

The jukebox stopped, clicked and whirred. "Deep Purple" dropped into its slot and the first notes began.

The slam of a back door brought Hutch's head up. Toots' high heels clicked from the bar through a door behind the bar. Straining, he could hear a man's deep voice and hers over the music, but not the words. Footsteps returned. A man's tread, once to three of hers.

"Damn it, Cobb, you can't do this to me!" Toots' voice was shrill.

"Now, Toots, calm down. Expenses have gone up. Times are getting rougher for us all."

"But you're the smart ass talked me into putting out hamburgers!"

Hutch peered cautiously around the edge of the booth.

Cobb was leaning across the bar, facing the irate owner. "It built your business. Doubled your income. Made you money," he said.

Her chin jutted out in anger and she snorted, "Some business! See any crowds in here? Damn you, Cobb, sixty's too much."

Cobb straightened and Hutch ducked out of sight.

"There's others would be glad to get the meat. No ration stamps. No questions asked. And the good liquor brands without having to load up on rum, either."

Hutch felt his ears twitch. If she was buying meat from him, where did he get it? And it was the law you had to take a bottle of rum with every bottle of the hard stuff, if you could even find it these days. That wasn't legal, selling it without. How could he do that?

Snitched them out of the NCO Club! That had to be it!

"Now just a damned minute, Cobb." Toots' voice held a strained note. "First forty, then fifty, and now sixty. How the hell much higher is it going? I've got a partner to consider, you know."

"And she can make more than that on her back in one afternoon any day of the week, including Monday."

"On her...."

Silence stretched between them.

"What she does is her business." Toots sounded defensive.

"And a nice little business it is, too, my friend." Cobb's voice had a laugh in it.

Once more Hutch peered around the booth. Cobb rested one narrow spit-shined shoe on the brass rail. How does he stay so neat, Hutch wondered, watching the tall lean figure. Toots moved down the bar toward the cash drawer. Hutch was struck again by her hair. Was it because her face was so white that it looked so black?

"How'd you know about Vernita?"

"Every GI on the base knows about Vernita and where to find her. You run a nice messenger service here, Toots. Might say you have a diversified business."

Hutch stifled a gasp and shrank back into the booth.

"Single girls got to make their own way. It's a tough world out there." Her voice held a whine.

"Time this war's over, I figure you and Vernita will own the prettiest house of ill repute in the South. Maybe in New Orleans? Or you figure on getting further away? No, I reckon not. Best stay with regular customers."

Hutch ran a finger around his collar, suddenly too warm.

"Oh, shit! Take your damned money and get out of here, you son-of-a-bitch!" The cash drawer opened and banged shut.

"Thanks for the business, Toots. See you same time next week."

Hutch drew himself into the corner and watched Cobb stride toward the street door, thumbing the bills in his hands. Apparently satisfied, Cobb folded them over, tucked them into a breast pocket of his uniform and was gone.

The clink of glasses was a lot louder now. The music stopped for a moment, then "I'll Be Seeing You" flooded the room, accompanied by muttering from the bar. The sound of breaking glass was followed by a string of oaths Hutch had never heard from a female before. He waited until the music ended and the room was silent again before he eased out of the booth.

Toots gave a startled gasp when he straightened. "My god, I forgot you were there!" Her eyes narrowed. "Heard it all, didn't you, soldier?"

"Heard what?" For once Hutch was glad he had a round innocent face. "Got some heavy thoughts on my mind," he said, trying to look burdened.

Toots eyed him up and down, then relaxed. She wiped the bar in slow circles. Apparently she'd decided he was harmless. Revealing the gap where an incisor had been, she smiled. "Another beer?"

"Thanks, no. Gotta go."

"Come again, you hear? Quiet tonight but usually there's a mob in here." Her voice followed him out into the dark street.

Down the empty sidewalk his footsteps echoed from the closed shops. Over a cast iron safe in the furniture store a night light illuminated chairs and sofas like huddled dark beasts.

Might as well take in a movie, he thought. The lights of the Bijou shone like a beacon in the next block. Two GI's were leaning against a poster of Dick Powell as he turned in toward the ticket booth. They each had their right foot propped against the brick wall behind them, heads together in conversation.

Inside the booth the cashier filed crimson nails. She laid down the emery board and patted the drooping red cotton flowers in her brassy hair. Her commercial smile revealed crooked teeth beneath a short upper lip. "Movie's out in five minutes. Want your ticket now, soldier?"

"One, please." Hutch shoved a quarter through the half circle in the glass.

She pushed a green cardboard ticket toward him and as he turned away her smile diminished like a Cheshire cat's.

Inspecting posters of coming attractions, he wondered if Louella would come with him sometime. Voices built behind the double brass doors with glass portholes. A tired-looking young boy in a gold-braided jacket three sizes too large pulled the doors open and kicked at the metal props. The first of the crowd spilled onto the curb.

Three GI's pushed past Hutch. "I say let's go to the Daisy May." "Fine with me. Nothing else to do in this burg on a Monday night." They headed back the way he had come.

A hand touched Hutch's arm and he smelled woodsy perfume.

Brenda smiled at him. "Imagine meeting you here." She linked her arm in Eddie's. "Good picture."

"Yeah," agreed Eddie, "even if it was about the Navy."

"Come with us back to the apartment," Brenda urged. "I'll make sandwiches."

Hutch fingered the movie ticket he'd bought. Realizing Louella might be home, he shoved it deep into his pocket. "Fine," he said and fell into step beside them. On the way back to the base in Eddie's car, he listened until their conversation about the movie died down.

"Heard something in the Daisy May. Saw Cobb."

"Watch the road," Brenda ordered Eddie as he turned to look at Hutch. "What happened?" she asked.

He repeated what he had overheard.

"How about that?" Brenda pinched Eddie's arm.

"Good work, Hutch!" Eddie slapped the steering wheel. "One more piece in the puzzle. We'll get him booted out yet." The muscles in his jaw bunched. "I'd rather catch him in a dark alley but maybe the slow way is the best way."

"Be sure you don't say anything to Louella about this," Brenda warned Hutch.

In the darkness beside her, Hutch frowned. He was afraid to ask too many questions. Afraid of the answers, maybe. Against the night he saw Louella's face. There was something sinister he must protect her from, even if he didn't know what it was.

Two nights later, Brenda sighed as Eddie parked at the curb outside the apartment. It was their custom to find an excuse to leave the housing unit most evenings, a time to be alone together. She found it the sweetest part of each day, painfully aware the time of decision drew closer every twenty-four hours. Her mind flinched away from the thought.

She'd have to talk seriously with Eddie. Later. Not just yet. His arm was across the back of the seat, hand on her right shoulder. Her thoughts were on the curve of his upper lip, but his words brought her to attention.

"Got an idea. What if there's something wrong with what Cobb's selling on the black market? Say there's maggots in the meat."

"Yecht!" Brenda shuddered.

"What'd that do to Cobb's business, huh?"

"Yeah, but where'd you get the maggots?"

"Garbage can."

Brenda grinned. "I can just see you picking 'em out, Eddie."

"Anything for our Louella," Eddie laughed.

"Or maybe the sugar could be doctored," Brenda offered.

Eddie snuffed out his cigarette and straightened. "That, too. Salt. About half and half. Maybe a little flour."

"Sure make a mess in a cup of coffee."

Brenda's hand was on the latch, ready to slide out. Eddie bent over and turned on the ignition.

"I think we've got something," he said. "Poor old Swartz spilled it all today. Dumb guy thought he'd just make enough extra dough to cover some doctor bills at home." Eddie shook his head. "By then Cobb had him, wouldn't let him off the hook. Swartz'll do anything for us now."

"Pick maggots?"

"Maybe." He grinned. "How's your own garbage can? In this heat a few flies will...."

"Not even for Louella!"

"Just kidding, Bronx." Eddie shoved the gear into neutral and took her into his arms. He kissed her lightly. Then his arms tightened and the kiss deepened.

Brenda felt her body go limp. Just a damned kiss and she came all unglued. How am I ever going to be able to tell him, she worried.

Eddie's breath was coming faster and he turned the ignition off again with one hand.

Brenda took a shaky breath of her own and shoved against his chest. "Eddie, we've got to talk. About us." Her palms were suddenly wet.

His left hand kneaded the back of her neck. In the dim light the black curl on his brow held her attention.

"What about us?" he asked, eyes on her lips.

How to start? The butterflies in her stomach had grown to the size of bats. "I...I heard from Flint today," she began. "He's coming home. Got enough points and then some for all his service time, ready for discharge."

Eddie's hand stilled on the back of her neck. She turned away, unwilling to look at him.

He swiveled to stare stiffly out the window at the housing units across the street. "How long did you know him before he went overseas, Bronx?"

"Three weeks. We married — and I meant those vows before the judge — and a week later he shipped out. What's that got to do with anything?"

"I was thinking about how long I've known you. Seems like always." Back against the door, he turned to face her. "But it's been, what? Going on two years now?"

"You trying to say I know you better than my own husband?" It was true. Flint had dimmed into the past and she could not bring his face into clear focus.

"I know all this started as just a little fun between us, Bronx. Lately, though, I keep thinking about the war ending." Eddie was silent for a moment. "Been thinking you and I could make it, have some fun. Even kids one day. Blonde. Like you."

"Brunette, then."

"Yeah, that's right. I forgot."

"But I'm not Catholic." Her breathing was getting difficult. "And I'd be a...divorced woman, even if Flint let me go."

"It's been done before." His face was sober. "Think about it, Brenda."

Her skin prickled. He's never called me by my name before, she thought, always it's been Bronx.

He drew her back into his arms, easing her head onto his shoulder.

"I've got to admit I have thought about it some," she said. "But I made a vow to...." His breath warmed her cheek, his lips nibbled her earlobe. "Damn it, Eddie, you know I can't think when you do that!"

"When you're thinking, don't forget about that, either. It's good between us, Brenda." His hand stroked her breast.

"I know it, damn it! But I'm...not free."

"Three weeks against two years?"

Brenda sat up and pushed Eddie away. "All right, I'll think about it." She slid over the seat and left the car.

Eddie moved to her window. "One thing more to remember, Brenda: I love you."

Her body tensed and she bent down expecting to see a grin on his face, but there was no smile. He meant it. She gripped the windowsill and leaned in to kiss the black curl.

"Not fair. Not fair," she whispered, pushing the curl from his brow.

Her walk was unsteady up the sidewalk. It was not until she closed the door behind her that she heard his car start up and drive away.

CHAPTER XXII

Louella looked up from her sewing as Brenda entered the apartment. Her roommate was leaning against the door, head tilted against the small pane of glass, apparently oblivious to the surroundings. Louella's hand stopped pulling thread in midair. She had heard Eddie's car leave. Had they quarreled? Something had happened.

Eyes glazed, Brenda released the door knob and started across the room. When she finally saw Louella, her expression changed. "Oh. Hi, honey."

"How was the movie?"

"Fine. I guess." Brenda sat on the nearest chair and lit a cigarette. She took a deep drag, intent on the spiral of exhaled smoke.

Louella remained silent, attentive to her sewing. If her roommate wanted to talk about it, she would. Over the murmur of the window fan she could hear the tick of the old Westclox alarm clock in Brenda's room.

"Heard from Flint today." Brenda's words were abnormally loud. "He's coming home."

Louella kept her voice noncommittal. "You're happy about that?"

"I should be, knowing he's safe." But there was no joy in her Brenda's voice. "The thing is...." She inhaled deeply. "Thing is, there's Eddie and...." Again her eyes held the blank look and she whispered. "And I think I've fallen in love with the lug." Louella laid the hand-me-down dress she was remodeling aside and stuck her needle into the padded arm of the couch. "What are you going to do?"

"Damned if I know. I meant it when I said that `until death do us part' thing. But I knew Flint only three days before we married. Then three weeks more here on this hick base before he shipped out." Her gaze flickered toward Louella and a flush crept up her cheeks. "Sorry, honey. It just slipped out."

"I know this isn't New York, Brenda."

"Seems like that was a hundred years ago and all this time there's been Eddie. At first he was just someone to pass time with, waiting for Flint." Brenda snuffed out her cigarette in the green glass ashtray. "But, hell, we're alike, Eddie and me. There's times he says something I'm thinking, you know, like we share the same crazy brain." She leaned her head back and stared at the ceiling. "God knows we both like a good time — and then there's the bed thing. My god, we're wonderful together, Louella!"

Warmth spread up Louella's throat. She hoped Brenda didn't go into details.

"Flint, now, the way I remember it was more like a wham-bam-thank-you-ma'am. Eddie, well, he wants me to be content, too."

Realizing Brenda needed to talk aloud to sort out her feelings, Louella picked up the dress again, threaded her needle and returned to the hem-lowering job.

"Flint comes from Wyoming...ranches, horses and all. Hell, Louella, I wouldn't know which end of a horse to feed. I know I'd hate it out there. Of course he might decide to stay in the service, but I don't think I'd like that much better."

Louella looked up as Brenda shifted in her chair. Now her roommate's face was brighter.

"Eddie, now, his family's got a little bar in Brooklyn and that's more my style. Maybe we could get a small one of our own. See my family sometimes on Sundays. Make the shows." She leaned forward. "Benny Goodman. Paul Whiteman. Lots of big bands come to New York and we could go dancing. Not with records or radio but the real thing." She kicked off her pumps.

Louella took five more stitches before she asked, "What do you think Flint will say about all this?"

Brenda stood and paced the floor. "That's the thing. I...don't...know!" She folded her arms around herself and rocked her body. "Flint's about twice the size of Eddie. Still, Eddie outranks him." She headed for the kitchen. "Oh, hell, Louella, I just don't know what to do." She left the room, padding in stocking feet with a slow drag.

Louella heard the icebox door open, the fizz of a beer bottle uncapped.

"Damn it, why couldn't I have met Eddie first?" Brenda was pacing again.

Louella bit off her thread, shook out the dress and asked, "Did you love Flint when you married?"

"Love? Hell, I didn't have time to find out. By the time I came to, we were already here." She swallowed half the Budweiser. "Flint's overwhelming. Made me feel helpless, like he was a knight on a white horse and all that, you know?" She snorted and wiped her mouth with the back of her hand. "Me helpless? Hell, I've been knocking guys away since I was twelve. I wasn't going to end up in a cold-water flat with a bunch of snot-nosed kids like some I know." She turned the bottle between her hands. "But in wartime, seems like everything's different. All the excitement. `Our brave boys' and all that propaganda shit!"

Brenda dropped the empty beer bottle onto the table and announced, "Oh, hell, I'm going to bed. Not that I'll be able to sleep."

"`Night, then, Brenda. I'll press this before I turn in. Want to wear it tomorrow."

Thoughtfully Louella set up the wobbly ironing board and connected the heavy iron, jiggling the plug to make sure it heated. Dress smoothed over the surface, she picked off a bit of thread where an embroidered flower had been. Somehow she liked things not quite so bright. Probably a hangover from her plain-jane days at home and The Religion.

What if it were she who was married to Stith, and it wasn't great like she'd dreamed it would be? Then what if Cobb came along? Louella shivered. Just seeing Cobb in the PX office had made her aware of her body's response. She knew the danger but how she would like to dance with him again, feel his strong arms, his chest hard against her breasts, their bodies in rhythm with the music. Just to dance again. That's all.

His cool face was clear in her mind as she tested the iron with one damp finger. Bemused, she pressed it too long on the hot sole, then jerked it away. That hurt! Maybe that was a warning. Stay away from Cobb or you'll get burnt.

She smiled to herself. Pretty childish thinking. Still....

Pushing the iron across the lengthened hem, she thought, with an extra beat of her heart, "But Stith, I still love you. I just can't help myself."

A tear rolled down and sizzled on the hot metal.

Hours later Louella stirred in her dreams. Stith's face bent over her. Again and again she heard him say, "I love you, Louella. I love you!" His hands stroked her thighs, his lips were on her throat, her breast, hungry on her mouth. Waves of feeling built like a stormy sea as they carried her higher and higher until her body convulsed.

It was the final spasm that brought her fully awake. Eyes half open in the dim light that told of early morning, she cupped one breast with her palm. She tried to sink into the dream of Stith, but his face had faded. It had happened before, that sweet passionate dream. If her body had learned such pleasure from Cobb, what utter joy it must be with the one you love.

Wide awake now, the memory of Stith's real visit brought a stabbing pain. Stith no longer loved her. She curled into a tight ball and pushed her head deep into her pillow as the tears came. Life was not beautiful, as she'd expected. Life was hard and cold. The only warmth she'd found came from friendships, an occasional laugh or two and the artificial glow from a glass of wine with her surrogate family from the office.

Of course, there was the security of payday, too, the satisfaction of knowing Cora Sue and papa were comfortable and their telephone worked.

She pushed herself to a sitting position on the bed. Doing something — doing anything — might lift her spirits. She heard the first flight of pre-dawn fighters pass overhead. No chance of any more sleep now.

She walked into the kitchen, the linoleum cool against her bare feet while she put the coffee on. Somewhere down the block a door banged and a dog barked once. It would be a few minutes before the housing area stirred to life. She dug out the iron skillet, careful to set it on the stove without waking Brenda. Only three strips of precious bacon remained. She dropped them into the pan. Grease collection was today, but she would put back a little for frying meat — if they were lucky enough to have any. The odor of coffee perking permeated the apartment. She cracked four eggs into a bowl and whipped them with a fork. Time enough to scramble them when she heard Brenda moving.

Flame low under the sputtering bacon, she walked into the living room, straightened a pillow and stacked some magazines on the coffee table. At the top of the closed flowered drapes, fingers of sunlight showed. She pulled the curtains aside and peered out at the empty street.

What was Cora Sue doing right now back home? Probably bringing in eggs still warm from the nest. And papa? Was he awake, one naked eye staring at the ceiling, hating me? Best face things as they are. She was no longer a child.

Wrenching her thoughts back to practical matters, she tried to call up the schedule for the day. Today's Friday, November 10th. With a start she realized it was her twentieth birthday. She shrugged. No one would celebrate the day her life began. No one knew. With a rueful grin she turned the bacon.

Highs and lows in a lifetime. How many highs? How many lows? Did they eventually even out over the years? Too early to tell. The thing was to hang on during the lows and wait for the highs, she knew that much.

Intent on her thoughts and the bacon, Louella didn't realize Brenda had entered the kitchen until she felt her quick hug.

"Happy birthday, honey," Brenda said in her ear.

"You scared me! How'd you know? I never told anyone and I just remembered myself."

Brenda wrinkled her nose and grinned. "Never try to keep anything from a good secretary — and I am the best! Looked it up on your job application." She stretched toward the ceiling, yawning. "Got something for you." She pushed Louella into the dining room where a large box wrapped in floral paper with a big green bow waited on the table.

"Oh, my!" Louella said.

"Unwrap it, honey."

Louella neatly untied the green ribbon and carefully rolled it up. She was taking pains not to tear the pretty paper when Brenda insisted, "Lord, Louella, hurry up! Rip it open. I want to see your face."

Finally lifting the lid, Louella saw a dress in its tissue paper nest. She gasped and held it high to admire the teal blue fabric and hugged it to her. "It's beautiful. Like a mallard's wing."

"Go try it on. I want to be sure it fits. Had my Uncle Jake send it out and it didn't come until yesterday. I was holding my breath." Brenda, back in the kitchen, slid two slices of bacon onto Louella's plate, and devoured the third strip before she poured most of the fat from the skillet into the grease collection can.

From her room, Louella heard the splutter of eggs in the skillet as she pulled the dress over her head. The soft fabric flowed like water over her body, clinging to her legs. In the wavy mirror the reflection of its color made her eyes almost green. She whirled to watch the nylon skirt bell out around her ankles.

In bare feet she danced to the kitchen door and assumed a model's pose, one hand lifted, one hip jutting.

When her roommate looked up she said nothing for a long moment. "You're really something in that, Louella. Time you had something beside the red taffeta to dance in." She carried their breakfast plates to the table. "Do you have any idea how much you've changed? It's like someone coming to life."

"Sometimes I don't recognize myself," Louella said.

"That dress will be perfect for the Officers Club. Real elegant. Or are you dating officers these days? I notice there's been more GI's around lately."

"Officers make me uncomfortable," Louella said, "always talking about college and famous people I've never heard of. And their rich relatives."

"Probably trying to impress you," Brenda said.

"Last month when I went with Hutch to hear Kay Kaiser's band here on the base, Lieutenant Smythe gave me a lecture on never dating anybody below the rank of Warrant Officer." Brenda snorted.

"I told him it was my business who I went out with."

"Looks like your spunk is finally sprouting." Brenda spread a scant spoonful of marmalade over her toast.

"They're all after the same thing, anyhow," Louella said, "and I feel more comfortable with the GI's. It's a lot less strain than always worrying about my manners and feeling stupid." She headed toward her bedroom. "I don't want to get a grease stain on my new dress."

When she strolled back into the dining room she wore her old black lisle stockings and the rosebud dress with long sleeves. She had brushed back her hair and pinned on the long braids she had saved.

Brenda's face went blank and then she threw her head back to laugh, peal after peal. "You can't do it, Louella, you know that? You can't go back. You even look different in your old clothes. The change is inside, honey." She waved her knife, tears of laughter streaming. "Good god, those black stockings! How I hated them!" She slid a slice of buttered toast toward Louella's plate. "Thank god the butterfly came out of the cocoon!" Louella dropped onto her chair, grinning at the success of her masquerade. Then she sobered. It was true; she could never again be the innocent she had been. That four-mile walk to the base last June had changed her forever. Perhaps each ordinary action every day changed you in some way. Simple actions, taken without thought. Conversations. Taking one street and not the other. It was a frightening thought. How could you ever know which was best? If you stopped to weigh all the possibilities, you couldn't act at all. Chaplain James had said, "Keep on trying." Donald Monahan said, "Begin anew." Both older and wiser, they had said the same thing.

Louella reached for the marmalade jar. Birthdays were time for taking stock, but she intended to enjoy this one, not look too far ahead. She had a feeling Chaplain James would list not being able to see the future as one of God's blessings.

"Birthday or no," Brenda said as she took a last sip of coffee and carried their plates to the sink, "you'd better hurry and dress. It's almost time to go."

On the walk to the PX, Louella breathed deeply of the autumn air. The sun's rays were still not high enough to touch the street, but they glinted on windows, coating them in gold. Foundations of buildings blurred in gray light. Ahead of her, Brenda's hair blazed in sunshine, but her feet were dim in the shadows, giving the appearance that she floated. Louella smiled to herself. Everything today seemed a little unreal.

But reality waited in the office with the stack of invoices on her desk. It was good to know there was work to be done and be competent to do it, part of a worldwide team winding down this war. She smiled at the fantasy. How ridiculous, really, to think she'd had the slightest effect. Still.... Perhaps her work was one of the actions with unforeseeable consequences, too. If the gross of bolts the flight line had special ordered was the wrong size or defective, that could make a difference somewhere. Maybe it did all matter. Certainly nothing was as simple as it had seemed six months ago.

Nine-thirty came, time for coffee break. And the whole office descended upon her desk. Louella felt a great wave of affection, looking up at their smiling faces.

Frances held a small cake with one thick red candle towering over it. She shoved aside the invoices and set the cake down before Louella. Twice as tall as the cake, the candle burned with a fitful flame that wavered when they sang the birthday song. In very bad harmony, Hutch and Mr. Monahan added, "And many more."

"It's a magic candle, my young friend," Donald Monahan said, dancing around the desk to plant a kiss on her cheek. "Make a wish."

"It's the smallest candle I could find. Ain't that a lick?" Frances said.

Louella laughed and then sobered. So many things to wish for. With all her heart she wished for Stith. And there was papa and Cora Sue. But Stith was the deepest wish in her heart. The odor of smoldering wick was fragrant in the room when she closed her eyes and blew out the candle.

Brenda polished a letter opener and handed it to Louella with a pad of obsolete government forms. "Here's your cake knife and plates. Serving cake on these makes more sense than what they were printed for."

Louella carved the small cake into six pieces and handed them around on the limber `plates.' When Frances filled everyone's coffee mugs, the crew settled down in their usual places. "Hey, this is delicious!" Hutch popped a crumb into his mouth. "Haven't had cake that didn't taste like bread for ages. Did you make it?"

"In my room?" Frances replied. "Landlady doesn't even let me heat a can of soup." She licked a finger. "Got it at the bakery in town. Dun no how they manage, but they seem to have plenty of sugar and their stuff is really good." Brenda exchanged a smile with Glen Hart.

"Bet I've gained five pounds on their sweet rolls. A cup of tea from hot tap water and a Danish is breakfast every morning."

A shadow fell over the hallway door. Cobb entered, his pale eyes surveying them. "What's the celebration?"

Frances wrinkled her nose. "Louella's birthday. Cake's all gone."

On the heels of Frances' words, Glen Hart demanded, "What do you want, Sergeant Cobb?"

"Still looking for the other half of the order for napkins and paper plates. But if it came, I see you didn't use any of them." Cobb's voice had an edge to it.

"Maybe Monday." Hart's tone was brusque.

"Damn!" Cobb turned and moved toward Louella. "Congratulations," he said. "If I'd known, I'd have sent flowers for the fair." Then he spun on his heel and turned the doorknob. Over his shoulder, he added, "Call me, Hart. I need them. Now." The door closed behind him.

As he disappeared, Louella found she had stopped breathing and she took a deep breath. She heard Hutch muttering and was surprised to see his face was beet red.

"Why do I feel the devil's paid us a visit?" Donald Monahan asked no one in particular. "Anybody smell brimstone?" He took Louella's hand and clicked his heels together. "Speaking of the devil, I hate like the devil to leave, but duty calls. Be happy." He squeezed her fingers, winked one green eye and departed.

Louella dropped her makeshift plate into her wastebasket. Then she announced, "I think I'll keep this red candle to remember you all and my twentieth birthday. You are the finest friends I'll ever have. Thank you."

Her eyes were stinging as she turned back to the invoices, wondering which of her birthday wishes would come true. Or would none of them.

CHAPTER XXIII

Technical Sergeant Leon Cobb hung up the telephone in the booth outside the Post Exchange. As he lit another Camel, he could not stop the trembling of his hands. He let out a long plume of smoke and stood head down for a moment to calm himself. He'd almost achieved the goal he'd set so long ago. Soon he'd be somebody, somebody others would have to reckon with. The option on the night club in Florida was finally his—except for the last payment and he had most of that already. Maybe it was outrageous to come up with ten thousand earnest money, but this was the nightclub he wanted, needed. There was no question it would be his, no way he'd lose that ten thousand. When he raised his chin, the reflection in the glass of the telephone booth returned a grin.

It was pure luck on his last leave home that he had seen the `For Sale' sign. A great location near the largest, plushest hotels, right on the beach. Of course, now those hotels were full of servicemen in Air Corp training programs. But when the war ended, they would be flooded with fat wives and rich husbands who'd made it big on profits from World War II.

Cobb closed his eyes and saw the face of the club's present owner, a swarthy man with eyes like black stones. The Mob? Maybe. He suspected the club was for sale because of too much government surveillance. MP's kept on top of establishments near training centers. Well, if he didn't know his own way around regulations by this time, he never would.

He unfolded the glass door of the booth and stepped outside, the gravelly voice of the club owner echoing in his mind.

"You got until the 15th to get up the rest of the dough. If it ain't here then, you can forget the whole deal. And kiss the earnest money good-bye."

Maybe it wasn't a full month he had. More like three weeks. His pulse raced. Sugar. He had to sell more sugar. Swartz would come around. It would be a pleasure to put a tighter squeeze on that fat boy.

If worst came to worst, Toot's at The Daisy May would be good for a short loan, no questions asked. One word from him in the right places and she knew the MP's would put her bar off limits, shut her down tighter than a cork in a bottle.

With what he could skim off the NCO Club, it would be enough. But time was running out fast. He stood for a moment in the small circle of light from the telephone booth to cup his hands around his Zippo lighter and a fresh Camel. Would it be worth it to branch out into cigarettes? Maybe. But it was riskier. There was a closer rein on smokes. Still...nonsmokers who bought a carton at the PX for almost cost were happy to get the bonus he'd pay, which left plenty of profit at the going civilians' price.

He dropped the lighter into his pocket and threw his shoulders back. The air was cool on his face and it was a night to celebrate—even if no one else knew why. To either make love or fight. Not fight; that might jeopardize his NCO Club position. He bit into the cigarette and grinned around it.

Remembering the celebration at the PX office for Louella that afternoon, his eyes narrowed. She was damned beautiful since she quit wearing those Halloween clothes. A beautiful broad on his arm—he'd need that when he opened the club. Cobb shrugged as he strolled down the sidewalk. There'd be plenty of good looking broads around then. Louella had been only one notch better than the flop-and-straddle floozies he'd had lately. If she'd learned how to dress, by god she could learn how to satisfy him too. Practice is what she needs.

Cobb tossed his cigarette onto the path a foot ahead beside the painted trash can, then ground it under his heel on the next step. He thumbed his nose at the `Hit It or Pick It Up' sign.

Low ground fog early the next morning greeted Louella as she closed the apartment door quietly without disturbing the sleeping Brenda. Everything was either black, gray or a luminous pearl color. Solid objects seemed to move forward, then retreat and advance once more in the fog wraiths before dawn. By the time she'd reached the kiosk at the base's gate the sky had added faint pink in the east. Sounds from the parade ground and the flight line were soft, then loud, in and out with the fog.

"You're off to an early start," the guard said, eyeing the brown paper bag she carried. "I'll have to inspect that, Miss."

"Just some clothes and things," she said. The black and white MP band on his arm made her uneasy and her voice rose. "I'm going to visit my family and change when I get there." Now that papa was mostly unconscious he probably wouldn't even know she was there, but it would give Cora Sue and Cloteel some relief. Maybe they could get away for an hour or two.

He took the sack and peered inside. "What's this?" He pulled out a plait of black hair.

"That's my switch. Papa likes me in braids." She bristled. It was none of his business, but she'd be prepared if her father woke up while she was in his room.

"Okay." He handed back the sack.

"Did you think I was stealing airplane parts or something?" she asked.

The young guard grinned.

Not a bit of stubble showed on his fair skin. Too young to shave but not too young to die in a war, she thought, her annoyance gone. He was just doing his job.

The sound of a car approaching made them both turn. It was a blue Ford coupe. The thin-faced blond driver saluted and drove through the gate, the crunch of gravel under the tires counterpoint to the sound of the engine.

"Sergeant Cobb," the young guard informed Louella. "Sure keeps funny hours. Never know when he'll show up. He was off and on this base twice last night since I reported at midnight. Must be nice, coming and going when you please. And having your own car." He yawned and looked at his wristwatch. "I'll be glad for sack time. My replacement is late."

The last word was muffled by the screech of brakes. From the fog the Ford emerged, backing toward them.

Sergeant Cobb rolled down the window and stuck his head out. "That you, Louella? Thought I recognized you. Hop in. I'll give you a lift into town."

His face was so close, she caught a whiff of shaving lotion.

"No thanks. I'm going home for a visit." She was repelled and attracted at the same time by his handsome face. "Home's in the opposite direction."

"Hop in, anyhow." he said. "I won't bite."

He was making fun of her and it rankled. Given half a chance, she'd show him she was not to be used and tossed aside. She felt her eyes narrow as she considered. Maybe this was the time.

"Gas tank's full. More where that came from. Might as well see some of the country around here." Cobb blew a perfect smoke ring out the window.

Going by car would save at least two hours' time, Louella thought. Brenda had warned her, but she had to learn sometime how to handle men like Cobb.

The door handle was wet from fog droplets. Louella climbed in and wiped her hand on the brown paper bag.

When they stopped at the highway, he asked, "Which way?"

"Turn right, then right again at the first unpaved road," she said, sliding closer to the door. His shaving lotion was stronger in the enclosed coupe. She wished she had not put on her Evening in Paris perfume. No use giving him any more ideas about her.

Until they were well off the highway, neither spoke. On the rutted road between the thick pines, they plunged back into foggy night again. Only faint light penetrated the heavy branches overhead. The headlights burrowed through fog patches. Two red dots shone for a moment as a vague shape slipped through palmetto fronds.

"How far?" he asked.

"Another three miles or so."

When she turned, his profile was sharp against the dark trees. It was as if there were no other people in the world, just the two of them in the fog and darkness before full light. The reflection from the headlights revealed the hollows and planes of his face.

He has a strong face, she thought, a firm chin. She watched his long fingers on the steering wheel and shivered, remembering his touch on her bare skin.

"Cold?" he asked in response to her shudder, then grinned and patted her thigh, sliding the nylon skirt up higher.

Louella gritted her teeth, captured his hand and planted it firmly on the steering wheel. She shivered again and felt a line of perspiration on her upper lip.

"Just thinking," she said.

Cobb snorted and laughed. "About VJ Day, I'll bet. Had some kind of a time, didn't we?" When the car swerved in the ruts, he turned his face back to the road.

Louella tensed, watching dark trees speed past.

"You were all gussied up in that red dress, flirting and flinging it all at me. Couldn't ignore an invitation like that, now could I?"

Louella ducked her head and took a tighter grip on the paper sack. She had been defiant that night, trying to show Stith.... No! That wasn't being honest. She had been trying to prove to herself others were attracted, even if Stith had rejected her. That she could function without him. Well, she had functioned all right. Functioned herself right into something she regretted. If Cobb called it an invitation, then she'd better think about future actions. Apparently one man's `friendly' was another man's `flirt.' She raised her chin to fend off the words of the man beside her. She was not guardian over anyone else's mind. Just her own. But she was vulnerable to Cobb and she had to work on her defenses.

The light was stronger and the fog thinned in the tunnel of road and trees.

Learning how others thought, now that was something valuable. She had invited him, wanted someone to replace Stith, someone to love her. She'd seen other heads than hers turn when this disturbing man walked through the PX, so cool and neat in the humid air. Not at all like the other sweaty, noisy soldiers. She remembered the waitress at her first meal in the Post Exchange. She now had more in common with that brassy girl than she wished.

Suddenly aware of her surroundings, Louella said, "Stop by the mailbox just ahead, Sergeant Cobb. Here's my home." She was relieved to be ending this trip.

In the dim light the old house was shadowed by the large magnolia and persimmon trees. A few fog swirls, like gray chiffon, curled around corners. Faint light gleamed from Cora Sue's window. Good, she was already up.

Louella turned toward Cobb as he braked to a stop. "Thank you for bringing me. It saved a lot of time." She reached for the door latch.

"What about my pay?" His grin was sardonic.

"Pay? I...I didn't think you were expecting pay, but I'll be glad to chip in for gas." She was thinking of the dollar she'd saved for her sister.

"Not that. This."

He pulled her to him and pushed his mouth on hers, tongue searching. For a second he held her, hard against his chest, then he pulled at the neck of her peasant blouse, his lips moving on hers. Fingers found her nipple and circled it.

Louella felt it harden and she groaned, knees weak. With both hands she pushed him away, wrenched her mouth free and pulled at his wrist. "Stop it, Cobb! Leave me alone! You've got no call to be so free with me."

Cobb merely grinned. With a quick movement he pinioned her against the car seat, dipped his hand into her brassiere and freed her breast. His lips pulled at her nipple.

She could not move, her body gone limp. She felt the heat of desire demanding....

Finally he lifted his head, pale eyes gleaming. "Just one sip from the honey pot today. I gotta go. But we'll get together again real soon." He pulled her blouse into position with a final fondle. Reaching across her body, he opened the door and gunned the motor. "See you."

Louella went rigid, mouth open. With the realization she was free, she slid out of the car and slammed the door with all her strength.

Cobb gave her a mock salute and wheeled the Ford around in the road. It disappeared through the gray fog.

Louella bit her lip. Anger had filled the hollow of desire. Once more he had used her. How could she have made love with him that night? It certainly had not been love he felt. She drew a quivering breath through clenched teeth and whirled to stomp up the walk with steps like hammer blows. At the edge of the porch she stopped to regain her poise and adjust her blouse.

She was disgusted with her body's responses to Cobb and her weakness. He could have had what he wanted, she realized. I don't think I could have...would have stopped him.

CHAPTER XXIV

Louella's foot was on the first porch step when the door opened. Cora Sue ran across the wooden floor, face shining. "Oh, you're really early. I heard the car. Who was it brought you? I'm so excited!" Like a small child, she rose to her toes and teetered back and forth, hands clasped behind her back. Suddenly she stopped, peering closely at her sister.

Louella embraced her. How fresh and untouched she was, protected from the Cobbs of the world. Her hug tightened and Cora Sue stiffened.

"Is something wrong, Louella?"

"Wrong?"

"You look...funny...all flushed."

"Heavens, Cora Sue, I'm just glad to see you." She drew her toward the door. "Come help me put on my braid. Is papa awake?"

Up in their bedroom, it took a while to fix Louella's braids in place. In the long pier glass with its tarnished gilt trim, Louella saw the ghost of her former self. The long skirt and high neck of the rosebud dress she'd brought in the paper sack contrasted with ribbed black lisle stockings and flat slippers. Her face, scrubbed of makeup, was pale under the crown of ebony hair. Brenda is right, she thought. I can't get back into the old cocoon. I don't know who that girl in the looking glass is, but today I'll do some play-acting for Papa.

Perched on the high bed under its faded canopy, Cora Sue swung her legs. "You look just like you used to," she said cheerfully.

"Hope Papa thinks so." Louella tied on a blue apron. "Let's go see Cloteel." Armed in her old clothes, she buried thoughts of Cobb.

Downstairs Cloteel was buttering toast hot from the oven. She dropped a chunk of butter on the bowl of grits and added a cup of coffee to a chipped blue tray. "There 'tis." Then she turned and saw Louella. "Law, you looks like you never been gone," she said.

Louella hugged her mammy. "I'm starved for some of your grits," she said.

Cloteel beamed. "Now you all go on and feed your papa while I gets you all's breakfast. You ain't et yet, has you?"

"And miss your grits? 'Course not."

Carrying the tray to her father's room, Louella's heart beat faster. Would he be awake and aware? Cora Sue was close behind. When she opened the door, she saw him sitting in his old blue plaid robe in the heavy walnut rocker beside his bed, facing the window.

"I wanted to surprise you," Cora Sue said and steadied the tray for a startled Louella. "He's lots better."

He did not turn from the window, head cocked, listening.

Louella took a deep breath and set the tray on the edge of the bed. She pulled a small table close to his chair, but she did not look at him until she shook out the worn linen napkin and laid it in his lap. As she gazed at his twisted face, she swallowed hard and said, "'Morning, Papa."

"Do listen to that old mockingbird. He's been singing most of the live long night and still at it." His voice was husky and slow, his gaze still on the tree outside. "Sometimes I think mockingbirds have crazy spells. Other times there's nary a peep out of them. Why do you think that is?"

No longer did the right eye glare at Louella; the lid drooped over it. His thick steel-gray hair was long, almost to his shoulders and the stubble on his jaw had grown into a full beard. It's as though he, too, was hiding behind a disguise, Louella thought, from a life too much changed.

"I always figured mockingbirds were fun, papa," she answered. "They laugh all night long sometimes."

"Wonder what they think's so funny." He mumbled the words and fumbled with his right hand on the napkin. "Not much to laugh about in this world."

Could he feed himself, Louella wondered. She looked at her sister with the question in her eyes.

"Ready for some grits, Papa?" Cora Sue picked up the spoon from the tray. "Cloteel says they're extra fine this morning."

He waved her away. "Cora Sue, go on about your chores. Louella can do it."

With a gleam of triumph the girls smiled at each other and the younger sister slid out of the room, quietly closing the door. Louella was grateful he gave no sign anything was unusual. If memory is one of God's blessings, surely forgetfulness could be another. With each spoonful of grits her father took, Louella made a grateful prayer.

Finally he pushed her hand away. "No more."

She wiped a toast crumb from the corner of his mouth, flicking away the last of the grits from his beard. On impulse she patted him on the cheek, his heavy beard tickling her palm. "I love you, Papa," she said around a lump in her throat. All the resentment, all the anger at her father was gone. What was it Chaplain James had said? Each soul fights a lonely battle every day and you can befriend the whole world when you know that.

She knelt beside the rocker and put her arms around her father's waist, her head on his lap like a child. His trembling hand brushed her cheek, moving up to pat her head. Remembering the precarious braids, she stood, his dark eyes watching.

"Real pretty. Like your mama." He let his hand drop onto the armrest. "Tired now. Let me rest." His seemed puzzled. "You haven't been here for so long. Where was it you went? I don't remember." He leaned back against the polished walnut of the rocker, eyes closed. "But I'm glad you're home again."

Louella quietly picked up the tray, her eyes and throat burning with threatened tears. Lately she'd cried with sorrow and now it was joy, she thought. Same reaction to both. More tears.

Downstairs she set the blue tray on the round oak table in the kitchen and hugged Cloteel hard, then swung Cora Sue around the room.

"Papa welcomed me home. I'm so happy I could burst or cry or scream!"

"That's mighty happy news, honey chile." Cloteel clapped time as the girls danced, her loose bulk jiggling in waves under her purple cotton dress.

"Now, then," Louella announced as she released her sister, "we're going to celebrate. Cora Sue's going in to town for some fun today and you must have a holiday, too, Cloteel. This is a good time to visit your kinfolks. I'll take care of Papa and you both can have a good time for a change."

In thirty minutes they had finished breakfast and Cora Sue and Cloteel headed out the door. Louella watched them turn out of the gate and start down the sandy road side by side, shoes and purses under their arms. Cora Sue skipped every three steps, then slowed to a walk beside the plodding Cloteel in her battered black hat with its orange plume. Cora Sue's blue sailor straw kept slipping back on her shining braids with every skip and she straightened it with a free hand.

How wonderful I feel, Louella thought. She seated herself on the top step to enjoy the rays of sun on magnolia leaves. Snowball appeared out of the shadowy bushes batting at a grasshopper, poking it into frantic leaps with her nose.

"Home." Louella tasted the softness of the word on her tongue. She touched the wide planks of the porch beside her. Perhaps now her nightmares would be gone for good. Papa was no longer a threatening, thundering giant but a tired, weak old man who needed love, too. Strange how she'd switched from being the child to caretaker for the helpless man upstairs.

She walked down the path and began to pull dried seed heads from the marigolds that lined the brick walk. Her apron was full by the time she'd reached the mailbox. She gathered the corners together and took the load around the house to the burning barrel. Over the fence Lightning worked his jaws slowly over a mouthful of grass. She stroked his soft nose for a few minutes before re-entering the house.

The quiet inside was the silence of a good friend. In the hall she turned to the right and stepped into the parlor. The tall walnut folding doors squeaked in protest, as though they resented her. Heavy floral drapes beside the narrow windows hung like sentinels alongside drawn blinds. She could not remember when the blinds had not been drawn. Faintly through the years she heard a soft voice say, "Sun fades the carpet." Her memories of this room were of company come to call—or the preacher. Company was rare but Preacher came often, always bearing away a contribution after a long prayer.

Suddenly the room seemed oppressive, void of life. Window after window, she raised the blinds until the room glowed with morning sun. Arms behind her, fingers interlocked, she noticed the horsehair fabric on the sofa and chairs gleamed like pewter against the carved rosewood. She remembered wriggling to keep from sliding off when she was small.

The large gilt mirror over the mantel reflected green from the persimmon trees outside. But something felt wrong here. Her memory stirred again. There had not always been a mirror. Instead there had been...yes, there had been an oil portrait of her mother as a young girl in a rose colored gown, holding a magnolia blossom! If she could see it again, perhaps she could revive the memory of her mother's face. Where was it now? Who had taken it away? And why? It certainly wasn't anywhere downstairs. Perhaps the attic?

On the second floor she cracked her father's door to peer in. He was as she had left him, his eyes closed, head against the heavy rocker's back, his mouth open. Still sleeping. She eased the door closed.

At the top of the second flight of stairs she shoved twice at the smaller attic door before it opened. Three steps led up to the attic floor. Through the tiny windows under the eaves the sunshine illuminated dancing dust motes.

A baby's cradle and a trundle bed were shoved against the wall under the slanting roof. Three round-topped trunks huddled nearby, all three locked, but the painting would be too large for a trunk, she realized. Behind the trundle bed she found a stack of pictures in grimy frames. Sneezing from the dust, she wiped away cobwebs and dragged them out.

The first was a framed wedding certificate with a border of blue roses. It was dated 1925, the year before she was born. "Brent Tolbert, age 35 years...Mary Carol Lawson, age 19 years...."

She sat back on her heels to consider. Her mother had been younger than Louella was when she married Papa. And Papa was sixteen years older! Parents look so old anyhow to a child and she'd never realized the age difference. Louella could not imagine marrying anyone sixteen years older than herself. There was too much about her parents she did not know.
Maybe when Papa was stronger she would ask.

She found three framed photographs of stern-looking couples. Ancestors, probably, she thought and smiled at the strange clothing. Sour-looking old women and grumpy-looking burly men. Not knowing them in person was nothing to be sorry about, she decided.

She recognized the ornate carving on the heavy frame at the bottom of the stack. Her breath caught. At last! She carried it upside down to the small windows before she turned it over — and gasped. Slashed from top to bottom and side to side, the face was obliterated. Only flakes of flesh-colored paint remained on tattered fragments. One triangular piece curled toward her at the bottom, a hand holding a magnolia blossom.

Who had attacked it in such a murderous rage? And why? Louella shivered.

She leaned the frame against the nearest trunk and stroked the fragments into place, attempting to visualize the beautiful face she only half remembered.

Cloteel knows about this; what has she been protecting me from? I must know and I'll make her tell me as soon as she comes home, she decided. She picked up the gilded frame and carried it downstairs to the second floor. The wide, heavy frame blocked her view as she felt for each step with her foot.

Past her father's room, she started at a sound. Over her shoulder she saw his door was now open. Leaning against the doorjamb, weight propped upon a heavy gnarled cane, right hand limp at his side, he stared at her.

"What's that you have, Louella?" he demanded, waving his cane at the picture.

"It's...I don't really know what it is, Papa," she answered in a small voice. "I found it in the attic. I remembered a painting in the parlor and went looking for it." She felt like a five-year-old caught with a finger in the frosting. Hesitantly she turned the slashed painting toward him.

A long silent minute he gazed at it. He seemed to shrink in size. Finally he heaved a great sigh.

"Help me back, daughter."

Obediently, she propped the painting against the wall and guided him back to the rocker. He flopped down as though his strength had vanished, but his voice rang clear and strong when he said, "It was a long time ago. I used to hate but now...it's too late for hate." He pulled his right hand into his lap with his left. "Bring it in here, Louella. Let me see it again."

By the time she had propped the heavy frame against the bed in front of him, her heartbeat had returned to normal.

With his cane her father pushed the triangle of canvas up to reveal the hand with its blossom. "Mary Carol...."

Louella had never heard a human voice express such sadness.

"Long ago." He struggled upright. "Time now to tell you, Louella. Owe you and Cora Sue that much." He did not look away from the painting. "Too good for the likes of me. But I wanted her and she chose me in spite of her family. Hardhearted folks they were. Closed her out when we married."

Louella sank down on the rug at his feet, her arms circling knees drawn up to her chin.

"It was a hard life I gave her. But we were happy at first." He nodded to himself, then turned to Louella. "When you came along, seemed like I was so happy I'd burst of it. And she was so proud of you." He was silent, remembering. "Dressed you up fine once and took you back to see her family. She never said one word about the visit when she returned." He shook his head. "Then Cora Sue was born and your mama was happy again. Things were easier for us by then, the price of cotton was up, the weather good for growing." He stroked the head of his cane.

"Then the evangelist singer came." His shaggy eyebrows met in anger and he thumped the cane twice.

Alarmed, Louella put a calming hand on his knee, but his words poured out.

"It was at a week's camp meeting that fall. Preacher got him all the way from St. Louis. Your mama sang in the choir. Should have known something was wrong long before that week ended, but I never...." He thumped the cane again. "I never made preaching any night that whole week. A man gets too tired in the fields right at harvest time." His sigh was a groan. "But I was there the last Sunday night, sitting between you girls, listening to your mama sing a duet with him. "In the Garden," it was. Seemed like angel voices and her face just shone."

His head began to shake, a palsy that crept down to his numb hand. Louella moved to stop him, but he waved her away.

"It was next morning Doc came and told me. She'd crept out in the night and gone with the singer. Left us all without a word." The hand in his lap leapt and fell as though it had a life of its own. "They never got far, just up to the next county. Doc said his car must have stalled on the tracks. The night train came around a curve on them but there was no way the engineer could stop it in time." The right hand danced until it was captured by the left. "They brought her home again for the last time, what was left of her, and I just went crazy." Shock had paralyzed Louella's vocal cords.

For a long time he sat with bent head over his struggling hands. Finally he lifted his head and said, "Now you know what happened to your mama. Don't ever reach above you, Louella. Marry one of your own."

Louella felt his pain in her own heart as she brushed away the tears that rolled down his beard.

"I nearly went out of my head again when you ran off, Louella. I'm sorry for those terrible things I said to you, but when you left it seemed like proof I couldn't keep nobody I loved. When you came back so changed, I knew you were gone for good. Cora Sue, too, one day." He leaned his cheek against her palm. "Since I've been in this room, though, with nothing to do but think, I've realized it's your time for finding your own life, daughter. But it was soft on my heart when you came home today.

Hidden behind Louella's own tears, his face grew dim. She still could not speak.

"Louella, I need your promise now that you'll look after Cora Sue. She needs some tending yet to help her vine grow strong and not too clingy." His voice weakened. "And don't forget Cloteel. Her family and ours go back to my great-great-granddaddy. She's family, her and 'Lijah. When your mama died, it was her held us all together somehow." His head sank onto his chest.

"So tired, daughter. Be good to sleep forever soon." He silenced her move to protest with a wave of his hand, eyes on her face. "You promise?"

"I promise, Papa." She gathered his shaking hands in hers and kissed them. "I'll sit here by you, Papa. You're going to be fine and strong again." The words had come easily but she knew they were not true. "I love you, Papa."

His head relaxed against the rocker, his eyes closed and a crooked smile moved over his lips. The hands she held shook slower and slower, then stilled. His breath deepened, retreating into slumber.

Louella leaned her head against his knees. After a long time her thoughts cleared and she heard a mockingbird singing, running through his medley of songs. She smiled when she heard him mock the squeak of the barn door. She'd taught him that one herself last summer, swinging the door open and shut while he attempted pitch and imitation. There was a pause, then the bird repeated his repertoire.

Louella's eyes drooped in spite of her efforts and she yawned. It had been very early morning when she left the apartment. She was home now and Papa loved her.

A sudden change in his breathing and he stirred. A sound like a snore startled her. She released his hands and stood.

The rocker tilted backward as his head jerked and he turned toward Louella, arms thrown upright, hands stretched out. His eyes opened wide and she saw recognition in them. He caught a deep breath, a look of astonishment crossed his face, then a smile of obvious delight. The strange sound came again and his hands dropped into his lap. For an instant he quivered and she saw his eyes glaze. The shaggy head fell forward and he started to slip out of the rocker.

"Papa!"

Frantic, she tried to push her father back into his chair, which tilted forward toward the floor, his limp body sliding against her. His weight pulled her down with him, his head over her shoulder like a sleeping baby.

Terrified, she struggled to keep from being pinned under him. Scrabbling like a crab away from his chest and dangling arms, she dragged herself free, gasping.

Now he lay full length on the floor, his head against the gilt frame of her mother's portrait, his chin tipped back, glazed eyes turned upward. The torn flap with its painted hand rested on his forehead. In the crook of his arm were Louella's braids, wrenched away in her struggle.

Louella sobbed beside him, hugging herself and rocking on her knees, fear and sorrow intermingling. Her father was dead, but a long time passed before she could see clearly through her tears. A last sob shuddered through Louella as she closed his dark eyes, straightened the blue plaid robe over his nightshirt and replaced a missing slipper. But now he had no need of slippers.

She picked up her false braids and went to call Dr. Cutler. There is no need to hurry.

With his last breath her father had seen something—or someone—that startled and delighted him. Something that brought joy to a man who had not smiled for many years. Now he looked peaceful. Maybe it had eased him to tell her about the sorrow he'd carried alone.

What had been in her mother's heart and mind that last Sunday night? Had she planned to come for her daughters later when she was settled somewhere? Had the singer been like Sergeant Cobb, a magnet that pulled, until she gave herself completely?

She puzzled over her father's words: "Don't reach above yourself." What was "above"? Weren't people just people, after all? Some smarter or luckier than others, but all reaching for a dream.

She was thankful she had not denied her father and herself her last words to him. "Papa, I love you."

CHAPTER XXV

Brenda poured another cup of coffee, lit another Camel. Only three left in the pack. She should have bought another carton when she left work, damn it. Now she'd have to stretch those three until morning. In stocking feet she padded into the living room with her cup.

Kaltenborn enunciated the evening's news in his typical style, two notches below excited. Lux Theater would be next. Idly she thumbed through the movie magazine closest to hand. Clark Gable in uniform looked back at her. Damn, wouldn't it be great if he came to Seacomb Air Base? Hell, all the women in the PX would faint in rows every time he walked in. Me, too, she thought, grinning around the cigarette.

It was a surprise how much she missed Louella. Poor kid had about had it these last two months. Stith dumped her, Cobb took her cherry, then her Pa had a stroke and now he was dead. Life always does come in bunches, like grapes, she thought.

With the toes of her left foot, she rubbed the arch of her right, loosened her belt and tossed it across the back of the couch. Tonight she'd be sloppy. Eddie had gone to the NCO Club to enlist Sam, the cook, in their plans, then he would pick up Louella at her home. If she was ready to return. By that time, Brenda planned to be asleep.

She stretched and carried a bed pillow to the couch. Flopping full length, she adjusted the pillow and installed a large ashtray on her stomach, ready to enjoy Lux Radio Theater. But by the first commercial she had lost interest and wandered into the kitchen to refill her mug.

The loud knock at the door startled her and the hot coffee sloshed over her hand. Damn! Must be Eddie. She rooted around for her shoes and found them kicked into the corner.

At the second knock she shouted, "Just a damned minute!" She ran her hands over her hair, grabbed up the belt and tied it. At the third rap, she jerked the door open, annoyed.

Her husband Flint stood on the top step, his leather-billed dress hat pushed back, grinning at her. He stooped under the weight of the duffle bag slung over his shoulder, the porch light gleaming on his lieutenant's bars and a chest full of ribbons.

It took a heartbeat for Brenda to catch her breath. "My god, Flint, why didn't you let me know when you were coming." She stood back to allow him to enter, staring up at this tall man she barely knew.

"'Home is the hunter, home from the hills,' he quoted and tossed the duffle bag into the corner.

I'd forgotten he was always quoting poetry to me, Brenda thought, and it made me feel stupid because I didn't know what he was talking about nine-tenths of the time.

He held her at arm's length. "Just let me look at you for a while, baby. You're more beautiful than the dreams I had of you in all those foxholes for four damned years. How I've looked forward to this moment." He gathered her in and his kiss was long and sweet. "I love you, baby. Oh, how I love you."

Don't, Brenda thought. Please don't say you love me. That will make my decision harder than ever.

He pulled her down onto the couch beside him. "Four long, wasted years," he murmured, nuzzling her neck. "Woodhue," he said, "I remember your perfume. Some nights I would dream you were beside me so clearly that I smelled it, but when I woke up there was the same old jungle rot. First thing I'm going to buy for you is a quart of it."

Brenda felt rigid beside him. Had he really been so damned handsome? He was as tanned as saddle leather from the Pacific sun, which made his teeth gleam whiter. His hair had bleached to a rusty gold and he looked like an Arrow shirt model. She was stunned. My god, he really loved her. Had she loved him too? She squirmed, aware the thought had been in the past tense. There had been so much wartime hysteria, so many soldiers reeling out lines like "I may die, babe, so how about letting me make love one last time." So many pleading "I need a sweetheart to fight for." Dozens of her girlfriends were marrying uniforms. Had she, too, been caught in the hysteria, marrying to keep this man happy before he left for the front? Four years was too far back to remember.

Or had it been too much good sex and booze? Or the fact she was swept off her feet after years of standing on her own. What a snarled mess, Brenda thought, blinking to erase the specter of Eddie.

"Let me get you a beer, Flint," she said, sliding out of his arms. On her way to the kitchen she asked over her shoulder, "When did you get in?" Her knees were unsteady.

He followed her to the door and leaned against the wall. "Just long enough ago to get off the troop train and make it to the base. Kind of forgot where our apartment was and wandered around some." He accepted the Budweiser and circled her waist with his free hand.

He can't keep his hands off me, Brenda thought, so what am I gonna do now?

"You seem kind of nervous, honey. Aren't you happy your hunter is home from the hill?"

"Sure, Flint. Of course I am. It's just sort of sudden."

"Life is full of surprises. I'm sick of the bad ones. And I intend to enjoy the rest of our interrupted honeymoon." His kiss was beer flavored.

"Flint, we're going to have to talk."

"Lots of time for that, lovely bride." He scooped her up and carried her into the bedroom and eased her onto the bed with a kiss on the top of her head. "Lots of time for loving, lots of time for talk," he half sung, fingering the buttons at her throat. "Oh, I have great plans, honey. World geography. We're going to learn it firsthand"

Brenda gasped. All the years stuck on this South Carolina base she'd been gritting her teeth, waiting to return to New York City. "Now, Flint, honey, we'll have to talk about that, too."

As though she hadn't spoken, he went on. "Where shall we go first? Somewhere where there's been no war. Canada maybe? Start at Niagara Falls and just keep going?"

His fingers had undone the bottom button and her dress fell open.

If it had felt like adultery with Eddie that first time, suddenly it felt more like adultery with Flint. I'm really screwed up, she thought.

"Hold on, Flint," she demanded. "You're coming on too quick. Let a girl catch her breath, for god's sake. And I need another beer." She slid off the bed. "As they say in the movies, I'll just put on something more comfortable."

She closed the bathroom door behind her and leaned over the sink, staring at her face in the wavy mirror. What in hell do I do now? she wondered, the thought battering her. Maybe those wedding vows turned out to be only temporary when she made them, but how lapsed a Catholic did you have to be before you could forget what the nuns drilled into you when you were a kid? And how could she hurt Flint, who clearly loved her? Why had Flint come into her life first? Why couldn't it have been Eddie?

Trembling, she reached for the sheer nightie hanging on the door. Once she had made marriage vows with the man who waited in her bed. Four years ago—another lifetime. She sank to the stool lid to roll down her hose. He looked like any girl's dream. He still did. With a great body. And she remembered stamina. Memories of the few nights they had had and their last afternoon revived. But was it enough?

She had made a contract and a payment was due. Opening the bathroom door, Brenda accepted the cold beer bottle Flint handed her.

Eddie set Louella's cardboard suitcase down on the steps and triple rapped lightly on the apartment door. It was very late and he didn't want to wake the neighbors.

"Sure do appreciate you bringing me back," Louella said, arching her back and stretching. "Saved me a long walk, come morning."

"'S nothing."

The window remained dark and he rapped again, louder this time. An inside door opened and a sliver of pale light gleamed briefly through the curtain. He heard the inside light switch click.

"Stay where you are. I'll get the door, damn it." It was Brenda's voice but who was she talking to?

Eddie stiffened. Had someone else come into her life in the few hours he'd been away?

"Who is it?" Brenda demanded through the closed door.

"It's me and Eddie," Louella answered, stifling a yawn.

The door swung open to reveal Brenda tightening the belt of her robe. She looked rumpled, lips swollen, face flushed.

Eddie moved forward with the suitcase and Brenda placed one hand firmly on his chest and pushed him back. With a glance over her shoulder, she stepped outside and pulled the door almost closed, one hand on the knob.

"He's back," Brenda said.

Eddie stared at her, frozen in place.

"Flint's come home?" It was Louella who broke the silence.

"You got it."

"Damn it!" The words escaped Eddie with his sigh. "I hoped you'd make up your mind before then, Brenda." Her flushed face, the full lips—they swelled like that when they had made love. He pulled Brenda hard against him, dropping the suitcase.

"I won't let you go, not without a fight. You know that."

"Hush, he's coming."

Flint pulled the door wide open, ruffling his blond hair. He wore only his uniform pants without a belt. His yawn completed, he looked first at Louella, who stood in the bright light flooding from behind him. "Saaay," he grinned, "you've gotta be Louella. Right? Come on in. I've heard so much about you."

Eddie realized the light had not touched him and Flint was unaware of his presence. Should he turn and go? Certainly not. This was the enemy and he would stay to reconnoiter his opposing force. Damn it, did the guy have to be so good looking? Following Louella inside, he brushed Brenda's arm away when she tried to stop him.

Flint led Louella to the couch and stood before her, bare toes wriggling. "You don't look much like the roommate Brenda wrote me about. Too pretty."

Louella glanced at Brenda, then stared up at Flint, her mouth open in surprise.

Brenda sank down on the couch beside her and picked up Louella's hand. "She's changed a whole bunch since she came to Seacomb." Louella winced and Eddie saw Brenda relax her white-knuckled grip on her fingers.

Positioning himself directly behind Flint, near enough they would be face to face when the taller man turned, Eddie sized him up. Flint was only a couple of inches taller, but he looked like a well-honed athlete, his midriff a lean washboard. Eddie wondered about the long scar that wandered down his right shoulder toward his spine. Bayonet? Damn, the guy might be a hero, too. Whatever the odds, he'd fight for Brenda. And I've got the best reach, he thought.

Eddie spoke directly into Flint's sunburned ear. "Eddie O'Brien," he said as he thumped down Louella's suitcase.

Flint jumped and whirled in a crouch. The pupils of his eyes had dilated, his hands clenched. Eddie wondered if he had jujitsu training. Probably.

"Who the hell are you?" Flint asked as he relaxed his stance. He glanced at Louella. "Your date? A little old for you, isn't he?"

Over Flint's shoulder Eddie saw Brenda's eyes widen. "He just brought her home, for Pete's sake. Don't make a big thing out of it."

"She's just back from burying her father," Eddie growled, hoping to throw him out of balance.

Flint reddened, to Eddie's delight. "Aw, hell, I'm sorry to hear that." He reached for Louella's free hand and stroked her fingers. "It's pretty late. Maybe we'd better start fresh in the morning."

"Before I go...." Eddie spoke, then stopped. Brenda's hand had gone to her throat and she shook her head, white-faced.

Eddie ignored the unspoken plea. Pushing his garrison cap back on his forehead, he moved his feet apart. "I met Brenda two years ago. And I've asked her to marry me."

Flint turned on Brenda, who was on the edge of the couch, her hands clenched between her blue chenille knees. "Man comes back after four years sweating the Pacific and finds another guy's fouled his nest?"

Brenda leaped to her feet, mirroring Flint's stance, her eyes blazing. "What the hell do you want me to say? Damned few letters for four years and you come busting in telling me you're going to drag me all over the world, telling me a wife's got to do what her husband decides, go where he goes — and clean up after him. Well, I've had it — up to here!" She sliced the air a foot above her ruffled hair. "A girl's got rights and I don't see anybody standing up for mine. By damn, I'm stating right here and now that I'm sick of being pushed and pulled around." She sputtered to a halt. "So just quit crowding."

Brenda turned her glare onto Eddie, who already regretted the confrontation with Flint. "And you shove off! Damn it, Eddie, I told you I wasn't sure. You're not pushing me into any corner for a snap decision. I made one when I married Flint and look how that's turned out. Just beat it!"

She revolved back to Flint. "Hell, I thought you were God's answer to females that weekend in the Bronx. You're a throwback to some bull-of-the-woods who likes women barefoot and pregnant."

Flint touched her shoulders and she shrugged them off.

"Why in hell would I be different from when you met me, I wonder," Flint answered. "Nothing's happened to me but four years in a foxhole, living with gooney birds and spiders, fighting sneaky yellow-faced snipers, jungle rot and snakes. Why wouldn't I look forward to a wife who'd believe in my dreams?"

"That's the trouble right there," Brenda spat out. "Your dreams. What about my dreams? You don't even know me."

"I know I've come home to a faithless woman who's already shacked up...."

"It was not like that, Flint. Eddie's a good, decent guy and we didn't plan to fall...."

"...time the boat pulled away from the dock!"

Brenda's face was mottled with rage and Eddie caught his breath. Her hand was swift and a red welt bloomed on Flint's cheek.

Flint caught her hand and squeezed.

For a second she stood rigid, then began to bend toward the pain. She wrenched her hand away and rubbed at her wrist.

Eddie moved closer to Flint. It had been too swift to intervene but that man would never hurt Brenda again. He jerked Flint around to face him. For a long minute the two men stared at each other.

It was Louella who broke the silence. She stood up and bent to pick up her suitcase. "It's been a long day," she said. Holding the handle with both hands, she moved toward her bedroom. When no one answered, she added, "Goodnight," and closed the door.

"Men!" Brenda spat the words. "I hope to hell she got a real good look at what they're all about. Right this minute I hope I never see another pair of pants." With a stiff finger she pointed at the front door. "Out! Both of you."

"You can't throw a man out of his own apartment. Didn't you know that? Seems to me I've been taking a cut in pay all this time for your housing allowance." Flint laughed and moved away from Eddie, taunting Brenda.

Her mouth worked in anger. "You'll get every damned red cent back, you cheapskate." She stomped into her bedroom and Eddie dodged as Flint's clothing flew through the air to fall in a mound beside the chair that held his uniform jacket.

"Head for the hills! The dam just burst!" Flint was laughing harder. But Eddie saw his face sober as he bent to put on socks. He drew on his shirt and threaded his belt through the pant loops without looking at Eddie.

Still ready for a fight, Eddie dropped back to his heels, puzzled. While Flint was present, he'd not leave Brenda unprotected. Not moving from his position at the center of the room, he stood at parade rest, watching.

Fully dressed, tie adjusted, Flint looked around the room, then hoisted his duffle bag over his shoulder by its rope drawstring. Eddie heard him say softly, "Reckon this is all I came in with," and saw Flint's eyes were moist as he went through the door.

Something moved in Eddie. That Flint loved Brenda also hadn't figured in his thinking. Someone was going to be hurt. Hurt bad.

A solitary car passing outside left a deeper silence in the room now his opponent had gone. The familiar surroundings seemed to Eddie like a stage setting when the play was over.

He set the pushbutton in the doorknob and snapped off the light as he pulled the outside door closed. Curtain down. But no applause.

CHAPTER XXVI

The odors of cinnamon and yeast followed Tech Sergeant Cobb out of the bakery. He let the door slam shut behind him, balancing the heavy carton on his shoulder on the march to his car. Goddamned fat German! What in hell had he been yammering about? He dropped the box into the trunk and slammed the lid closed.

The baker's thick accent echoed even in the Ford coupe. "Nein, nein, no more yet! What for you want ruin my business? What for you spoil so much vun whole batch raisin bread yet? Sugar I ask. Mit salt I get!" His fat belly had vibrated with indignation, floured hands waving, then doubling into fists. He shook them at Cobb, who had been too astonished to say anything. "Nein, nein, take back dat stuff already. Better yet I make sweet with honey dan with salt yet!"

Furious, Cobb turned on the ignition and stomped the gas pedal. Tires skidded from the curb. How in hell did salt get into the sugar? It had to have been Swartz in the mess hall. No one else had touched the stuff. Irritably he honked at a slow car, then pulled out to pass. He cut back in sharply, forcing the driver to brake. This was not going to be one of his best days. The telephone call that morning in the booth outside the PX had started it off wrong.

"More time? What you mean more time?" He could hear the husky voice rasp in his ear again. "Two weeks left, soldier boy. That's it. Or kiss your equity money goodbye."

He had held the receiver to his ear long after the man had hung up, listening to the buzz of the dial tone before he dropped it in its cradle. Six weeks had seemed plenty of time to make the loan and get the equity. But he was perilously close to the deadline now and the bank was fiddle-farting around over the loan.

He turned onto Seacomb's main street, shifting uneasily on the car seat as he pulled over to the curb in front of the Daisy May Club. Maybe Toots would be good for a temporary loan. He couldn't expect much out of any poker games he could find. Too far from payday.

Car keys still in his hand, he stood before the Daisy May and was jarred out of his thoughts to see the door was closed. Closed? The Daisy May never closed. He blinked at the white square of paper tacked to the exact center of the red door. Lost the bakery as a customer and now something was wrong at the Daisy May.

He thought of the twenty-five pounds of ground round and the case of booze — half Southern Comfort, half Chivas Regal — in the trunk of his car. Had the MP's put the club off limits? God, that was all he needed now. He blinked again, clearing his vision enough to read:

CLOSED BY ORDER OF THE BOARD OF HEALTH

There was some gobbledygook about an ordinance number in smaller print underneath.

What the hell was he going to do with twenty-five pounds of ground meat on a hot day? He looked up and down the street, considering. Some months back he'd felt out the one grocery store in town and run into one of those hard-shelled Baptists who gave him a lecture on patriotism and the black market.

A trickle of perspiration oozed from his armpit as he turned back toward his car.

A battered white Chevrolet squealed its brakes and lurched to a halt in front of him in a fog of blue exhaust smoke. He caught a glimpse of Toots' distorted, flushed face behind the wheel. She shook a clenched fist at him.

"Now what?" he wondered.

Toots threw open the door and he leaned into the powerful odor of jasmine perfume. She grabbed his tie and jerked him into the passenger seat beside her. Her fists, like sharp-edged clods, pounded his chest with surprising strength.

Still astonished, he pinioned both her wrists. "Whoa now, Toots."

"What're you trying to do to me?" It was a shrill female echo of the fat German's voice.

"What're you talking about? And what's with the Daisy May?"

"It's all your fault, you big promoter, you!"

"Just calm down and tell me."

"You and them damned hamburgers. I knew you'd screw me up somehow." She jerked her wrists free and wrung her hands. "Last night about nine this long lanky kid comes in with an MP I recognized. The kid'd been in before. Name's Sandane but they call him Ohio. He ordered a hamburger; the MP had a beer. The MP was off duty, of course, but I recognized him even without the armband." She swallowed. "The place was full, everybody having a ball when this Ohio starts yelling, `Worms! My burger's full of worms! You trying to kill American soldiers?' And he just keeps on yelling."

"Can't be," Cobb said, stunned.

She glared at him. "Hell, you know it's kind of dark in there, but all these GIs crowd around with Zippo lighters and the MP, he's got this flashlight, and there they are. Cooked, but you could tell."

"There was who?" He had the strange illusion hair rose on her head.

"Worms, you idiot!" She beat his chest again. "You sold me spoiled meat with maggots in it!"

Numb with surprise, it was several seconds before he grabbed her fists. "That meat was fresh, right out of the NCO Club's kitchen. It's some kind of trick."

"No trick." Toots tried to pull away. "The MP made for the back room and when I looked over his shoulder, I seen them worms crawling over that meat."

Cobb tightened his grip on her wrists.

"Then he made a phone call and pretty soon there was MPs all over the place. The GIs all left when they saw Ohio's hamburger."

Cobb caught his breath. His time was running short on the loan and now this.

"This morning the Board of Health guy showed up and didn't say nothing until he nailed up that notice on the door and then he told me," Toots gulped and glared at him, "told me they may take away my license."

Well, there went the ballgame for any more ground round, Cobb realized. He released Toots and considered his options. Maybe he could get the baker back if he threw in some butter to sweeten the deal, but Toots was definitely out of the market for meat. The booze alone wouldn't meet his money deadline. His dream of being somebody was moving farther from his reach.

A strangled sound brought his attention back to the small woman beside him. She had leaned forward, head on the steering wheel, beating her knees with clenched fists.

"If they take away my license that means no place in Charleston when the war ends. Vernita's and my only chance gone — and you're the reason." She lifted a ravaged face and turned toward him. Two wet streams coursed down her pancake makeup. A black mascara tear joined the trail.

Silence boomed in the little car. Cobb saw her face change again, harden like concrete setting up. Her features sharpened, eyes narrowed into black slits, chin sliding forward. He was astonished at the raw hate that faced him, a condensation thick as tar.

"Go...to...hell!" she enunciated coldly.

He saw her utter stillness, a cat before it leaps, but there was no room to dodge before she struck. Her nails clawed five burning streaks down his cheek.

Cobb leaped out onto the sidewalk. His left hand covering the stinging wounds, he leaned on the roof, staring in at her.

The motor roared into life and the car jumped away from under his hand. Down the street it raced and turned the corner on two wheels.

Cobb realized his breath was coming too quickly. He straightened, teetering on the curb of the empty street. No time for panic. He had to think, find the money.

Back under the wheel of his Ford coupe, he drove slowly toward the NCO Club, mind racing. What was he going to do with twenty-five pounds of ground round? Of course! Old Sam was going to be real surprised how generous the Supply sergeant had been this week. Now Sam wouldn't have to stretch the hamburger meat with bread crumbs. Maybe that would stop the old guy's muttering.

But that didn't solve the equity problem. No way to touch Toots for a loan now. He'd make the weekend poker game, but that was only good for a hundred or so in the middle of the month. Tomorrow he'd scrounge some butter for the baker. Butter him up. A big batch of better batter made from the best butter. What a pitch for a sale. Better butter would make the batter better. He tried it aloud.

By the time he'd pulled into the parking lot at the NCO Club he had forgotten Toots' tirade—except for the sting of his cheek.

CHAPTER XXVII

It had been a morning of strain, like a dance around a hand grenade, nobody knew when Brenda would explode. Louella nibbled at her pencil, watching her roommate from the corner of her eye. Brenda's blonde head bent intently over her typewriter, a frown engraved between her eyebrows. Breakfast at the apartment had been silent, her face set in a grim expression that recommended no light chitchat from Louella. At the office Brenda's mood had not lightened. Once Frances peaked her eyebrows at Louella to express a question. Louella shrugged in answer.

In refuge behind his pipe, Mr. Hart's grave eyes were on his secretary every time Louella glanced his way.

After one sharp answer from Brenda, Hutch scuttled out of the office, throwing a comical grimace Louella's way. The back of his neck was red.

Noon-time. Louella laid her pencil down.

As if she had caught the thought, Brenda turned off her typewriter and pulled hat and purse out of her desk. Veil adjusted, she dropped a mirror into the center drawer and slammed it shut. "I may be late coming back. Legal business in town." Her statement brooked no inquiries.

Hart pushed the pipe stem to the other side of his mouth. "Going in to town myself. Be glad to drop you."

Brenda regarded him coolly. "Well, okay. It will save some time."

After they left, Hutch entered and ambled over to Louella's desk. "She's a thunderstorm at harvest time! What's riling her?"

"Personal problems," Louella answered, dodging the question. "Give her room."

"Sure. Okay. Well...hamburgers, anyone?" Hutch aimed the inquiry into the air midway between Louella and Frances.

They nodded simultaneously and followed him out the door.

Trailing Frances and Hutch to the lunch counter, Louella struggled with her thoughts. Maybe all men were not like Eddie and Flint or Cobb and Stith, who seemed in relentless pursuit of their own benefits without much consideration for the women close to them. Hutch seemed vulnerable and sensitive to moods, a humble, cheerful soul. And perhaps the men she was quick to judge weren't so self-sufficient either. Maybe they too were full of doubts, camouflaging feelings behind protection they'd built, like oysters around grains of sand.

Maybe it was women, after all, who were the self-sufficient ones, despite apparent fragility. Women had to have steel inside. At least Brenda shows steel, Louella thought. Not a tear last night. None today, either. "Legal business in town." The words roared in her thoughts.

They had reached the PX counter and Louella shook herself mentally and placed an order.

"I almost forgot, Louella," Hutch said suddenly. "There was a letter for you. I stuck it inside my blouse so I wouldn't forget...and I did anyhow, doggone it." He pulled out the crumpled envelope, straightened it on the counter with his big hands and pushed it her way.

It was from Stith. And this time the APO number was from the Pacific.

Louella paid for her hamburger and scooped it up with the letter. "Please excuse me. I'm...going back to the office," she said, sliding off the stool. The thin envelope with its red and blue airmail edging sped her down the hall. At her desk, she slit it open to flatten the airmail stationery with its single attached thin second sheet. Stith's handwriting was firm and clear.

"*Dear Louella,*

"It's been a while since I saw you at Seacomb. Been doing a lot of thinking. Time is all I've had since the boat left the dock. Duty is light on this island since we got the foxholes dug.

"I guess I made a bad mistake with you, Louella. I remember all those letters I wrote and all those promises made about getting married. A man is only as good as the promises he keeps and I wouldn't be much of a man if I broke mine to you.

"I must have been real crazy that day, mixed up from what I've seen and done. Thought I was telling you the straight of it, about not being good enough for you and all. That's probably still true but I won't break my word. Now I'm willing to come home, raise cotton, start plowing again, something normal. Maybe I was just meant to drag a cotton sack.

"Could you answer right away? Someone else might have come along for you. If that's happened, then I'm released from my promise and I hope you'll be happy. Don't blame yourself if you've made plans that don't include me.

"There's some scuttlebutt about points and getting out of service if you have 36 or more. Near as I can tell, I've got a lot more months than that, so maybe it won't be much longer.

"Please write as soon as you can. I have to know. – Stith"

Louella's hands shook so hard it was difficult to read the last words. She placed the thin pages flat on the desk and read them again, then closed her eyes to picture Stith's face. And failed. Dark eyes and curl of auburn hair on a wide forehead, but she had lost the essence of the man himself. How could she answer yes to a stranger, share the rest of her life with a man whose image had faded so quickly? Good looks were nice but they weren't enough to make a marriage.

But how did you ever know what it would take to have a good marriage until you were already in it? How you felt in someone's arms wasn't enough of a test, either. Cobb had sent her reeling among the stars once, and from that moment in the car she knew he could do it again easily, given the chance. But that hardly made him husband material.

The tone of Stith's letter made her uneasy. Then anger flashed. He actually offered to marry her like a man chained to a bad promise! The fourth time she read it, she realized the word love had never been mentioned.

Louella flounced away from her desk. Did he really believe she would wind up forsaken, withered on the vine if he didn't marry her? The nerve! She realized she was not sure she ever wanted to see Stith again, let alone marry him.

I've changed more than he, she thought. I'm eager to leave the piney woods for city life. Pulling cotton and scrubbing floors and pots? There were easier lives and she knew how to fend for herself.

"I've got to talk to somebody," Louella said aloud into the empty room. She refolded the letter and tucked it into her purse.

The doorknob rattled and Brenda stepped inside the office. She pulled off her black pillbox hat, her air of belligerence gone. To Louella, she seemed only sad when she dropped her hat and purse into a lower drawer.

"Well, I tried." Brenda leaned back in her chair like a figure carved from wood.

"Tried?" Louella let the word hang between them.

"Went to see a lawyer about divorcing Flint. Man seemed pretty sharp for this little burg. Convinced me he knew what he was talking about, in spite of his hush-my-mouth speech." She heaved a sigh. "Honey, there just isn't any way you can divorce a soldier in service without a big fight and lots of trouble about how long you've lived in Seacomb and all." She lit a Camel and blew out the match with a puff of smoke. "And cause for divorce. Right there he had me." Brenda slumped over her desk. "I can't prove a thing about Flint fooling around and it wouldn't take much for him to pull Eddie into it. Eddie doesn't deserve that and I won't see him getting hurt, too."

Louella had no words.

"It's not as though I'd still be in a rush to marry Eddie," Brenda continued. "Right now being single feels just fine to me.

Marry and you give a man all kinds of holds on you." She frowned and tapped her cigarette against the ashtray.

Louella could think of nothing to console her roommate.

"I'm not giving another guy license to shove me around where he wants. Not anymore. And if Flint thinks he's going to do any shoving, he's got another think coming!"

After a moment's silence Louella's thoughts were on Stith's letter again. "I've got a problem, too," she said. "It just came up."

Brenda swung her chair around to face Louella, obviously glad for a subject change. "Yeah?"

"Got a letter from Stith."

"Changed his mind, I'll bet," Brenda smirked.

"Yes, he did," Louella said, surprised at the apt guess. "Said he was all mixed up when he was here before. Wants my answer right away."

"Sure he does," Brenda said sarcastically. "I'll say this for them: We can't seem to live with or without 'em." She stabbed at the air with her cigarette, punctuating words. "For me, I'm sure as hell going to try the without part."

"You mean – Eddie hasn't a chance?"

"I need time." Brenda snubbed out the Camel viciously.

They sat in companionable silence for a full minute.

"Brenda, do you believe marriages are made in heaven?"

"Oh, hell. Religion again?" Brenda's face softened. "Sorry, honey. I do have a few beliefs myself." She cocked her head. "Made in heaven? Sure, along with thunder and lightning." She grinned. "It gets pretty confusing when we start thinking everything that happens is pre-destined, honey. Maybe Flint and I were destined all right, if you knew how hot the chemistry was that weekend in the Bronx." She picked up a pencil and doodled on her steno pad. "But for marriage? I dunno. Maybe it was supposed to be Eddie all along and I got antsy too quick." She tore off the page and wadded it into a ball. "Might be a good thing if you didn't answer Stith right away. Think about it more."

"I just wish it was over." Louella ran a hand over the surface of her linoleum desk top. "I hate to keep him wondering over there in the Pacific."

Brenda lit another Camel and snorted, her breath disrupting the spiraling smoke. "That's another male trick. Make you feel sorry for them and up comes your mothering instinct. Why must they get everything they want, the minute they want it."

"I'll think about it." But I'll make my own decision, Louella thought to herself.

It was well into afternoon before Hutch came through the hall door, both hands behind his back. He marched to Brenda's desk and held out a slender glass vase holding one long-stemmed red rose. "This was delivered to Headquarters for you and I brought it over," he said.

Brenda stopped typing and stared at the blossom. She pulled a card from the asparagus fern spray that softened the bare stem of the rose. After she read the message, she jerked the flower out and shredded it into her wastepaper basket, grim faced, and hurled the vase after it. The glass shattered against the metal basket. "Sons-of-bitches!" she snarled and ran out the door.

For a moment after she left everyone remained fixed. Then Louella rose to lean over the white card left on Brenda's desk. The message was brief.

"Brenda,

"You have to choose. Give one of us something to be thankful for by Thanksgiving Day."

No signature. Louella took a deep breath and followed Brenda, knowing she'd find her in the ladies room.

Glen Hart waited until the door closed. To Frances and Hutch he said, "It's Brenda's problem. Give her room."

"Eddie gave me the rose," Hutch gulped. "He said there'd be another every day until Thanksgiving. Dunno whether I want to deliver them or not."

Glancing at his desk calendar, Hart said, "That's only a week away. You could hand them over and then dodge."

"Thanks a whole bunch!" Hutch said.

Hart dropped his voice so Frances wouldn't hear. "How's the Cobb project coming along?"

"Eddie had a good idea," Hutch answered. "He got some maggots for Sam at the NCO Club to put in hamburger meat, except for packages he'd marked. He was pretty sure that's where Cobb's been getting the meat."

That's why the Daisy May closed, Hart realized.

"Eddie thinks it's stirred things up considerable. He's got this friend in the Military Police he's been talking to and they're doing some nosing around too. Washington is real hot about black market and Headquarters keeps nudging the MP's along."

Hart leaned back, hands behind his head. A good long jail term for Cobb would make him feel better. Be practical, he chided himself. It won't make Louella a virgin again. Lately he'd noticed a speculation on her face, a look he saw Louella turn on men who entered the office. A look that said, "How do you make love? Is it different or the same?" It was only a matter of time before a line formed. He wondered whether his wife Irene kept close tabs on June. Was there some 4F Cobb in Texas about to violate their oldest daughter? Bile rose in his mouth. He brought his thoughts back to the boy before him.

"How're you getting along with Louella?" Hart asked.

Hutch examined his hands as though they were new to him. "After you and I talked that time, I told her."

"Told her what?" Hart tried to remember their conversation about Hutch's infatuation with Louella.

"Told her I thought she was...special." Hutch turned scarlet.

"Thinking about marrying her one of these days?" Hart noticed Hutch's fingernails were gnawed.

The boy's face came up startled. "Marry!" He stuttered over the word. "For gosh sakes, I'm too young to get married." He dropped his chin and mumbled but Hart caught his words. "Gotta be able to shave every day first, for gosh sakes."

"Thought you were in love with her," Hart prodded gently.

Hutch threw him a wary glance. "Just...admire her. Well, not admire exactly. I mean she's so...pretty and all." He stretched his neck out of his collar. "When I marry...well, it takes a pretty strong girl to help run a wheat farm, you know." His face was serious. "Louella's like something in a jewelry store window. Somebody you'd just treasure, take care of; not somebody who'd help with the harvest and all."

"That's a long speech," Hart said without expression. He sighed and relaxed. Let God play God.

But it certainly would be a pleasure to rub Cobb's nose in the dirt. I want to be there at the finish, Hart thought.

CHAPTER XXVIII

Two evenings before Thanksgiving Louella announced, "Brenda, I've been thinking about Cora Sue and the holiday and all. School will be out. Would it be all right if she came to visit?" She picked up another potato to peel. "Cloteel could visit her own kinfolks. My sister's never seen the base. Doesn't even know you, except for seeing you at Pa's funeral."

"Can't imagine why we never thought of it before," Brenda said.

"I'd be glad to pay...."

"Oh, hell, honey, don't talk about money. You didn't even have to ask." She spun to face Louella, who was bent over the kitchen sink. "Damn it, Louella, I know I've been a bitch these last few days, but, hell, it's getting to be a terrible strain."

"You look thinner, too," Louella said, giving her roommate a long look.

"It's gotten so I can't think straight. Or sleep. I smoke too much." Brenda stuck her burning cigarette under the running tap water, then dropped it onto the pile of peelings. Under the bare ceiling light bulb Louella noticed her hair was dark at the roots, a first for Brenda.

"Flint's got to leave soon. His enroute furlough is about up."

Louella felt another pang of concern. It had been a long time since she'd seen a smile from her roommate. Brenda's lack of energy worried her.

"What gets me, though," Brenda continued, "is that they're together in this thing. How can they even be speaking to each other? And where the hell are they?" Brenda slumped into a dining room chair. "You'd think they'd come around, one or the other, so I could heave something at them."

"They do send the roses."

"Which Hutch now delivers to the infirmary for whoever the nurses elect Sad Sack of the day." Brenda moved to the couch, body tense, nibbling nervously at her lips. "Just the thought of the roses burns me. They're pressuring me," she said over the back of the couch. "I do miss Eddie some. He used to jolly me out of black moods. But if I was dumb enough to marry him, we'd never have a dime. He can think of too many ways to have a good time. And that all costs money." She pounded the upholstery with one fist. "On the other hand, Flint wants a cook and housekeeper and somebody in bed. `Keep 'em barefoot and pregnant.' I've heard him say it."

Louella took one look through the kitchen door at her troubled roommate and returned to her potato peeling.

"The goat believes it, too. Still and all, I meant those vows when I made them. There ought to be some way to make it work, make him listen to my needs, too."

The only sound was the clatter of the pot Louella removed from the shelf, the splatter of water over the chunks of potato as she filled it.

Brenda flung herself to her feet and strolled back into the kitchen. "Tell you what. Forget all that and let's plan something special for Cora Sue. I got this hundred-year-old Southern pound cake recipe from Barbara before she left...."

It was good to hear her roommate plan something again, Louella thought. "If you think I have lots of hair," Louella said, "wait until you get your hands on my sister's." She set the pot on to boil.

"Keep an eye on the potatoes, will you?" Louella asked as she untied her apron and tossed it over a chair. "I can't wait to tell Cora Sue the news. I'll go down to the PX and call her now."

At the gate Thanksgiving's Eve, Cora Sue looked like a small stiff statue to Louella. Her sister clutched an overnight bag. A blue sailor hat rode the coils of her brown braids above the sprinkle of amber freckles on her pale face. Approaching from behind her, Louella squeezed her waist.

Cora Sue whirled. "Oh, Louella, I'm so purely glad to see you! It all seems so strange. It took me longer than I figured, time I put Lightning out to pasture where he could eat and get to water and nobody would have to come over special to feed him and all. Time I got to the highway I'd missed the bus and had to walk the whole way and that man there said I'd have to wait and I surely thought I could have gone right in and found you. But I guess I wouldn't know just where to go and all that. You'd think I was a spy or something!"

Trembling under Louella's hands, Cora Sue had run out of breath and words simultaneously.

"No matter. You're here and it's all right."

Her sister's flat black slippers were dust covered, her black lisle stockings severe under the blue and white plaid long cotton dress with its round white collar and cuffs. Her cinnamon braids had been wound so tightly into their coronet that skin was stretched at her temples.

Louella turned to the grinning guard. "She's going to need a visitor's pass for the weekend. Do I take her to the MP's?"

"Right." The guard's lips twitched.

Louella realized he was contrasting the way they were dressed. Today she felt especially well-groomed with her new upswept hairdo — the very latest from the movie magazines — and her smart gray suit, tailored to fit by her own hand from one of Brenda's hand-me-downs. Her platform shoes — an extravagance before Pa died — were still presentable and she was well aware how the high heels called attention to her slim ankles.

By the time they had obtained the visitor's pass, it was past closing time at the PX office. Louella led the way to the housing units. Nearly dusk, the buildings around them were washed with gold from the setting sun. Laden with moisture, the air was still, the November evening unusually warm. When they reached the parade ground, a company of men stood beneath the flag at the tall silver pole. The sunlight touched metal on their uniforms, giving off sparks of gold. The bugle began to play "To the Colors" and the company snapped to salutes.

Louella halted and put down her sister's suitcase at their feet. Cora Sue's eyes grew round when Louella placed her hand over her heart, and she copied the salute. A few other khaki-clad figures froze to attention on the sidewalk ahead of them.

The old, old tradition gripped Louella by the throat. She blinked back tears while the flag slid down the pole into the hands of the two waiting soldiers. With the last notes of the bugle, the flag was folded and the men executed an about face and joined their company. At the order, the squadron marched away across the turf, the cadence of their feet a soft amen to the ceremony.

Bending over to pick up the bag again, Louella saw two tears slide down Cora Sue's cheeks. It was a reminder of her own first days on the base. "I never get used to it, either, Sister," she said. "Yonder's the chapel where they have preaching. See the white cupola? We'll go on Sunday, you and I."

Cora Sue turned her attention back from the marching men now far down the parade grounds.

"Tomorrow, though," Louella continued, "there'll be something new for all of us. We've been invited to eat turkey and dressing with the men in their mess hall."

Cora Sue's head seemed to be on a swivel. Twice she turned completely around, ogling at everything. It embarrassed Louella to watch her staring at passing uniforms. But that's exactly the way I was less than five months ago, she thought.

Again she was aware of the changes in herself. What moment do you change? she wondered. Is it this second or the next? Is it between thoughts or following actions? Cora Sue's visit to the base would change her sister, too. In some slight or maybe important ways she never would be the same again.

At the apartment's door, Cora Sue burst out, "Oh, my goodness, I've looked so much I'm plumb dizzy already!"

The door swung open to reveal Brenda's smile. Louella recognized her mixture of dismay and laughter combined when her roommate eyed the black stockings.

"I know, Brenda, and I bought her a pair of nylons yesterday."

"You did? Oh, Sister!"

Brenda laughed and reached for the overnight bag. Behind Cora Sue's back her face sobered and she whispered in Louella's ear. "A showdown. Eddie and Flint sent word."

"Well...!" Louella put her arm around her friend's waist. "Have you decided yet?"

Brenda shook her head. One way or the other, Louella knew Brenda would feel better when the choice was made.

Later Louella said to her round-eyed sister, who was seated on her bed, "Tonight we're going to the Non-Commissioned Officers Club and you'll need something special to wear." She pulled a green nylon dress from the closet. "You're about my size but shorter and there's a pair of pumps that'll fit close enough not to cripple you for life."

When they had dressed that evening, she was not prepared for Cora Sue's transformation. The green fabric brought out red glints in Cora Sue's hair and turned her eyes faintly emerald. The flush of excitement on her cheeks and Louella's soft rose lipstick brightened her features into real beauty.

Cora Sue bent again to slide her hands down her legs. "My, they feel so smooth and cool like. I do declare it's just all so pretty and I feel just like a queen, sort of." She pranced around the room, stumbling in the heels.

They both had passed Brenda's inspection when the knock sounded at the door. Brenda jumped and stiffened. "You answer it, Louella." Her hand shook as she fingered a rhinestone earbob.

But it was Hutch who ambled in, carrying two small corsage boxes. A gardenia for Louella, dusty pink carnations for Cora Sue, who had a hard time keeping still long enough for them to pin on her flowers. All four stood in a huddle deciding which shoulder and how high, when a double rap reverberated from the door.

Brenda took two backward steps and froze, an icy hand on Louella's wrist. "Don't go just yet, please?" she breathed in her ear.

It was Hutch who opened the door. Eddie and Flint stood side by side on the top step.

CHAPTER XXIX

When the door finally closed on Hutch and the two sisters, Brenda did not move from her seat on the couch. It was all Flint's and Eddie's idea and by damn they'd start it off, she vowed. For the first time she looked clearly at the two men opposite her.

Eddie looked pale. Maybe he'd had an upset stomach or something. She stifled her concern and focused on Flint, who had a defiant, chip-on-the-shoulder attitude. At least she knew her husband well enough to realize it was the way he faced most situations, like a boy with his fists cocked. Again she stifled a warm feeling.

Let them sweat a little, she decided. Uncrossing her legs, she re-crossed them the opposite way, then slid off an earbob to study the flashes of light reflected from the floor lamp beside her.

Flint cleared his throat and she looked up. He remained silent.

Eddie opened his mouth. And shut it again.

Maybe the oafs couldn't get it going. She stood up and clipped the earring back on her left lobe. "Budweiser, anybody?"

"Good," Flint and Eddie chorused.

The sound of caps being removed was sharp in the quiet. She handed them the bottles, opened one for herself and returned to the couch. Flint's throat worked as he swallowed down a third of the beer. Eddie only turned the frosty bottle in his hands, his head lowered, a dark coil of hair drooping over his forehead.

Finally Brenda gave up. "How come you haven't been around for a week? What kind of dumb conspiracy was that?

And all those stupid roses!" Angry heat began to build. Better to say nothing more. She had to remain in control.

Eddie glanced at Flint. "Even enemies negotiate," he said. "We agreed to give you some space, not put any pressure on you, Bronx. We both...."

"No pressure?" Brenda snorted. "What in hell did you think those damned roses did?"

Eddie shifted, meeting Flint's look again. "That was my idea." A mottled scarlet crept into his face. "Red roses for love, you know," he whispered.

"Sentimental sort of guy," Flint commented, revolving his Budweiser bottle as though he shaped clay between his large hands.

"Flint's got the legal claim." Eddie sounded miserable.

"Yeah, sure," Flint said. "A spur-of-the-moment wedding, a hot wartime romance. Since death didn't us part in the war, maybe we'd better think it over some, give it a little chance to breathe. Forever is a heck of a long time." The chair creaked under Flint as he moved. "So is four years apart. One thing about foxholes in the Pacific: they're great for thinking between skirmishes, thinking about what you want out of life if you live through the war."

It was the longest speech Brenda had ever heard from Flint and it shook her.

"I've got this hankering to see the rest of the world before I settle down, now I've finished Uncle Sam's tour," Flint continued.

Brenda was indignant. "You mean you want to go galloping around sightseeing while I sit home waiting on you like some goddamned slave waiting on Massa's return?"

"You could come along, you know."

She pounced. "Live out of a suitcase? Eat strange food? Pick up some foreign disease somewhere and you can't tell the doctor where it hurts in his own language?" She was appalled at the thought. "There's plenty of the United States I haven't seen yet and the natives all speak my language." Her anger had risen another notch. "How about spending some of that money you're planning to scatter all over the world to build a home and put down some roots?"

Flint mauled his beer bottle. "What's a house? Just walls and a roof. Live in one, you've lived in them all. If you're so gung-ho about a house, there's one waiting back in Wyoming for you."

"You're not going to dump me on your relatives and then take off!" She thumped herself on the chest. "You look at me like I've got WIFE branded on my forehead. Damn it, I'm me! I may have a lot of titles in a lifetime like SECRETARY and maybe someday MOTHER and MOTHER-IN-LAW, but I'm always me! BRENDA." The heat had reached the boiling point. "And you don't have the vaguest idea of who BRENDA is!"

Eddie seemed to shrink in his chair.

Flint gave her a long look of appraisal. He stopped the rolling motion of his empty bottle, holding it still between his palms. Thoughtfully he set it down beside his right foot and bent forward, hands on his thighs.

"Brenda baby, I keep hearing something under all this that says you and I made us a mistake a lot of months ago. Seems like we disagree about more than we agree on." He stood before her. "Maybe we'd better wind it up now before the fighting gets dirty and messes up the good we had once."

Brenda returned his straight gaze, putting her thumb over her lower lip. "You might as well know I went to see a lawyer in town last week."

Flint dropped his shoulders and sighed.

"Didn't seem any way I could bring off a divorce."

Flint reached for her hand and pulled her up. "I'll check it out with the legal beagles in the Provost Marshall's office. No contest; no kids. If we go together, it shouldn't be a problem."

Brenda felt a sudden letdown, realizing he had made his decision before this night. It was a mixed relief and regret. She glanced over Flint's shoulder at Eddie, who had lost his drawn look.

Suddenly she was overwhelmed with a sense of loss, of failure. She and Flint had begun their marriage with light hearts. Somewhere they had missed the way. And it hurt. The war had acted like a clothes dryer. After the heat and the tumbling, maybe you came out clean without too many wrinkles, but maybe you came out shrunken and blistered. Their marriage had not been wartime proof. A hot tear rolled down her cheek before she could touch it away.

Flint pulled her into his arms. "Aw, hell, Brenda, no tears now. We gave it a try and it just wasn't right for us. I guess I took me a wife too soon, can't imagine a city girl traipsing along with me, anyhow. Tomorrow we'll find somebody to get us untangled," he said, resting his chin on her head. "I've still got five days before I report to my next post in Texas. That's time enough to finish all the paperwork." He gave her a gentle squeeze and released her. "You're a hell of a woman, Brenda, and I wish you all the best."

Brenda snuffled, trying to dam the flood that threatened.

"It's good we're parting friends. Let's keep in touch, okay? I'd like knowing things were going well for you and – maybe Eddie?"

"Nobody...," Brenda stuttered. "I couldn't stand going through all this...twice." The last word came out in a sob.

Louella realized the evening at the NCO Club was not a complete success for Cora Sue. Her sister sat woodenly upright, slender neck turning in tiny jerks, taking in her surroundings, her mouth a prim pucker. It was obvious she felt she was in a "den of iniquity," as Preacher used to shout.

Louella waved away the first three soldiers who asked her to dance. Finally she realized Cora Sue would never relax and decided there was no use in being miserable herself. The music moved her feet beneath the table and she accepted the next man who asked.

Her partner was lithe on his feet and she picked up a new dip step from him. She did not ask his name. The good dancers didn't bother with details, only wanting someone to dance with. The band had been playing together long enough to echo the famous music of Glenn Miller. Once Louella and her partner paused at the edge of the bandstand to watch the drummer. A soldier from Massachusetts, he was drenched in sweat, his tongue at the corner of his mouth keeping time with his sticks. It was some time before she returned to the table.

Hutch looked up just as the soldier pulled out her chair. Louella caught the bunching of his jaw muscles. In amusement she realized he struggled to hold back a yawn.

Cora Sue's mouth was a tight pucker and she gave her sister an acid glance. One hand clenched her cola glass and her eyes were enormous in the candlelight.

"What time is it?" Louella asked.

Hutch peeled back his cuff. "Ten-thirty. Suppose she changed her mind about coming?" "Does that surprise you?" Louella asked.

"Maybe we ought to leave," he suggested.

"Just a few minutes more, Hutch. I haven't finished my wine." She bit her lip to hold a smile. "She probably wanted a little time alone with...whichever it turned out to be."

Hutch looked so bored that Louella gave up any thoughts that Cora Sue and he might hit it off. There was time for a single sip from her glass before another pair of spit-polished Air Corp shoes approached. He was not very tall and his face looked like fried grits. But you could never tell. Some of the homeliest ones were the best dancers.

Not this time. Through the odor of ancient garlic and cigars he counted aloud through the jitterbug. It won't last forever, she consoled herself. When their table swung into view, she saw Hutch rise, speak in Cora Sue's ear and head for the men's room. Perhaps she should go back. Louella started to speak when her partner landed his full weight on her right foot.

With a gasp she bent, unable to catch her breath. The bones felt pulverized but her pump showed only a smear of dance wax. She hobbled two steps to the wall and leaned against it, eyes closed, until the initial pain subsided. Some of Brenda's four-letter words formed on her tongue and she bit them back, waving away her partner's garlic-and-cigar scented apologies.

Leaning on the grit-faced soldier, eyes on her throbbing foot, she willed it to carry her back to the table. Sinking into her chair, she motioned the offender away and eased off her shoe. When the pain had cleared enough to restore her vision, she discovered she was alone. Hutch not back. Cora Sue gone! She stared at her sister's half-finished cola.

When the door closed behind Flint, Brenda drew a quavering breath and turned on Eddie. "Well, where's the old happy-go-lucky `New York, New York'?" Where's the guy always telling me life's for laughing and don't get solemn and nothing's worth being sad about?"

"Bronx, come off it!" Eddie replied. There was no smile. "So maybe I finally found something too important to kid about." His mouth twisted. "There's nothing funny about living without you and it scared the hell out of me." His eyes were moist. "How'd you do it, Bronx? How'd you get past the joking and the fun in bed and find something in me so deep down I can't breathe without it?"

Although he kept his voice low, his words thundered in Brenda's ears. She steeled herself against them.

"I think there for a while I tried to hate you, Bronx. Hate you because Flint came into your life first. Makes a lot of sense, doesn't it?" Eddie began to pace. "If I'd met him a couple of years ago in New York, we'd probably be buddies."

Brenda gritted her teeth. "And do I gather you two chummed around all week?"

"He left for home the morning you kicked us out. Just got back this afternoon."

"And where were you all this time?"

Eddie's green eyes narrowed. "Maybe I'm not Haaavaard educated and all that, but we'd agreed to give you some time and it wouldn't be fair...."

"Okay, okay!" Brenda jerked off an earbob and turned it under the light.

"...and I stuck with it. I may not be a gentleman born...."

Suddenly Brenda could not look at him.

"...but by God, I'm a man and a man's word is...."

He did not finish and she turned her back, hearing the squeak of the chair as he sat again. Somewhere down the street a dog barked once. A door banged.

Brenda could not sort out her feelings for Eddie. The past week had alternated from rage at him to depression, never settling into anything like normal. Yet somewhere deep down she realized she would not be content alone. Like the Chinese symbols Yang and Yin, day and night, black and white, she recognized a missing half.

She stole a glance at Eddie. His usual grin was gone. His face looked longer, corners of his mouth sagging.

"Flint's gone, Brenda, out of your life," he said. "Couldn't we just...." He leaned forward, hands clenched between his knees. The chair squeaked again when he jumped to his feet.

Her earbob clattered to the floor and bounced under the couch.

"I...I need you!"

Brenda stiffened. Sure, get me into bed and you might talk me into anything, she thought. No way today.

He caught her thought and his eyes widened. "Not like that! I mean I need you for always. I want to wake up every morning and see you asleep beside me." His hands trembled on her shoulders. "I want to be there when you're sick. And hold your head. Be there when you're happy to laugh with you." His eyes brimmed. "Build you a house somewhere in the suburbs — maybe Scarsdale — and make some kids and...." Like a crystal drop, a tear lay on his black lashes. He turned away from her.

But the word need had unlocked everything for Brenda. If no one needed you, why exist at all? A voice inside said, "Better be sure." Another answered, "You're in luck; grab it!" She gave a shuddering sigh.

"Scarsdale? That would be a long ways to commute, wouldn't it?" Her voice shook as a glow began inside that swelled higher and higher, a healing sweet peace.

Like sun from under a cloud, Eddie's grin appeared. He gave a shout that started the dog down the street barking again. Lifting her up, he swung her around. His kiss was both sweet and violent and lasted a long time.

Finally Brenda drew back to pat her hair into place. Her lips felt bruised and wonderful.

Again he grabbed her waist to swing her in a dizzy circle around the room. "I love you! This is the finest night of my life. Oh damn I'm happy!" He stopped the swing to hold her close. "My god, Bronx, we've got to celebrate!"

When he released her, she dropped to her knees beside the couch. "Where the hell did my earbob go?"

Eddie knelt beside her to kiss her again, slowly and thoroughly. "Forget the earring," he whispered into her ear and shifted against the couch, holding her close.

Brenda sagged against his chest and ran one finger around the curve of his ear. "An earring can wait," she whispered.

Louella looked up as Hutch returned to the table.

"Where's Cora Sue?" they asked in unison.

"You don't know, either?" Louella asked in alarm. "That oaf stepped on my foot and when I got back she was gone. I'll check the ladies' room."

Her shoe refused her swollen foot. To heck with it, she thought, and began an up-and-down gait towards the restrooms.

But the opened door revealed only Glodeen yawning beside a small table holding a stack of folded paper towels and a saucer of silver coins.

"Glodeen, did anyone come in just now? A young girl in a green dress?"

"Ain't been nobody for some little time now, Miz Louella. Mighty slow this evening." She rattled the dimes and quarters through black fingers. It was a skillful hint.

"Yes. Well...I'll come back and see you later, you hear?"

"Yessum." Glodeen dropped her hands back into her lap. Another yawn threatened to snap her neck.

Toes now numb, Louella hurried back to Hutch. "Where on earth could she have gone?" Worry increased. She shoved the injured foot into her pump with a grunt of pain.

"Cobb?" Hutch's gaze locked into hers.

Instantly she was up, nearly to the staircase before Hutch joined her. Together they ran up the stairs without a word. A dim light showed on the faded hall carpet under the door ahead. Hutch's rap reverberated down the corridor.

"Yeah?" Cobb's voice.

Louella threw open the door. Cobb and Cora Sue sat on the chaise lounge, his arm around her shoulders. He turned to stare at them, eyes like lake water on a cloudy day, black pupils dilated.

Cora Sue rose. "Oh, there you are, Sister. I really didn't think you'd mind, Sister."

Again Louella was struck by the fact her sister no longer had a child's body. The green dress fell softly over a woman's curves. Small firm breasts, a slim swelling of hips. The soft flush in Cora Sue's cheeks made her eyes sparkle.

"I reckon you already know Mr. Cobb—I mean Sergeant Cobb," Cora Sue continued, her flush deepening. "He told me he was the one who brought you home that time, Sister. So I felt like he's a friend of the family. And he offered to show me around this lovely old house...."

Insolently, Cobb slid his feet out, crossed them at the ankles and lit a cigarette. "How you doin', Louella? Been a while since you've been up here." He blew a perfect smoke ring and pushed a finger through it, facing Cora Sue. "Lovely girl, your little sister."

Louella took a deep uncertain breath. Fear and rage mixed in an explosion. Hands clenched, she ran across the room toward him. "You...you...!"

Hutch stepped in front of the man on the couch. Chin out, he shouted, "Get up!"

Cobb blew a second smoke ring and pushed the lighted cigarette through it, careful not to break the circle. Ignoring the stocky soldier, he turned to snub out the Lucky Strike on an ashtray.

Hutch grabbed Cobb's khaki tie, braced himself and pulled with both hands.

Cobb came to his feet, jerking at Hutch's hands. Hutch released the tie and jammed his right fist squarely into Cobb's left eye.

Louella saw a look of mingled pleasure and astonishment cross Hutch's face. He dropped his arms limply to his sides.

Both hands over her mouth, Cora Sue leaped to her feet and screamed.

Cobb staggered backward one step, legs against the faded blue brocade. In a cold fury, he regained his balance and made for Hutch. His first blow hit the pudgy body low, doubling Hutch over. The next straightened him, jerking his head upright. Hutch gave a soft moan and slid like a collapsing balloon to the floor.

Fists still cocked, Cobb maneuvered around the fallen boy. When he raised his foot to kick him, Louella grabbed his elbows from behind. "No more! Even you won't kick a man when he's down," she shouted.

Off balance on one foot, Cobb whirled on Louella and regained his equilibrium. His movement threw her against him. Instantly his face relaxed and his sardonic grin appeared. He aimed his cocked right fist at Louella's chin.

Cora Sue screamed again.

Cobb's fist lightly brushed Louella's chin, then he pulled her to him, one hand cupping her buttocks. He grabbed her hair with his free hand and jerked her head back. For a second Louella felt her neck would snap.

Then he released her, adjusted his tie into place, flicked a bit of fluff off one cuff. "The party is now over," he said in an icy voice. "You may take your fat friend home, Louella. Next time bring someone with better manners — or come alone." He did an abrupt reverse turn and left the room.

Cora Sue locked her hand on Louella's arm, her mouth a circle of dismay. "It's all Hutch's fault, Sister. Why did he hit him?"

Ignoring the question, Louella knelt beside Hutch, who rocked back and forth, holding his stomach. "Oh, Hutch, he's hurt you! Will you be all right?"

But his face was radiant. "I hit him! I really popped him a good one, didn't I? Oh, man, but that felt good!" He rubbed his right fist. A red discoloration on his jaw marked what would be a black bruise tomorrow. Fingering it gingerly, he struggled to his feet and caught his breath, but he did not lose his smile. "Boy, I'll bet he's got a shiner tomorrow, all right, boy!" Leaning on the two girls, he chuckled all the way down the staircase.

It was a silent ride in the taxi back to the guard's hut. Walking through the damp November night, a disapproving Cora Sue trailed them, registering righteous indignation. The only sound was an occasional sharp breath from Hutch.

Her arm around his waist, Louella could feel him flinch when the pain stabbed. At the apartment door, she asked, "Are you sure you don't want to see a doctor?"

"I feel great!" Hutch answered, although he winced when he touched his jaw. "I never hit anybody before."

Without a word Cora Sue disappeared through the door.

Hutch waited until it closed behind her. "I was always scared what they'd do to me. Boy, I never felt so good in my whole life!" He leaned toward Louella. "The trick is, you see, you gotta get the first lick in. Element of surprise. Learned that in Basic." He was still smiling as he walked away.

Louella entered the apartment, took her sister's arm and led her firmly to a chair.

"Louella, it was so terrible!" Cora Sue burst out. "Hutch hit him! They were fighting! And all those people were dancing and drinking and...and...and I just never had such a terrible time in all my life!" Her mouth was a pious pucker. "Mr. Cobb...Sergeant Cobb, I mean...he's such a gentleman. He kissed you, sister. Does that mean he's your boyfriend? Hutch never should have hit him...."

"Just hush, Cora Sue. You and I have to talk." At the sharp tone her sister's eyes widened.

"That Cobb...," Louella took a deep breath to gain control. "Not everybody is good, Sister, and he's...."

"But, Sister...."

"You listen to me. Nobody ever told us about men like Cobb and you aren't going to have to learn the hard way, like I did."

Cora Sue's eyes were huge as she leaned forward. "You mean he did something to you? Did he kiss you against your will? Was it like that?"

Louella gnawed her lip. Had she also been that innocent such a short time ago? She felt inadequate to go into the subject only six weeks since she'd graduated from Brenda's one-night seminar. Tomorrow she and her roommate would conduct a short class on sex education with a student body of one.

"More than that," Louella answered tersely. "Not having a mama is a disadvantage to a girl, but I reckon we'll survive. You just stay away from Cobb, you hear?"

Louella tugged for a full minute at her right pump. Her swollen instep bore a sharp red line when the shoe came loose. "Let's get some sleep now," she said, limping toward the bathroom. "Tomorrow's Thanksgiving and it'll be a full day, for sure."

Two hours later Louella was still awake beside the sleeping form of her sister, wondering where her roommate was. Which had she chosen? Or was it none?

When the outside door opened and the light switch clicked, she waited to be sure Brenda was alone, then slid out of bed and hobbled into the living room, squinting in the light.

Brenda stretched both arms toward the ceiling, her face soft. One hand dangled a red belt.

Louella whispered, "I couldn't sleep, wondering which one." Brenda lowered her arms and gave Louella a quick squeeze. "Honey, I've just gone through the worst and happiest night of my life, bar none." She sat on the couch and crossed her legs, arms spread against the back. "Lord, when those two came through the door I thought I was through with men forever! Outside of making babies, we really don't need them, you know, cuss 'em!" She gave a soft chuckle.

Louella curled her feet under her in the chair, rubbing her swollen toes.

"I almost told them both to get lost." Her eyes flashed, "Flint had made plans without talking to me. He was going to spend a year going around the world after his discharge and let me just sit and wait on his majesty until he decided to come home. If he did." Her face changed. "He's not so bad, really. We're just wrong together."

"Then it's Eddie? Oh, Brenda, I'm so happy for you." After a pause, Louella added, "So what happened?"

"Flint's going with me tomorrow to start a divorce, since there's no kids and he wants it, too."

"And Eddie?"

Brenda's face was soft. "I tried to throw him out when Flint left, and you know what?" Her eyes were round with wonder.

"He said he needed me. And that did it." Her smile grew wider. "That was the key that unlocked it for me. The question was: Did I need him? And, yeah, I guess I do. I need him needing me, if that makes sense."

Maybe the words didn't, Louella thought, but her roommate's face told it all.

Brenda yawned. "Sorry about not turning up at the NCO Club. Did Cora Sue have a good time?"

"Listen, Brenda," Louella said. "Tomorrow you've got to do something for me. That Cobb...well, Hutch and I found her up there in his office. It couldn't have been more than ten minutes, but.... Will you help me explain things to her?"

"That damned Cobb again? Well, we've got some surprises for him."

The statement puzzled Louella but before she could ask Brenda continued.

"Sure I'll talk to your sister. Might even make a career out of giving talks on sex."

"Oh, and you'll never believe this: Hutch got into a fight with Cobb. Hit him hard, right in the eye." Louella grinned in satisfaction, then sobered. "Cobb hurt Hutch, though, a lot. But Hutch is so proud. Imagine Little Brother Hutch doing something like that."

"Looks like everybody's growing up all at once, honey." Brenda covered another yawn with her hand and glanced at her watch. "Geez, it's four o'clock in the morning! Eddie and I have been driving around. Watched the moon come up over some pines somewhere. And talked and talked. It was so good to be together and too nice a night to stay inside." She moved toward the bathroom, unbuttoning her dress. "Can the rest wait until morning? I'm pooped."

For a long time Louella sat curled in the chair, thinking.

Was Cobb really so bad? What he had taken from her, was it so important? Hadn't she given it more than him stealing it?

Without the hope of Stith, being a virgin didn't mean much. She saw the flush on her sister's cheek again and curled tighter. Not yet for Cora Sue.

Cobb's kisses stirred her, of course. But they were not like Stith's that first time, being held like precious porcelain, kissed softly, gently and with love. But that Stith was gone, had died overseas in the European Theater, leaving a red-eyed stranger who talked wildly of death and evil. And now there was the Stith of the last letter, who sounded rational again. He wrote he wanted to come home to her, that he'd made a mistake. Did that mean he had changed back into the old Stith? Or could she ever trust him to be that man again?

She limped into her dark bedroom and felt for the letter by the dim light shining from the living room. Cora Sue murmured and rolled over. For a moment Louella stood still in the darkness, listening until her sister's breathing resumed its deep slow rhythm, then she returned to the couch.

The letter did not sound like the stranger in the rose garden. It echoed the old Stith.

"...Now I'm willing to come home, raise cotton, start plowing again...."

Louella sat up straight. Even if it was the old Stith, there'd come a day he'd blame her for chaining him and he'd throw the sacrifice up to her. Such a marriage couldn't possibly work.

But did she care one way or the other now? The wound had healed. There were other fish swimming in the seas around her, like Brenda said. Pretty interesting fish, with all kinds of colorful lives. Maybe she'd marry a Yankee — or not marry at all. But her dreams about babies resurfaced, little faces with reproachful brown eyes and auburn curls. Yearning for them grew as she tried to clear her thoughts.

If Chaplain James is correct about God and He is a good father, then I need His advice right now. She slid off the couch and knelt beside it, elbows on the floral fabric, her eyes closed.

"Dear God," she began in a whisper. "I'm so confused. Stith wants my answer and I don't know if I love him anymore.

Nothing's like it was before I came here. Tell me what to do, please, God. Tell me now so I can write Stith."

Motionless, she concentrated and squeezed her eyes tighter. No answer came. Aware of the silence, she heard the squeak of springs as Cora Sue moved.

I've got to decide this and I'll wait until God answers if it takes the rest of the night. "Hurry up, God. I'm waiting for You," she whispered toward the ceiling.

Minutes passed slowly. A cramp formed in her right leg. Impatiently she shifted her weight.

Music formed in her mind, a popular tune that became stronger while she struggled to concentrate on her prayer. The cramp forced her to her feet. Well, He's not going to answer me and I was silly to ask, she thought as she rubbed the cramp away. Funny how a pop tune can begin to run through your mind like that, unasked.

Irked, she limped back to her room. Lying beside Cora Sue she sighed in disappointment. Sometimes prayer didn't help. It was childish to expect God to be concerned with her problems in all His enormous universe.

Mentally she hummed along with the music in her head, then stiffened. "Do nothing 'till you hear from me...." That was the tune.

She had an answer after all. Or did she?

CHAPTER XXX

Thanksgiving Day dawned clammy and gray. Rain threatened. Without the prodding from the clock, the three girls took a long time dressing. Brenda wandered in a pink cloud, but she roused herself when it came to Cora Sue's hair.

"Ever think of doing it another way besides braids?" she asked, watching Louella brush the shining brown cascade. "How about a chignon?"

"I reckon I don't know what that is," Cora Sue replied, her voice muffled behind her hair.

"Let me give it a try," Brenda said. "I used to fix my auntie's hair like this." She fingered the tortoise shell hairpins on the bed beside the girl. "These are gorgeous. Where'd you find them?"

The Tolbert sisters looked at each other in surprise. "I don't know, actually," Louella answered. "They've been around as long as I can remember. Probably they were Mama's."

Brenda twisted Cora Sue's brown hair into heavy coils, anchoring them with the hairpins at the nape of her neck. "There now. Doesn't look half bad." Brenda stood back and cocked her head to one side. "Makes you look older, though."

"It does?" Cora Sue raced to the mirror.

"You look at least eighteen." Brenda winked at Louella.

Later, walking the three blocks to the company mess hall, Brenda watched the sisters ahead of her and smiled. Louella's customary long stride was hampered by a slight limp, her slim ankles wavering in her alligator platform shoes.

Cora Sue tipped forward, skipping an occasional step. It took Brenda a moment to realize the girl watched her own nylon-clad legs. Brenda chuckled silently. "Another pair of black lisle stockings bit the dust," she thought.

Cora Sue was half a head shorter than Louella. Her pale blue dress was too long but it was brightened by Brenda's yellow sweater on loan. Cora Sue reached up to pat her chignon, pushing it higher and securing a loose pin.

Hope to god it doesn't fall down, Brenda thought and crossed her fingers. I'll have to teach her to do it herself, but it's a shame she doesn't cut it. Was it true all your strength went to your hair? The sisters had masses of it but they weren't puny in the least.

Brenda caught the curious stares of male khaki figures lounging near the mess hall door. Hutch and Eddie leaned against the building together. Just the sight of Eddie made Brenda's heart race. Still several yards away, she could see a large bruise on Hutch's chin.

"How's my favorite boxer?" Brenda asked him as they all drew even.

Hutch flushed. "My jaw's a little sore, but I reckon I can eat turkey and dressing."

Brenda felt Eddie's arm around her waist, but she could find no words when she looked into his face. Sometimes words weren't necessary. He seemed taller today, his head thrown back, face shining from a recent shave. His black hair sprang into curls as he pulled off his garrison cap as they entered the building, tucking it under his belt with one hand, not relaxing his hold on her waist. He was establishing their relationship to his entire company, she realized.

The mess hall looked much like the other gray and white-trimmed buildings that neighbored it, although it was one-story among two-story barracks. Inside, long tables stretched with benches on each side. From open rafters hung orange and brown crepe paper streamers. Each table held a centerpiece of burnished red grapes, purple eggplants and small shining pumpkins on white cloths. The crew on KP had certainly tried, Brenda thought.

At the far end of the room behind the serving table Sergeant Tony Palermo ruled his kingdom, a white apron stretched around his girth. His grin was wide, his square face glistening with perspiration. He waved a large spoon in their direction and returned his attention to the food, barking orders at sweating GI's who scuttled at his bidding, their aprons not so pristine.

Brenda noticed two other women in the room, both very young and clinging tightly to the arms of the soldiers beside them. Probably wives here on a visit, she thought. For an instant she wondered where Flint would eat his Thanksgiving meal. Was he really thankful for the way things had turned out?

"Hungry?" Eddie asked. The trivia of the question revealed another message of love that she read in his eyes.

"Starved." The odor of turkey, onions, pumpkin pie and coffee was a sharp reminder she'd had no breakfast.

Chaplain James leaned over a table to rap once on a water glass with a spoon. "Gentlemen—and ladies who grace our meal today—let us begin with thanks to Almighty God before we celebrate this feast."

Out of the corner of her eye, Brenda saw heads bow in waves and felt Eddie's fingers seeking her own. She returned the pressure. He was one thing she was damned sure glad about this Thanksgiving Day. Now just get us out of this war, God! Let us go home to New York and my world will be perfect. And if that is a prayer, then let God hear.

At the "Amen" a line formed quickly at the serving table until Palermo roared, "Ain't you guys got no manners? Ladies first! Guys what brung gals, you come on up here. Get in line ahead of these bums."

When Brenda set her filled plate on the table beside Louella and Cora Sue, she slid down the bench to leave room for Eddie and Hutch. Hart and Monahan nodded welcome across the vegetable centerpiece. A table of friends. People she would never have met in a lifetime had there been no war. Like the Bingo cubes that tumbled in the caller's cage in the basement of

St. Anne's church back home, their numbers had popped up in her life.

"I'm impressed," she said to Eddie. "Even white tablecloths."

"Bed sheets, if you look close enough. Tony conned them out of Supply." He gestured toward the arrangement in the center of the table. "I hope we don't have to eat his vegetable centerpieces fried all next week. Promise me you won't ever fix eggplant or...or the wedding is off!"

"Scout's honor," she said with a grin, folding under two fingers and raising three.

There was a curious music ringing through the mess hall, a combination of flatware against thick china with a faint harmony of fifty people chewing and swallowing together and an overbeat of murmured voices:

"Pass the salt."

"Butter this way, please."

"Where'd the rolls go?"

Brenda could feel her own happiness, a tangible thing, a warm bubble that held her and Eddie, expanding now to include their friends. But beyond their table she sensed a kind of gray fog, a heaviness from faces placidly chewing. They're homesick today, she thought, their hearts with their families, only their bodies here. Geez, has being in love turned me into some kind of tearful softie she wondered as she sliced off another bite of turkey.

At the NCO Club office Technical Sergeant Leon Cobb poked at the plate of half cooked chicken on his plate. It took heavy pressure from his knife to slice the drumstick from the thigh. The ooze of red blood finished his appetite. He slammed down his knife and fork, grabbed up the plate and headed for Sam in the kitchen.

At the foot of the stairs, anger still rising, he caught a glimpse of himself reflected in the mirror behind the bandstand. The sight brought him to a full halt and made him wince. Beneath his left eyebrow a miniature purple thunderstorm swelled the lid almost shut. It was blackest over the bridge of his nose, fading to deep mauve at the temple. Hutch and his damned lucky punch!

Anger now trebled, he threw open the kitchen door, bouncing it off the wall with a bang. Sam's black face jerked up from the onions he was dicing, startled whites of his eyes showing. Instantly his face resumed its impassive mask.

"Sam, what the goddamned hell are you doing to my food?"

"Just fixed you fried chicken like you asked, suh." Sam's soft voice was one degree short of insolent.

Cobb shoved the plate under the black man's nose. "The stuff is raw. Bleeding. You see that?"

The dark face didn't change. "Dat's the juices, Sergeant, sir. Too much frying makes it dry...."

Cobb's violent temper grew. He heaved the plate with all his strength straight at Sam, who took one dignified step aside. The china shattered against the wall, chicken ricocheting into the sink. Mashed potatoes began a slow slide down to the floor.

"Now you clean up that mess and fix me something fit to eat!"

Sam resumed his onion chopping, unaffected by the fumes surrounding him. Without looking up he said softly, "Heard tell they's turkey and dressing in the mess halls today, suh. Reckon you might like to have pumpkin pie and all with your friends?"

"Shut your black mouth and fix my dinner before I slit your ugly gizzard!"

Cobb saw Sam's muscles bunch in his dark forearm. His hand tightened on the chef's knife he held. For a second Cobb tensed.

Sam relaxed and shrugged. "Just what you got a hankering for, Sergeant Cobb? Little bit of steak? Rare, like?"

He's laughing at my black eye, Cobb fumed. Tomorrow Sam would be gone and good riddance. Maybe he couldn't hang the insolent nigger and get away with it today, but it hadn't been too long ago he could have made an example of him. Lurid stories his father had told flashed through his memory.

Cobb drew a steadier breath. Tonight Sam was needed, since the club would be full of GI's celebrating the holiday. Tomorrow he'd have the pleasure of firing his black butt out of here.

"Fifteen minutes. I give you fifteen minutes to get me a decent meal up in the office." Cobb whirled and had reached the swinging door when Sam's words stopped him.

"Heard tell Sergeant Woods 'bout all healed up from the doctors cutting on him. You heard that, Sergeant Cobb?"

Once more Cobb felt the pinch of time running out.

By late afternoon the third day Cobb could see definite signs the color around his eye had ebbed. Probably Toots had makeup that would cover it. Now that she'd promised the Health Department no more hamburgers would be served, the Daisy May had reopened and she'd come around to half way friendly, since she needed the booze he supplied. It might take a while, but GI's would soon forget there had been trouble and be back in her place full force. There had been no mention of meat between them and he wasn't about to pull any trigger with the word hamburger.

Being cooped up three days in the NCO Club's office had made it harder to bite back words aimed at Sam. Until he saw whether Woods was really coming back so soon, he'd best get along with the black bastard. No use riling Woods now. Give it time and he'd find a legitimate reason to dump the uppity cook.

Cobb unlocked a small drawer in the desk and slid out his notebook labeled "Cobb's Cove." He leaned back against the complaining springs of his chair. Ain't it amazing, he kidded himself, what a tech sergeant could do on his pay of $117.90 a month? He laughed aloud. It would be a close fit, but he'd be able to make the balance of the loan's first payment over and above meeting the $10,000 money already sent to Florida. Then it was a matter of coming up with cash for a manager and staff until he could get untangled from the Army Air Force.

Flipping a page he ran his finger down the column of figures under "Daisy May Club." Outstanding balance $298.50. Time to collect when he delivered another case of scotch. Supply was unloading the NCO Club's booze downstairs this very minute. The scotch for Toots was already tucked away in the trunk of his car.

He caressed the account book like the flesh of a woman, his mind on the dim lights inside the Miami Beach club. Cobb's Cove. A real good name for his place. Tied in with nets and seashells and the tank of live lobsters that was the first thing you saw when you came through the door.

Maybe he'd get a girl in a mermaid costume to curl up on top of the tank and kid the customers. Might be a real good drawing card. Toots, now, she was just the right size and she'd be good at stringing suckers along. Too old. Still, if the lights were real dim....

The knock at the door startled him. He shoved the book back into the drawer and locked it away. Sliding the key into his pocket, he shouted more loudly than he'd intended, "Yeah. Who is it?"

"Me. Woods."

Oh, damn, Cobb thought, not so soon! He threw open the door.

Woods smiled at him, his pale face covered with perspiration. He leaned weakly against the door jamb. "Talked the docs into letting me convalesce back here. Convinced them

I'd heal a whole bunch faster in my usual surroundings. And they bought it!"

It was a struggle for Cobb to hide his dismay, but he managed to mumble, "Hey, that's great. Sure. Fine." He shoved down all the reasons it was not at all fine. No more girls up here. "I'll get my things out of your room," Cobb added.

"Don't bother. I'll just bed down next door in the smaller room for now. I'm not quite up to taking over just yet. They won't release me for active duty for a while." Woods stood more erect. "Got strict orders not to climb these stairs more than once a day. Climbing them this time made a believer out of me."

To have Woods cooped up on the second floor was a slight relief.

"Bring the ditty bag on up, Sam, will you?" Wood called downstairs. He moved across the threshold into the office and sat heavily in the nearest chair, turning his head to observe the room. "Damned good to be back," he said. Looking at the Betty Grable poster, he added, "See you've added a little decoration." "Yeah, well..." Cobb could not read Woods' expression. "There is that faded spot on the wallpaper and I, uh....."

Woods cocked his head to one side. "She's an orthopedist's dream, isn't she?"

Cobb flushed. Throwing big words at him, was he? He bit his lower lip.

"I mean bone doctors must wish everybody had legs that straight, right?"

Was he being condescending now, letting him know what an ortho-whatever was? Suspicious, he eyed the little man, who gazed out the window at the scarlet bougainvillea blooms. Well, give him the benefit of the doubt. "Yeah, sure," Cobb said.

At the door Sam appeared with a small duffle bag, his face a shining black moon over his white neckerchief, a jack-o-lantern grin splitting his face. "Ain't this just so fine, having Sergeant

Woods back?" Not waiting for an answer, he disappeared down the hall with the bag.

"Sam?" Woods called after him.

"Yessuh?"

"Got a hankering for some of your fried chicken."

The black moon re-appeared around the door. "You just rest yourself, Sergeant Woods. I'll bring it right on up to you, yessuh." Cobb heard Sam's descending footsteps on the stairs.

Narrowing his eyes, Cobb considered the fact that Sam would be appearing on the second floor of the club at odd moments now that Woods was back. Not such a great idea. Maybe Glodeen, being slow and stupid...well, he'd figure it out later.

"Now," said Woods, settling deeper in his chair, "tell me all about the club. Sam says the GI's have been packing the place."

Cobb sat in the chair behind the desk and pushed the club's ledger over for Woods' inspection. What else had Sam told him? Did he mention the pop inspections twice this week? He'd have to trust his own ears for the faintest hint of trouble for him. Keep Woods on the second floor and Sam in the kitchen and he'd manage this unexpected turn of events all right.

"He's beginning to squirm like a worm in hot ashes!"

Brenda was surprised at the excitement in Eddie's voice when he walked into the apartment on Sunday afternoon.

He tossed his cap onto the chair in the corner, picked her up and swung her around, then kissed her lightly and set her back down.

"Cobb you mean?"

"It's all beginning to take shape, Brenda. We'll burn him yet."

She leaned away to stare up at his face. "Yeah, but I been thinking...."

"That'll give you wrinkles." He laughed.

"He won't even know why, that it's because of what he did to Louella. He'll think it's just getting caught with the black market stuff."

Eddie pulled her closer. "But we'll know, Bronx. We'll know."

His arms were warm and she relaxed in the comfort of his embrace.

"Guy like that, he wouldn't even think Louella was any big deal. Probably collects virgins."

Brenda sucked in her breath. She pulled herself away and reached for an envelope on the side table, then pulled out the folded pink stationery. "Found out something else today," she said. "I've got an older cousin, retired and moved to Miami in Florida, place near where Cobb came from. I got to thinking about all his talk about buying a club down there. I asked Cousin Bart to sort of dig around, see what he could find out.

"He got kind of a kick out of playing detective, gave him something to do and he loves mysteries. I just got his letter today."

Eddie ignored the letter, listening.

"Seems like a few folks in Cobb's hometown remember him all right, but not happy memories. Bart said none of them would ever come right out and say anything. One guy, who works at the bank, said Cobb put in for a big loan last month. He's really buying this nightclub on the beach, a real fancy place. The guy at the bank said the seller was a syndicate-type but the loan still isn't closed."

"Syndicate?"

"Then Cousin Bart checked with friends there in Miami and there's something funny about the club, too. Seems like it's been sold a bunch of times but it always falls through at the last minute with the owners ending up with all the earnest money. Something about not getting up all the cash in time." She pulled Eddie down to the couch beside her.

"I dunno much about real estate, but Bart said the owners collected a bunch of money every time. A realtor told Bart it was all legal, but just barely. He figured the owners had found a way to milk suckers."

Eddie laid the letter beside him, dug out his lighter and a pack of Camels from his blouse pocket. He lit two and handed one to Brenda. "And this is the same place Cobb's raised mortgage money on?"

Brenda nodded. "Maybe that smart soldier found somebody smarter than he is?"

"He's found a whole bunch of them," Eddie said through a smoke ring. "Louella's friends, too." He nodded toward the second bedroom. "Where is she, anyhow?"

"Oh, she went to `preaching' as usual. Sometimes she takes off and goes home for the afternoon. I think she's going to the movies with Ohio today, but I'm not sure. We don't keep track of each other on Sundays."

"You never mentioned that before," Eddie said as he snubbed out his cigarette and reached for her, encircling her knees as she stood up. She read the spark in his eyes.

"Now, Eddie, don't get any dumb ideas. She could walk in any minute, too. Sometimes she just grabs a bite in the PX and comes on back." She tugged Eddie to his feet. "Besides, you promised to take me to see the Bette Davis movie in town."

"Oh, hell, Bronx, you and your sobby movies!" He kissed her long and lovingly, then released her. "Why not? Let's go, but bring your own handkerchief. Mine mildewed last time." As she passed him through the door, he made her a deep bow, head near his ankles. Maybe Eddie would never deck her in furs and jewels, but he sure as hell knew how to make her happy and keep life interesting.

I'm a damned lucky woman, she thought as they moved down the sidewalk to his car.

CHAPTER XXXI

That Sunday morning, after Louella shook Chaplain James' hand at the door of the chapel, she started for the Post Exchange and a sandwich. The sermon had been about resuming rightful places in the world, now the war was over and soldiers were returning home. It was growing very close to the time she must leave the base, a sobering thought.

How did one go about getting a job in a strange city? Brenda had urged her to visit the Bronx, be there for the wedding when Eddie was discharged. Somehow Louella felt she could not spare the time, that it was more urgent to find her own niche.

What to do about Cora Sue? Should she uproot her sister, take her along while she searched for work in Charleston? She rejected the idea. Better to leave her home under Cloteel's care until she found a home for all three of them — and a place for Elijah. School would not be out until May and it was only December now. Rumors flew about the base closing in January.

December. Taxes coming up on the home place — and no money to pay them. She'd just found out they hadn't been paid for the prior years and foreclosure threatened. Brenda had contacted a friend in the antique business in New York who phoned about some of the furniture. It hurt to think about selling part of her heritage. I'll just have to accept both the guilt and the money, Louella thought.

Maybe she should see a realtor, put the place on the market. But not yet. They'd best hang onto it until something came through in Charleston.

Louella crossed the street, joining men who walked toward the Post Exchange.

Sergeant Cobb leaned against the building, paring his nails. When Louella approached, he dropped the knife into his pocket. Gripping her elbow, he pulled her away from the foot traffic moving up the steps. His pale eyes were intense.

"You're just the one I was looking for," he said.

For a change, Louella thought he looked less sure of himself, more vulnerable. Like the rest of us mortals, she thought. Conscious of his lithe body, an electric charge from his hand on her elbow flowed up her arm.

Lately she had learned the power of silence. If it lasted too long it could be painful to some people. She said nothing and waited.

His eyes flickered after a moment. He released her but bent close to her ear. "Heard you're looking for a job when the base closes. I've got a friend with a place in Charleston who's hiring."

Louella held her face still but felt her heart accelerate. What kind of job? She fought her curiosity and held silent.

"Oh, come on, Lou! You still mad about the thing with your sister? You didn't really think I was going to take her, did you?" He moved to peer into her face. "Hell, she's just jail bait. I'm not that stupid." His sardonic smile was back. "That dumb kid friend of yours was just showing off and I had to put him down, don't you see?"

Although a week had passed, Louella could see a slight puffiness around his eye. The faint yellow stain strangely softened her. What could it hurt to talk about a job with this friend of his? "Come on, Lou. It's a pretty day...."

"Don't call me Lou. My name is Louella." She walked away, Cobb pacing beside her.

"I promise hands off," he pleaded, holding his palms shoulder high.

Louella stopped and faced him. "I have never believed your promises, Sergeant Cobb." She lifted her chin prepared to leave him, but her needs for the future overwhelmed her resistance.

"Call me Leon."

"I'll give you this one chance, but if you so much as...."

"I'll not lay a finger on you," he vowed again. "But I remember a time when you...."

"Sergeant Cobb!"

"Leon. I'm sorry. That just slipped out." Again he took her elbow, propelling her down the sidewalk at a faster pace. "Car's down by the gate. Let's go."

They were well down the highway towards Seacomb before he spoke again. Hunched over the wheel, he wriggled his body into a more comfortable position. Without looking at her, he asked, "What's it all about, Louella? What're your friends trying to do to me?"

Astonished at the questions, Louella stared at his blond profile. "I really don't know what you're talking about, Sergeant Cobb."

"Leon." He threw her one glance before he faced the road again. "Every time I turn around Warrant Officer O'Brien shows up for an inspection at the NCO Club. In the Daisy May I see that Corporal Hutchinson glaring at me. Donald Monahan followed me out of the bakery in town today. Hart asks questions about supplies for the club. Your friends are bugging me."

Louella's mouth dropped open. It was news to her. Or was this what Brenda had hinted about? "You're probably seeing ghosts where there aren't any. Eddie O'Brien is assigned to Supply and who knows what Headquarters orders him to do? Why shouldn't Hutch be in the Daisy May? Every other soldier on base is. I happen to know Mr. Monahan keeps sweet rolls in his room for breakfast...." When he gave her a scornful glance, she let her words trickle away. Cobb probably made it all up, anyway. Probably just paranoid. He really is a strange man, she thought.

The coupe raced down the highway past the gray shacks. Louella kept her eyes on the white square pasted to the windshield with the black letter "C" plainly visible. How had he managed to get an unlimited ration for gasoline, she wondered. Most folks had "A's" which entitled them to three gallons a month. "B's" got less than ten. The only other "C" sticker she had noticed was on Dr. Cutler's car.

She stared at Cobb's impassive face against a row of dark trees. A dangerous man, full of mystery, this Leon.

It was another mile down the road before he asked, "How'd you like a steak, good and thick, broiled just right? Little salad on the side. Nice baked potato...."

"Oh, my," she said involuntarily. "It's been a long time since I've tasted any steak...." Saliva welled and she swallowed. "Where in Seacomb can you get—"

"Trust me." Cobb smiled.

They had passed through the business section of town, when Cobb stopped the car before a white frame house. "We're here."

A small pale woman with inky black hair answered the door and smiled at them, exposing for an instant a missing incisor. "You did bring her, then," she said. "Come on in."

They walked into a living room with walls calcimined a pale lime green, which intensified the red of the plush heavy sofa and matching bulky chairs positioned on a carpet of red roses.

"So you're Louella." The woman's black eyes shone like glass. "Glad I've finally met you, honey." Over her shoulder to Cobb she added, "You're right. She is a stunner."

"Vernita not around?" Cobb asked.

"She might be here later. That Captain came by early this morning, the one with the convertible. God knows what he had in mind this time. He's a little spooky, if you ask me, but he pays her so well...." The words trailed behind her as she headed for the kitchen Louella could see beyond an arched dining room. At the threshold she turned. "What'd you like to drink, honey? Cobb'll have his usual bourbon and branch water."

"Noth...nothing for me, thanks." Louella was rigid on the sofa beside Cobb. "This is really an imposition," she hissed at him. "I really must insist you take me back to the base. To drop in for a steak like this, I surely believe it's wrong to – "

"You heard her say she had wanted to meet you," Cobb interrupted. "She's a good cook, if that's what's troubling you."

Louella ran gloved fingers around the edges of her purse and stared at the little Christmas tree on a window table. The red balls, silver tinsel and cellophane icicles were hard and bright on the glittering tree.

Silence was broken by the clatter of high heels. The woman returned with a tray holding two glasses showing ample depths of brown liquid. She splashed in water from a small pitcher and handed one to Cobb. "Mud in your eye," she said and drained half the contents of her glass.

"Yes, indeed," replied Cobb.

The small woman hitched her chair closer to the end of the sofa and leaned forward to pat Louella's knee. "Now, honey, I'm Toots and you just call me that. What my folks named me I won't repeat to nobody." Again the dark gap in her teeth appeared in a smile that did not reach her eyes. "That slob beside you don't have the manners of a goat. What's the rest of your name, honey?"

"Louella Tolbert," she said, cringing from the woman's touch.

"Nice name for a tall Southern gal. Cobb tells me you work in the PX office. What you going to do when the base closes?"

Louella squirmed. What a rude question. It was none of this stranger's business. Still it was a question everyone she met asked these days. "I really haven't decided. I hope to find a secretarial position in Charleston." She rubbed at a smudge on the first finger of her glove.

"Well, now, ain't that a coincidence!" Toots waved her glass at Cobb. "Ever hear tell of a better coincidence than that?" She turned back to Louella. "What I mean is, honey, me and Vernita, we're starting a business in Charleston. Lots of class. Real fancy. Not like the Daisy May."

Louella stiffened at the mention of the bar.

Toots finished her drink. "More like a private club. And we're going to need help."

Louella remembered things she'd heard about this woman who owned the Daisy May. She stared intently at the small figure perched on the red chair. It was a pert, wise face that looked impervious to attack. Laugh wrinkles at the corners of her eyes were deep and so were the lines that bracketed her mouth. She won't see forty again, Louella decided. That Toots had seen a lot before forty showed in her face. But somehow she felt drawn to the woman. Toots appeared to be a survivor misfortune had not drowned. If I'm going to survive, I'll have to learn some of the things she knows.

"I don't reckon I could work in a club," Louella said slowly. What would Preacher say? Probably preach a whole sermon about her.

"Not much to it, really," Toots said. "What we're looking for is somebody to greet folks at the door, show 'em to a table, that sort of thing. Somebody in a long fancy gown. Somebody to answer the phone real elegant and make reservations." Toots directed the next words to Cobb. "Found a guy who'll handle taxes and paperwork." To Louella she continued, "Maybe you'd sit with some lonesome salesman from out of town once in a while, you know." Her face with its black marble eyes was a mask. "Nothing else, honey. Some of these guys, they travel a lot and just want to have a pretty girl to talk to for a little while."

Toots looked at Cobb and there was a flow of silent communication between them Louella could not read. She stripped off her left glove and kneaded it into a tight roll. She needed a job— and soon. Taxes had to be paid before the state claimed the home place and there were three hungry mouths.... Charleston, South Carolina had been her own choice. Maybe it would be all right. Just until she could find a real office job. "I...I've been making $36.50 a month since my raise," she said tentatively and was startled by the sudden laughter from the other two.

Cobb straightened his face. "Big deal!"

"Some of these guys will give you a tip bigger than that." Toots regained her composure and wiped her eyes. "Vernita and me could start you at thirty-five and whatever you got in tips would be your own. And Uncle Sam don't need to know nothing about that part, either."

A tip bigger than a whole month's salary? How rich those lonesome men must be. Would it be different than having coffee in the PX with some of the soldiers on the base? She could sure use that money.

"Take a little time and think about it, honey. No hurry. Vernita's going to Charleston Monday and the club won't open for another three weeks." She picked up tray and empty glasses and headed for the kitchen. Over her shoulder she said, "I figure on opening New Year's Eve with a big bash. After we eat, I'll show you the ads. Real showy place. Gotta bunch of girls lined up for the stable that'll knock your eyes out, too."

Cobb's head jerked toward Louella. Was he watching her for some reaction, Louella wondered? Toots had said stable? Would those girls be dressed like jockeys, then? Or would there be actual horses? Louella realized this was another world and she knew nothing about it.

All Cobb said was, "Let's eat." In the dining room he pulled out a chair for her.

The smell of the cooking meat made Louella's mouth water. She pushed back her qualms. I'm not obligated if I eat a steak, she thought. It's already cooked and shouldn't be wasted. And I don't have to decide right this minute. But a tip as big as a whole month's salary!

On the way back to the base Louella was quiet, struggling with the decisions that faced her. For five miles Cobb said nothing, then he half turned toward her. "See, that wasn't so bad, now was it?" Louella did not reply.

"I mean you and me. Half the time I get the feeling you wish I'd drop dead and the other half...well, you don't do a very good job hiding it when you've got a little yen to...."

"I do not!"

"Come on. Who you trying to kid?" He grinned, concentrating now on the highway. "Probably all that religious garbage you were weaned on keeps you from having a real good time." After a moment he continued above the singing of the tires. "We might even be good together, you know. One day real soon I'm going to be a pretty important man, owner of the best club in Miami and I'd rather have you work for me instead of Toots."

"I...what?"

"Be a team. Guess you wouldn't mind being hitched to a rich man, would you?"

"Hitched?"

"Yeah. Maybe permanent."

"M-marriage?" Was this a proposal or a proposition?

"Wouldn't mind having your shoes under my bed. Before or after, what's the difference?"

"Sergeant Cobb!"

"Leon." He put his hand on her left knee and she jerked it away. "Don't get sore. Why is it women set so much store on that one piece of paper?"

Louella clamped her jaw shut. No law said she had to answer. When he pulled to the curb in front of the apartment, she jumped out quickly before he could shift into neutral and make a move in her direction. She slammed the door and stood for a moment with her hands on the window's edge. After all, he had taken her for a job interview. Sort of. And a steak.

"I...I appreciate your taking me to see Mrs. Toots," she said. "I'll let her know what I decide."

"What about my offer?"

"To put my shoes...."

"Okay, okay. If a gold ring means that much...."

But Louella did not wait to hear the rest. She ran up the steps and into the apartment. Another attempt to use her? Well, two could play at that game and she had responsibilities to three innocent others.

But a rich man's wife? Wouldn't that be something!

CHAPTER XXXII

Louella tacked the last strand of twisted green crepe paper to the opposite wall and crawled down from the wobbling dining room table. "Beginning to look a lot like Christmas in here, Brenda," she said, hugging her roommate. "It's not too much against your religion, is it?"

"Christmas decorations are pretty, honey, and some Jews have decorated trees, too. They call them Hanukkah bushes. Don't worry about it." Brenda stuck another small branch of holly into the flat-sided potato and stood back to admire the centerpiece. "Where'd you get the idea for using a potato as a base, Louella?"

"We've done that ever since I was a little thing. Something about the potato keeps the green stuff fresh a long time. At least until Christmas. And that'll be our Christmas tree, since we don't have room for a big one."

"I never saw a holly Christmas tree before I came south." Brenda winced and stuck a finger in her mouth. "Damned things stab you to death. I miss the smell of evergreens."

"Next time I'm home, I'll bring some pine boughs," Louella promised.

When the rap at the door sounded, Louella was closest to answer it. Hutch stood on the step, sack in one hand, a V-mail letter in the other.

"Hey. Somebody sent word I had a package and when I stopped by the mail room, there was a letter for you, too." He pushed it into Louella's hand.

The handwriting made Louella tingle. Odd, she thought. If I don't love Stith, why do I feel this way just seeing his letter? She laid it on the table.

Hutch handed the sack to Brenda. "Thought you two would like some of what my folks sent in my Christmas package.

They've got a couple big pecan trees on the place and this is a good year for them."

"Great honk!" Brenda exclaimed. "I've been hoarding sugar and now we can make Christmas cookies. Sit down, Hutch; you can help crack 'em." She rummaged in the kitchen drawer. "But what can we use for that? No hammer. No nothing."

"I thought of that," Hutch said. "Picked up the last nut cracker at the dime store in town."

Louella finished the miniature holly Christmas tree while Brenda assembled cookie ingredients. Her thoughts on the letter, Louella gasped as she pricked a finger, tasting the coppery flavor of blood. The other two were deep in conversation, so she picked up the envelope and entered the privacy of her own room.

Dropping onto her bed, she opened the single thin sheet.

"Dear Louella,

"I haven't heard from you since I wrote from the island. Tomorrow I board ship. They added up my points and the total was way over thirty-six. So I'm coming home. Maybe not hearing from you means you've made plans with someone else, but I've got to see you. Give me that—even if it's the last time. I'm not asking for more than this one visit. If that's the way you want it."

His signature wavered. Perhaps his hand slipped at just that moment.

Louella wondered what paths the letter had followed to reach her. From what strange port had it been mailed? Had it flown part way or all the way? The envelope in her hand had been places she would never see. It seemed to have a life of its own.

Leaning back into her pillow, Louella closed her eyes. Stith's face appeared in her mind, smiling warm brown eyes under a stubborn lock of auburn hair that fell across his brow. Rubbing her eyes, she wiped away the picture.

Stretched full length on the bed, hands behind her head, she stared at the water stain on the ceiling which looked like a flying pig. Knowing that the decisions she soon would make would shape the rest of her life was alarming. Whichever road she chose, it would never again meet other possible roads.

Two decisions, really. There was Stith. And there was what to do when the base closed. The second hung on the first. If she decided to pick up the threads of her life with Stith, then the second choice was already made. But Stith was a stranger now.

Louella realized she was not ready to give up her future to any man, whether she loved him or not. And love was still a question as far as Stith was concerned. Something pulled deep inside when she thought of him—but which `him' was it? Certainly not the red-eyed man she'd seen last. Maybe not the sweet boy who'd asked her to wait an eon ago. She did not want a sweet boy for a husband but a grown man who met life head on. Such a man would father her children, and for such a man she was willing to wait.

Cobb's face emerged to obscure the flying pig on the ceiling, a disturbing smile in his pale-water eyes. Cobb took life head on, chose what he wanted and cast everything and everyone else aside. Such a man could wind up millionaire, deadbeat or convict. Probably a rich man. If it's wealth I want, I'd better latch onto him. He'd half offered marriage already...if she could trust his words.

But is money what I want? Certainly she needed more than she had right now. It was hard to think about riches, since she'd never had any, except for Uncle Sam's paycheck, a kind of skimmed-milk riches. It might be nice never to worry again about expenses, about the care of Cora Sue, Cloteel and Elijah.

A light breeze from the open window moved across her body. The memory of Cobb's touch made Louella tingle. Defensively, she rolled into a tight ball, then sprang up from the bed. That wasn't love. But it had its own glory, still. The thought of being his wife made her sigh. Then she grinned.

Married to him she wouldn't need shoes; she'd never be out of bed.

Louella picked up a brush and stroked her hair. Brushing had always soothed her. Her first memories of Cloteel were her soft voice and the bristles moving gently over her scalp.

Quit skating around the issue, she ordered herself. If only Stith were a strong man, how proud she would be to match her future with his. The brush bit down and his face vanished again. I don't know him anymore, she thought, but I do know I can manage without him or any other man to shape my life. Suddenly confident, she dropped the brush.

Right or wrong, I'll make my own decisions. And the first one is to see Stith face-to-face. She owed him that much. The sweet boy who wove the grass ring was a pleasant dream from her childhood, a part of her growing up. Somewhere a strong man waited who would take the place of that dream.

As to getting work in Charleston, since the employment agency she had contacted by letter had no offers, it seemed logical to go along with Toots' job. She could spend daylight hours hunting for an office position and have the income she needed right now. On the other hand, Cobb's offer for his club in Miami rang false. Probably another way of making a pass, she thought.

But she shivered once, wondering where the road she chose would lead.

Leaning against the door jamb in the dining room, she announced to Hutch and Brenda, "I've got some news for you two."

Brenda held a yellow bowl against her waist, stirring its contents. Her wooden spoon stilled. Hutch laid down his nut cracker and gave her full attention.

Suddenly anxious about their reactions, Louella fumbled with the belt of her dress, twisting it around, then back into place.

"Um, Brenda," she said, breathless, "do you reckon your uncle in ladies wear would let me buy some evening gowns? Long ones...."

"Sure, honey. But what...?"

"I found this job in Charleston that pays well and I'll need them."

"What kind of job?" Brenda's voice had sharpened. The wooden spoon had not moved.

"Well, I'll greet folks at the door, show them to their tables and all like that. Make them welcome. You know."

Visibly Brenda relaxed. "A restaurant?" She began to stir.

Louella's heart beat twice before she answered. "Not exactly." The clatter of the bowl when Brenda thumped it down on the table startled her.

"Then what exactly?"

"Well, it's a private club, like. Lots of class."

"`Lots of class'? That's not the way you talk, Louella."

Brenda wiped her hands on her red apron, leaving white flour smudges. "Who offered you this wonderful job?"

"Her name is Toots." Louella threw back her head and faced them squarely. "And it's going to be real nice, she said. She and her partner Vernita, well, they made money during the war with the Daisy May Club and they're going to have this fine place in Charleston...."

"Whore house!" The words burst from Hutch, who blushed a fiery red.

Louella was shocked. "Oh, my, no, Hutch! No, no. It's going to have a big band and everything." She swallowed. This was not going well. "And all I'd have to do is seat folks." Might as well tell it all. "And maybe sometimes sit with some lonesome guy who just wanted to talk."

"Uh, huh, sure." Brenda's voice was sarcastic. "How dumb can you get? Haven't I taught you anything?"

"But Toots said some of those fellows would give a tip bigger than my whole month's salary just for talking with them. And you know I need the money. I couldn't make that much working in an office, although I do plan on looking for an office job in the daytimes. It's only temporary, you see." She raised her chin. "Besides, we're going to sell the home place as soon as Cora Sue graduates. Then we'll have enough money for a long time."

"Louella, I...uh, I've got some saved and until you sell your place, why don't I just...." Hutch's face had toned down to a mottled flush.

Her pride touched, Louella lifted her chin. "You're very sweet to offer, Hutch, but I couldn't take anything from you. We'll manage. It'll only be a short time."

Brenda beat the contents of the yellow bowl furiously. "How'd you meet this Toots? You go in the Daisy May?"

"Of course not!" The idea shocked Louella. "Sergeant Cobb...well, he took me to her house in town Sunday after preaching."

Brenda glared at her as she dropped the bowl onto the kitchen counter. "Cobb again. Cobb forever! Why'n hell can't you stay away from a snake like him?"

"Do you really think he's evil?" Louella asked. "He's a strange man, for sure, but there's something...well, something that's sort of...well, magnetic."

"Yeah," Brenda said, "and you spell it s-e-x."

Hutch's ears blossomed redder and he picked up the nut cracker and went back to work on the pecans.

Louella laughed. "Oh, now, you two. Let's don't get so serious. Maybe something else will turn up." She pulled up a chair beside Hutch and began to pick out nut meats into a cup. Intent on her work, after a while she said, "That was a letter from Stith that Hutch brought me."

"Oh?" Brenda's voice was softer. The odors of the spices she added to the bowl filled the whole apartment.

"He's on his way home and wants to see me."

"That's nice," Hutch said. "That's real nice!"

Louella frowned at a stubborn bit of meat lodged in a shell.

"I'll meet his train, even though I don't want to."

"Aw, now, Louella...."

"Who needs him, Hutch? I can make my own way." Louella tossed the curls back from her face. "Besides, there's lots more fish in the sea." She grinned at the boy beside her. "Maybe I'll marry you, little brother Hutch. How'd you like that?"

To her surprise he had turned a sick white, his round cheeks sagging.

"Oh, don't you worry," she hurried on. "I was just funning you." Poking at the nutshell, she added, "I probably won't ever marry, anyhow. Who needs a man?"

"Hurry up with those nuts, you two." Louella was surprised by the anger in Brenda's voice.

Hutch lifted his left wrist and peered at his watch, red spots in his blanched cheeks. "Time for me to go." He stumbled to his feet and shook a piece of pecan shell from his khaki tie. "Brenda, would you save a cookie or two for me? I forgot about having to do something this morning...."

Puzzled, Louella closed the door behind him. "That was awful sudden," she said.

"Louella, sometimes you can be so dumb! That was plain cruel of you to tease him like that."

"What?"

"That boy's so crazy about you he can't see daylight."

Louella's jaw dropped, shame flowing through her. She remembered Hutch's face on VJ Day when she had kissed him on impulse. Little brother Hutch. Only he didn't think of her as a sister. She fingered the nut cracker, then lowered her head onto her hands at the table. "I never knew. I swear to you, Brenda. Whatever shall I do? Apologize?"

Brenda bent over the oven. The sour smell of gas filled the apartment for an instant before the flames popped. "Best you can do now is never mention it again. Leave him his pride."

For a time there was only silence broken by the sounds of Brenda using an empty beer bottle as a substitute rolling pin on the cookie dough, plus the tiny plunk of nut meats into the cup.

Louella struggled with embarrassment. Her affection for Hutch was as deep as her love for her sister and she ached to retract her careless words. She had almost filled the cup when Brenda spoke.

"About that job in Charleston. I knew a girl back home took a job like that. Wasn't long before she decided to make some of the big money the girls upstairs got." Brenda sank onto a chair beside Louella and took her left hand. "Saw her once after that, about five years later. God, I almost didn't recognize her. The dew was sure off the rose by then. She looked harder than chrome-plated steel." Brenda's grip tightened on Louella's hand.

"It was her eyes I remember most. They were so empty. Like they'd seen so much, they couldn't bear to look any more." A tear rolled down Brenda's cheek. "I couldn't stand it if something like that happened with you, honey." She jerked her red apron up to blot her face.

"Goddamn it, Louella, now look at what you made me do. Me that never cries about anything. Ever." Brenda smoothed the apron over her lap. "You'll unhinge me yet. Guess you take the place of all those snot-nosed kids I haven't had yet." Brenda grinned. "Now. Let's get these cookies finished and you think about what I've said, damn it!"

CHAPTER XXXIII

Glen Hart carefully aligned the single sheet of paper with the corners of his desk, smoothing his hands over it. One piece of paper and it all came to an end. One single sheet of Army directive, like a thousand others that had moved across his desk in the last four years. He read it again.

"Effective 0600 Monday, 31 December 1945, the Post Exchange will close. All existing stock, fixtures and supplies, including office and kitchen equipment, will be transported by truck to the Post Exchange at Barksdale Field, Shreveport, Louisiana. Move to be accomplished by Seacomb personnel under the direction of Major Ben T. Williams."

"And a Happy New Year to you, too," Hart said softly. Why on earth were they shipping it all to Barksdale? There were closer permanent bases. He shrugged. DO IT THE HARD WAY was the unwritten motto around here.

Directive in hand, he shoved his big frame up from his chair to search for Donald Monahan. Better to tell the office staff later.

The end of the war had brought on a flurry of buying from anxious GI's, stocking up on scarce items unavailable to civilians. Nylons and cigarettes from the PX. Butter and sugar from the Commissary. GI leather shoes beat the plastic-and-cardboard footwear off base. He would have to maintain enough stock to keep GI's happy and not leave too much to be hauled off to Barksdale Field, the country club of the Air Corp. Maybe it wouldn't matter in the long run, but he liked to leave things neat.

He found Monahan bent behind the hosiery counter, lifting lids on boxes and muttering to himself. Beside him a skinny girl clerk bit her fingernails, anxiety apparent. Hart had reached hearing distance when Monahan raised up and faced her.

"And now, me darling, would you be admitting how many pairs of nylons followed you home all by themselves?" Monahan's white eyebrows peaked at the girl, now visibly shaking.

"Swear to God it was just the one pair, Mr. Monahan. Just one pair. For Mom's birthday, it was." She clenched her hands together.

"Your Mom's birthday, indeed!" The eyebrows bristled.

"That'll be coming out of your paycheck, indeed."

The girl ducked her head and nodded.

"Thieving's not for a young thing like you, my darling." Monahan's face changed as he caught sight of Hart over her shoulder. "Let this be a lesson to you. No thieving allowed by Donald Monahan or else you'll be sternly disciplined. Sternly!" Monahan turned away from the relieved clerk and joined Hart.

"Time for a cup of coffee?" Hart asked, hiding a smile.

Monahan glanced around his domain. "A fast one." On the walk to the lunch counter he dropped his voice. "They're just kids, you know. And there's that temptation of nylons they're handling all day long. Nylons civilians can't get without standing in line for hours...and maybe not then." He was almost running to keep up with Hart's strides and the big man slowed down. "She's a good kid and it caught her at the weak moment. She won't do it again."

"At least she won't have much time left for it," Hart said.

Monahan's bushy eyebrows shot up. "You weren't suggesting I fire the poor child.... Aha! It's something you've heard!"

"As of 31 December it's all just a memory, friend." Hart handed over the directive.

"As soon as that!"

After the waitress set their coffee mugs down and walked away, Hart continued. "Heard from the Ford Motor Company, myself. They're expanding dealerships, gearing up for automobiles again. I've been offered my old franchise."

"Congratulations!"

"And I congratulate you, too, Donald, on your new position with the Ford Motor Company." They grinned at each other.

Hart felt a wave of warmth for the little man beside him. He knew without a doubt that his wife and daughter would welcome him. Stirring his coffee, he asked, "So I suppose you'll be heading to California soon to get your sister ready for the move. Maybe you'd like to come to Texas with me first, look the place over. Find a house."

"Aye. And meet your fine family as well." Monahan pushed his empty mug aside. "Right this minute I'd best get back to me chores. It's busy I'll be until then."

"Don't sweat it too much, Donald. Now it's official, the Air Corp will pick up the pieces."

"But first we must see the boys have a fine Christmas," Monahan replied, dropping a nickel on the counter for the coffee. He hurried away, heading for a clerk who was signaling him.

Taking his time, Hart finished a second cup before he returned to the office. Time to make the announcement. When he entered the room, Frances was center stage, her brown face animated.

"...and he's on his way! Ship landed yesterday. Charlie called me as soon as he found a phone and he'll be here this afternoon! We're leaving Seacomb tomorrow!" She threw her arms up, her wiry body stretching toward the ceiling, prancing in her sensible shoes. "He's coming back! We're going home. To the desert!"

"Now who on earth could she be talking about?" Hart asked with a grin. "Looks like we're going to have to fire her. Brenda, I think you'd better make out a termination report and final paycheck request."

Frances whirled and hugged his arm. "I am going to miss you. You've been great." Her voice dropped to practical tones. "I might have to work for a little longer, until we get everything going again. Could you write me a letter of recommendation?

Muroc Air Base is only about twenty miles from our place...."

"Be glad to." Hart turned toward his desk. "Bring your notebook, Brenda, and we'll do it right now for everybody before we get churned up in closing this office."

His words did not sink in immediately but, as he had expected, Brenda was the first to react. "Close the office?" she asked.

Eyes wide, Louella moved closer to her roommate.

"December 31st. New Year's Eve."

"Why, that's...that's only two weeks away! Great honk!"

The door popped open and Hutch hurried in. "They're closing the base! I just heard it at Headquarters. The last day of December." He stopped for breath. "There'll be a cadre or two left to wind it down and I'm being transferred to Headquarters the day after Christmas!"

"Well, this is certainly news day," Hart commented.

Brenda smacked her forehead. "I just realized!"

"What?" Louella asked in alarm.

All that damned packing! God, I hate moving!" Brenda tucked a pencil behind her ear. "Maybe I'll set a match to it and walk out." She turned to Hutch. "Didn't hear any news about Eddie's assignment, did you?"

Hutch pursed his lips. "What'll you give me?"

"A rap in the mouth if you don't speak up."

"Okay, you scared me," Hutch said in mock terror. "He's heading up the Supply cadre."

"Great! Maybe I can still camp out here after they turn off the lights and water until he ships out. I sure as hell wish he wasn't in what they call a `necessary' category. Another month and they can't hang onto him, anyway. I hope."

"What about you?" Hart asked Louella.

She ran a fingertip around Brenda's desk top. "Oh, I...plan to go to Charleston and take a job. Got an offer I'm considering." Hart saw her exchange an odd look with Brenda.

"Later I'll sell the home place, if anybody wants it, and move Cora Sue and Cloteel up there, too." She was still looking at Brenda. "I wrote another employment agency last week and they sent me an application. It's in the mail to them now." Her lack of enthusiasm puzzled Hart.

"I reckon I can't tell you how much I'm going to miss all of you."

Hart caught a glisten of tears as she dropped her head. "Now, none of that," he said briskly. "We've got another two weeks and we'll save the farewells for the big party."

"Which one?" Brenda asked.

"You were thinking of more than one?" Hart asked.

"We've got to give Frances and her Charlie a good send-off tonight, you know."

"Of course."

"Our place. Eight o'clock," Brenda said.

"Now Charlie can meet all the people I've written him about," Frances said, beaming.

"What'll we bring?" Hutch asked.

"Nothing. We'll give you the privilege of chipping in when we figure the cost later." Brenda picked the pencil from behind her ear and waggled her notebook at Hart.

He sat at his desk, locked his hands behind his head. "To Whom It May Concern," he said. "Frances Maynard has been an employee of this office for the last...."

Another part of Hart's brain was recording how sorry he was it was ending. It felt like a death in his family. How long would it be, he wondered, before they all faded from his thoughts.

It was the 23rd of December when Stith reached Louella on the office telephone. His voice was faint under loud static and she shoved the receiver closer to her ear.

"What? I can't hear you."

"...coming...train on Christmas Eve...Columbia...please..."

"You're coming by train from Charlotte on Christmas Eve?" Louella was conscious of Brenda and Hart listening. "What time?"

Static covered his answer and she gave up. "Never mind. I can find out the train schedule. But I already have plans for Christmas Eve. I don't know...."

There was a garble of atmospheric interference and then a single word of his: "Please...."

"I can't promise, Stith. Maybe. I'll see. I have to go now." She replaced the receiver in its cradle.

"That was Stith, of course," Brenda said.

He wants me to meet him." Louella kept her attention on the telephone. "I really don't know." She shook back curls from her face. "I've changed so much I really don't think we have anything in common anymore." She turned toward Brenda. "You said it once: You can't go back."

Hart stirred in his chair. "Maybe he's changed, too, Louella."

"He has. Now he's a stranger to me." Louella moved to the coffeepot and filled her mug. "It's getting strange around here, too," she commented, stirring sugar in the brew with the office's community spoon. "I miss Frances. Lots of faces gone already. The empty barracks stare at me on the way to the apartment. It's spooky." She laid the spoon beside the tarnished coffeepot.

"Be a ghost town soon," Hart replied. "You've got to expect spooks."

Brenda changed the subject abruptly. "Been thinking about that gross of nylons that arrived too late and — well, instead of shipping them on to Barksdale, how about if Eddie and I bought 'em at the PX price?" She revolved a pencil, her face serious. "Uncle Sam couldn't care less and at the going civilian price, Eddie and I could clear enough for three months' rent in the Bronx. How about it?"

"Well,..." Hart frowned.

"Oh, come on. Nothing illegal about it. Or immoral, either, other than I'd be buying more than the rule of two pair. And that's only Monahan's idea." She tucked the pencil above her ear. "And he's leaving, too. So that rule doesn't make sense anymore."

"Tell you what," Hart said. "Six pairs apiece for Louella and me and I'll agree. No way I could go home to three females waiting in Texas knowing all those nylons had gone to the Bronx."

"You're on," Brenda grinned. "I'll figure up how much we owe and give you a check."

"Under the circumstances, make it for our cost."

"Great honk, boss! Thanks a bunch."

"Call it a bonus for a job well done," Hart answered, "and while I'm at it, I haven't dictated your own recommendation."

Louella hooked her heels over the rungs of Frances' stool and tackled the Kardex records. With the exodus of most squadrons, PX work had tapered off. The overhead drone of planes was rare now. A single fighter passing over now lifted heads, where before the sound had been unnoticed background. On the flight line, solitary Mustang aircraft looked oddly tiny on the expanse of concrete apron, like birds deserted by a flock. More and more Louella felt herself drawn to the flag ceremonies at sundown. Perhaps she and the others who came were reassuring themselves they were not alone on the base, which now echoed footsteps in the empty streets.

The office door flew open and Hutch hustled in and dropped in the nearest chair. "Boy, I'm tired! That's the last crate I pack today." His round face was damp. "Won't be long now," he added, mopping his forehead with a khaki handkerchief. He glanced at Louella, perched on the high stool. "Frances get off okay? It was a nice party you all had last night."

"Her Charlie is a good man, isn't he?" Louella did not lift her head from her work.

"This letter came for you, Louella." Hutch unbuttoned his blouse pocket and handed her a damp envelope. For an instant Louella thought of Stith, then saw the return address of the Charlotte employment agency. The single sheet was neatly typed — and to the point.

"Thank you for your application for employment through our agency. Although your work record is brief, the references we have been able to contact have been most complimentary.

"We regret at this time we do not have immediate prospects to offer you, since many servicemen and women are now returning and, as you know, have first preference. However, we will retain your application and will immediately be in touch with you should there be any change in the labor market here in Charleston."

Louella's hand shook as she returned the sheet to the envelope. The time had come to call Toots and accept.

CHAPTER XXXIV

When Sergeant Cobb approached the Daisy Mae he found a long black Packard parked at the club, forcing him to park in front of the furniture store next door. Three occupants in identical black fedoras swiveled as one to watch him enter the club.

He blinked for a moment to adjust to the dimness inside. At the bar Toots straightened to face him.

"I seen the hearse; where's the funeral?" he asked.

"You got a visitor. Maybe he knows." Toots jerked a thumb toward the corner booth.

"How'd anybody know I'd be here...?"

Toots shrugged.

Waiting in the booth was a large swarthy man in a pinstriped suit with white shirt and tie. The black fedora shadowed his face but as he turned toward Cobb the flash of the red neon beer sign caught a scar from temple to chin, making it a bloody gash.

Joe Guernsey from Miami. What was he doing here? For a moment Cobb paused, then slid into the opposite seat. "What brings you to this burg?" he asked, trying for nonchalance. A trickle of perspiration drained down his side. "You're a long way from home."

"We got business all over." The eyes in the expressionless face did not blink.

"You got the money; we're square," Cobb said. "Did you bring the papers?"

"Not so damned quick, Cobb. We're square on you buyin' the club. Don't mean you own the furniture."

It took a moment for Guernsey's words to sink into Cobb's apprehensive brain. "What do you mean? That don't include the furnishings, the tables and chairs?" Cobb's voice had risen to a shout. He glanced around at Toots, who was leaning on the bar, listening.

Cobb hunched forward, lowering his voice to a hiss. "You told me twenty grand bought the club. What the hell are you...?"

"The club, yeah. Them fixtures ain't free, you know. We ain't some kind of benefactors, you know, giving stuff away." He dropped his voice to a bass whisper, his hand a vise on Cobb's wrist. "Tell you what. My partners out in the car ain't going to like this, but I'm a real generous guy. Say I give you another three days to come up with ten C-notes?"

Cobb's stomach lurched, shutting off his breath. A thousand more in three days! Should have had a lawyer, damn it. "It'd take a week at least!" he answered, his own voice sounding strange. He shifted uncomfortably in his damp shirt and glared at his opponent. "For that price I can buy new!"

The big man laughed, a nasty chuckle deep in his throat. "Uncle Sam's been pampering you so long you ain't got no idea about the real world, buddy. Where would you get all that stuff?"

Cobb tried to imagine the club he now owned empty. It would take weeks to furnish it again. The base was ready to close and with it, his resources. He couldn't afford to wait weeks to open. "Seven hundred," he said lamely. "And that's firm." The four hundred now in his bank account was meant for a manager's salary and bar-tending staff. Somehow he'd have to scrape up the other three.

The big man did not move. Then he pushed back the fedora, revealing a crease across his forehead from the hat brim. "You don't know from `firm,' buddy," he growled. With one heavy hand he gestured toward the window. "`Firm' is outside in that there Packard, buddy. You're lucky I'm on your side."

Drops of sweat swelled on Cobb's forehead and he brushed them away.

"Get it up or forget your equity, friend." It was not a friendly growl. The big man slid out of the booth and towered over Cobb. "You'd better get scratchin', pal."

"How...," Cobb swallowed hard. "How do I get in touch?"

"We'll be around." Like a dancer the dark figure moved across the floor and was gone through the street door without a sound. There was the purr of a well-oiled motor pulling away and then silence.

Goddamned bastards! They had him over a barrel and there wasn't a damned thing he could do about it. In a fury, he pounded the table. The half empty beer mug rolled on its side and sloshed a river toward him. Cobb jumped to his feet and headed for the street.

"Hold it!" Toots stood between Cobb and the door. "He left without paying. You owe me twenty cents. Two beers."

"The hell I do!" His right arm swept Toots aside in a thrust that sent her half way back to the bar.

When he started his car, he was trembling all the way to the base. Fumbling in his pocket he withdrew the small black notebook of phone numbers and entered the telephone booth outside the PX. Twenty minutes later he had regained his composure, but he was two hundred dollars short of his goal.

Looking up, he was surprised it was almost full dark already. He turned and hit the folding door. It did not budge. Two figures, one fat, one thin, leaned against it.

Fury regained, Cobb hit it again and the door opened six inches. He blinked to clear his vision, staring at the pot belly that blocked his way.

"You Sergeant Cobb?" the burly man asked through the crack.

"So?"

Tech sergeant stripes were stretched tight across the muscular arm holding the door. The thin corporal had stepped back.

"Palermo here. Glad ta meetcha." The fat man backed away just enough to let Cobb slide through.

The thin blond stuck out his hand. "Sandane, Sergeant, but call me Ohio."

Cobb ignored the hand. Where had he heard that name recently?

"Picked up a little rumor you was in business." Palermo bit the end off a fresh cigar. "Swartz told me about your, uh, sugar arrangements."

Cobb had tensed to fight his way free, but the words stopped him. He looked closer at the big man, aware the slender corporal was grinning.

"Ohio and me, well, we been thinking we'd like a seat on your gravy train." Black eyes were watchful.

Cobb stiffened. "Don't know what you're talking about." Was this a threat or two greedy hands reaching for his pocket?

Palermo grabbed Cobb's right arm in a painful squeeze. The thin GI clamped onto his left and they marched him down the street away from the light from the telephone booth.

Better hear them out before he sucker punched both of them, Cobb decided.

"Smoke?" Ohio produced a pack of Camels.

"Uh...yeah."

When cigarettes were lighted and Palermo had his cigar going satisfactorily, the fat man said, "You're wasting your time with small fry like Swartz. Hell, man, I'm the company cook." The pudgy little finger of his left hand carefully nudged off a thin ring of cigar ash. "You got any idea how much goes through my kitchen?"

Cobb's ears pricked.

"Ohio and me, ever since we got this, uh, idea, me and him we've started a little stockpile, you might say. Porterhouse steaks. Few tenderloins. Butter. Sugar. You name it." Palermo dragged on the cigar, the exhaled smoke blurring his swarthy features. "Ohio, he makes a good delivery man, if you know what I mean. We wouldn't charge much. This time. Just a drip in the bucket, you might say."

Ohio's grin was fixed around the Camel clenched in white teeth.

Cobb's thoughts raced. Ten C-notes. One big score might be enough. "How much?"

"Base's closing pretty quick now. We figured we could use a boost in pay from Uncle, you might say. But we ain't greedy." Palermo's smile was oily. "Say ten percent off the top?"

"Apiece?"

They looked at each other, smiles wider.

"Naw. Ohio and I'll split the ten fifty-fifty." Palermo blew a cloud of smoke into Cobb's face. "We're, you might say, new in the business. Learners' wages. This first time."

Cobb swallowed. Maybe Lady Luck had returned, towing them his way. With a three-day deadline.... "I'd have to have it all by tomorrow night, Christmas Eve," he said firmly.

"No sweat. Just tell Ohio where." Palermo's little finger was busy with cigar ash again. "Time's running, but the cadre will be around ten days or so and we can rustle up another, uh, shipment in a couple of days."

Something about their smiles made Cobb uneasy. Instinct said "no," but the echo of Guernsey's gravelly voice — and an unspoken threat to involve MP's if he didn't agree — overcame his hesitation.

"All right. Back door at the NCO Club. Christmas Eve. Nine o'clock sharp."

Eight-fifty. Christmas Eve. Cobb's nervousness grew. Wouldn't you know tonight would be the night Woods decided to join the crowd downstairs? Cobb had installed him in a chair near the bandstand, made sure his attention was on the GI's. Then he slipped out the kitchen door past Sam, who was shouting orders to two young black helpers.

He shivered in the cool night air. Unable to keep still, he paced on the dark back lawn. Where the hell were they? He unlocked the trunk of his car, lifting the lid and unscrewing the revealing light bulb inside. Five minutes to load and he'd be gone from here. Calls had been made. Besides Toots at the Daisy Mae, three others stood behind their doors, greenbacks ready.

At the sound of a footstep, he whirled. In the dimness he saw a thin Santa Claus carrying boxes stacked to the white cotton beard on his chin.

"Ohio?"

"Merry Christmas," came the answer.

With a grunt Santa Claus lowered the packages into the trunk of Cobb's coupe and straightened. Cobb shoved down the lid, but it would not close. Damn! He shifted the heavy cartons and tried again. Too many. Cobb removed the top box and shoved it onto the front seat, then locked the trunk.

"See you tomorrow," Santa Claus whispered.

"Where?"

"We'll find you." The white beard and thin costume had already merged into the darkness.

Cobb eased into the driver's seat and turned the ignition, surprised to find his hand trembling. Suddenly he was blinded by a reflected glare in his rear view mirror. A car crunched to a stop on the graveled driveway behind him. What the hell?

"Stay where you are. Hands in sight."

MP's! Cobb's pulse skipped, then raced. It was a setup, but no trap was going to catch him! Goddamn Palermo and Ohio! He revved the motor and spun wheels across the back lawn. Passing the building he caught faint strains of music and laughter. The tires churned through the flower bed in front of the NCO Club and bounced over the curb into the street.

Speeding down the highway, his thoughts moved faster than the car. This was not a coincidence, the MP's arriving the moment the car was loaded. Palermo and Ohio. Where had he heard that last name? Toots' voice. Ohio was there when they closed the Daisy Mae. A drop of sweat oozed into his right eye and he blinked it away. My god, he had to get rid of the stuff in the trunk! He glared at the black letters spelling `butter' on the box beside him. He couldn't dump it all in some bayou. He needed it to meet Guernsey's deadline. All that green just waiting for this.

Eddie O'Brien. Palermo and Ohio. Hutch. Monahan. Inspections and people spying on him and now this. They were all friends of Louella's. She had to be the key. It didn't matter why they were out to get him; he had to get to her. Make her pay, by god.

The gas pedal hit the floor and the car rocketed through the night. He caught a glimpse of a startled face in an approaching car that flashed by. Maybe he had time to make the Daisy Mae delivery. He had to! But he'd better be quick. It was the first place the MP's would hit, looking for him.

Back at the NCO Club Palermo and Ohio were still laughing as they entered. "Man, did you see him rip right through that flower bed?" Palermo gasped. "I turned on the headlights and yelled, `Stay where you are; hands in sight' and he thinks the MP's are right behind him. Ain't nothing chasing him but his guilty conscience."

Ohio bent double, fighting for his breath, as they joined Eddie and Brenda at their table. "Man, oh, man, you should have been there!" he said, slapping Eddie on the back. His red peaked cap slipped sideways over one eye. He was laughing so hard the Camel he was smoking dropped into his snow white beard.

It was mass confusion until Eddie doused the smoldering cotton with the contents of a ginger ale bottle.

"It won't be long now," Eddie grinned. "He's running and he'll make mistakes."

At the edge of town Cobb slowed and pulled his wet shirt away from his body. God, he hoped the single town cop in the only cruiser was on his usual nine-thirty coffee break on the school grounds. Streets were empty of traffic. Everybody was either at home celebrating this Christmas Eve or at the Daisy Mae already.

At the alley's entrance he cut lights and ignition, coasting to the back door of the bar. He listened for a moment. Was that a faint siren he heard?

Leaping out of the car, he rapped on the scarred metal door. "Hurry up, you goddamned broad," he muttered.

The door opened. Toots was outlined against the inside lights.

"Be quick," he ordered. "I ain't got but seconds." He fumbled his key into the lock of the car's trunk.

Toots reached around him to pick up a package wrapped in butcher paper from the top carton. "These steaks better be good, Cobb."

"Shut up and get inside." Arms loaded, Cobb pushed into the room behind her and dropped cartons onto the wooden table. "No time for inventory now. Give me the three hundred you owe for this and your back bill." He stuck out his hand, impatient to be gone.

"Well, look, Cobb. This all came up so sudden and I don't have...."

"What the hell do you mean, you don't have it?" He shook with rage.

Toots' eyes widened. She took two steps back from his reach, jerked open a drawer beneath the crusted sink and lifted out a stack of bills. "Here's two hundred seventy-two, all I could scrape up that quick and on a holiday, too. I'll have the rest before the night's over." For the first time she seemed intimidated.

Cobb grabbed the money. "You'd goddamned better have it."

An idea blossomed and he swallowed his anger. "Matter of fact, I'll settle for this and the rent of your garage for a couple nights."

Her eyes narrowed. "Somebody chasing you, Cobb?"

"Mind your own business. Take it or leave it."

Toots pursed her mouth, then shrugged. "Why not? I leave my car in the drive, anyway." A smile glimmered and faded. "Be my guest; paying guest, that is."

"Where's the key?"

"Ain't locked."

Before she ended the last word, he had closed the door and regained his driver's seat. He'd have to get a padlock on it before Toots got her greedy little hands into his stock. Then he'd have to move it in a hurry. Even in December in South Carolina, meat and butter wouldn't last long. Ten minutes later he had off loaded the last carton and shut the door on the small frame building behind her house.

Back under the wheel of his coupe, it took two attempts to bring the flame of his Zippo to his cigarette. He exhaled the first drag and waited for his thudding heart to calm down. So far so good. His disappointed other customers would get a call later.

Once more anger built. Who the hell did that Louella think she was, conniving with her friends to catch him like a bug in a jar? He dragged in smoke. There had to be some way to save his club, some way to repay the bitch, to get out of this jam. His pulse slower, his thoughts became more coherent.

If the MP's pulled him in, he'd have to convince them Louella was the mastermind in the black-market deals, so he could be released to meet Guernsey's deadline.... Sure. That would net all her friends at the same time. Palermo, Ohio, Warrant Officer O'Brien, Hutch. How many more? Right now he knew she was at the train station meeting an old boyfriend. Good thing he'd kept close tabs on her lately.

He shifted on the seat, feeling the comfortable bulge of bills in his pocket. Cigarette butt flipped out of the window, he spun gravel backing to the street. The siren was a lot closer now, howling in the silent night. No way they could track him in the next thirty minutes.

The night breeze through the window dried perspiration on his face. Cobb licked his lips, tasting salt. There was enough stockpiled in that garage to add to the four hundred in his bank account to pay off the club furnishings. If he will be free to disperse it. If he can find Louella in time....

Thirty minutes would have to do.

CHAPTER XXXV

The rock and sway of the train had lulled First Lieutenant Stith Bonham into a lethargy he couldn't seem to break. Bayous had multiplied, speeding past the windows, turgid brown water that gleamed between palmetto spears and heavy vines. Home was not far now. He shifted in his seat carefully, not to disturb the girl sleeping on his shoulder. A glance at his watch showed nine-forty.

He looked down at the girl's disheveled black hair. Such a scared but determined child. In the crowded train they had been seatmates for half a day before she relaxed enough to speak. On her way to meet a husband she had not seen for four years, a man she'd married and told good-bye in two swift weeks. Her story was the same as a dozen others he'd heard before.

Stith longed for the luxury of a soapy shower after his day and a half in this dirty, stuffy coach. At that he'd been lucky to have a seat.

The dull thud at the door of the car announced the entrance of the conductor. He watched the man fight his way down the aisle, moving around those standing passengers, who clung to seats for balance, past the drowsy man crouched on a suitcase whose head bobbed with the movement of the train.

"Seacomb! Next stop Seacomb!"

The conductor stopped to shake the shoulder of a man in a plaid sports coat. Stith caught the gleam of a Ruptured Duck emblem in his lapel. Some soldier home to stay who didn't wait to shed his uniform. Nobody he knew.

When Stith touched the arm of the girl on his shoulder, she roused quickly, lifted her head and blushed. "I'm...sorry."

Amused at her embarrassment, he said, "No problem, friend.

This is my stop coming up. You'll be okay the rest of the way. Right?"

"Of course." She had the dark eyes of a doe. "Thank you for helping me change trains in... wherever it was."

He dismissed the thanks with a wave of his hand.

She swept back wispy hair that curled damply at her temples. "I'll be fine as soon as I meet Marvin."

Stith pulled his duffle bag from the rack overhead, easing it down into the seat. Realizing Stith's place would soon be empty, the man swaying in the aisle was suddenly friendly. Stith inspected him carefully. Too old to be a threat to the small brunette seatmate. He waved the elderly man into his place, inching past him.

Stith hunched over, watching the first gray shacks at the edge of town slide past. The wail of the train reinforced his mood. He had hoped never to see this burg again, but he owed Louella. Would she be here waiting?

The train clanged to a stop. A plume of steam obscured his vision for a second, then he saw Seacomb's small station with its white lettering. Before he could force his way to the door he heard the ring of metallic steps descending and the thud of a wooden stepstool the porter placed on the weathered boards of the platform. When Stith pushed through the door, the whoosh of air in the damp night was a mixture of fresh oxygen and the smell of hot metals.

Clanging down the steps, he took three strides toward the station door, swinging his body around under the weight of the duffle bag to look back at the coach windows. He waved his free hand at the pale oval face before he turned away.

Light and shadow alternated from the bare bulbs down the length of the platform. Where was Louella?

Near the train the man with the plaid sports coat was surrounded by a thin brunette with tired eyes, two small children and an elderly couple.

"Welcome home, fellow," Stith muttered to himself. "Hope it's as good as you've remembered."

A heavy man brushed past, rotating a cigar in thick lips, wrestling two bulging suitcases. Salesman, probably, Stith decided. Poor bastard, having to fight his way from town to town in crowded trains. That's another job I don't want, he reminded himself.

A large bleached blonde, dressed totally in yellow from a wide picture hat to spike heels, descended the train steps and paused for a moment. Aware of the porter's grin, she pushed out her chest like an actress waiting for applause. Stith was amused to see Plaid Sports Coat eye her over his own wife's shoulder. The blonde had dropped her shoulders until she noticed the attention; instantly her breasts came up again. Her gaze roamed the platform and then she shrilled out, "Toots! Hey, Toots, honey, over here!"

Stith dropped his duffle bag at his feet and tugged out a Camel. Hands cupping a match, he turned to see whom she greeted.

A small woman dressed in a bilious green suit had entered through the street door. Her hair was impossibly black and she advanced with jerky steps like a starling working over a scattering of crumbs.

"I see you, Vernita. You don't have to tell the whole damned town."

"Oh, honey, it's just so good to get home and all! Wait until I tell you about the club. It's going to be fabulous!"

The bilious green suit almost disappeared in the big blonde's hug.

"There may not be any club, Vernita. Damn it, let me go and let's get out of here."

"Not be any club?" The blonde's voice rose an octave before the street door swung shut behind them.

People-watching had developed into a hobby for Stith. Idly he wondered about the club-that-might-not-be. Sometimes he felt like a peeping-tom. Always he felt curious about brief glimpses of lives. Sometimes a vignette hinted of a story, like this one.

The train huffed away down the track, picking up speed and wailing. He shouldered the duffle bag again and pushed through the station door. Only a few people remained in the dim waiting room on this Christmas Eve. The ticket window was a brightly lit stage. A clerk in wire-rimmed glasses stamped a long roll of tickets with a thump and clatter under a faded red honeycomb Christmas bell. He beat time with "White Christmas" coming from his portable radio.

That old guy hasn't aged a week since I left, Stith thought. But I've aged years.

No Louella. He propped one foot against the wall, closed his eyes and brought up a clear vision of her. Braids, severely restrained. Slender face, gold-flecked gray eyes and thick black lashes. So earnest and so...prudish. And, my god, but she was religious.

Well, he'd found religion, too. In a foxhole. Atheists were scarce under fire. But on the other hand he intended to do some living before he died, find some laughter. Maybe he could teach Louella life could be fun. She hadn't had many giggles in her life before they met.

Surveying the room, Stith saw a tall brunette with her back to him in the corner near the street door. Her legs made him catch his breath, the slender ankles and the gentle slope of smooth calves gleaming when the light caught her nylons. Their dark seams carried his eyes upward. When she moved, he caught a glimpse of the indentations behind her knees at the edge of a blue hem. Those were the sweet parallel lines in the curve that always knocked him out on a great pair of legs. Let other guys rave over a pair of knockers; he was definitely a leg man.

The brunette faced a soldier who clutched her arm. His mouth was cruel, his face a mottled, sweaty red. Curved white streaks on his cheek looked suspiciously like fingernail wounds that had healed. Had the girl done that to him? And why? The thin sergeant was really telling her off.

She wrenched her arm free and took a single step backward. Dark curls bounced under her veiled navy blue hat. Great hips, too, Stith noticed, not bound by any Iron Maiden girdle. There was a sway that spoke of lush fullness below the small waist. If only Louella were like this girl! Suddenly Stith wanted to see her face.

The thin sergeant in the sweat-stained uniform grabbed her arm again. Over the tinny Christmas music Stith caught phrases. "...lose my equity...your goddamned friends..." The brunette jerked away a second time and Stith caught a glimpse of her profile. Even across the room he could see a full lower lip outlined in moist red. Better and better.

Stith lit another cigarette from the butt of the first, grinding out the last half inch under his heel on the dirty tile floor. Was Louella ever coming? He'd give her thirty minutes more.

The only figure on the long worn bench that centered the area was a fat man who sat, elbows on knees, steadily cracking peanuts and tossing them into his mouth. His jaws worked without pause, the pile of shells a growing mound at his feet.

When the street door opened, Stith turned in anticipation. It was only a young mother dragging her howling small son behind her. Inside the waiting room, the echo of his own cries intimidated the child and he closed his mouth around a soiled thumb. His mother began a conversation with the ticket agent at the lighted window.

The family with Sports Coat in its center moved in through the platform door. An entity with many feet, it moved as a single unit across the room and disappeared through the street door.

Stith turned back to the pair in the corner. The sergeant's blond widow's peak under his stiff crewcut vibrated with anger. He thrust his chin within an inch of the girl's and then shook her, his voice loud.

"Goddamn you, it's all your fault! It's a plot to get me and I won't stand for it. You hear? You're going to call off your dogs and you're going to tell the MP's...." Over her shoulder the angry man caught Stith's stare and abruptly lowered his voice.

I know better than to get involved in this, Stith reminded himself. He moved to drop his second cigarette butt into the ashcan at the end of the bench near the fat man, who did not look up from his peanuts. Once more Stith consulted his wristwatch. There was no point in waiting any longer. Obviously Louella wasn't coming. Perhaps it was just as well. But the twinge somewhere near his heart told him the truth. He still loved her.

He bent toward his duffle bag and caught the scent of something that spoke of moonlight and flowers. A hand touched his sleeve.

"Stith?"

He turned to face the girl in blue, the angry sergeant close behind her. He stared through the hat's veil at the wide gray eyes and black lashes that had filled his dreams so long. Louella!

"Now just a goddamned minute!" the soldier shouted, grabbing her elbow. "You can't just walk off when I'm talking to you." Stith stiffened. What the hell was going on here? The face before him was lovelier than the one in his foxhole dreams. This was Louella? What had happened to the prim girl in tight braids, the one bogged down with screwy religious ideas? Maybe he wasn't the only one who'd changed.

"Louella! Glad you came." He ignored the tense man beside her and reached out his arms to embrace her.

She flinched and moved back a step.

Stith dropped his arms and felt his face fall as well.

"I can only stay a minute," Louella said. "I came to tell you face-to-face that things have changed, Stith. I'm not the girl you left and there's no way I can go back to being the girl you made the grass ring for."

"Thank god!" Stith replied with a wide smile. "I like what I'm seeing right now."

Her hair spilled over her white collar when she bent her head, clutching a red purse in both hands. "I don't plan on marrying anyone, Stith. I'll have a job in Charleston when the base closes and I don't need to marry. I can make it on my own just fine." She turned away. "And that's what I came to tell you." She added over her shoulder, "Good-bye, Stith. I hope you find a good wife. Somebody who deserves you."

The sergeant grabbed at her arm and she jerked it away. For a moment she hesitated, then moved through the street door without looking back, the sergeant pacing beside her.

It was a heartbeat or two before Stith collected his wits. There was no way he was letting this mesmerizing woman out of his life. He grabbed his duffle and raced after her.

CHAPTER XXXVI

Outside, Stith saw the blond sergeant dragging Louella down the sidewalk to a blue Ford coupe. She beat at him with her purse and cried out as her right ankle turned. He fumbled with the car door, opened it and tried to push her inside.

Stith dropped his duffle and in two steps grabbed the man's shoulder and spun him away from Louella, who limped back toward the station.

"Looks to me like the lady doesn't want to go with you, soldier. So why don't you just get the hell out of here?" Stith suggested in a calm voice.

Red-rimmed pale eyes glared at him, pupils dilated. "Mind your own goddamned business." The man wrenched himself free.

"The lady is my business."

"Yours and every pair of pants on base." The thin mouth sneered.

Stith took a convulsive breath. Not Louella! Not that innocent girl who had worn his grass ring. He grabbed the man's arm in a grip that made him wince. "You heard me the first time. In your car and be gone or I'll...."

"You and what company of Marines?"

There weren't six inches between them and Stith staggered from the blow that hit his midriff and robbed him of air. But he let go of the man's arm and his own swing connected with a satisfying crunch on the fellow's chin.

Stith heard a grunt from his opponent but the man was instantly away, running toward Louella. Stith managed to catch him around the throat with one arm, pinioning the sergeant's wrists, a combat skill he'd used effectively before.

But the man was an eel, who whirled and brought up both wrists in a collision with Stith's chin. He felt his teeth crack together just as the knee hit him in the groin. Gasping, Stith doubled over as the sergeant disappeared into the station after Louella.

Reckless fury built as Stith felt blood roar in his ears. Pain forgotten, he lunged through the station doors and grabbed the sergeant by his collar, whirled him around and smashed at his face and then his solar plexus, relishing the change from rage to astonishment on the man's face. For good measure he swung at the bloody chin with an uppercut he felt all the way down his arm.

The man sagged in sections like a carpenter's ruler, his eyes glazed. His head hit the dirty tiles with a hollow thud. One hand scattered the mound of peanut hulls at the fat man's feet.

The huge bulk on the bench stopped chewing, his eyes frightened in the folds of his skin. He heaved his mountainous body up and surprised Stith how fast he sprinted through the platform door.

Stith sucked the knuckles of his right hand, then wiped away moisture at the edge of his mouth. Glancing at his fingers, he found blood. Out of the corner of his eye, he saw the clerk replace the telephone receiver on its hook. Damn! That meant there would be MP's on the scene.

The scent of flowers surrounded him. Louella touched his mouth with her handkerchief, intent on his split lip. She folded the cloth to a dry spot and applied it again.

"I'm sorry he hurt you, Stith," she said. "Cobb's a...a strange man and not very nice."

Stith nudged the unconscious figure at their feet with his toe. "How'd you ever get mixed up with him?" He couldn't read her expression clearly through her veil.

Louella shrugged and turned away.

Stith touched his midriff and winced. "Let's get out of here. The MP's are on their way, for sure."

They had reached the sidewalk and his duffle bag when two husky uniformed figures approached, their black and white armbands prominent.

"Oh, hell," Stith muttered as the MP's blocked their way and moved them back into the station.

Two sets of eyes, alike as four peas, flickered over Stith, Louella and the man on the floor behind them. "That's him," said one MP, sotto voice, pointing with his nightstick. Stith tried to ease Louella toward the door.

"Just a minute, Lieutenant. You, too, Miss."

Stith felt Louella stiffen beside him and he led her to a bench, dropping his duffle at her feet.

The bulkier of the two policemen stood before them, slapping his billyclub into the palm of his hand. The second bent over Cobb. "You two know him?" the first asked, nodding over his shoulder at the man on the floor, who showed signs of recovery.

"Never saw him before," Stith answered. In the large room his voice echoed. "I just got in on the train thirty minutes ago." Conscious of his appearance, he tucked his khaki tie carefully between the third and fourth buttons of his shirt.

"Looks like you two went to Fist City. Why?"

Stith thought quickly. There was no way to keep Louella out of this. Honesty right now might keep things simple.

"He was trying to force this lady into his car."

"That right?"

Louella nodded.

Cobb made it up to a sitting position, bracing with his hands on the floor.

The second MP said, "We'll all go back to the base and sort things out." Facing Louella, he added, "I know you. You're Louella Tolbert. I've seen you in the PX."

Does every GI on the whole base know Louella, Stith wondered with a pang. Shouldering his duffle, he winced again. If he didn't get into a hot shower soon, tomorrow would be a painful day. He followed the MP's outside. Each held up the wobbly sergeant by one shoulder, jerking the man along like a puppet. By Stith's side, Louella was rigid. She still had not said a word.

As they passed the blue Ford coupe, one officer asked, "That the car?"

"Right." Stith bit the word off.

One repeated the license number aloud, probably memorizing it, Stith realized. They heaved Cobb into the black van parked near the coupe. One took the driver's seat in front of the steel mesh that separated the interior. The other pushed Cobb down the bench in back and sat beside him, jerking his thumb at Stith and Louella to take the bench opposite.

Stith could feel the venom in the glare the sergeant sent toward Louella. Motion of the vehicle told him they were on their way toward Seacomb Army Air Base.

The MP opposite seemed to be studying them. Finally he said to the man beside him, "Been a while tracing you down, Cobb. You've been a busy boy lately. Here and there. Loading and unloading. Paying off and collecting." He clicked his tongue. "My, my!"

"Just doing what she told me to do, that boss lady," Cobb sneered.

Stiff as stone beside Stith, Louella blurted out, "That's not true. I don't even know what you're talking about."

"Well, sugar, don't you worry none," the MP said, his black eyes measuring her. "We'll let the Provost Marshall sort it all out."

"Yeah? Well, you'd better not wait until she dumps the evidence, wise guy," Cobb snarled.

The MP's face changed. "You want to hand over your purse now, Louella? Or wait until we subpoena it?"

It was Stith's turn to stiffen. Was she involved? Did this girl he thought he knew so well have a dark side, too?

"There's nothing in my purse except what belongs to me," Louella said firmly, clutching her red bag.

"If you've nothing to hide, then let me see."

For a moment she did not move, then she tossed the purse at the MP.

With two thick fingers he released the catch and lifted the flap. An expression Stith could not read flickered over his face. "You usually carry a wad like this?" He withdrew a thick packet of greenbacks.

Louella's mouth dropped opened. "What...? That's not mine! Where did that come from?" She leaned toward the MP, protesting, "I only had two dollars and fifteen cents when I left home. I don't know anything about that money or how it got there."

Stith caught the sardonic grin on the face of the man called Cobb before he dropped his head into his hands. It wouldn't have been too hard for this snake to slip the wad into her purse earlier. It must be black market the MP had hinted. It had been months since he'd seen Louella and she'd certainly changed. Did he really know she wasn't deep into something illegal?

Louella tugged at his sleeve. "Tell him, Stith. Tell him I wouldn't do black market! That's like stealing; I wouldn't do that!"

He placed one hand on her cold fingers. Her eyes were so dilated they were almost totally black. Fright? Afraid of a false accusation or afraid she'd been caught? Fighting his thoughts, he could not answer her.

The van swerved right as they entered the base. Quick braking jostled them all together. When Stith helped her down from the van, Louella whispered, "Cobb's an evil man. Please tell my roommate Brenda where I am. She's in Unit 19 in the housing area. Please?"

Though her fright and the sweet fragrance of her perfume worked on Stith, his brain sent warning signals. Getting word to her roommate wouldn't compromise him, but it sure as hell didn't look like he'd have the opportunity very soon, he thought, following everyone into the Provost Marshall's office.

But it was a surprise how quickly he was released. Perhaps they didn't want to confuse the charges they already had.

"Lieutenant Bonham, you may go. But stay out of trouble."

"Yes, sir!"

Stith felt an electrical current in Louella's gaze as he shouldered his duffle bag. He gave her a tight smile as a promise and she slumped back against her chair.

After a twenty-minute hike to the housing area and a ten minute search, he found the apartment. He dropped his duffle on the stoop with relief.

A blonde with heavy makeup answered the door in a wave of musky perfume.

"Brenda? I'm Lieutenant Stith Bonham. Louella's in trouble and needs your help."

CHAPTER XXXVII

Louella watched Stith Bonham go through the door of the Provost Marshall's office, longing to leave with him. With a sigh she turned again to face the captain, who looked like a tired banking official, his face long and serious. She had told the truth, surely he believed her. How could anyone doubt the truth?

As the door clicked shut, Technical Sergeant Cobb jumped to his feet.

"Sit down, Sergeant," the officer said sharply.

Ignoring the command, Cobb pulled on his garrison cap, adjusted it on his crewcut carefully and turned to leave. Instantly the two MP's, who had lounged like Tweedledum and Tweedledee against the wall through the interrogation, were beside him.

Cobb reached for the doorknob. "I can't stay around here," he announced. "I've got business. There's only twenty-four hours left." He pulled his dirty cuff away from his wristwatch. "Less than twenty-four hours. I've gotta go."

Without a word, the MP's revolved Cobb's thin body back to his seat, sweeping off his garrison cap and dropping it into his lap.

"You're not going anywhere, Sergeant, not for a long time." The captain's eyes were like stainless steel.

"You don't understand," Cobb said earnestly. The bones of his cheeks seemed near to piercing his taunt skin. "Cobb's Cove. If I don't get the thousand by tomorrow night, they'll take it all back." Again he rose. "So I don't have time for all this...." He spread his fingers wide, half hunched over the captain's desk. As two pair of heavy hands flopped him back into the chair, Cobb began to pant.

Louella had a quick thought of frightened chickens back home, just before Cloteel wrung their necks.

Cobb clawed at the desk, struggling against pinioning arms. He threw his head back, straining neck cords, looking wildly at the corners of the ceiling. "Cobb's Cove," he shouted.

Frightened, Louella drew farther into her chair.

The panting grew louder in the room and Cobb began to rock back and forth, still clawing the desk top, his head now hanging.

"Sergeant Cobb!"

Louella flinched at the roar of the captain's voice.

Slowly Cobb lifted his head, his neck unsteady, and stared at the officer.

"I have named your known, uh, customers. Do you deny having transactions with any of them?"

"Seashells and nets. The lobster tank." Cobb's head wobbled toward Louella. "You will wear the mermaid costume." He drew out his black notebook with shaking hands. "I must place the order today. Give me your size."

The room was silent except for his panting. Cobb's face had become unrecognizable to Louella, his eyes now completely black and blank. She turned toward the captain for reassurance.

"I said, `Give me your size,' you bitch! Now!" Cobb slapped the notebook on the desk and lunged at Louella. In an instant he was immobilized by Tweedledum and Tweedledee.

Louella's heart slowed, but she eased her chair farther away.

The captain lifted the notebook and began to read. "Dates. Names. Quantities." A crooked smile lifted a corner of his mouth.

"Mine! Mine!" Cobb shouted, straining to grasp the book. Great drops of sweat welled on his forehead. The struggle against the restraint of muscular arms became silent. Suddenly Cobb collapsed, head down. "Gone. All gone. Nobody again. Nobody. Cobb's Cove gone...," Cobb's words slowed to mumbles.

Louella had the sensation he had suddenly shrunken into a frail old man between the two MP's.

Abruptly he threw back his head, cords of his neck writhing. "Cobb's Cove! Cobb's Cove!" It was the hoarse cry of a rooster, repeated endlessly. "Cobb's Cove! Cobb's Cooove!"

The captain looked up from the black notebook and stiffened. "Lock him up," he ordered. "And get Captain Trammell from Medical over to sedate him. Apparently he's gone 'round the bend."

A single sob escaped Louella's lips. Gone was the cool, confident man who had made love to her. This was a skinny scarecrow with a demented clown's mouth and lolling tongue that the MP's half lifted through the inner door. Pity had overcome her anger. Long after the door closed behind them, she heard echoes down the hall of his cries, "Cobb's Cooove...."

Brenda eyed the tall lieutenant on her doorstep. His uniform looked soiled and there was a streak of white in his auburn hair. His accent was Southern. Eddie had moved to stand beside her and she was conscious of Glen Hart and Donald Monahan listening from the couch.

Luella went to the station to meet her old boyfriend." Brenda spoke the thought aloud at the exact moment his appearance and accent connected in her mind. "You're Stith Bonham. Where is she?"

"At the Provost Marshall's office. There was this sergeant named Cobb...."

Brenda did not need another word. If Cobb was involved, her roommate needed help. She snatched up her black evening bag from the table. "That goddamned bastard!" She glared at Stith and announced, "The party's off. Let's go!"

Donald leaped to his feet. "You all go on. I'll find Hutch and meet you there. We're all in this together."

"Hurry!" Eddie jerked the door open impatiently.

Donald was the last to leave. He snapped off the light and set the lock, then disappeared into the night toward the barracks.

Stith trailed Brenda and Eddie, pacing beside Glen Hart. No one spoke, each deep in troubled thought. Suddenly Brenda could not stop the stream of words that welled up.

"That son-of-a-bitch fouls everybody he touches. If I'd only realized how much she'd drunk that night, I could have stopped...fix that bastard good...." With an effort, she clamped her jaw shut. Every time I get really mad I either spout a fountain or can't say a word, she thought, glancing at the profile of Lieutenant Bonham, who had moved up beside her. It was a face familiar from the large photograph Louella had had on her dresser. I'll check you out later, bub, she thought, see if you're good enough for her.

"Look, Brenda," the lieutenant said, "I don't know you all, except through Louella's letters. But I've figured out you're all good friends of hers." They had crossed the street in front of the PX when he continued. "Guess you all know Louella and I had...had an understanding someday we'd be married. After that, things happened to me and I'm different now." He dropped his voice to add, "I guess I had to change or shatter."

Brenda steeled herself against sentimentality and stumbled over uneven ground. "These damned high heels," she grumbled. She jerked them off. Thank god I had just painted my legs with fake hose tonight, she thought, running faster in bare feet, keeping pace with the others.

"Looks to me," the lieutenant continued, "Louella's had things happen to her, too. Things she couldn't do anything about. Maybe her changes were all to the good, but maybe not. How could I know? Maybe she's really deep in this mess with Cobb...."

Brenda grabbed his arm, jerked him to a full stop beside the empty flagpole on the parade grounds. "If you think that, you don't deserve even to see her again!" She glared at Stith, his face a pale oval in the dim light. Hands on her hips, she squared off at him. "You broke that girl's heart when you dumped her last August. I was the one glued her back together again. Men!" Brenda spat the word at him. "She's got it all together again and she sure deserves better'n you, you damned Confederate!"

Three feet ahead, Eddie and Glen Hart had stopped to listen. Brenda stalked on and joined them, grateful when Eddie drew her close with one arm around her waist. Without a backward glance at Stith, the three paced on toward the Provost Marshall's office.

Stith hastened to catch up. "I didn't think she'd gotten involved deliberately. Not Louella." Brenda heard the chagrin in his voice. "I figured Cobb for a conniving son-of-a-gun who wanted a handy victim to dump on."

Brenda's anger escaped like air from a child's balloon.

"I reckon you all are the only ones who can tell me what really happened," Stith continued. "Seems like I'd need to know that before I can help her."

The silence that followed was deeper in the darkness, broken by a querulous cry from a sleepy bird. Several paces further Brenda relented, but it was Eddie who spoke.

"If she hadn't drunk champagne like water that night she could have seen what a slime ball he is. We were all celebrating VJ Day and she'd never tasted champagne...." Eddie looked at Brenda and was silent for a moment. "After that night, seems like he kept popping up too often."

One by one they took up the story, the words seeming to wrap them all deeper into the darkness.

"...so after her papa died, now she's responsible for Cora Sue and Cloteel. And probably Elijah as well," Glen Hart added.

"Brent Tolbert died? I never knew," Stith whispered.

"With the base closing," Brenda said, "she's worried about finding a job to support them all. The only job she's found is with Toots, that dame that runs the Daisy May in Seacomb. Toots's opening a new club in Charleston. At least they call it a club." She checked Stith's face in the dim light to make sure he had caught her insinuation.

"Oh, hell," he said.

They had reached the Provost Marshall's office and Brenda struggled back into her shoes while Eddie held open the door open for them all.

Blinking in the light of the bare outer office with its government-issue benches and desk, Brenda ran a finger under each eye. "Damn it, my mascara's running."

Eddie and Stith joined her on the bench and Glen Hart took the chair facing. When Stith reached for her hand, Brenda jerked it away. Pulling out a handkerchief, she blew her nose. "Man, you really touched a button, didn't you?" she asked Stith. "I gotta hand it to you. You really listen."

"Anyway," Eddie continued the story, "Mr. Hart and some of us planned this trap for Cobb and it was supposed to close on him tonight. Something went wrong when Louella got caught in it as well."

Composure regained, Brenda said, "He's been raking in all this black-market money. Toots at the Daisy May is one of his customers and the Board of Health closed her place for a while last month because some of his black-market meat was bad."

The outside door opened and a nervous little woman in a bilious green suit entered. When she caught sight of them, she glared and said, "I heard my name."

"What're you doing here?" Brenda demanded.

"The MP's brought me in. Cobb's got two hundred and seventy-three dollars of mine and...." Her shrill voice broke off. "You don't have to look at me like I'm dirt," she snapped. "I want that son-of-a-bitch more'n you do." Brenda narrowed her eyes.

"She's right," Glen Hart intervened. "If she's a witness against him, it'll help Louella."

"Without what she's going to say, they may not have much of a case," Eddie said.

Glen Hart rose to his feet, his Texas drawl pronounced. "It won't help Louella if we get to fussing amongst ourselves." He smoothed down this thick hair which sprung up again in a pepper-and-salt cowlick. "Mrs. Toots, we're grateful for your help," she said, offering her the chair beside his own.

"Yeah, well...." Brenda was not about to back down quickly. "She's going to get Louella working in her whorehouse...."

"Hold it right there, babe!" Toots' black eyes snapped. "I ain't asked her to do nothing she don't want to do. She's got to eat and there ain't no other jobs waiting. Figure I've done her a favor." She tossed her black hair. "It'll be a respectable place and...."

Brenda released a weary sigh and subsided. "Oh, shut up! If they jail you for black market, you won't have any club."

The outside door burst open, Donald Monahan's and Hutch's momentum carrying them half way into the room. They skidded to a halt.

"Where's Louella? What're they holding her on?" Hutch's round face seemed leaner, his chin firm.

With one accord, everyone looked at Stith.

"The MP's found a big roll of bills in her purse," Stith answered.

"Damn!" Brenda breathed.

"My money," Toots snorted. "They'll give me immunity or I won't talk. No way I'll lose that club in Charleston."

"Cobb was arguing with her when I first saw them at the station. I think he slipped them in...."

The inside door opened as the tired-looking captain entered. He took his time, looking at each of them. When he came to Toots, Brenda saw his eyes flicker. Turning aside, he spoke through the open door. "Miss Tolbert, can you identify these people?"

When Louella entered, Brenda shot out of her seat to gather her into her arms. "We're here, Louella, honey. We're here for you."

"Oh, thank God!" Louella whispered in her ear. Her face was strained, but composed. Turning to Stith, Louella said, "And thank you."

"Do you know all these people?" the captain asked.

"They're my friends, Captain Edmonds."

As though a conductor had dropped his baton, they all began to speak at once.

"Hold it!" Edmonds raised his hand. "We'll take you people one at a time." He turned toward Brenda. "You are...?"

"Brenda Bernstein, her roommate."

The captain faced each in turn for identification. When Toots said, "I run the Daisy May," Brenda caught Edmonds' reaction, quickly shuttered.

"Your name is...?"

"Mildred Brattagan."

No wonder she calls herself Toots, Brenda thought, seeing a twinkle in Eddie's eye.

"Please step into my office Mrs. Brattagan."

"Miss," Toots said as she disappeared through the inner door.

Captain Edmonds consulted his watch. "It's Christmas Eve and almost midnight. We'll make this brief." He turned to Louella. "I think we have all we need with your deposition, Miss Tolbert. You may go, but remain on the base."

Louella frowned. "But my family expects me home."

"Out of the question."

"See here," Glen Hart interposed, standing to tower over the shorter captain. "I can vouch for Louella. Her home's not far. I'll see she's available, should you need her."

"You'd take that responsibility?"

"Of course."

"It's on your head, then, Hart. The rest of you remain, except for Lieutenant Bonham."

Eddie leaped to his feet. "I have a car. How about letting me drive Louella to her home and then I'll return. It's only about four miles from the base."

For a moment Captain Edmonds hesitated, his hand on the door's knob. "Make it fast, then," he said and closed the door behind him.

"I'd like to hitch along with you, if you don't mind," Stith said to Eddie. "Our place adjoins Louella's."

"Why not."

After Louella hugged her and left, Brenda took a deep breath. Hutch sank onto the bench beside her and patted her hand.

"Aw, jeez, poor Louella," he sighed.

Somewhere deeper in the building Brenda heard a strange cry, rather like a hoarse rooster crowing.

CHAPTER XXXVIII

Christmas dawned clear and cool. There had been no sleep for Stith Bonham. His happy parents, roused from deep slumber when he arrived, had spent the remaining hours celebrating his return over cups of chicory coffee.

But his joy at greeting his parents had been tempered. Had he never noticed the gray in his mother's hair, the lined forehead of his father, the slowness of their movements as though time had unwound a spring for them? Had they been that way before the war?

"Morning so soon?" his mother asked, pulling up the blinds in the familiar kitchen. She reached for her apron and opened the icebox. "What for breakfast, son?"

"Make it a big one, Mother," his father said, relighting his pipe. "Our son needs a man's nourishment now."

Through all the good conversation they had, Louella's face was the screen through which he saw them. He had not mentioned her plight, but it was a constant thought, making concentration difficult.

He shoved back his chair and straightened his loosened tie. "None for me, Mom," he said. "I'm having breakfast with Louella."

His father chuckled around his pipe stem. "Like I said, Mother: Our son's a man now."

His mother closed the icebox and straightened slowly, wiping her hands on her apron. "But...Christmas and only six o'clock. This is your first morning home."

Stith moved up behind her and teased her with a tug at the wisps of gray hair on the back of her neck. "I know. There'll be lots of time later to be together."

"But you've known her all your life. Your first morning home couldn't you just...."

"Let him go, Mother. Louella's a fine girl."

He's right but what would he have thought if he'd been with me last night? Stith wondered.

He stopped only long enough to change into a fresh uniform and find the small package in his duffle. It was good to walk through the fallow fields again, noting changes on the way to the Tolbert home. Small trees were taller. The ivy on the west wall of the old house reached the eaves. To Stith the building seemed to lean a little, weakened by time. Like my parents, he thought with a pang.

Walking through the pasture he found Lightning cropping grass through the fence. For a moment he stopped to pat the horse's nose. Lightning, too, showed the effects of four years.

Stith rapped at the Tolbert's weather-beaten kitchen door and entered. Cloteel shoved her bulk up from the chair where she'd been drinking coffee.

"Mr. Stith! I do declare! My, but you's growed some!"

"Hey, Cloteel. How's my favorite girl?"

"Miz Louella?" The black face sagged. "That gal seemed kinda puny when she come back home last night."

"Not Louella. I meant you, you dark hussy!" He grabbed as much of her waist as he could encircle and hugged her.

"Go long wid you, Mr. Stith!" But her round face split in a toothy grin.

The footsteps down the hall made them turn. Head down, Louella entered.

"Just look who come for breakfast with you, honey," Cloteel ordered.

Louella looked up. For a moment her face brightened. "Stith. How nice." But her tone was disinterested, aloof.

Cloteel glanced from Louella to Stith and back again. "If'n you two intends on eating this mawning, then scatter and find me some fresh eggs." She winked at Stith. "Now, shoo. Both of you."

Louella shrugged. A silent Stith followed as she picked up a pail from the porch. She didn't speak until she had placed the first warm egg in the bucket. Stith leaned against the henhouse door, watching.

"It's no use, Stith. I told you at the train station." She jerked her hand from under the speckled hen that squawked and pecked. "Ouch, Hildegard! Doggone it; she gets me every time."

Stith laughed and took the pail from her. "Here, let me do that." Expertly he slid his hand under the hen, dodging her beak and withdrawing a large brown egg. Moving down the row of nests, he soon completed their task. "Why call her Hildegard?" he asked, keeping his tone light.

"There's always one that pecks," Louella answered, smiling in spite of herself. "We name that one Hildegard after a cranky Sunday school teacher Cora Sue and I used to know."

When they left the henhouse the sun had reached high enough to gild the treetops, leaving their feet in shadow. The hens had settled down, quiet before the new day. Together Stith and Louella started for the house.

"You hungry?" Stith asked.

"No," was her answer. "I didn't sleep much last night, what was left of it." She turned toward him. "Do you think my friends will be in any trouble because of me?"

Unable to reassure her, Stith said, "I'm not hungry, either. Let's walk."

Handing in the pail of eggs to a protesting Cloteel, he joined Louella, who took the lead down the sidewalk to the road in front of the house. At the mailbox she stopped.

"Where to?"

"This way," Stith said.

It was very quiet on the sandy road. The day promised warmth but in the shadows of the live oaks, Louella pulled her old blue sweater closer. They had reached the first curve before she spoke.

"Your folks okay?"

"Fine." Walking beside her a space away, Stith glanced at Louella's profile against the gray beards of moss swaying in a light breeze. "Mr. Hart told me your papa died."

"A couple months ago." She added nothing further.

"I'm sorry I didn't know." After a moment he tried another subject. "I've walked over a lot of different kinds of earth since I felt South Carolina's good old sand under my feet."

They had reached the path he sought and he held aside a branch and motioned her forward.

"You'd have had a finer welcome at home, than you did at the train station, Stith." Her words followed him as he bent to avoid hanging moss. "I'm sorry about what happened." As he straightened she asked, "Is your lip better now?" Her hand moved toward his face, then withdrew before she touched him.

"I've forgotten it already," he said.

"I truly am sorry about all this. What can I say? But I haven't changed my mind." She ducked a branch he held aside for her. "In fact, I'm more sure than ever that I don't want to marry. You nor anyone else. I don't want to drag anyone into my problems and I sure as the dickens don't need to take on anyone else's."

They had reached the bayou. Thick brown water flowed past a tattered canvas stool. He saw Louella's eyes fill.

"This is where...."

"Yes."

"It's been a long time since that Sunday...." Her eyes were on the brown ripples. She swallowed hard and turned toward Stith. "How could we know war wasn't just waving flags and women knitting socks for their `brave boys,' giving up sugar and saving grease for the war effort? That it wasn't glory and triumph for the men who fought either?" Her grin was lopsided. "Just dumb sweet innocents caught up in a war we didn't understand."

Stith bent to brush a twig from the canvas stool. At his slight pressure, the fabric parted. He sighed and shrugged. "Even this has changed."

Louella kicked at the dead grass near the bayou. "I still have the ring you wove for me." Her laugh sounded strange. "If I were superstitious, I would have known when it broke apart that everything would end."

Stith said nothing, drawing a length of what had once been blue ribbon out of his pocket. It was faded and streaked with brown. "I've kept this, too," he said softly. "You dropped it by the canvas stool that day." He smoothed it through his scarred hand. "Used to tie it on my wrist when we went on patrol. Got a little blood on it when the bayonet went through my palm." He curled it around one knuckle and let it spiral into her fingers. "Thought it was gone when I was in Paris, but it turned up at the bottom of my barracks bag out in the islands."

"Oh, Stith," Louella breathed, holding it tightly in both hands.

The water murmured at their feet in the sudden silence between them.

"All those times I thought of you when I looked at my grass ring, all those times you thought of me when you looked at this ribbon. Were we thinking of people who really didn't exist? I wonder."

"Perhaps," he said, his throat dry.

"It sorrows me, Stith, it purely does, that life just isn't like I thought it would be." Her eyes were huge and brimming over. "People hurt each other. People die sometimes, when their hearts have been broken long enough. War cripples people in their bodies and sometimes inside where it doesn't show. Dreams...." She swallowed and blotted at her cheek with the back of her hand, like a child. "...dreams are only for reaching for. They don't come true for most folks." She lowered her head, hiding her eyes from him.

"Maybe, Louella," he began, "maybe they just need help from someone who loves them."

"I had such a beautiful dream! A white wedding...so many flowers and candles." When she looked up her face glowed. "And...a little house and beautiful babies, and the worst worry would be new ways to fix rice and beans until my husband was rich." She turned away, gazing out over the water. "I dreamed of candlelit dinners, cooking fine meals in a ruffled blue apron...."

When he caught her hand, their fingers tangled in the stained blue ribbon. "Most of those dreams could come true, Louella." He grinned and tightened his grip. "Candles don't cost much and I could probably find you a blue apron in Charleston."

Her smile was tight but her eyes had a cold glitter. "Oh, Stith, quit it. Some dreams I've outgrown. Some I've learned are silly, childish. But all my dreams were built on love and loving and I...I really don't know any more what love is." Her sigh was deep. Silence lengthened, broken only by the sounds of the bayou, before she continued.

"Bringing babies into this world? Folks say we've got maybe five years before Russia drops the atom bomb on us. Who wants to bring children into that? There's nothing left to dream about in this world, Stith."

Stith kept his eyes on the blue ribbon stretched taut between them. "What is it you want to do so badly you can't do if you marry me?" he asked.

"Well...there's nothing so particular." She was silent for a moment. "Yes, there is, too! I want to make my own decisions, Stith, about my own life. It's taken me so long to learn how and I'm not ready to give that up."

"That's a valid reason," he said with a sinking feeling. "But if we married, you still could. I'd be there to talk things over before you decided. It helps sometimes." He leaned close enough to catch her scent. "What else?"

"I...I want to work. It makes me feel good to have an income of my own, to support Cora Sue and Cloteel and Elijah...."

"That decision would be yours, too, Louella. But if you wanted to quit and stay home, you could do that, too. When you decided to."

A silent gray bird flew down the bayou. It lit on a branch over the water and stared at them with one bright eye.

"That's not fair, Stith! That's...bribery." She turned her back on him. "I want to be stronger, not weaker. And I don't know you anymore; we've become strangers." She twisted the ribbon around her fingers.

"Louella," he began, then stopped to clear his throat. "I've got a confession to make. When I got off that train I was all set to make the big sacrifice, to marry you just because of a promise I'd made to a young girl. Thought it made me more of a man to honor that foolish promise." He could not control the flush he felt creeping up his face. "But when I started to leave the station and saw you, I saw a woman, not a girl. A grown up, warm and beautiful woman with spirit." He dropped his head. "And I saw the future, too. Empty without you."

"I don't feel so grown up," she said in a small voice as she turned to face him. "I feel helpless much of the time."

"All of us do," he whispered. "I reckon just picking up and trying again is the grown-up part." He placed his hands on her shoulders and looked into her eyes. "Marriage to the young girl I said good-bye to would have been a life-time sentence at hard labor to keep it going." His hands tightened their grips. "Marriage to the beautiful woman I see now is a dream I had in foxholes under fire. A woman who'll let me be a grown man." When she did not speak, he continued.

"I'll tell you a secret, Louella: Sometimes a grown man needs a shoulder to cry on, too."

She tilted her head and narrowed her eyes at him.

"Okay, you don't have to believe me. Sometimes when a man's cussing and stomping, it's his way of crying. When he sees understanding in a woman's eyes at a time like that, he knows she's found his soft underbelly. If she protects it, he's bound to her forever."

Behind his back he heard the whir of wings. The bird soared down the bayou over Louella's head.

"Seems to me you and I have changed in similar ways. I know now I'm not the sterling fellow I once thought I was. Things happened to you, too, I reckon."

She did not answer, shredding a leaf with quick fingers.

"So maybe we're both a little damaged with a bunch of scars, some of them pretty ugly, that maybe time won't ever smooth out." With an effort he faced her squarely. "Maybe a damaged guy like me lost his shiny ideals somewhere among folks he saw struggle just to eat any way they could. Thirteen-year-olds feeding their parents on what they picked up Saturday nights hanging around bars. Thirteen-year-olds with sixty-year-old eyes." His throat was tight but he forced the words. "When a guy's drunk enough to forget what he's seen in combat, he can forget how young they are. When he remembers again it's too late and one more thing to forget."

She knows it all now, he thought, and he'd probably lost her for good. His eyes were on the movement of the cattails in the turgid brown stream when he felt Louella grasp his right hand. "Things happen sometimes." Her eyes were luminous.

"If you have scars, too, I know I love you even more than I was capable of before, Louella." Again he tried to reach her with his words. "You're a survivor. Together we could survive anything life throws at us."

A long shuddering sigh shook her and he drew her into his arms, sheltering her gently. Gradually she relaxed until her head found a hollow on his shoulder. He stood very still, savoring the moment, careful not to press his luck.

"I remember holding a young girl whose name was Louella once long ago," he whispered into her hair. "A beginning for us that day in this very spot."

She did not move. Was this also a beginning...or an ending...he wondered.

"You went through a lot yesterday," Stith said. "I won't ask for an answer right now." He dropped his arms and stood back. Reaching into his pocket he pulled out the small square box, opening the lid to reveal a ring of dark green jade, carved into a lovers' knot.

"I found this at the port the day we embarked for America," he said. "It reminded me a little of the grass ring I wove for you."

Louella's hands trembled as she accepted the box. Stith was lost in the beauty of her gray eyes. He spoke hurriedly, suddenly terrified of rejection. "I love you, Louella. But you must chose on which hand you will wear this ring."

With a single finger he lifted her chin and leaned forward slowly until her eyes blurred from his vision and he felt the warmth of her breath, the sweetness of her lips on his. With an ache in his heart, he straightened and waited for her words.

"I can't promise, Stith," she whispered. "I don't know if we can begin again or...."

"Whichever it is, can't we just let it happen? I want to remember this Christmas with you as happy for the rest of my days."

"Look, Stith," she said, her words a little breathless. "Our own Christmas tree."

He turned. Behind him stood a holly tree, a perfect tall cone of shining green leaves and heavy red berries. Had she changed the subject so abruptly to avoid hurting him? Or was it a sign of sharing? Whichever, it had broken the spell.

Louella closed the small box and held it toward him.

He motioned it away. "When I see it on your finger, I'll know your answer, Louella. You hold both our futures in your hand."

Eyes on his face, Louella pushed the box into the pocket of her full blue skirt. "We'd best go home, Stith. Cora Sue will be up. She and Cloteel need my help." Carefully she wound the stained ribbon around one finger and tucked it away with the ring.

Watching her, Stith's heart felt a surge of hope.

When they entered the kitchen, the good smells of roasting turkey, pumpkin pie spices and onions filled the room. Cloteel met them with an expectant look on her broad black face. She looked at each of them carefully and sobered. "'Bout time you two was gettin' here," she scolded, hands on her ample hips. "Miz Brenda done called. Dey all be here most any time and you out gallivantin'. Get yourself upstairs, Miz Louella, and pretty up. Cora Sue setting a place for you right now, Mr. Stith." With a start, Louella realized how much time had elapsed. Hurrying through the door, she called back to Stith. "Of course you're staying. It's time my friends got to know you." Before he could answer, she gave a quick wave to Cora Sue through the dining room door. "Wait'll you see the present I've got for you," she called as she ran up the stairs.

Alone in her room, Louella faced the long pier glass with its faded gilt. Is this ache you feel and the warmth in your heart love? she asked the girl in the mirror. She shed blouse and skirt and pulled on her new emerald green velveteen dress. She kicked her old slippers under the bed and buckled on T-strap black leather high heels. A dusting of powder over her nose, a glide of lipstick and she faced the mirror again with her brush. Two strokes and she dropped the brush to find the ring box and ribbon in the discarded skirt pocket.

As she lifted it from the gray velvet box, a ray of sunshine caught the ring, the jade glowing like a live thing in her fingers.

A strong man's love, Stith had said. Wasn't that what she had been seeking all along? Was it just the gentle kiss that had melted her doubts? Firmly she slipped the ring into her velveteen dress pocket. The sounds of a car approaching the house gave her only minutes for a quick brush through her hair.

Descending the stairs, she heard the laughing chatter rise on the porch. Cora Sue raced past her to the door; face flushed with excitement, she returned buried under a pile of Christmas presents they unloaded on her. As her friends shed hats and jackets, their voices were a happy hubbub in the hall. Looking a bit uncertain, Stith entered from the kitchen.

"Have we got news!" Brenda burst out, hugging Louella. Her red dress was a bright contrast to the drab uniforms of the three soldiers, the charcoal gray of Mr. Hart and Donald Monahan's dark green. From all their faces, Louella took hope.

Eddie grabbed Louella away from Brenda and waltzed her down the hall into the parlor, the others crowding behind. "Toots did it; she really did it, my friend!" he announced. He stopped their spin in front of the Christmas tree. "That black-haired bitch really came through! Two hundred and seventy-three dollars and..." He swept up Brenda and revolved her around the room, avoiding the stack of Christmas presents, pumping their arms in a tight circle.

"She did what?" Louella asked, confused and breathless.

"It was Mr. Hart's idea," Hutch answered. "She marked all the bills she gave Sergeant Cobb with a purple dot in the guy's eye in the middle and...."

"What guy?" Her confusion deepened.

"Washington or Franklin or whoever. The guy on the bill!" Hutch's thick fingers waved in excitement. "They're bringing charges against just him, and Toots is getting off with a hundred dollar fine and...."

"That means you're free," Stith explained.

She took a deep, cleansing breath and exhaled, releasing all her tension and fear. The mirror over the mantel reflected all their smiles. The Christmas tree sparkled in the sunlight pouring through the window. It's as though this room has come to life again, she thought. And so have I.

Glen Hart grinned down on her when she took a seat on the horsehair couch. "Being in at the end was all I wanted," he said. "There's the court martial to come, but no doubt how that will turn out." He threw back his thick mane of hair. "You're my extra daughter, Louella. Even though we couldn't undo all the damage, vengeance tastes very sweet."

"Did you...see Sergeant Cobb?" Louella asked, remembering his face, the demented crowing.

"Captain Edmond said he was...not in very good shape," Glen Hart replied after a moment. "He's under medication and probably will be sentenced to a psychiatric hospital after his trial." Watching Louella's expression, he added, "At least for a time."

"I never saw anybody before who...disintegrated like that." Louella let her words die.

"He made the choices," Brenda said, her voice brisk. "How can you even think about him after what he did?"

"Look at it this way, Louella," Donald Monahan added, "after he gets some help he might have a better life." The small man looked up at Glen Hart and placed a hand on his arm. "Sometimes all you need to get off a crooked path is to get a clear look at yourself."

Cora Sue whirled in the doorway, her blue dress fluttering around her knees. Teetering on tiptoe in the parlor door, she announced, "Dinner's served. Cloteel says you all come to the table now."

Last to leave the parlor, Louella was conscious of Stith beside her. His nearness was soothing, warmer than the presence of her friends, she realized. Was it only friendship she felt for him, then? Or something deeper, something resurrected? Even to Brenda she'd never been able to talk about her own dreams. This morning with Stith it felt comfortable.

In the dining room there was a general flurry of finding seats at the long mahogany table, which was spread with her mother's fine Havilland china and crystal. Once more the chatter became celebration. When Stith pulled out her chair at the head of the table, Louella felt the tug of sadness. This was my father's chair; now I'm head of this family. Unfolding her napkin, she looked around the table at the cheerful faces. Probably this would be the last time they all would be together. In two weeks her friends would have scattered.

Stith eased down into the seat to her right and leaned forward. "Everything okay?"

He senses my unspoken thoughts, Louella realized. Something deep inside responded to his concern. How could she close this man out of her life, the one person who cared enough to share her dreams?

"Better'n okay," Louella whispered through the convernation that flowed around them. Under the table she drew the ring from her pocket and slipped it on her finger. With her heart in her smile, she reached her left hand to him, displaying the jade on her third finger. In the noisy room, the moment was theirs alone.

Stith glanced at her hand, then his eyes sought hers, his face glowing. Without a word, he lifted her left hand to his lips, then held it tenderly to his cheek.

Louella clearly recognized the feeling that had revived deep within her. Joy! Still clinging to Stith's hand, she rose to her feet.

Entering the room from the kitchen, bearing the turkey platter, Cloteel stopped. Cora Sue, Hutch and Monahan looked up, their uncertain harmony to "Jingle Bells" fading away. Glen Hart stilled the knife clinking against his glass in rhythm with their song. Eddie dropped his arm from Brenda's shoulders, ending their whispered conversation. Behind Cloteel's shoulder, the grizzled head of Elijah appeared.

"As some of you know," Louella began, smiling at Brenda's lifted face, and "I did not buy a Christmas gift for Stith. So," she went on, her voice suddenly tremulous, "I'm giving him something I could not wrap in a package. My love."

Knees weak, she sat abruptly in the stunned silence.

Just before the tumult broke out, through the thunder of her own pulse, she heard Stith say, "The gift of a lifetime."

The End

Acknowledgments

When you are in a group of vital women writers who encourage you, reveal your mistakes, compliment your writing when appropriate, and keep you producing, it's Nirvana for a writer.

Such a group was The Gadflies, bless 'em. There was Lynda Haller, who writes great articles about the Southwest and its artists; Bette Widney, a published author; plus too many former members now on The Other Side. Writers need support groups who can criticize without wounding the author. We were all blessed. And we knew it.

Most of all, there is Marcia Preston, who has six or seven great books of her own. She became the godmother of Her Innocent War. Without Marcia, it would have been forever entombed in my desk drawer.

34522971R00211

Made in the USA
Lexington, KY
09 August 2014